Secret
of the
Hindu Kush
A Novel

Anthony Stone

Cover design by pro_ebookcovers
Printed in the United State of America

DEDICATION

To my beloved grandmother, Bibi Gul Zekrya

For my son

To my wonderful wife, Karen
And to our cat, Whimzy

I must inquire whether there is a God as soon as the occasion presents itself. And if I find a God, I must also inquire whether He may be a deceiver for without a knowledge of these two truths, I do not see that I can be certain of anything.

- *Descartes*

- Part I -

The Beginning

1

The Witch

One hand on the adobe wall, the witch crept around the back of a tent where our village doctor hurried from one cot to another carrying a lantern and a bag of hope. A guard surprised her, but he bowed and gave her the formal greeting befitting her status before moving on, although he may have wondered why his Lord's youngest wife wandered the outer courtyard at this time of night. I followed the witch while my brother tugged on my coat sleeve, urging me to retreat to our warm and cozy room.

"Look." I pointed at a tall man striding across the courtyard, squatting near campfires and talking to the refugees. He looked up and seeing the witch, he waved her over to join him near the black gates. She gestured and nodded at the giant. He stood with jaw muscles flexing and arms crossed. She hissed and yanked her cloak tight around herself while he shook his head back and forth, leaned down and wagged a finger in the air. I pulled my brother along the wall and searched for a hole or a shadow to hide us.

"What are they doing?" my brother asked.

"Don't know. Nothing good," I said.

"Should we tell father?"

"Quiet, they will hear us."

The giant held something out for the witch. A thin sheen of blue gleamed.

"Look," my brother said.

"Be still."

The witch reached for the blue bauble, but the man pulled it back and stuffed it into the folds of his coat. He leaned down and whispered to the witch, whose hands fluttered and fidgeted, long fingers spinning nightmares and terrors in the air.

Just then ice crunched beneath our feet. Faces turned, their eyes searched the courtyard. I lunged into a shadow and pulled my brother down next to me. We crawled until we reached the remnants of a collapsed wall that once formed part of an old stable.

They returned to their argument for a time. Then the giant walked away and vanished through the gates while the witch turned her hooded face towards us and smiled.

♦ ♦ ♦

2

The Day After

Scuttling chickens squawked and chortled. Frost-coated yaks moaned outside our gates, and the horses in the stables stomped and whinnied. As the sun broke over the eastern mountains, the old man began the prayer. Father walked out on the balcony and gazed at the refugees settled around the courtyard.

"Baba?"

"Yes, son? You have a question?"

"Why doesn't God stop the war?"

He smiled and ruffled my hair with his hand. My question hung in the air unanswered while a rainbow spread across a patch of clearing sky.

Laughter came from the doorway behind us. My brother ran out and jumped on me. We wrestled. Baba laughed and pulled us apart. My brother ran from wall to wall, making snowballs, tossing them at me and Baba. He burst with energy today, one of those strange sun and snow days when men whisper in their beards of omens and shadows and evil spirits.

In the courtyard, the old man sang out the prayer. Refugees faced the west and held out their hands, palms facing the sky. For a few moments, we watched the people kneel, stand and gesture in mesmerizing unison. A slow dance of forlorn spirits. Then the wind rushed across the walls and engulfed everyone in a cloud of snow. Baba took us by the shoulders and steered us down the walkway to the back wall where he pointed and recited the names of his horses that roamed free near the stables.

Clouds gathered and thickened, dark bellies drifting close to the ground. I heard a woman weeping, but Baba pointed and said, "That one is Jaheel. Tomorrow you will meet my newest stallion, white as a poppy blossom, the fastest horse in all three valleys".

"But someone is..."

"Yes, she is crying."

"But we must help her."

"We will."

I turned and watched the stallion prance, toss his mane and circle the field. Two men chased the stallion to bring him back to the stables. Then wind gusted and snowfall obscured everything.

The witch's cloaked form drifted past Baba's balcony and down the other side of the battlements. Tingles spread down my spine as her enormous eyes swung my way. Her shape faded inside the rush and swirl of ice crystals, yet her presence remained, warning of nightmares yet to come.

Heavy steps echoed on the walkway and Uncle appeared, limping from that bullet still lodged in his leg. A pink scar ran from his ear to his chin. Another line cut down his neck and vanished into the collar of his shirt.

"How goes it, brother?" said Baba.

"Three villages destroyed. Survivors arriving. What will we do with them all?" Uncle said.

"Same as we always do. Feed them, clothe them, build more homes in the village. Take the orphans to the mountain?"

"What mountain?" I said.

Baba glanced down at me but ignored my question. The mountain remained a mystery I would not solve for many years.

"Enemy attacks the pass with tanks and gunships," said Uncle. "They drive more families from their homes."

"The Lion will stop them," said Baba. "The day is short. The Lion will roar when darkness falls."

"He calls for more of our men."

Baba looked back from the ponies.

"I will go. You stay," he said.

"I can still fight."

Baba smiled and looked back at the ponies. "When I fall, you can kill them all for me."

Uncle nodded. We stood in the falling snow and listened to the soft sounds of prayer. Uncle and Baba stared at each other for a moment. Then Uncle nodded and hobbled away, leaving us in the icy embrace of winter.

◆ ◆ ◆

3

Yaan

Our village had no school and so Baba paid Yaan, a second uncle by marriage, or maybe a third cousin, to live in the fortress and to give my brother and me lessons in mathematics and science and the history of war.

Yaan showed us art and the world in secret. He brought pictures of Moscow and New York and we marveled at the enormity of the world, the deep shadows of gray buildings, birds that gathered along black lines and long gray avenues, and tree-filled parks. The birds seemed drawn to lines, and so I drew them until Yaan taught me how to see light and shadow on paper.

Yaan had a little gray beard he twisted between the burned skin of his fingers. His hands had pink scars and the skin on his arms had melted over and under older skin and great welts gouged his neck and face, making his age unknowable, his expressions enigmatic. He once sold firewood in a town along the border, but the enemy destroyed his town, killed his wife and three daughters, blowing them into dust.

Sometimes in the afternoon, when Nargis brought us tea, Yaan's eyes would cloud over, and I knew he passed into the land of memories and lost himself in his old life. Occasionally he smiled, and that helped him continue with the lesson.

One day my brother and I kneeled near an old chestnut tree stump we used for a table. We drew Baba and his great black beard and his eyes full of storms. For inspiration, we used a large photo of Baba as a young man, sitting on a bear's chest, rifle in hand. Baba stared at us from there, on the first day of his manhood and the day he earned his sobriquet, "The Bear". That day he felled a giant bear with a single shot straight through the heart, a feat unequaled in our mountains.

Baba came in while we kneeled there drawing, and before we knew anything, he picked up Yaan by the back of his vest and threw him against the old wall.

"Art? You are teaching them art?"

"Just a drawing. They are children and children love to draw."

Baba shook his head.

"They must learn history, politics, science. Pictures will not feed the people. Will art keep that pig Hassan on his side of the river? Will art defeat the enemy who murdered your family?"

"Forgive me." Yaan held out his palm. "No more drawing."

Baba blinked at Yaan, who lay crumpled against the wall. Then Baba spat on the ground and cursed the fathers and mothers of enemies everywhere. Spinning round to face us, he glared for a moment before holding a fist to his forehead and then stomping out of the room.

My brother and I rushed to Yaan, helped him up off the ground and brushed off his shirt. Yaan stood straight and pulled his little red vest tight around his slender chest and lifted his chin.

"You may continue to draw now boys. Your Baba won't be back today."

We did not draw that day or the day after or ever again during our lessons. We dared not risk Yaan's life for a simple drawing that would not feed any people, kill any enemy, or keep that pig Hassan on the other side of the river.

◆ ◆ ◆

4

Night and the Buzkashi

The full moon turned the stallion into a silver beast and Baba rode this beast, swung him around and pounded him down the field in pursuit of a horseman who held the headless calf across his lap and rode for a distant chalk circle and fame that would spread across the whole of Badakhshan.

"That's Daoud," said my brother, "he won last year in Mazar."

"His horse is slow. Baba will catch him," I said.

We laughed, entranced by the vision of Baba entering the field, a rare happening and certain to bring riders from the ranks of our soldiers and from every nearby village.

Baba caught up with the horseman and struck him from the saddle with a blow to his chest. As the man tumbled backwards over the rump of his horse, the calf fell into Baba's hands. Riders closed in on Baba from all sides, but the stallion surged ahead and swung around the field while the pursuit faded amid groans and shouts for fair play. Baba laughed and held the headless calf up, taunting the riders, whose numbers had grown to nearly a dozen, and soon from all corners of the valley came the echoes of unshod hoofs. The mountain pass filled with moonlit clouds of fog and ice swirling over everything.

Soon a storm of riders surrounded Baba, but he did not relinquish the calf. He stopped Jaheel and reared him up, kicking his forelegs in the air. Shouting their intent, they closed in on him. Whips snapped. Fists thudded, bones cracked, and bodies fell. Men abandoned their horses to throw themselves at Baba, wrestle him to the ground and tear the calf away. While men held him down, one snatched up the calf and thundered away from the pack.

Baba emerged laughing from the pile. He jumped on his stallion's back and joined the fun and it went on like this, while Mother watched from her narrow window in the tower with her hair bleached quicksilver in the rays of the winter moon.

Then I heard the drummer banging out another beat, this one louder and closer than before. I looked to the fields but saw no one. I turned towards the village. Still, I did not see him. The beating of his drum melted into the thunder of hoofbeats.

Then I saw the giant lurking in the distance. When he noticed us, his lips curled to reveal a row of blackened teeth. I pushed my brother. Look, I said, the giant comes. Sikandur smiled and turned to face the tallest man I had ever seen. With thick dark hair matted to his head and a scar running straight across his face from chin to ear. His cloak swung open and revealed dark clothing.

"Which one of you is the boy named Omar?"

I stood still, my heart beating fast while my brother ignored the giant and turned around to face the horsemen whose shouts drew ever closer. I stared at the man's teeth and felt a cold trickle of sweat sneaking down my back.

"Well, which one of you is Omar? Tell me quick, I am a busy man."

"I am."

The man stared at us for a moment.

"I did not realize you are twins. How will I know which is which?"

I shrugged. At that moment, I heard Baba shout, and I turned to see him riding towards us at a gallop. When I turned back to the giant, he had vanished.

"What did he say?" said Baba.

"He wanted to know which of us is Omar," my brother said.

9

Baba nodded and swung Jaheel back around and rode away, but within a few steps, he turned and shouted, "Do not talk to him again."

We did not see the giant again that night.

For hours they rode and blood mixed with earth beneath a sky full of stars so close that it appeared a man riding might reach up and brush them away.

Dawn approached. The eastern sky turned into an indigo ribbon that stretched across jagged black peaks. Impenetrable, powerful spirits of our ancestors standing guard over our valley. Baba rode over to us with Uncle. They picked us up and rode to the stables where grooms took their horses and rubbed them down, fed and fussed over them, treating them like beloved children. No one said anything about the man still lying in the field, his family tasked with the removal of his body. The rumble of hoofs continued, the pack growing and shrinking, yet never entirely disappearing.

"My sons must have guards," said Baba.

"Don't be ridiculous," Uncle said. "He is just a man like any other man."

Baba shook his head. "I do not believe that and neither do you.

◆ ◆ ◆

5

Fatima, the Witch

My mother claimed, with some fury, that Baba had robbed a poor family of their child by marrying Fatima. Baba laughed. My brother and I avoided her. However, her duties as Baba's second wife included watching over us while our mother attended the household, the servants, and the day to day. When mother walked by, the witch would bow her head and mumble a stammering hello which mother ignored as she should as first wife and mother. She held all the power.

Yet, mother abandoned us to the witch ever since she appeared in our lives with painted nails and sparkling jewels and her body full and firm. Baba watched her, and I watched him and feared for mother as the witch peered from huge black eyes full of sparks and flames and she swung her long hair with the eagerness of a colt and Baba loved his colts so very much.

When alone with us, she pinched and jeered us, and if we told Baba, he ignored us and if we bothered him too much he exploded. Sitting outside, observing the construction of new homes in the village, he often spoke his frustrations to Uncle while we played nearby, my ears attuned to the timbre of his voice.

"Why does God hate me so much that he curses me with this life?" Baba said.

"Perhaps because you hate God," said Uncle.

"I have reason to hate God."

"I know you do," Uncle said, "We both do."

We walked downstairs for dinner served on the long table with chairs and plates, a foreign style and something Baba insisted we adopt. We sat in a fragile silence laced by soft stepping servants carrying steaming trays of rice and chicken. My brother and I on one side, our mother whispering to Baba on our right. Across from us sat Bibi Shirin, our auntie, and Uncle who rarely ate at the big table for he disapproved of foreigners, silverware, and everything new or modern.

Yaan's silence haunted me through the meal. He rarely spoke since Baba's moment of rage, and I understood his heart and wondered how it could ever heal. At the far left of the table sat the witch, her ebon eyes darting this way and that, chicken grease smeared around her glistening lips as she tore meat from bone, cracked open the bone, sucked out the marrow and filled the room with grinding slurping sounds.

"Have I told you the story of the man with two wives?" said Bibi Shirin.

"No, you haven't but I'm sure you will," said Baba.

Bibi Shirin smiled. "Long time ago, in a town not far from here, there lived a man and wife who had grown into middle age without giving birth to a child. One day, the man married a young wife, hoping that she might provide him with sons. At first, life went on without incident, as life sometimes does, but soon all that changed. One day, the quarreling began and soon after that, the women came to blows, which he stopped while he was in the house, but as he went out the door to begin the work of each day, shouts and screams started and he imagined hell could not contain more horrors than his poor home. Well, things got worse. He could not contain the wrath of both wives and so, to calm and appease, he slept alone, laying his *sandale* in the kitchen where he hoped to find some peace. Peace would be harder to find than he imagined. For at night while he slept the young wife would enter and pull a white hair from his head, thinking in this way her husband would appear always young. In the darkness of early morning, the old wife would creep in and pull out a black hair, so that her husband would appear ever older. Soon the man lost all his hair and with his hair went his fortune. Within a year, he had to return both wives to their families. He became a beggar, cursed to wander the streets alone until the end of his days."

She stopped, and then with a chuckle, she continued. "They say he died beneath a donkey's hoofs, covered in excrement."

She wiped her mouth with one of Baba's fancy napkins, lily white bordered in gold, and set her fork on her plate and smiled at mother. Baba roared with laughter. Uncle smiled and placed a hand over Bibi Shirin's hand. Baba did not stop laughing. He rose from the table and laughed all the way to the stairway, and as he ascended toward the towers and battlements, I heard his laughter still echoing. Glancing to my left, I saw the witch smiling, and I shuddered.

♦ ♦ ♦

6

Older by Three Minutes

Some nights, when I could not sleep, I sat in the hallway next to the door of Baba's room and listened to their voices while the wind ran through the old fortress, whistling through cracks and shaking windows.

"Do you not fear God?" Mother's voice slipped from the gap beneath the door.

"Sometimes I convince myself there is a God. Other times there is just darkness."

Baba's voice forced its way through the door.

"Then why do you not bend your knees and pray?"

"You pray my love, perhaps God will listen."

"Am I your love?"

"You are the light in the darkness."

Her voice died to a cracked whisper. "Yet you married her."

"I need the treaty with her father. I need his men. You know this."

"Then why did you sleep with her? Why?"

"Her father expects it. If she had complained, her father would ask for the dowry."

"I do not care about her dowry or her stupid father. I came not from my city to this old fort so you could marry another."

Wind battered the narrow windows at the end of the hall, creating a rattling din that invaded the corridor and shook the oil lamps set high in the walls, their gold light wavering against the old gray stones. As a strange dread gripped me, I folded my arms around my curled knees and listened.

"Forget your city. Out here, everything is different. They pass stories of my faults from mouth to mouth. Imagine the shame if I had refused her. This is not like the home you knew. This is a... tough world. Our world at war."

We rarely spoke of my mother's family or where they came from. All I knew is that Bibi Shirin came with her, sitting among a caravan full of gold and jewels, horses and yaks, all her dowry glittering in the sun like a vast imperial treasure not seen in these mountains since the days of ancient lore. That is how Baba told it to us, and that is how it must have been.

I imagined my mother arriving like a princess to our broken-down old fortress. What did she think when Baba rode out to meet her upon his war-scarred mare that still, by some miracle, possessed enough speed and strength to take him from battle to battle? What did she think of the poppy in the eastern fields, the horsemen thundering past day and night, and the two old soldiers patrolling the compound?

Some nights she sang wondrous songs and recited poetry and told us stories of men and women who fell in love only to die in wild battles, hearts broken by dark magicians and cruel kings of distant lands. My brother and I fell asleep to her stories. I missed them now. She no longer told them since the witch arrived. I waited by their door to hear them speak the way they did before Fatima arrived.

"I know you hate God."

"God hates me. It is Fate that we should hate one another."

Their voices lulled me, sending me drifting, but not asleep.

"I know it breaks your heart. I have done everything I know to heal your pain, but still you suffer. You suffer in the day, your back bending beneath a great weight. Then at night, your voice cracks with this pain. Why can you not let it go?"

Wind and soft rattling windows. Their voices. The ever-present murmurs of my life so comforting.

"Once, I loved God. Then my mother and father murdered by... I cannot forgive... I cannot forget the sight of it. Now, I only know that I must prepare my sons for war. I must ready them for the horrors of this world. Tomorrow I will take Omar to the battle. He must see and understand the meaning of war."

"You want them to see what you saw and suffer what you have suffered? You want them to live constantly haunted by tragedies? No. I want to take them back to my home where they will be safe."

"I will take Omar. He is the elder by three minutes. I will leave you to coddle Sikandur until our return."

A sudden gale blew through the fortress, ripped open a window and tore up the hallway. Rushing to the window, I slammed it shut and fastened the hook to hold it firm. Then I returned to the doorway because although I heard it all, I thought it must have been a dream.

"Send the girl home, Ali."

"Yes, one day, when the war is over, I will send her home."

That night I dreamed of forests, a white mountain, and a city of lights. In the distance, a beast roared, a drummer drummed, and red rain fell from a black sky.

♦ ♦ ♦

7

Sikandur and the Ghosts

Wrapped in a white sheepskin coat, she watches the long line of men and horses trek towards the mountains. Tears slip down her pale cheeks. He pulls her down and hugs her. The wind brushes her long thick hair, the sound of willow leaves rustling. Together they watch Baba and Omar lead the horsemen towards the pass.

"Where are they going, Mother?" he says.

She takes a fast breath and pulls him to her chest, holding him tight. Uncle limps out from the shadowed doorway and stands nearby. Sikandur runs to a cannon wheel and climbs. Snow swirls in the distance, an approaching storm. In the courtyard, Baba's fighting chickens preen, scuttle, and squawk inside their kennels.

Spread throughout the compound and beyond the outer walls, villagers help refugees tend campfires that burn soft in the morning haze.

He turns around. Mother sways in the wind. Her face shines, touched by wetness, simple and perfect. He can almost see through her, as if she is not there at all.

"Come Sikki. We go for a ride," says Uncle. "Give your mother a hug."

She hugs Sikki tight and then walks back inside. After a moment, Uncle picks him up, sits him on a wide shoulder and limps towards the stairway leading down to the courtyard.

The stable is full of men talking and laughing. Tools clang, hammers strike anvils, fires roar and blaze. Hands reach for him, ruffle his hair, and a dozen voices intertwine in cheerful labor. The air feels thick and warm and he loves it.

"This is Jaheel. He will sire many stallions for your father," says Uncle.

A ghost white horse looks down. The long face lowers, and he reaches out to touch. Rough skin feels cold. He shifts around behind Uncle's leg and peers up into the enormous eyes. The horse comes forward and nuzzles against him.

"He likes you. Interesting. He does not like anybody. Not even your father, really."

He steps out and hugs the stallion's face and laughs.

"He likes me, Uncle."

Uncle cinches a lightweight saddle on the stallion and swings up.

"Hand me the boy."

"Are you sure, lord? He is very small. He could get hurt," said the stable master, Jovan.

"Pick him up and hand him to me. He is not too small. You and I rode at his age."

Jovan nods and picks him up and places him in front of Uncle. Together they ride over the hill and along the river to a slender waterfall where mist wraps them in a cold cocoon. Everything crystallizes into the roaring falls, the howling wind and Uncle's arm tight around his chest. Yet there remains an emptiness, some integral piece of the universe missing. He senses his brother moving away. Omar, the quiet one, the careful one.

Jaheel stomps and shakes his head. Uncle tightens the reins and turns Jaheel away from the water. They canter through soft snow that muffles the sound of Jaheel's hoofs. Uncle whispers a prayer and the boy looks up. Tears slip down Uncle's face. His eyes shine and he looks free from the pain of his many wounds.

For a time, they ride along the river's edge. Then a shadow glides through the air just above their heads, wings beating against the wind. Uncle leans forward, clicks his tongue, and the stallion breaks into a run. The shadow moves away, then just ahead, another shadow stands upright. A lean tall man stands in the swirling snow, wild hair matted to a massive head, black holes for eyes sitting in a bearded face, a cloak bound around his body.

Give me the boy, the man shouts. His voice thunders into the wind.

Uncle veers Jaheel away, but the man appears again. Wind slaps Sikki's face. Dark shapes slip past in the flying snow. Once again, the shadow flies over their heads, then alongside. Wings hammer against thin air. They cannot outrun the shadow, nor can they escape the voice, a drumming voice. A pounding voice, a voice relentless in its calm, deep certainty.

"I must have the boy. Give him to me."

Smaller winged shadows appear in the whiteout. The river rises, trying to flood the banks and wash the horse, boy and man away.

Uncle shouts and turns Jaheel. In the distance, gray walls stand out against the flurries. Uncle whispers in Jaheel's ear and the stallion speeds through the storm. They come to a jolting stop inside the stables and dismount.

"Who is that man, Uncle?"

"Just a man."

"A wicked man?"

"Just a man, like any other man." Uncle shakes his head and mutters as they walk back to the fortress.

Sikki and Uncle spend the day with Yaan, looking at books full of paintings and sculptures. A woman painted by Da Vinci, a name Sikki likes to repeat until Yaan shows him a picture of a statue without arms. Venus de Milo, says Yaan, by Michelangelo, an even better name.

Yaan and Uncle talk about art and old men while they play chess. He tries to draw Venus on paper, but without his brother, his drawing falters and remains half done. Uncle and Yaan argue about who betrayed the country more, the king or the generals. They move on to singers and drummers and play chess. They laugh, shout, and shake their heads. Sikki struggles with his drawing until late afternoon when they stand up and descend the long stairs for dinner.

Arriving in the main hall, they find the witch perched at the far end of the dining table. Shifting lamplight dances inside her black eyes, large as the eyes of the giant horses of the northern plateaus. He turns away from the witch and waits for his mother.

"Where is Mother?"

"She is unwell," says Uncle. The witch who leans away from the table and curses the cook who scurries back to the safety of the kitchen.

After dinner, Uncle takes him to his room, tucks him into bed and then leaves. The thick door shuts and darkness settles into corners. He stares at firelight flickering over the ceiling for a moment before he rises and counts the army men on his shelf and then runs his hand over a long smooth piece of driftwood.

Hearth fire crackles and logs slip and crash against each other. The shifting embers pull his head around and he checks the shadows for things that should not be there. In one corner of the room, where black shapes float and coalesce, two enormous eyes gleam. She emerges from the shadows with a log in her hands. He smiles. The log makes no sound as it cuts through the air.

♦ ♦ ♦

8

The Lion

We rode through frosted valleys and across frozen streams. Heavy gray clouds swallowed mountaintops on both sides of the trail. Riders sat loose, small riding whips gripped between their teeth, eyes squinting against the flurries. Baba and I rode in the middle while others rotated back and forward, bringing word from nearby villages. Baba nodded and kept the pace at a trot. Buried in the white horizon, big guns thundered and the ground shook. As we approached the pass, I imagined an enemy hiding inside every shadow and behind every boulder.

The storm faded, the clouds moved off and stars decorated an obsidian sky. A pale blue moon climbed out from behind a peak and transformed the snowfield into a dazzling blanket of crystals. Ever higher into the mountains we rode, ever closer to the jeweled sky.

"Baba, look. Our shadows in the moonlight," I said.

"Yes, I see."

I asked where my shadow went in the darkness.

"Is it still there, hiding in the dark, or is my shadow gone to some other place until a light brings it back?"

Baba did not answer. He flicked his whip in the air above his warhorse's ear and the old mare snorted and sped away, kicking snow into the air. It felt good sitting in front of my father, his arm tight around my chest. I wished this night might never end.

We came to the pass from above and looked down upon a quiet battlefield. A rider arrived, told Baba about a cease-fire, reported numbers of the dead and wounded. Baba nodded.

"Now you will meet a warrior," said Baba, "even though he is not of our tribe and he comes from the North."

Baba spat in the snow at the mention of northerners. "In times of war enemies become friends."

I had not met a northerner, nor did I understand Baba's dislike of them. For now, my excitement grew at the prospect of meeting the man everyone talked about, this famous general.

We descended towards the pass, a gorge littered with the wreckage of a tank, long barrel bent and stained. Smoke curled from rocks where gnarled helicopter blades clawed the air. Men scrambled from wreck to wreck. Fires burned in every direction, and a poisoned stench arose as they poured gasoline and tossed torches on the dead. We rode up a ridge and around jagged cliffs to a pristine snow field surrounded by tall thin pine trees where Baba gave orders to pitch camp. Men raised tents along the edge of the forest, and jeeps rumbled up from below with generators and food. Baba showed me how to raise our tent and as we unzipped the old green flaps, a small man surrounded by a chattering mob emerged from the forest and hurried towards us. Atop a sparrow's face and a sparse little beard, he wore a faded green cap while army fatigues and high black boots blended him into the crowd of men who shouted out his nickname, "Lion of the North". Baba leaned to shake hands and kiss the Lion on both cheeks. The Lion's eyes shined in the moonlight as he spoke of victory while his men cheered and shook their guns in the air.

"There is a cease fire," the Lion said.

"There have been many cease fires," Baba said.

"This one will last."

"It won't last, they never last," Baba said.

"We must make certain it lasts. Did you bring men?"

"Of course. You can trust me."

"Yes, I know I can trust you. We are not enemies. All of us here in the North are one people. Do not take offense my friend."

Baba spat in the snow, a hole burning in the pale blue ice crust.

We devoted the night to celebration, and a man brought me soup and warm bread, steaming in the night air. On a raised platform, one man sang while another played harmonium and a third kept beat with the tabla. The clan leaders danced in a large circle around the campfire, and soon all the men danced with their shadows. Laughter filled the field and forest. Hundreds of campfires where men danced around, many carrying torches and flashlights. I asked Baba about the dance and he called it "Atan", our national dance, and said that he would dance it with me at my wedding. Back then, I did not know about dancing and weddings, but I nodded as if I did so I would not disappoint Baba with my ignorance.

A man walked into the forest and returned with a young ewe that he pulled to a large campfire. Baba walked into our tent and came back carrying his long battle knife, a straight blade thick in shank and serrated along one edge. Grey metal flashed in the moonlight as Baba strode through the camp, this extension of him as natural as his thick black beard. He walked to where two men held the ewe, kneeled, and laid the ewe's neck to the ground. Her bleat echoed a thin thread of fear beneath the rough, heavy beat of the drums. My head felt hot and my eyes burned. I climbed atop a large ammunition crate, securing a vantage point to see over the other men. Baba rested the blade against the ewe's neck. The drums pounded louder. A shortness of breath took hold of me as Baba drew the silver blade against the white neck and a dark streak sprang forth, arcing across the snow. The ewe struggled, its moonlit eyes dancing a wild rampage only to stop and stare directly at me as if asking me to save it, perform a miracle and send it back to the forest. The heat of its panicked gaze burned my skin, and suddenly I felt nothing but the frozen bite of snow against my face. Two men laughed and picked me up. The beat of the drum pounded into my skull and I sat down, burning with shame.

The Lion sat beside Baba who sat next to me with one heavy calloused hand around the back of my neck, rubbing heat back into my soul while they talked. Baba nodded and spat many times into the campfire. Men tromped through the camp, rattled their long guns, and whispered in the darkness between flickering tongues of firelight.

Our men and the Lion's men did not mix, for ours came from the midlands where we lived at higher altitudes. Men from mountains full of scorpions and bleached bones of war machines where orphaned children made their homes in discarded tanks and burned out trucks. Baba took us last year, and we trekked back with a thousand refugees, back to our high pastures where each family settled, built new homes and lived under Baba's protection. They came to raise wheat, children and the poppy. The one thing nobody dared take from them. The Lion and Baba discussed last year's march, this year's crop, and many other things while I fell asleep by the fire.

In my dreams, I heard my brother calling my name. I tried to wake and call Baba, but demons plagued my sleep, pulled me down into a darkness filled with echoes of my brother's voice. I tossed, turned and heard noises all around, but my eyes refused to open. I struggled. I know I did, but since then I have wondered just how much.

The next morning Baba and I woke before dawn. I told Baba about my dreams and noticed dark circles beneath his eyes. Before the rest of the camp stirred, we saddled Baba's warhorse and rode home through a fresh snowstorm, arriving in our courtyard to a whirlwind of chaos. Men shouted and rushed about, pulling at their beards. Bibi Shirin wandered in a daze, calling my brother's name and crying. Baba took me in his arms and ran inside.

◆ ◆ ◆

9

A Brother Lost

He often woke me by jumping on my bed or running around the room or just by sitting and waiting until my eyes opened. Flashing a smile, he would pull me out from under thick quilts and lead me on a romp through Baba's summer garden, sitting between the four high walls of the battlements. He would leap into Baba's arms, bounce on Baba's knees and laugh, while I stood beneath a willow tree and watched, pain and happiness, two edges of the same knife cutting into my heart.

Then he would run back and pull me from my curtain of willow branches into the sunshine. We sailed sticks down Baba's little stream and stepped on Mother's tulips and laughed. But not this day.

Mother sobbed while Baba flexed thick cords of muscle in his jaws and men stomped through rooms and hallways, shouting, growling, and swearing vengeance. Guns clattered and scraped against walls. Servants wailed as the men questioned each one. Two men dragged Fatima out of her room and brought her to us. Eyes wide, she shook, cried and beat her hands against her chest.

I remembered part of a dream from last night and it startled me in that moment, as forgotten dreams sometimes do. I felt a pain in the side of my head and my eyes clouded so I hid from her black eyes, pulling my coat up over my chin and mouth, covering my nose. I moved to the corner and sat behind a soldier who let me hold his Kalashnikov, the metal cold and dead. I peeked around the soldier, though I did not want to.

Mother shouted, slapped Fatima across the face and had her dragged away. For a long time, I thought she died. Then came the day of crows.

◆ ◆ ◆

10

Sikandur and the Leopard

A roar pulls him from a deep and painful sleep. Head throbbing, he tries to move but cannot. Struggling beneath a thick wrapping of furs, he pulls one arm free and rubs his eyes.

Where am I?

The furs keep a chilly wind from his body, but his face feels frozen. His skin tingles with numbness. He reaches up and feels a cloth wrapped around his head while straight ahead, shadow and light blur together. Black shapes shift against a white background. A figure approaches through the haze.

"My head hurts."

"You will live."

He rubs his eyes, but they do not clear.

"How do you feel?"

Who is this? Why is it so cold?

"I cannot see."

"Soon you will see again."

"What are those... moving shadows?"

A gust of icy air carries an awful stench. The quiet lingers, interrupted only by sounds of breathing and a rising thunder inside his head.

"What is your name?"

"I..."

Pain in the side and back of his head grows to a pounding between his ears. He feels sick to his stomach.

"You are not the boy called Omar?"

"I cannot remember, but... I do not know."

"Then I will call you boy until you remember your name." The voice sounds irritated, and a shadow moves into the light and fades away.

Time passes. He sleeps, wakes, and sleeps again. His eyes improve little. He can see only darkness and light, and from this, he knows the days pass too fast to count.

"Who are you? Where are we? Is this my home?"

"One day, when you heal, I will take you to a new home. You will be warm and your mother will feed you and take care of you. You are my son."

"I am?"

"Yes, your name is Omar. You have forgotten. That is why I asked you. To see if you could remember your name. I found you on the mountain. Hurt. You must have fallen and hit your head. Soon you will remember again."

"Am I going to die? I cannot see."

"You will not die. I will not allow it." The voice belongs to a man who pulls the blankets tight around the boy and puts a warm cap over the boy's head. "They took my sons. I won't let them take you."

"Take me where?"

Dark and light and dark again. Wind howls all the time. The man keeps him wrapped in blankets. The days pass. The man whispers strange words and then hums a soft melody, soothing and lulling the boy towards sleep.

"He owed me a son. I warned him, but he did nothing. Now the debt is paid."

The man mumbles for another moment before settling to a silence broken by heavy padding steps, occasional rumbles and soft growls.

He dreams of a woman with long hair. She stands in the narrow window of a stone tower and gazes at snow-mantled mountains with one hand above her eyes to shield against the blazing sun. She sings a gentle song and climbs out the window to float above a snowfield towards a long silver waterfall that plunges down between ice-crusted black cliffs. He shouts for her to turn around, come back, but she fades away inside a cloud of swirling, glittering crystals. The crystals turn dark and then catch fire and then the outside world burns, yet he stands alone in a circle of darkness. He wakes up screaming and tears burn trails down his face.

The man brings warm soup, chants and whispers and then blows the words in a breath over the boy's face and body. Every day the man does this.

"What are you doing?"

"These words are magic. Now nothing can hurt you. You are... invulnerable. That is unless they separate your head from your body. In that case, you die."

Magic words. Headless bodies. This is...

Over time, his vision improves, and he struggles to regain his feet. One day, as the sun splashes a sharp brilliance into his world, he rises on wobbling legs, leans against the cold sharp stones of the wall and edges forward towards a white curtain that lays at the end of his vision. Something brushes against him. He turns to face yellow eyes and teeth longer than his hand. He looks down. Pieces of a man lay strewn across the ground. An arm lies next to a pale head that stares at him from white hollows. The ground shifts beneath his feet and he falls. He wants to run, but his feet slide, and he lands on his back. A huge white cat stands over him, sniffing the air and licking its face the way cats do. He squeaks out a call for help, but only the frail echo of his own voice responds.

The air turns frigid cold. He swallows hard. Throat aches and teeth rattle and bang against each other. He backs away from the cat, sliding on his hands and knees. The cat trots forward and yawns. The gaping red maw with long, sharp teeth startles him. The boy cries out and hurries toward the light. He falls into the shimmering curtain and tumbles down through soft wet clouds. Sometime later, he comes to a stop. The world darkens and the echo of magic words fades into nothing.

♦ ♦ ♦

11

Searching and the Day of Crows

Uncle and I searched for my brother every day. I rode on his lap from village to village, through ice and snow, over mountains and across rivers, questioning farmers, smugglers, and ragged starving Mujahideen.

Have you seen a boy like this one?

There are many boys like that one.

I mean just like this one. A boy with a face exactly like this boy. Have you seen one?

I have not.

The story remained unchanged no matter how far we rode, how long we searched, and my dreams grew terrible.

On the night my brother vanished, I dreamed of a black-winged demon with a terrible face, leathered wings and massive stained claws. The monster snatched our soldiers from the battlements and flew to a great coliseum where it clawed them open from belly to neck, spilling entrails over stone pews, columns and arches all around. Often, I saw the demon with my brother gripped in its talons, his face stained with tears and a huge white cat with yellow eyes watching from the peak of a distant mountain. I woke up shaking.

Uncle calmed me and fed fresh logs to the fire. He said the flames would drive the demon from my dreams, but fire possessed no power against the demon for as I fell again to sleep, he roared and from his mouth spewed an inferno and he tore his claws across the sky ripping it open and from this gash dropped winged beasts that consumed the stars and moon until nothing remained but darkness. In that darkness I trembled, waiting for my end. Daylight became my refuge, and I faced the nights hoping to stay awake, listening to the darkness, watching shadows shift and wander in the moonlight.

We went on this way, days melting into nights. Uncle kneeled upon his prayer rug and begged God for my brother's life with prayers and promises. We sacrificed a lamb in every hamlet, giving the meat to the poor and needful. The weeks wore on. His prayers remained unanswered.

One night, as we sat next to the fire, a man shouted out and hailed us. Uncle bade him enter the camp and warm himself. He carried an old flintlock rifle, and a stained bag smelling of acid and a certain enigmatic sweetness.

He kept looking into the shadows where Uncle stood, kneeled, and bowed his head, then back at me, his eyes like shifting beads of black reflecting the campfire. Then he asked me why I did not pray. I replied I did not know the prayer and why did he not pray. A scowl darkened his face. He said he prayed just moments ago, and he pulled the bag closer to himself, scraping it over rocks with a heavy dull sound.

Roasting lamb shanks dropped grease into the fire, and the sizzle drew his eyes that way. He spoke about God and a reward for killing unbelievers. I asked him if God created both the believer and the unbeliever and he replied, God created everything. Then I asked him why God would create both and then have one murder the other. He shook his head and called me a name I did not understand. His mustache twitched and his voice strained as he cursed unbelievers. He reached back into the shadows behind him where the old flintlock's tarnished barrel reflected gold and dark, blood and fire.

It happened fast and loud. The bullet tore into his head and out the other side. I scrambled around a boulder until I saw Uncle standing tall and fierce. Tears wet against his face, reflecting fire, golden rivers flowing. Then he dragged the man's body into the dark and tossed it over the cliff. I listened, but I did not hear it hit the bottom. We opened his bag and inside we found a woman's head, bloody and bulging. A putrid essence careened us back against the rocks.

Uncle took her into the shadows, buried her, and said a prayer. He came back to the fire, sat down, and carved a slice of lamb for me. My hand trembled as I reached out and the meat fell to the dirt. Uncle held out another piece, but I had no stomach for food. From that night on, Uncle's shoulders slumped even more. He bent beneath the weight of his great burden as we rode from village to village.

We searched for so very long. The seasons changed. Summer heat baked the earth and battles raged all around us. The daytime air filled with the stench of death and at night, vast numbers of fires burned on mountainsides, men camping in small separate groups. In the fall, a month-long ceasefire came and went, and as fall ended, the bombs fell again. I had not yet seen a Russii, although we passed Baba several times as he rushed into battle, riding his old mare, leading men into gorges or across valleys. We watched, waved, shouted, but he never heard us, never looked up.

Long months passed, and we found nothing. When winter filled the valleys with snow, Uncle turned Jaheel around and began the long journey home.

We crested the pass and rode through the village. Crows circled our four stone towers. Black dots against the bruised sky. Bad omens, the villagers said, and pointed up. They had built new mud brick homes in the village, but still the western fields held many tents full of refugees. Many wandered between the campfires. A long stoic line of fishermen waded along the riverbank with poles and nets and spindly arms reaching towards the heavens while the wounded hobbled around, and the rest sat on faded rugs and stared at the sky with empty eyes.

We entered the main hall to a bustling mass of confusion and noise. Servants ran with bed sheets and pots of boiling water. My mother's face shined with tears as she ran to me, held me by my shoulders and stared into my eyes. Then she ran her hands over my body, squeezing, pulling, and hugging me close. Together we pushed our way to Fatima the witch's room and stood in the narrow hallway outside. Many toiled inside, including the village doctor whose instruments gleamed ominously on a tray by the long narrow window. A large crow sat on the windowsill until a woman shooed it off.

"What's happening Mother?"

"She's having the baby."

She had a girl. Baba named her Shaima. Just then, Shaima smiled. She won me over immediately. Her skin shone lighter than her mother's and her eyes set wider and more beautiful, but most of all, her hair took my breath away. Magic in its color, the hue of sunset, copper-gold, thick and shining like a treasure found.

♦ ♦ ♦

12

Christians

He wakes between cool sheets. He can see again. A woman in a long black gown touches his face with a warm hand. Standing in a soft ray of sunshine, she shimmers and a golden glow surrounds her face. The woman speaks and another woman like the first walks over and looks down at him.

"Am I dead?"

They laugh. "No, you are not dead. Rasul the hunter found you wrapped in a snowball and brought you to this orphanage."

"Or-phan-?"

"A place for lost children."

She leans back, her blue eyes sparkle, and she smells like flowers sitting in a window somewhere but he cannot remember where for a pain the side of his head keeps pounding and no matter how much he tries to remember, everything he knows fades away.

"Thank you," he says. He slips back into a deep sleep laced with strange images. He dreams about a mountain, a fortress, and a boy who stares at him from familiar eyes. The women take turns pressing cold and warm towels against his face. A round faced man brings needles that sting as they sink into his skin, but after a time, he feels better. One day he wakes and the women help him walk. Soon, he walks alone.

Life turns brutal. He has the disadvantage of small size and bigger boys beat him, take his shoes off and force him to walk barefoot in the stone courtyard. They laugh while he hops about. A woman rescues him and retrieves his shoes, but in the morning, the shoes are missing. The beatings continue and the days run into each other, never changing.

"What is your name, boy?"

"I don't know, I can't remember."

They name him Snow Boy, laugh and push him down. He gets up and fights back. They overpower him, hold him down and pummel him. Another woman dressed all in black sends the boys running.

"Are you all right?" she says.

"I think I am alive."

"My name is Mary."

"Mary."

They call the women Sisters. Their black gowns cover them from head to foot, every inch except their faces. They talk about Jesus and forgiveness and saving lost souls. He does not know what any of it means. They work hard taking care of the boys and girls but often lose track of him and so he slips from shadow to shadow, hiding from the bigger boys.

Some mornings babies arrive in boxes or baskets at the front door. Many of them curl up and die. The Sisters cry, wiping their eyes with little white kerchiefs. They bury the babies in a field behind the orphanage where a vast number of small wooden crosses lean like crooked scarecrows in a wheat field. A fleeting image scratches at the edges of his memory.

"Is this heaven?"

"No, this is a graveyard. Heaven is high above."

He looks up but the sisters say heaven is somewhere far above the clouds and only righteous people may go there, only good Christians.

"Other people cannot go?"

"No. Only good Christians may go to Heaven."

Good Christians. What does it mean?

The seasons change, Snow Boy grows out of his clothes. The Sisters bring him new pants and a stiff collared white shirt that buttons down the front, a new style for him. Snow melts, fresh grasses poke through the mud, and a stream bubbles through the field. Flowers grow near a white picket fence. Yellows, blues and purples burst thick and fragrant. Laying down among the flowers, he studies thin clouds that float across the sky. One cloud is in the shape of a woman. Yellow hair cascades down her back while she hums and leans over bright flowers in a tall, narrow window. The scent of her haunts him. He aches for her to turn around, but she never does.

Sister Mary tends the flowers in the field next to the orphanage. She waters them and places a fresh bloom at each cross on Sundays. She has a pretty face. Skin hued a pale pink-lavender and clear blue eyes that often fill with tears. She reads aloud from a tiny book, whispers words over graves and draws crosses over her face and chest. She does this every afternoon until the sky turns red.

Snow Boy hides in the long grasses and watches her black robes flutter and snap in the afternoon wind. Sometimes Sister Mary scares him. Her thin black profile melts into a copper sky, and when the sun dips behind the horizon, she vanishes. Then Sister Jean calls for the evening meal, a thin voice beckoning from afar. Sister Jean smiles from a moon round face, stands in the doorway and waves, her arms sweeping back and forth above her head.

One scorching summer day, Kumar arrives. He claims to be of royal blood and that his parents will come and take him home. Kumar slithers and crawls. His eyes bulge and he sweats even on cool days. Kumar has the benefit of size and age, and he uses these advantages against the smaller boys and girls. Snow Boy hides under his bed, but Kumar finds him. Snow Boy hides in a box, but Kumar finds him and punches him in the side of his head once, twice, three times. His eyes cloud and the entire world turns gray, but he does not cry. He learns to hate Kumar, but hate does not keep Kumar away.

"I am strong. You are weak. It is my right to take what is yours and make you my slaves." Kumar smiles while saying this and the children hide, and Kumar walks the courtyard alone.

At night, Kumar turns into a monster. He smells acid sweet, and Snow Boy drowns beneath the monster's weight. After a time, Snow Boy loses himself in a dreamland. A gray field of black stemmed flowers and white petals melting in long liquid teardrops. Shadows haunt his sleep from behind curtains of glittering white. Sometimes he dies in his dreams, suffocating beneath the sick-sweet, heavy stench of Kumar. He wakes soaked in sweat. Soon he fears sleep and the monsters that visit him in the dark, so he stays awake and follows Sister Mary, hiding in cupboards outside her room at night, staying close to her during the day, avoiding the other children, avoiding Kumar.

Sister Mary grows ever thinner until one day she falls to her knees among the flowers, rolls over and stares at the sky. Her blue eyes turn to glass and reflect clouds that suddenly burst open and send down a torrent of water and lightning strikes. Kneeling in the thick pounding rain, Sister Jean reaches out and closes Sister Mary's eyes. The next day, beneath a clear sky, they bury her in the field. Snow Boy sits beside her cross and waits for her to come out and go to heaven. She never does.

Time passes. Sun, moon, and stars streak the sky in an endless blur of color. He dreams of mountains, snow, and a stone fortress. A white horse prances by a silver stream, purple flowers sway in the soft wind, and smoke rises from the chimneys of a snow-covered village. The dream haunts him every night until one morning he leaves the orphanage to search for this place. He goes only a short distance through the woods before he sees Kumar sitting beneath a tree with a spoon in his chest. He nods and passes, knowing.

The day burns hot. So hot the air sizzles and rocks groan and dragonflies fall to the dirt. Cracks open in the earth, long thin mouths begging for water. The ground burns his feet until they bleed. He has no shoes, so he pulls his shirtsleeves off and uses them for socks and wraps the extra pieces around his feet. He limps pasts burning villages where bodies smolder in black holes and naked children wander through the dust whirls. He knows he can do nothing for them, so he turns towards a range of mountains shining in the distance.

At night, he curls up between rocks still warm from the sun and pulls a tattered piece of canvas over himself. In his dreams, a woman's voice sings from far away and drifts ever further. He tries to remember the singer's face, but his memories have withered and new terrors have taken up residence.

Hands push and pull him in different directions. A dark face mocks him. A spoon flashes in the moonlight. He tries to resist the terrors but they grow stronger, so he sleeps less and some nights not at all, preferring to struggle on towards the mountains.

As daylight breaks, he comes to another small village where the people live in shacks and holes cut deep into hillsides. They give him bread and tea and he eats some, saves the rest for his journey. He continues towards the mountains, unable to resist the strange pull of fading memories. Along his path, lines of beggars without limbs sit, mutter, and rattle their cups. They stare, hunger screaming in their faces.

He finds refuge in a dark forest, stopping for a day. At night he listens to bursts of wild screaming, feet scurrying through the underbrush, voices muttering and whispering. None of it matters to him. He finally sleeps for a few hours and then walks on, his feet blistered and bleeding.

The next evening, before darkness falls again, he leaves the forest behind. After two days, he arrives at the base of the mountains, but weak and starving, he can hardly walk. He finds a thin blue ribbon of water trickling through a desolate canyon of black and gray rocks. Drinking and then resting, he sees a flat rock that leads behind a small waterfall. Tiny fish swim beneath the falls, trapped in shallow pools by thin ice. Eating them raw while standing in the water, he feels like a giant. The fish gives him a bit of strength, so he plods on.

He walks for one more day, climbing ever higher into the mountains. Far away, a drummer beats a slow cadence that echoes from canyon to canyon. His eyes close and he stumbles along, lost within the drummer's beat. The hours pass, he collapses, rolls down a hillside and drifts into the dusk between life and death.

♦ ♦ ♦

13

Arad

Baba brought me a tall black horse, not a pony like the other village boys rode.

"You will ride this horse. His name is Arad."

Baba strapped the saddle to the horse's back and tightened the cinch. He did not smile. He had not smiled since Sikandur vanished two years ago. I thought he hated me for not finding my brother. Perhaps I hated myself. Still, I rarely looked into Baba's granite face anymore.

"Come here, Omar," Baba said.

I nodded, and Baba helped me to the saddle. He slapped Arad's flank. Arad shuddered and jumped, shook his black mane and surged forward. I hung low and threw my arms around Arad's neck and whispered to him, do not let me fall. His ears perked and his dark muscles flexed, and after a time, I sat up and took a normal breath. I could not reach the reins for fear of falling, so I held on and let Arad decide where to go. This displeased Baba. He stormed up next to us on his stallion and snatched me out of the saddle.

"Use the reins. Do not let them dangle. The men are watching you. One day they will be your men. Earn their respect."

Then he dropped me on the ground and galloped away. I looked up from the dirt towards my mother's window. Set high in the eastern tower, it caught weak rays of sunlight. Birds ate from the feeders that hung below the window. Mother kept these stocked with various bird foods. Glancing down at me, she waved and then held her hands pressed together. A gust of wind pushed the hair back from her face and she waved again. I did not wave for fear of what Baba might say.

I often thought of the day she would take me to her home, the mysterious city she spoke of when we sat by her knee. Sadly, when she told us stories of her hidden world, Baba would walk in and frown and would not have it. Yet she often whispered to me in secret. You and I will go, we will leave this cold mountaintop and we will live with my people.

I got up and looked around for Arad, determined to seize his reins and ride well enough to survive the day. He stood in the tall grasses by the stream, his black coat like a brother's shadow, calling. A distance to my right, Baba sat atop a prancing, posing Jaheel. A good number of his men stood around him with guns slung over shoulders, some laughing and some just watching me with cynical eyes, waiting. In the Buzkashi field, young boys rode their ponies and fought each other for possession of a rag bundle shaped to resemble a headless lamb. I smiled at this, my time coming.

The drum thumped in the distance. Still, I had not found the drummer. However, I often dreamed of my brother, and in those dreams, I became him, I saw flashing images, faces and colors. I felt a constant pain in my head. An aching pain in the side and I knew it to be his pain and when I closed my eyes to sleep, I became him, or perhaps, he became me, I do not know. I wanted to pray for him, but I did not know how. I thought to ask Yaan, but if Baba found out, it might go bad for Yaan. Therefore, I kept my silence and waited for the day I knew in my heart must come.

◆ ◆ ◆

14

The Girl with the Green Eyes

He wakes to laughter. Horses snorting and scattering gravel. His eyes refuse to open. A hand touches his cheek and a voice murmurs close to his ear. He tries to speak but fails. Something cold and wet touches his face. Then darkness pulls him back into a deep embrace.

Time passes. Shadows and light play on his eyelids and the warm heavy scent of baked bread drifts by. He feels a warm soft piece of bread against his lips, then against his tongue, but he cannot swallow.

Someone laughs, someone else whispers in his ear, yet he remains trapped within a world of scents, sounds and shifting patterns of light and dark. One day he opens his eyes and looks up at a green sky filled with tiny stars. When his eyes focus, he sees the threadbare ceiling of a tent.

A girl with blazing red hair, large sparkling green eyes and a gentle face sits next to him. She smiles and places a wet cloth on his forehead. He tries but cannot speak. His throat aches, his skin burns, and he shakes with chills. She says something, but he cannot hear over the roaring in his ears. She tilts her head and studies him, running her fingers across his brow. His eyes close and he sinks beneath cool wet waves that spring from her fingertips. The days go by like this, waking to her smile, bread and chai. A little at first, then more, then soup with lentils, yogurt, and small pieces of meat.

Many days pass before he gets up and walks out of the tent. The girl's father hugs him, ruffles his hair and kisses him on both cheeks. His rifle slides on his back, leather crackles on his chest and along his arms. He kneels and looks into the boy's eyes. The man has a burly thick mustache and beard, and warm brown eyes with deep fissures decorating the corners. The girl laughs and hugs the boy and runs her fingers through his hair.

They ask him his name.

"They called me Snow Boy."

They laugh.

"Ok Snow Boy it is."

The next day, she takes him to the village school. They entered a cave with a few rickety chairs and desks. In the mornings, he learns how to speak Pashto and read Dari. Afternoons they sit in another cave where a yellow-bearded man teaches English and tells stories of a shining wonderland called America, a place without war or hunger. Snow Boy thinks it a fairy tale, like the ones old men tell by the campfire every night.

They live in tents and caves high in the hills surrounded by giant fingers of white and gray rock and small groves of walnuts trees and patches of ground where villagers grow tomatoes, lettuce, and melons. He watches her knead dough and bake in an earthen oven. She hums and sings songs that remind him of places lost. Her green eyes sparkle with life and energy. Sometimes in the night, he hears the drum beating far away.

"Do you hear the drummer?" he says.

"Not drums. Bombs."

She works hard, taking care of the wounded. When they do not fight the invaders, they fight other camps and villages in the name of vendetta and honor. A man steals a cow and the villagers kill him for it. His family swears vengeance and two more men die in the night, throats cut by assassins. Snipers and bandits roam the hills, waiting for travelers to fall asleep. The bandits attack and then vanish into the mountains or southern deserts.

He worries about the girl, for she does not have the protection of magic words. To protect her, he learns to use the Kalashnikov, a gun as big as him. He sits atop a rusted old shell of a gunship and sounds the alert when the chopping clatter of helicopter blades drift up from the plains. Bombs fall, people burn. He stands over craters where dead lay scattered across the ground. Women shuffle from body to body, searching for their missing children.

When the men return, they bury the dead wrapped in white sheets and without crosses. He makes tiny stick crosses and places them on the graves so they will go to Heaven. At night, someone takes the crosses away.

Determined to protect the green-eyed girl, he follows her everywhere. She laughs. She sings and kneels beside the same grave once a day, and he kneels with her. She cries for a while, then rises, takes his hand and leads him beneath the trees where they sit and drink *dogh,* cool liquid yogurt with mint leaves and small chunks of cucumber. He studies her, enchanted by her wholeness. She smiles like a dream he once dreamed and he looks down ashamed, alarmed, knowing he cannot laugh or sing or smile like her. His world is empty of everything but her. He comes to think that if he can stay with her, he might one day become whole again.

Seasons drift into each other and he grows tall as the cattails by the river. The men talk about guerrilla warfare, and he learns that the girl's father commands the local Mujahideen. They fight against the Russii who have tanks, jets and helicopters, while they have nothing but old Kalashnikovs taken from the bodies of their enemies. They sometimes find missiles and mortars, and they learn how to use the enemy's weapons against him. Every day her father leads men into the mountains. At night, they return with clothes, faces and beards covered in dust. Some come back without limbs. Many die during the night, their eyes like black holes begging for light.

One night, the men gather all the women and children and march them high into the mountains. Panic takes hold as whispers run wild.

Russii are coming.

Tanks and artillery and killing machines.

They push and pull heavy-laden donkeys and horses up steep mountainsides towards a series of caves.

We will stay the winter here, says the girl's father. That night the men gather by the campfire and argue, curse and shout. They want to kill a certain Russii, but the girl's father says no, he is not a soldier and the others shout he must be a spy or a man of great importance. The men pack their horses and make ready.

The girl's father comes to her and kisses her on both cheeks. He claps a hand on Snow Boy's shoulder for a moment, then ruffles his hair, instructs him to protect the people and be vigilant. A long journey, he says, and she cries. When will you return, she says? He shakes his head. Only God knows, he says.

Days run warm, sun basting the mountains. The nights turn cold and frosted. Snow Boy sleeps with the girl, wrapped in the same blankets. They hold each other to keep out a frigid wind that blows into the caves and swirls rock dust and smoke from campfires into every pore, mouth and nostril. Bread and tea are running out, the meat consumed long ago, and the men have not returned. The women cry and the children sit in the sun and wait. Below them, stretched across the lower mountains and distant hills smoke curls high into the sky.

She says the Russii are trying to reach them and the men fight to stop them. When gunships clatter overhead, the women scurry to hide their children in the back of the caves where they huddle, their clothes now gray with dust. The falling dust tortures them, gathering within their chests where it causes endless coughing, bleeding from the mouth, skin sores.

The old women say to move the children higher into the northeastern mountain ranges where the air is too thin for gunships to fly. After much discussion and tears from the children, they decide the razor sharp and forbidding peaks loom too far away for a journey of women and children. Everyone settles in, the girl pulling Snow Boy by the hand, leading him everywhere, as if she fears he might vanish into the night, fall down a cliff, stumble on a cluster mine, or trip over the traps the men left all around the caves to catch intruders.

One morning they search for wood, descending into a glen of alpine trees and crooked, bleached trunks, gnarled stumps, and animal bones lying all around this bombed out stretch of dirt that once nurtured a thick forest. They tie the wood to a donkey's back and push and pull the braying beast back to the caves where it is unloaded.

At night, beside the campfire, old women whisper stories of a secret mountain and a city long forgotten by everyone but the very oldest. They call it Alexander's city and tell of endless caverns full of jewels and gold beyond measure. Nobody knows exactly where the city is, but they believe the old stories handed down by grandfathers and great grandfathers. Snow Boy loves the stories, falling asleep by the fire as the old women prattle them out, cackling and grunting as they warm their bones. Complaining as old people sometimes do, passing their prayer beads between their fingers, whispering their endless devotions, reading their tattered holy books and shaking their heads as one reads aloud, bringing tears streaming down their deep-creased faces.

The weeks drag on and the thunder of bombs draws ever closer. Then, in the cold of a moonless night, they hear horses and footsteps and everyone awakes, shaking, shivering, whispering. A voice calls out in Dari, but sometimes the Russii know Dari, so they sit quiet and listen. The voice again, this time recognized as the girl's father and she jumps to her feet and runs out into the night. Snow Boy follows a step behind, the old Kalashnikov gripped tight in his hands.

The girl cries and hugs her father. Women stumble across the rocks to their men who greet their families in hushed voices. A mother and her children bring candles and a hand lantern. The men's flashlights crisscross against the rocks. A tall stranger is with them, a shock of dull yellow hair, blazing blue eyes. Snow Boy watches the men push and pull the archeologist, a professor, a Russii, the first he has ever seen. The Russii, perhaps stunned by his circumstances, smiles at Snow Boy and in that smile Snow Boy finds no malice and then he wonders how men without malice can cluster bomb and fire rockets into villages full of women and children.

The morning brings the scent of battle, drifting up from below. Smoke fills the sky, and all eyes turn downward, waiting for the Russii to come charging up the mountain and rescue the professor. Some shout he is a spy and others shout he is only a professor. The arguments erupt into fistfights and curses. Through it all, the girl's father watches and remains silent, shaking his head whenever a man approaches and points a gun towards the Russii.

The father takes Snow Boy by one hand and his daughter by the other, and together they approach the Russii. This is my son, and this is my daughter, he says. They will feed you, bring you clean clothes. You are my guest now, and none shall harm you.

The girl, always outspoken, asks the Russii, why do you bomb us? Why do you hate us?

The Russii smiles and shakes his head. In Dari, accented only slightly, he says, "My child, I have never in my life bombed anyone or done anything to hurt my Afghan brothers and sisters, and I never will. My father is Afghan. I just want to find Alexander's tomb."

On that frozen mountain, as bombs fall and the skies fill with smoke, Snow Boy meets Professor Sergy Volkov and becomes his young friend.

The next day, as Snow Boy and the girl bring the Russii his breakfast of tea and bread, the Russii nods his thanks and pulls a small dirty notebook from his shirt pocket.

"Do you know what this is?" he says.

"A book," says the girl.

"No, not a book, a journal. A place to write your thoughts. Do you know how to write?"

"Yes, we both know how to write," she says.

The Professor talks about how he has searched for years, since before the war started, in the northern and eastern mountain ranges of Afghanistan and southern Tajikistan for a fabled city that holds the tomb of Alexander. He reads how he uncovered a statue of Alexander in a city he dug out from beneath twenty feet of dirt where it remained lost for years, and how the times changed from when Afghans greeted guests as friends to the years of warfare leading to mistrust.

Every day the Russii reads more of his journal for Snow Boy and the girl, and every day they sit longer and longer, listening to him tell of gold and jewels that he recovered from sites across the north. He shows them how to write their own journals and as he eats his meal, he questions them about their day, reviewing all they saw, all they heard.

As the weather warms, unknown men arrive at the camp. They speak different languages, wear long robes, and scratch their thin beards. They cannot conceal their pale faces. Villagers grumble and cast nervous glances their way. They bring new guns and the men love these. They give the girl's father a long gun that shoots a huge bullet with a white tail. Soon the night skies light up with a hundred blazing trails and the enemy falls like wounded birds. The people cheer.

One day, when Snow Boy wakes, he goes to find the professor, but Sergy's tent is empty. The girl says they took him across the border and released him where Sergy would find his way back home, back to his people. Snow Boy shakes his head and thinks Sergy will not survive to see his home, for many of the men hated him, many swore to kill him, and many of the men have left the village in the night.

The next week, the girl's father returns with his men and brings with him other men, dark faced, lean warriors from lands far away. They fight the Russii. Their language is guttural, ancient and sometimes beautiful, but often violent like themselves. These men live to fight, and when they sit by the fire, they do not laugh or smile or banter with one another. Their pale eyes flash hollow and distant.

Battles go on for days. Food is scarce. They eat lizards and boiled weeds, nuts and tree bark. The orchards wither in winter but in the spring, fresh fruits and vegetables emerge again, undaunted by the blood that fed the ground.

One day, a short man with a long black beard rides into camp. Men gather to bow and kiss his hand in greeting. People arrive from other camps and villages to meet the man they call *"Mahlim"*, the teacher. Suddenly everyone prays, young and old alike, but Snow Boy does not know the prayer and so he sits and watches the sun melt into the plains. Reds, purples and pinks blend into an indigo sky. The people rise and kneel, shadows against the liquid horizon as memories play along the edges of his mind. He hears a cannon's roar and children's laughter in the fading light.

After the prayer villagers celebrate, children running and chasing each other. Laughter and handshakes and slaps on the back for the adults. Cooks prepare a feast. The men cut the necks of young lambs, skin and roast them across deep pits filled with fire and glowing red boulders. Snow Boy creeps to the edge of a pit. The smell of meat cooking overwhelms his senses. He grows dizzy and almost falls into the hole, but a strong hand from behind pulls him away. He turns to face Mahlim standing there smiling down through an unbroken line of white teeth. Snow Boy runs away, straight polished white teeth being rare in his world, he thinks the man part cat or worse, a cannibal. He has listened to the stories told at night by the campfire, and he knows the terrors that frighten people more than death.

"Cannibals live in the tallest of mountains," one says, "where sane men do not wander."

"People disappear," says another, "never found again."

The side of Snow Boy's head hurts again and his eyes cloud over. He remembers a tall man chanting in a cave and a skull staring from empty eye sockets.

Magic words.

The bearded man tells the girl's father to train the young men to make bombs. He will pay if the men will die for Allah.

"Who is Allah?"

"Allah is the Almighty God, silly Snow Boy." She laughs and tickles him.

"I thought Jesus-."

"No! Jesus is a prophet. Allah is God and Mohammad, his very last prophet."

"What is a prophet?"

"A wise man blessed by visions from God."

"I don't understand. Why did the sisters say Jesus?"

"Because they are Christians and we are not."

"We are not?"

"No. We are Moslems."

"Is there a difference? The sisters wear long black dresses, cover their heads, and pray. Your women wear long dresses, cover their heads, and pray. Why is there a difference?"

She looks at him with her head tilted a bit to one side. Then she smiles and takes his hand and marches him down the hillside towards a small grove of trees beside the river. They pass an old woman baking with wrinkled dotted hands, children with old Kalashnikovs in one hand and ragged spelling books in the other, young and old without arms or legs lying in the dirt, hollow-eyed and pale, bleeding from badly wrapped injuries. The dying stare, moan, and cry out for God to take them to heaven. Snow Boy shakes his head, knowing that heaven cannot exist, for Sister Mary never left the dark ground where they laid her.

They walk to the river's edge where long thin chinar leaves dance on the glimmering liquid surface. They sit together and toss rocks at large fish swimming in the clear shallows. For a time, she is silent, facing the setting sun. Then she turns with a serious look in her eyes and her hands take a firm grip of his shoulders.

"You will learn the difference when you are older. But do not talk about Jesus here. It's not safe."

He nods and shrugs. Behind the girl, standing by the river, the Mahlim watches him with glowing eyes.

One day, the girl's father calls him over. He wears sadness on his face. Nearby, the girl cries, her head down. Her cheek bears roughened red marks, the imprint of fingers lingering on her face. Tears slip from her eyes and form clear bubbles in the sand. She rushes over and hugs Snow Boy and gushes hot salty tears onto his face and lips. It is in this moment that Snow Boy's love for her becomes everlasting.

"My name is Helena," she says.

"Helena." He repeats the name to remember. Her father looks down. Wet pools gather in the bottoms of his eyes, and he ruffles Snow Boy's hair and kisses him on each cheek. Her father takes Mahlim's paper money. He tells Snow Boy to go with Mahlim. He will take him to America, to a proper home. He says Snow Boy will eat nutritious food and go to a proper school. He will be safe from the bombs and gunships and the dying. Snow Boy nods and feels another piece of him tear off and float away in the raging river of his life. He wonders if he will remember this place and the girl with the green eyes.

♦ ♦ ♦

15

Lessons

The drummer drummed and I searched the hills and canyons, along the rivers and streams, but did not find him. Elusive and always distant. No matter how far I searched, his drumbeat stayed an equal distance from me. I determined never to end my search until I found the drummer. Yet nightfall came, and still nothing. No drummer. No brother.

Making everything worse, I grew frustrated with dreams of my twin, knowing that he suffered somewhere past our ring of mountains. At night, his life became my nightmare and I saw death, fire, burning rivers of blood and a girl with red hair. I asked Baba if I might travel alone and search for my brother, but he said no. He said Sikandur must be dead, for we did not find him all those years. I said he lives and I know it. I share his dreams. Baba cursed and said he did not believe in dreams any more than divine justice. I knew he lived and I knew one day I must find him.

"Lean down," he said. "Lean all the way down and snatch the calf up by his legs, like this."

He swept by, hanging from Jaheel's back. With one hand he seized the headless calf from the ground, tossed it over his lap and rode out across the Buzkashi field. He dropped the calf in the center of the circle, although the mark lay beneath three fingers of fresh snow. Having done this a thousand times, Baba needed no mark. Baba needed very little of anything. Only his beloved Jaheel, who whinnied, reared up and kicked out his forelegs and together they appeared majestic, ready to grow wings, leap into the air and capture the sun.

He leaned down, plucked the calf from the snow and galloped across the field at full speed. Jaheel's hoofs pounded and I shivered, pinpricks spreading over my back and arms. Baba stopped halfway across the carpet of last night's snow. He swung the calf up over his head and tossed it to the ground. He waved and I knew my task. Riding low across Arad's back, I begged for mother luck to keep me in the saddle, after all the calf likely weighed more than I.

Leaning, I hung my arm down. My fingertips cut through snow. Arad galloped, kicking snow in my face. My stomach tightened as we approached the calf. My hand closed on a leg and I pulled. I thought I had the calf, but the calf had me and while I lay on the ground rubbing my head and arm, Baba rode off through mist-filtered rays of the morning sun. The men followed, some casting cold looks back at me. He did not turn around or come back that day. A long day of tumbling, reaching, and numbing cold that turned my fingers into wooden sticks.

The next morning, Baba sent us out once more to search for my brother. Uncle and I rode for days, far into the east, from ice-clad mountaintops to the desert plains. We searched every village and town once more.

We came to a village on the edge of a thick alpine forest. The village contained a few mud huts with thatch roofs, hanging wash and children chasing after chickens and goats. Many children, too many for a single village of five huts. Uncle asked about a boy like me but they did not know, had not seen, could not imagine. The women looked at me and wept. The children laughed, too young to understand. We asked about the forest and any villages that it might hide, but the women said do not enter, the forest contained evil spirits. No one ever came back.

Uncle shook his head. We must enter and search, he said, and so we did. The women screamed for us not to leave, for their men had died and they needed us to help them prepare for winter. But they could not sway Uncle from the forest, his eyes lighting with determination and his chin held straight. I believe he found hope again that day.

We rode around the fence that separated the village from the forest and into the dim light. Shades of green and falling rays of sunlight mixing to form a new and ever-changing world. Shadows and mists shifted among the trees whose trunks grew sometimes thick as a horse and other times, thin as a man's leg. Covered in red needles, the ground crunched beneath Arad's hoofs while Uncle's spotted horse shook his head from side to side, eyes wide and frightened. We had never seen a forest like this, so thick and beautiful and yet mysterious, holding the secret of missing men and children who wandered too far into its heart.

The new pistol that Baba had given me for my last birthday, hung against my leg in a holster fashioned from leather by Uncle's own hands. The gun, an old relic that Baba oiled and cleaned and fired a thousand times before giving it to me and teaching me how to clean and aim and fire, shined gray in the shifting sunlight. I found my grip tightening as the forest grew dark and a mist thickened. Clouds of vapor drifted past, clearing for a bit, and then a new cloud engulfed us with wetness, hiding everything.

We rode into the forest for two days and nights, camping, gathering our wood, lighting the fire and keeping a watch for the forest loomed ominous and terrifying in the night. The stars and moon did not reach their light into this place, and worry crossed Uncle's brow day and night. The third day we rode even deeper into this green womb.

When we first heard the sounds, we looked around and Uncle shouted out that we meant no harm, that we came to find a boy, and that we came to help. Skittering, shuffling, moaning sounds emanated from everywhere within the mist.

Animals, said Uncle, and pulled his Kalashnikov and laid it across his lap. I did not know of any animals that made sounds like this. The mist shifted and I heard footsteps running, soft against the pine-needled earth and Uncle shouted out, hailing whoever, whatever.

Then it happened, not the first terrible thing nor the last. Still a thing so horrifying that to this day my dreams still hold me in that forest where screaming horrors sealed themselves inside my memory forever.

I felt a coldness in my leg and I looked down to see a gray black sliver protruding from my calf and small hand attached, and to this hand a thin gray arm and to this arm, a small gray face. The face torments me to this day, gray like death itself, eyes wide and bloodshot, hair long and unkempt, the mouth bloodstained and the teeth sharpened like razors. I screamed. Uncle turned to look at me but did not understand, for he rode on the opposite side.

They are attacking me, I yelled, and Uncle jerked his pony in front of mine and shot his Kalashnikov into the mist. The thing vanished. He came to my side and studied the blade still jammed into my leg before pulling it out and wrapping my leg in a piece of his shirt. As he did this, they attacked from above, dropping on us from tree limbs. Guttural sounds came from their throats, their faces gray and white and painted with dirt, their hair long and wild. So small, they seemed like a gang of children. One dropped on Uncle's back and raised up his Stone Age blade to plunge it in his neck and at that moment, my pistol went off, shattering that small gray face into pieces, blood everywhere, on my hands and face. I shouted and Uncle fired wild into the mist. He grabbed my reins and broke into a gallop back the way we came.

We did not stop that night or the next but rode weary and slow, making our escape from this demon hell, Uncle called it, full of devils and spirits that could not die. I slept as I rode, my reins in Uncle's hand, and I dreamed of that small gray face exploding into a thousand pieces and I wondered who I had killed back there.

We finally left the forest and came to what remained of the village. The huts lay burned and crumbled, the animals gone, the women dead in postures unwilling, and the children lay in a ditch, bodies piled and festering. Not one living thing remained. Uncle could not determine who had done this, Russii or raiders from across the border or those denizens of the forest we had left behind. We buried the dead and stood there over their graves, and I felt a terrible anger painting me a new color, changing my world forever.

When we arrived home, I asked Baba for a rifle.

♦ ♦ ♦

16

Snow Boy in America

School consists of a room with a chair, a small white desk with an English translation book, and a Koran. A bare bulb hangs from the ceiling, splashing garish light across white walls, which contain one tiny window the size of a small prayer rug. A mattress in one corner serves as a bed, softer than anything he can remember.

Mahlim instructs him to read Koran and pray five times each day. If he cannot do as instructed, two men take him to a room beneath the house, push him to his knees on a concrete floor and play a video in which a man reads from a gold-bound Koran. They tell him to repeat the words and learn humility. He refuses to say the words. They beat him with long, thin pieces of wood. Then they pick him up and chain him by his wrists to an iron beam in the ceiling. After he hangs for what seems like days, they take him back to his room and lock the door.

From the small window, his eyes explore a deep dark forest,. Treetops scratch the sky and trunks thick as a house stretch upwards. His tiny window sits a distance from the ground. Jumping means a broken leg, maybe two. The door remains locked. They do not allow him to open the window or to walk outside. As punishment for his refusal to pray, they nail hard black plastic over the window and Snow Boy's heart sinks further into darkness. They feed him once a day and he eats alone. The cook brings a plate of rice and meat and slips it through a barely open door. He never sees the cook's face. She keeps it hidden behind a cloth mask. He only sees her dark, fearful eyes flash behind the screen.

Once a week Mahlim comes to his room and orders him to recite the Koran. Since he has refused to learn the prayer, they take him down to the room under the house and hang him from the ceiling. Soon his punishments increase in measure and duration. One day, as he hangs from the iron beam, Mahlim uses a whip to instruct him in the words of Allah. The whip slices air. Blood splatters on walls.

"Allah is my God, and Mohammad is his prophet. Say it, boy."

The whip cracks and slashes his back. He saves his strength, knowing this too will end and he will survive. He has a strange faith in the tall man's magic words. Still, some days he is not so lucky, those days when Mahlim displays a heavy hand.

"Allah is my God, and Mohammad is his prophet. Say it, boy."

He holds on, clinging to his memory of Helena. He drifts in and out of dreams while Mahlim cracks the whip. The sound lingers, Mahlim's voice drones, flat, hard, hypnotic.

"So you will never again talk about Christians and Jesus," Mahlim says.

Days dissolve into nights. Time becomes a dark thing, dead, silent and unending. The room beneath the house has no windows, but fresh chains hang from the ceiling around a pole that Snow Boy comes to know well as his cheek rests on the cold painted metal. He no longer feels pain. His mind and spirit have left. Only his body remains. Memories fade, dreams crack and shatter, reality bleeds and pools beneath his feet. Years pass and Snow Boy turns to stone.

◆ ◆ ◆

- Part II -
The Adjustment

17

A Visit from Death

I stood beside my mother's bed, her hand in mine and Baba's hand tight around my other wrist. Wind rattled the windows and I imagined dark amorphous shapes floating over the bed, pulling her away from me. Uncle stood to my right, and Purdill whispered in his ear every few seconds as a soldier whispered to him and the messages passed from man to man like this out into the hallway where everyone rushed from room to room searching, swearing and cursing fathers and mothers of all assassins.

"They poisoned her," said our village doctor.

"I see that," Baba said.

Uncle's face shined a ghostly white. Mother's eyes never left mine.

"The tea," the doctor said.

Baba lifted the teakettle and smelled the still warm liquid within.

"No smell."

"A poison unknown to me, but a powerful potion prepared by a well-practiced chemist."

"No such chemist here," said Baba.

"Perhaps gypsies, traveling from the north. They could bring such a poison."

"Koochies? But why?" Baba whispered. "She never harmed a soul."

A shout in the hallway, the line of messengers leaned and whispered words traveled backwards finally reaching Uncle's ears.

"We have it," Uncle said.

Baba stood, and the great bear spirit that lived inside him growled.

♦ ♦ ♦

18

The Stoning

A burly pine thick with needles grew at the edge of an ice blue stream that meandered past the village, down through the poppy fields, past the high grasses where it straightened to form a deep trench between the cliffs and the wide Buzkashi field. The tall man stood there once again, wrapped in his thick overcoat. Baba nodded to him as we passed on our way to the Buzkashi field.

"Who is he, Baba?"

"I told you. He was a Pathan warrior, but tragedy drove him mad."

"I mean his name."

"His name is Abraham. They called him Abraham the giant. I want you to stay away from him. He has lost himself in his despair. Such things happen to men who lose those that they love."

When I looked back, Abraham had vanished and yet I still felt him watching from the mountainside where boulders and granite pillars stood separated by patches of wild grass and scree. The man raised a sense of familiarity. Scanning the fields, I did not see Abraham and so I let my eyes return to the horror unfolding before me.

She screamed. Uncle propelled her towards a thick post. She struggled against her bonds and flashed her teeth like Wolf the massive hound Baba recently chained in the garden outside my door for protection. She stopped and dug her heels into the ground. Uncle picked her up and tossed her over his shoulder. He set her down and bound her to the post. Arms tied back, she lunged to bite his hand and ram against his belly and shouted a litany of vicious curses and cast her gaze around the circle of villagers gathered for her punishment.

Floating in the giant white pools of her eyes, her black orbs landed on me with a hateful glare. Over the years, those fierce eyes had burned holes into my soul. The biggest, blackest, and most evil eyes in my world. Often I saw her in my dreams, a raised club in her hand, leaning as if she meant to smite me a blow. She swayed, her eyes glinted and the club flashed through the air and I knew then what she had done to my brother. Baba laughed when I told him about my dreams, and when I insisted she knew what happened to my brother, he swore by the white beards of our ancestors and said to stop bothering him with my stories.

So I watched her from secret nooks in the castle walls as she hummed a mournful tune and wandered through the hallways, rubbing the cold stones and mumbling soft words. From her first days in our land, villagers claimed she had the powers of a witch. *Jahdugar* they called her, and she truly looked like one. Wild black hair fell past her shoulders to an inchoate waist. I feared the strange woman who, my mother said, made a pact with *Shaitan*, the devil, to give him my brother. However, when she looked upon Shaitan, it drove her mad and she took to wandering through the hallways, whispering, waving her hands and casting spells on the walls.

Villagers closed the surrounding circle. Men cursed through frosted beards. Angry eyes gleamed. Some prayed, some did not, but all believed in omens and magic and the words of older, wiser men. She let loose a terrible shriek that pounded against my ears and I turned to run, but Baba held me firm and pulled me back in front of him.

"Steady boy. Be strong. Remember, this witch poisoned your mother."

He held my face in two calloused hands, keeping the wind and snow out of my eyes. I felt the rough edge of his sheepskin coat against the back of my head, comforting in that moment of panic.

Villagers raised their fists and shouted curses. Many called for God's wrath to strike down upon the witch who continued to scream in streaks, stopping only to catch her breath and then turn loose another long howl. Wind whipped her black gown to a frenzy and she moaned. Her thin lips turned blue.

I looked up at the fortress and saw my sister Shaima in the window of my mother's tower, looking down at us. The witch turned to the tower and screamed in a voice that cut through the wind.

"Shaima my daughter, do not forget this day. Escape these evil Pathans or you too will end like this."

She shouted this again and again until the crowd barked her down. She turned and hissed. The crowd flinched. A woman shooed her young children back towards the village.

"Yes. I killed her. Who was she? Nobody knows who she was or where she came from. Why should she be first wife and live in splendor while I, daughter of a warlord from Mazar, suffer like a slave?"

Her madness sent murmurs through the crowd. Roshan the saddle maker shook his head and stroked his beard. Khatim the farmer backed away two steps as she lunged from the post, straining against her bonds. Uncle took his place next to Baba and rested a hand on my shoulder. Baba lifted a hand to quiet the crowd.

"She poisoned Arya with this." Baba reached into his coat pocket and withdrew a small vial with a long blue ribbon tied around the neck. The blue ribbon fluttered in the winter wind as snowflakes swirled around us.

"Our laws are simple. If one kills another, their life is forfeit. The Koran says, 'take not life, which God has made sacred, except with justice and law. Thus does he command you so you may learn wisdom'. When I drop my hand, you will deliver justice upon this murderess."

Baba dropped his hand. Borak the butcher picked up a large rock and flung it at the witch. His son Abdul and I flipped rocks across the pond in nearly the same motion. This struck me like a piece of a puzzle that refused to fit. Then the villagers turned loose a barrage. I heard a crack like the snapping of a chicken's neck. She screamed and hid her face in the folds of her gown.

I looked around at the circle of my people, their faces changed from the friendly, cheerful faces I saw on Friday afternoons that often turned into celebrations with a carnival atmosphere. Peddlers raised their tents and hawked pots, pans, and clothing. Old men sat around fires and told tales of the old days and acrobats performed for the children. During the day, we had goat fights and in the afternoon varieties of birds and gamecocks battled each other in struggles of strength and endurance. By Friday's nightfall families gathered from the hills and mountains, musicians played and everyone stayed the night in our courtyard, singing and laughing, faces beaming in the light of campfires.

Now those same faces twisted and stretched, caught in a vengeful fury. Brutal minutes passed and I realized that I no longer recognized most of them, though I knew them all my life. Borak turned into a blackbird. His cloak became great hairy wings, and I knew I could never again see him as the friendly man who laughed and tossed Wolf his meals every day. My friend Kai turned into a four-legged beast scrambling for rocks, his face blurred and incongruous. Even the women transformed into dark wraiths, scrambling, bending, and arcing stones into the air.

She screamed when a large rock crashed against her face. Sagging against the wood, she slumped to the ground. Villagers turned wild, crazed, and unrecognizable as men or women or even as animals. They became chaotic shadows from some other world, distant from earth as the sun. Their uncontrolled rage taking them back to some primeval lust that even beasts do not share. I looked down, afraid of them for the first time in my life.

Soon a running red stream advanced on us in the shape of a pointing finger. From this crimson rill, slight puffs of vapor curled and my heart pounded in my head. Thinking the blood poisoned, I tried to slide away.

"Stand still, boy," Baba said. He shook my face with his hand, twisted my neck back around and forced me to watch.

"Stop, brother," Uncle said.

He sounded angry. I had never seen Uncle angry.

"He is just a boy. You shouldn't have brought him down here for this."

Baba stomped his feet, perhaps to keep them warm. My feet felt frozen to the ice.

"When you have a son, you can decide what to do with him. Omar is mine and I say he grows up strong. If he does not see this, how will he dispense justice when his turn comes?"

Uncle's hand tightened on my shoulder. Nobody talked back to Baba, the elder of the two brothers. Sometimes I feared for Uncle's life. Baba had killed many men. I witnessed executions from Uncle's window as squads fired and men fell into the abyss.

Baba's wrath invokes fear and terror from most. I often caught him glaring at Uncle from beneath thick brows, his eyes gleaming with the energy of some unknowable thought. Therefore, I feared for my Uncle while I watched my stepmother dissolve into a pile of black and red mud. She laid with her head back, mouth open, eyes bloodied. Rock continued to pile on top until only her ebony hair remained visible. For a moment, I thought I saw her spirit rise from her body, but it might just have been the frosted breath of demons. I tried to get away again, but Baba held me firm.

"Do not let the men see you turn away." He took a finger and wiped the snow from my eyes. "Pathans fear nothing, not even the angel of death."

Uncle cleared his throat and I thought he would say something or take me away from this, but he did neither. Demons raged and rocks fell. After a time, the demons grew silent and some wandered away. The rocks stopped and the demons stood still. I heard guns shift from hands to backs and the air smelled bitter and salted.

"It is over," Uncle said.

"It is not over," said Baba.

We stood there for a long time and the demons slowly changed back into human beings, none approaching the other. Perhaps they no longer recognized each other or even themselves. Somewhere in the distance, the drummer pounded a heavy beat on his drum, the sound drifting with each snowflake as it fell slowly to earth.

"Where is that drummer?" I said.

Uncle squeezed my shoulder. I looked up into a steel gray sky and snow fell in spirals, thicker and thicker until the sky vanished and only white remained.

◆ ◆ ◆

19

The Chess Game

In my dreams, my mother died before my eyes. Her blue eyes closed while her lips changed in degrees from pale pink to purple as the poison took hold and pulled her under. Her last breath taken, she stilled, but for many long nights, her cries echoed through the empty corridors. I searched for her spirit when sleeplessness drove me to wander the fortress. I kept remembering the night she died, when Uncle tried to take me from her room while Baba held a tight grip around my wrist, so tight that a bruise remained for a week.

"So you know death," Baba said. "Stare it in the face and do not flinch."

I think I hated him in that moment, and though I felt the guilt that accompanies hate, I reasoned that love and hate reflected each other and I had no real control over either. I also made a choice when her eyes closed and that last breath escaped her bruised lips. The unexplainable concept had bothered me since my mind awakened to the plight of the people and the horrors of war.

I saw my people without arms and legs, reduced to begging and waiting for death to free them from their misery. Afghans, who never smiled, never spoke. Silent statues with burned coals for eyes. I asked

Uncle for an explanation of this thing called jihad, holy war, and I asked why God allowed such devastation to fall upon his people who bound themselves to his spirit by praying five times a day and never moving without whispering "*tobah*", begging for God's forgiveness. Uncle talked of faith and belief, and yet I never saw a single prayer answered. Therefore, I determined never to believe in God.

A benevolent God would not have let my mother die in such a way. Oh, they told me about the devil. Yet God is greater than the angels, and so I still did not understand. Yes, they told me it should strengthen me, but it did not. My heart broke and our home became a silent tomb without her bustling through the halls and directing the daily tasks. She would comfort the children and laugh with the cook and sit for hours with Bibi Shirin, who clicked and clacked her knitting needles in the garden while I played at her feet. She told me stories of fearsome mountain men, famous bandits and bands of wandering gypsies. My mother sat with us, knitting a thing or two, drinking tea and laughing.

Bibi Shirin passed away soon after my mother, and we buried her in one corner of the garden beneath a willow tree of her own. Now their voices echoed in my heart while my eyes burned with unshed tears.

Uncle entered and cleared his throat.

"Come, they serve dinner in your Baba's room."

I turned from the trees that sagged beneath the weight of snow and followed his broad back towards my mother's rooms where I could hear my sister crying behind the door. I stopped and reached for the knob, but the guard moved in front of the door and glared down at me from beneath a white turban, his bearded face disapproving. Uncle took my hand and led me away.

"Your father has not decided what to do with Shaima."

Alarm rose in me and fear came with it.

"He isn't going to-"

"No, he won't do that. He will send her away, to her aunt in Moscow, for a while."

I loved my sister and though born from the witch Fatima, she had a trickling, skipping laugh that reached inside and touched me in a place very close to where my mother's face would always shine. The thought of her going away pained me, and I knew the days would turn even darker without her.

Hearth fire warmed the room, servants rushed in with platters of kabob, and Baba, wearing his black cloak and green sash, sat at his chess table. Uncle walked over, sat across from Baba and moved his queen pawn forward one space. I sat down in a chair beside the table, thanking mother luck for not having me play.

I glimpsed the Nuristani, Baba's assassin, sitting in the alcove half hidden behind a long curtain, sharpening his knives against a long black whetstone. He smiled through his blonde beard and mustache and I grimaced, knowing the deeds attributed to the man. I turned my attention back to the board and the waiting queen pawn.

Baba considered queen pawn openings a contrivance of the west. I think Uncle favored them for this reason. Uncle sometimes brought chess books to my room and we studied openings and made plans, but our plans never worked.

"I see you two have been conspiring. You think to defeat me with your Nimzovitch and Alekhine. I am an old warrior. It takes more than fancy theories to beat an old warrior."

An hour later, uneaten kabobs turned cold and Uncle lost his queen to a pawn, a foolish sacrifice he liked to make when trying to win with a stunning combination. As always, it did not work, and Baba chuckled and twirled the captured queen between thick fingers. They played again.

Farid the cook and his niece Nargis entered and sat by the fire as they often did after serving the meal. Baba enjoyed having people near. Nargis sniffled and tears streaked her brown face. Her Uncle pulled her close and ran his fingers through her curly hair. He shared a hand towel with her, wiping her tears away.

Girls have permission to cry. Boys do not.

"Tomorrow, we go on a raid," Baba said, "We will attack a column of Russii who retreat for the Amu River where they will attempt to cross back into safety. Omar will go with us."

"What will he do?" Uncle said.

"He will fight, like the rest of us."

"He is still a boy."

"Almost thirteen years old. We will treat him the same as any other boy. No special privileges because his father is Khan."

"Yes. However, the Russii run for the border. Peace will come soon. Omar can learn how to be strong without killing. For the boy's sake you should reconsider this action."

"You speak nonsense, brother. Your heart has always been soft. Omar must grow up strong to defend these mountains that have kept our home safe for two thousand years."

For a moment Uncle remained silent and turned his armchair to face the long narrow windows. Then, with a sigh, he finally spoke like a man who knew his argument would falter against the walls of Baba's insistence.

"But he is your last remaining son and like all children, he is a gift from God. How can you wish to corrupt such a gift?"

"See what your God did to our parents, our people, and our country. You are a fool and like all fools, you dream. I want you to stop filling the boy's head with your nonsense and let him grow into a man."

I said nothing. Danger lurked in Baba's voice, and I knew better than to jump in front of it. However, Uncle had found renewed energy. He turned back to the board and launched another attack on Baba's defenses.

"He is not you, Ali. He does not have your endless rage. His mother taught him to draw. He has a powerful mind and reads books that you and I do not understand. He could be a physician, engineer, artist, or play piano. We should send him to Europe or America for proper schooling. He can learn how to kill when he is older and understands."

"Enough!"

I trembled in the thunder of Baba's voice. It nearly knocked me to the ground, but I held on with my fingers clutching the edges of my chair.

"Is he a woman that you speak like this? Will piano defeat the Russii? Will art earn him the respect of his men? The men do not understand art. They only understand death and destruction. They make their homes in caves. Their fields burn, their children die, their parents suffer. What kind of leader do they need? One day they may need your philosopher king, but this is not that day. He will go with us tomorrow and learn to kill his enemy."

I kept my eyes down and watched Baba win another game.

◆ ◆ ◆

20

The Russii

Black and massive, loping across the field, the bear chased me towards the abyss that had swallowed so many of Baba's enemies. I ran along the crumbling edge, trying not to fall while the bear roared and came with a speed that rivaled a galloping Jaheel. Just as a cloud covered the sun and drowned the world in monochrome, I lost my footing and the beast came upon me, stood on its hind legs and swiped a massive paw at my throat. I leaned back and fell into the darkness, watching the gray sky shrink and then vanish.

The dream haunted me from this day on, in the morning, the last dream playing into the dawn.

I rubbed the sleep from my eyes. Morning sunbeams slipped through windows and fell on the chessboard where white and black kings stood on either side of a solitary pawn. Time stood still as the pawn and I watched each other like lost brothers. Uncle snored in his chair. Baba's chair sat empty. Purdill stood by the hearth. His brown eyes frozen open, staring at the air like a madman. Nargis slept beneath a blanket near the still warm fire.

I thought about the dream and wondered what it meant. My people believe in portents, omens, and unalterable fate. Getting up from my chair, I stretched and wandered out onto Baba's balcony.

Often from this high vantage, Uncle and I reminisced about the times Sikandur hurt himself leaping from the lower walls. He twisted ankles and broke a wrist, but these did not stop him. He laughed and jumped again. He belonged in the fortress. He fit here. He rolled in the dirt, bounced off the walls, and charmed everyone who came within a distance of his voice. We suffered through those nights, remembering our brave little man. Now we mourned my mother, and the nights showed no mercy.

The sun crested over mountains to the east and ribbons of pink, blue and violet gave chase to stars still glittering in the sky. Mornings started like this, clear and vibrant colors, but by afternoon the snow flew, the sun dropped behind the western peaks and the ever-present chill frosted the wild grasses. My eyes fell to the Buzkashi field where a mass of black and red lay covered in a fresh glazing of snow. I looked up from her body to the western horizon where a smiling sliver of moon followed Jupiter, sweeping stars across the sky. Baba's voice from the other side of our courtyard startled me.

"Get your lazy Uncle up and come down. We ride to battle."

Baba waved a hand at me, shooing me to the task. Leather bandoliers crisscrossed his chest and pearl-handled revolvers hung in a belt around his waist. His men stood near, checking weapons, leading horses from the stable and milling about. I waved and shouted that I would get Uncle and come down. As I turned to go, the drum pounded in the distance.

Every week I grew more determined to find the drummer. Every week he eluded me. As I searched the maze of canyons that perforated our circle of mountains, I sometimes heard a deep voice singing of Gods and war and stolen maidens. Other times, I only heard the boom of his drum, close and then far away, and I followed the sound until the cliffs stood between us, soaring into the sky. Today, the drum beat fast and heavy and though I craved to follow and hear his songs once more, I went inside to waken Uncle.

Several hours later, we huddled behind massive boulders alongside a gorge, waiting for the Russii to "show his face". My Kalashnikov grew heavy in my arms, so I rested the butt on a rock. Baba slapped me on the back of my head.

"*Khar*. Donkey. Point the gun down, not up. You could shoot someone in the head."

I turned the gun around and stuck the barrel in the ground.

"Don't stick the barrel in the dirt. If it fills, it can blow up in your face. Who will marry a boy with half a face? Where will my grandchildren come from?"

I sighed and slung the gun over my tired arm. The Kalashnikov hung heavy and my shoulder hurt, but I dared not move it from there, the only position that Baba had not challenged.

"Look there. I have placed half the men on the far side of the trail. They hide in the hillside while we wait here for the enemy to come down this gorge. I have also sent men behind the enemy to flush them into this trap. You will see how stupid the Russii are when on the run. Never fight the Russii in the open. Their weapons are superior. You must hide and strike when they least expect it."

"Yes, Baba," I said.

"Remember, take the high ground. Cliffs and mountains are your friends. You stay up here and your enemy down there will be at your mercy. Russii are too proud to learn tactics. They think their machines will overcome our mountains. Such a thing can never happen."

"I understand, Baba."

I knew what a Russii looked like, kind of because I went with Baba to war once before. We found only two Russii who ran and dived in the river to escape. Now, when I tried to imagine their faces, my mind formed images of winged demons from the north, dark capes swirling, faces a mass of blood and sharpened teeth.

Within an hour, the first of the enemy column rumbled down the trail. A charred tank crawled along, its long gray cannon's barrel cresting and leveling. It stopped at the far end of the gorge. Baba called for the RPG. A man ran down to us with a long-barreled gun and handed it to Baba. He aimed and the tank moved forward. The rocket left a white trail and blasted the tank with a ground-shaking explosion. The tank shuddered. Then it creaked and groaned and advanced, eating earth and spitting it out.

Grey soldiers emerged from behind the tank. They kneeled and fired. Our men fought back, one popping, shooting, and then ducking behind a rock while the next man popped up and fired. Two-man teams tricking the enemy, drawing fire and ambushing, Baba called the tactic, "the wounded duck".

The battle took on a rhythm of its own. They beat the drum, and we played the melody. Baba stood in the center, shouting orders, pointing and shaking his fist. How very much like a chessboard, pieces played and Baba winning.

Many Russii fell that day. Baba's men tore them to pieces and cheered as pale heads rolled, separated from their bodies by curved swords. They would not waste a bullet to finish a man, so the swords stabbed and sliced. I closed my eyes and tried to shut the screams out, but the cries bounced between the hillsides and the tank kept moving.

"Bring a mine Rashid," Baba said.

I worried whenever someone mentioned a mine. Too many lost lives or limbs to the monstrous devices. Some refugees arrived at our village incomplete, leaving a part of their body on a field full of these evil things.

Rashid handed Baba a gray mine. Holding the mine to his chest, Baba sneaked from rock to rock down towards the tank. He turned around once and gave me a look, then he motioned for me to fire my gun. I nodded but did nothing. Baba continued down the mountainside. A man sitting on the top of the tank fired at us while the long cannon blasted round after round into the hills. Our men scattered and ducked. The tank rarely found a victim.

A volley of gunfire broke out, Rashid fell next to me, his head cut in half and all that lived inside came rolling out. I held my stomach and blinked away tears. Uncle snatched me up by the scruff of my jacket and slung me under his arm. He ran across the ridge, skidded down behind a large boulder and dropped me on the ground.

"Stay here," he said.

He left me and I feared I would never see him again. I stayed behind the boulder and listened to the battle. I jerked with every explosion and cowered when the hammering rounds of the long barrel shook the mountainside. In my mind's eye, I kept seeing Rashid's brain falling from his shattered skull. I knew Baba wanted me to shoot my gun, but I could not bring myself to look up over the rock. I knew that made me a coward and I tried to force myself, but something held me there, frozen in the dirt with a squashed white scorpion lying next to me. I kicked the scorpion away and my eyes stung. I stood up, but nothing else. I cursed myself for my cowardice.

Soon, the grinding moan of the tank stopped. A few minutes later the gunfire died down and then Baba appeared. He stood there covered in blood and dust mixed with snow and looked down at me like a ferocious god.

"Come with me," he said.

I toted my gun on my arm the right way and followed Baba down the hillside. I thought I might get away with faking like I had done something and nothing bad would happen. But such things do not fool my father.

They had lined several Russii up against the side of the tank which now squatted, blown apart like a tin can with the top smashed in. I saw Uncle standing with many of the men, all staring at me. Baba took enormous steps, being such a large man, and I took five to his one, trying to keep up.

"This is what a Russii looks like. They look like us, only pale as ghosts," said Baba. "And they have no Gods, no belief in anything but the plunder of our land. Why should such invaders live and our people die?"

He pulled his pistol, approached a Russii, stuck out his arm and blew the man's brains all over the tank. He took two steps and did the same to the second man. I froze, stuck to the spot. Snow fell hard and blood mixed with flakes painting the side of the tank in dripping red and varied hues of pink and green. Baba turned around and held out the pistol.

"Take it and shoot this man," he said.

My legs froze and my Kalashnikov fell to the ground.

"Come, boy. Take my gun and shoot this man."

I shook my head from side to side.

"I can't." I did not know why, but I could not, though I desperately wanted to crack his stone face with pride. I knew my brother could have done it. He had Baba in him, pure Pathan, but me, I had something else and I knew this and it shamed me. Some of our men shuffled their feet while others murmured and scowled. Uncle stared at the ground, his short-trimmed beard white with smoke and snow.

"You can. You will."

Baba walked over, kneeled beside me, took my hand and placed the gun against my palm. He pointed with me at one man's face, slipped his finger with mine against the trigger and pulled. The gun kicked back and the man's head shattered. I felt sick, dizzy, and then I promptly threw up on Baba's arm. I felt his breath on my neck and I started shaking all over.

"Mukhtar take this... boy away before I kill him," Baba said. He wiped his hands on a rock, gave me a disgusted look, and at that moment I knew my father hated me.

Uncle picked me up, tucked me under his arm and carried me away. That night we rode home by ourselves. A week later, Uncle and I left for Dushanbe. Once there, we would fly to America.

"For a year or two of school," Uncle said.

Baba did not look at me again or say goodbye. He rode away, across the Buzkashi field on Jaheel, named for the stallion in a movie we watched a hundred times about a *chapandaz* and his son. I watched him for a long time, he and his beloved Jaheel prancing in the snowfield, their breath timed as one breath, frosted jets of vapor rushing forth. The sun crested and washed his face in gold. He reached down to rub the stallion along his muscled neck. He spoke gently to Jaheel and at that moment, I wished God had made me a horse instead of a boy.

The plane soared above the clouds, blue sky appeared and a weight lifted from my heart. Uncle read to me about Julius Caesar, told me stories, and we pretended to laugh. The echoes of our sadness lingered in my ears, and I thought how long it might take for that to change.

♦ ♦ ♦

21

Six Years Later, Snow Boy

In his dreams, Sister Mary cries long silver tears that melt into the field where he lies with black ants swarming over his body. Sinking into the darkness of a thousand tiny feet and pinching mouths, he shouts to her, "I am still here. I am still alive. Do not cry for me".

Dreams fade and life intrudes. Thick, sweaty hands pull and push while he drifts in and out of consciousness. They keep him alive in the lower room, chained to the ceiling while a recording drones on. They tell him to kill and they teach him how to use a knife to slash a man's throat. They show him by cutting into the skin of his arms and chest. The two men laugh. Sweat pours down their bearded faces.

Cuts heal to angry scars, half-moon slices he picks until they bleed. They wrap his arms in towels, slap his face, shout in their guttural language and then laugh, the sound echoing against the concrete walls. Years pass like this and shadows take complete control of Snow Boy's heart. His mind separates from his body. He watches himself from somewhere above while men cut him and Mahlim bends him to his black will. He cannot remember anything but the distant smile of a young girl. All other faces fade away. He knows only the icy touch of a stone floor and the taste of his own blood. One day, Mahlim gives him a name: Armon Badil. It will be his name from now on, Mahlim says. Snow Boy does not care.

One day, Mahlim does not come back. Nor do the guards or the cook. Snow Boy beats on the door, but nobody answers. He grows hungry and over the next few days, he withers and weakens. In the grip of a sudden desperate fury, he breaks a leg off a chair and smashes it against the doorknob until the knob breaks away. He wanders the empty house, eating what food remains in the cold white box and cupboards. He stares at a wide set of double doors for days, waiting for the courage to turn the gleaming knob. In the end, hunger drives him to it.

Armon Badil opens the door and looks out upon a shiny green wonderland.

◆ ◆ ◆

- Part III -
The Transitions

22

1998

"Open it."

She fishes a key from her jean pocket, sticks it in the register and pushes a button. The drawer opens. He snatches the bills, grabs some burgers from the warm glass case and runs out the back door.

Streetlights cast pale rings against the night. Tiny liquor stores and knick-knack shops perch on both sides of the wide avenue where during the day tourists gather like flies on a corpse. Reaching a side street, he turns the corner and mixes in with people stumbling out of bars. He shifts the black baseball cap on his head and dons a set of two-dollar sunglasses that make it hard to get around in the dark but keep his eyes hidden.

Head down, he drifts in the crowd like a drunk, weaving towards the old Camaro which has a few blue spots still showing between the hood and rusted fenders. It stands like a peasant's ox cart amid shiny BMWs and Porsches lining the streets. He jumps in, turns the engine over and heads south on the 101.

An hour later, he hides the car in some reeds and tangled bushes. He runs across several grassy knolls on a trail that leads down between black cliffs towards a violent ocean. Reaching the sand, he keeps along the cliffs and climbs. The cave sits in the cliff's side, some hundred feet above the rocky shoreline and crashing waves. He sits, dangles his legs over the dry edge of the cave and eats the hamburgers. In the distance, boats wander. Their lights like campfires strung along a hillside, a memory from long ago that brings visions of green eyes and red hair.

The wind turns stiff and the windbreaker cannot keep out the chill. He gets up and retreats into the cave. It curves left, dips down and widens to a grotto. He lights a kerosene lantern, illuminating all the things he owns. A cot and two blankets, a Coleman stove and propane tanks, bottled water, a yellow gym bag with clothes, a spear gun for fishing in the kelp that grows less than a hundred yards off the coast, a small mirror and shaving gear.

He stretches out on the cot, grabs a book stolen from the local library, "A History of the United States", and opens to a dog-eared page, "The Civil War". He has been learning about John Brown and Harper's Ferry. He stares at a rendering of John Brown, wild eyes and frothy beard. He recalls a man with eyes like that and a thick beard and pistols with pearl handles. He cannot remember the man's name or where or why, but he stares at the face, tracing it with one fingertip.

"Who are you?"

The wind shrieks across the cave mouth, a sound he is well familiar with. He pulls a blanket around his shoulders and reads about black slaves and white masters.

◆ ◆ ◆

23

Coming Home

Spitting dirt, I lunged forward to untie the ropes around my ankles. Purdill spurred Arad forward and knocked me back to the ground. My head bounced along the field raising a dust storm while Baba shouted from the back of his new stallion, also named Jaheel after the previous Jaheel retired to stud. This Jaheel, his son, stood even taller.

"Purdill, I said fast. We will teach this American what it means to say no to his Baba."

Arad snorted and dragged me around the same field where ten years ago I watched my stepmother stoned to death on a wintry September morning. Today Baba kept pace and flashed the same glare that sent me away all those years ago.

His face had not changed. He had not aged. He appeared even bigger, stronger and more determined than ever to break my will. Every summer I returned home and every fall I went back to Virginia humbled by my failure to rise to his expectations. I did not become the skilled Buzkashi rider he wanted. Nor had I become the leader and warrior he needed and wished for all these years.

"This is not America, boy. Here you are Afghan and you will do as I say. You will marry the daughter of Hassan Bey. I will not hear another no from your mouth. I am an Afghan father, not American."

He rode at a hard gallop towards the chalk circle where tomorrow the beheaded calf would fall to begin the Buzkashi and the celebration of my wedding. He expected me to win the Buzkashi. He trained me all these summers for this day and the many to follow, so he could say to his friends, "That is my son. He is a superb horseman."

"Pull him faster Purdill. Are you taking your grandmother to the bazaar?"

He still loved bazaar references. We did not even have a bazaar in the village. Strange thoughts go through one's mind when digging ruts with one's body. Thankfully, the men had cleared the field of rocks to prepare for the Buzkashi. God forbid the horses should suffer. The dirt had no pity for me as it tore my jacket, shredded my shirt, and left my naked back to fight the ground. I tried to think of something else.

Tonight, Ferooza and her father Hassan Khan would arrive and I would greet the father but not look upon the daughter for three days, until the wedding ceremony. They said her beauty could melt the sun and that she already had a thousand suitors asking for her hand. My problem lay elsewhere.

"You brought me back to marry a twelve-year-old child?"

During dinner, when I asked why he sent for Uncle and me in the middle of my second year at Georgetown University, he stood up and knocked me to the floor with a blow that I never saw coming. I should have.

"Yes, she is twelve. What of it? How dare you question me in the presence of my guests?"

"But Father," I said.

He kicked me in the ribs.

"Father? What happened to Baba jan? I am not American that you call me father."

He raged, his temper in full wind.

"Baba jan." I coughed. "She is only twelve."

"Idiot. My mother was twelve when she married. I was born when she turned thirteen. You think yourself better than your grandparents? You will marry this girl and you will live here. You will learn to protect and care for your people."

Then Shaitan must have entered me, for I uttered the unforgivable, "No" and that Baba would never tolerate.

"No? What do you think? That you are free? You are not a free boy. You are mine, like this fortress is mine, like the horses are mine, like this land, these people, everything you see... as far as you can see, all of it is mine. If I need to make a treaty with Hassan and you are the cost, then I will give that cost to protect my people. And you will not say no."

He dragged me to my room and placed a guard at my door. In the morning, they brought me here and now I lay on my back digging furrows through the field.

"So you learn who you are and what I expect from you," he said.

Purdill shouted something to Baba, possibly asking that he might stop, but the dragging did not cease. I felt blood running up my back and into my hair. Soon I would lose consciousness. I looked over at Baba, hoping he might relent and call an end to this. But he did not. He had grown accustomed to death on this field.

During the Buzkashi, men whipped and beat each other, hoping to unseat an opponent. Then they trampled those unfortunate enough to fall beneath the hoofs of their ponies. Each man for himself. They rode hard and fought over the headless calf, dragging, pulling, flinging it over their saddles. One more dead would mean nothing to Baba.

After all, this was not America. Nor was my punishment unusual. I once saw a father tie his son to a tree and whip him to death. Americans would call it barbarism. We call it discipline. I wavered, teetering between two cultures, horrified and yet calm, revolted and yet accepting without question, my father's punishment.

"Brutality is the essence of victory. The enemy must fear you or you will fear the enemy."

His voice reverberated across time from those summers I returned from Virginia when he trained me to lean with one leg hooked over the saddle and snatch the calf from the ground. Now the image of his face contorted with fury burned into my mind as stars flashed in a black sky.

I woke to my sister's frantic voice and her hands lifting my head from the dirt.

"Are you crazy, Baba? Do you want to kill him?"

Tears ran down Shaima's pale cheeks and fell on me. She wiped them off and smiled. In the background, I heard Baba's horse snorting and stomping, the clinking of his bridle and Baba twisting in the saddle. My eyes rolled around searching for him until he loomed up in the background, a massive shadow, white stallion and warrior. Had I skill, one day I might have painted them and attempted to capture on canvas the raw energy that sizzled all around him.

"You are a girl. You do not understand these things. More guests arrive soon. It is dangerous for them to see your head uncovered. You don't know who may watch," said Baba.

"I don't care, Baba. Do you hear me? I do not care what you say. I'm not leaving him here." She screamed at him and I feared for her, but he did not dismount and strike her down. Instead, he turned Jaheel and rode away.

"Stay still," she said, "I will get help."

Another shadow fell over me and I saw Purdill standing there. He kneeled beside me. A single tear decorated his angular face.

"I will carry him," Purdill said.

"Nobody will carry me." I tried to stand but fell flat on my face. Purdill turned me over and my sister brushed dirt from my eyes and mouth.

"Just stand me up." I spit out dirt and coughed. "I won't let him see me carried."

"Your back is bleeding," Shaima said.

I stumbled along between them while they held me up. I tried to focus on the fortress, but the gray stones of the keep and outer walls floated in my eyes like a mirage. I looked down at my sister, my arm slung across her too thin shoulders. She dressed in black like her mother, and I realized with a shock that I had never seen Shaima in any other color. Purdill had my other arm around his shoulder and in this fashion, we made our way towards the gate. I heard my sister crying.

"Don't cry. It will take more than this to kill me."

"Why don't you just marry the girl? He will kill you if you do not." she said.

"I don't think he will."

"I don't understand it. Can't he ever be nice to you? Every summer you come home and every summer he hurts you. One of these times he will kill you."

In America, I did not hear the drummer and he had slipped my mind. Now I heard him once again, far off in the distance, rapping out a marching beat that helped my feet find a rhythm and my mind to clear and imagine what Baba's life had done to him.

"It's not his fault. Years of war and death have twisted him like the root of an old tree. In America, we live in comfort while he fights his wars and sees his people suffer. He wants to show me his pain."

As we crested the hill, my eyes focused and my breathing calmed. In the distance, a group of men approached the gate through the line of welcoming tents and banners where elders drank tea and played chess in the shade and children chased each other, their squeals echoing across the field. The men stopped and chatted with the chess players for a moment before moving on towards the gates. One man stood taller than the rest. His head uncovered, his short blonde hair rustled in the wind and his eyes found us from the distance.

Purdill spat on the ground and spoke, startling me.

"Look, the Russii are here. Now that Talib bombed Kabul to pieces, the Russii are our friends. They sell us weapons and give your father advice. As if your father needed advice."

"The Russii," I said. "Baba sent me away for not killing them, and now they are here?"

The tall Russii wore traditional pants and shirt, baggy and fluttering in the wind. They carried no weapons and some wore turbans. The big man said something to the others and then ran towards us.

He asked, "Do you need help?"

I felt my sister tremble under my arm. She had nothing over her head and if seen like this, malicious words might spread through the valleys and reach Talib ears. Here a girl's honor is all she has, that and her family name.

"No. Please, you must enter the fortress so Sardar Ali may greet you officially," Purdill said.

I felt the tension across his shoulders.

"I am Sergy Volkov. I fought with your father against Talibs up on the pass. It is good to meet you. You are the daughter of the Bear?"

She nodded. I saw her glance at the man and smile. She trembled again. I spit out more dirt and shook dust from my hair.

"And why is this poor man covered with dirt? Can I help you transport him?" He approached, acting as if he would take Shaima's position. I let her go and leaned on Purdill.

"Thank you, I am fine. Please, you must not come closer. It would be dangerous for my sister. Spies may spread word to the Talibs. They are relentless in their blood lust."

His eyes flashed with understanding.

"I am sorry. I cannot see your face beneath the dirt."

He bowed slightly, holding his hand over his heart in the fashion of our traditional greeting.

"I do not wish to dishonor your sister." He took another step towards me. "May I assist you to the fortress?"

He spoke to me, but his eyes fell on Shaima and he cracked a smile. Any man's heart would break to her beauty. At sixteen, she had the face of a doe. Light hazel eyes angled slightly inwards towards a delicate nose and hair the color of coppery gold. Her lips shone with the pale pink of a certain rose that Baba grew in the garden and I knew men would crumble in her presence and for a moment, I felt sorry for the Russian. He appeared hypnotized and seemed not to care that all over Afghanistan, Talib shot men for looking upon the uncovered face of a woman.

For the sin of walking without the veil, a woman risked her life and from the field, the bloody stump where her mother died tugged at my eyes. I looked up at the smiling Russian who now appeared broken, like a puppet without its string, half hunched over and reaching for me.

Bristling at his attention and slow crab like movement, I took her hand, leaned on Purdill and staggered towards the open gate. I feared unseen eyes watching, noting, reporting. Last year, during my summer vacation, Baba caught a Talib spy who had lost his way and could not find the only exit from our high plateau. A search of the spy revealed a cache of notes and diagrams of the fortress and a half-finished map. Baba beheaded him in the field near Fatima's stump. I watched Baba's face as he swung the curved blade down and separated the man's head from his body. A wild wind tossed his thick black beard as his hands tightened around the hilt. He cried out as he swung his father's scimitar and a madman's fire burned in his eyes. And in that terrible moment, I realized that mountains of pure liquid anger simmered within his heart. That day I understood why those who approached him trembled like leaves in the wind.

Though he caught the one spy, Talib displayed nothing less than possessive fanaticism and we knew they would send others to sneak in during the ceremonies or watch from the mountains. Baba took ever-stricter measures since the extremists and their rigid doctrines burst upon Afghanistan like a bloody flood. Now I understood his aversion to religion and fanatical fervor. I too had seen it in their eyes, the crazed dog look. That hunger for death. The guarantee of paradise shone in their eyes like a brilliant star. What else did they have but that? Rocks, scorpions, a gun and a piece of naan. Who would not die for something, anything more?

We shuffled forward, leaving the Russian somewhere in our wake. I hoped the villagers had not paid attention and I sneaked a glance towards the gathering of old men. Their heads bowed over their chessboards. For these men, chess often ruled the heart in a world without a soul.

♦ ♦ ♦

24

A Fireside Chat

Pashtun wali, our code of honor which is over 5,000 years old is something you Russii would not understand. As I have taught my son, there are six major laws we must uphold. The most important is revenge. There is a saying: A Pashtun will wait a thousand years for his revenge, but he will not wait forever. The second tenet, Professor Volkov, is what allows a Russii to live inside the walls of this fortress. This is the law of hospitality, even unto our enemies. If they come seeking refuge, we must treat them as honored guests until they leave."

Baba's voice boomed through the halls and stone stairways. I often heard his code of the Pashtuns lecture during games of chess lasting deep into the night and daily rides into the maze of canyons and gorges surrounding our home. He led on Jaheel. I followed on Arad while he taught me the things I had to know to be Khan of his mountains and all his people. He had a name for everything, every mountain and every stream. His voice brought back those memories of summers past.

"Koh-i-Baba, named for one of your own forefathers, many generations ago," he said.

And we climbed Koh-i-Baba together, stood on the very peak, and watched old men limp by with their donkeys laden with sticks of firewood and yellowed bags of poppy and their faces wrinkled like the mountains they spent a lifetime crossing and re-crossing. We traveled and saw all the people of his three valleys, farmers and artisans, weavers and storytellers, Afghans young and old, and he knew each by name and their father's names and even their grandfather's names. He knew their cousins and uncles and aunts and all the marriages that took place over the years and I marveled at his mind, so nimble and strong enough to recall each face and the details of each life that I never would have thought to remember. Truly, he possessed the gift of leadership that I did not. Perhaps knowing my own shortcomings, I feared the years ahead. I could never be like Baba and though this hurt more than a knife in my heart, there remained distant precious pieces of my life that gave me joy and hope and I clung to these as I climbed the stairway towards my room. Dripping water from the shower, I shuffled through the cold hallways while the conversation drifted in from the main hall.

"And we thank you for that hospitality General. We are not enemies. You and I fought together for many years. Surely you have not forgotten."

"I have not forgotten. However, many Afghans will worry that you are Russii and most will prefer to stick your head on a pole. You must remember this when you ask questions about treasure and pry into our history. These villagers do not trust outsiders. They will tell you nothing."

"I am merely an archeologist. I only ask so I may document the history of your land and people and finally locate the mines of Alexander."

"The mines." Baba chuckled. "There is no such a place. Perhaps these mines are in Iran, where Alexander died on his march back to Greece, or in Egypt, where they placed him in a green sarcophagus. There are old lapis and ruby mines, but these have been useless for years, most valuable stones removed long ago."

"I have visited mines in the valley of Jerm. They are, as you say, empty of any genuine treasure. There have always been rumors of a single mine kept secret by the Khans for thousands of years. Some historians speculate that the body of Alexander may reside in this place. Though much of what we know comes from legend, but legends are often born from truths. For example, the Bamian and Kabul treasures and the rare antiquities which reside within the palace vaults."

"What do you know of the Bamian and Kabul treasures?"

"I have heard rumors of a massive treasure within the hollow sections of the Bamian Buddhas. Gold and jewels from as far away as Egypt and China. A cache estimated in the billions of dollars. The Kabul treasure, though smaller, contains priceless artifacts left behind by ancient man, some pieces reportedly 100,000 years old. Your secrets are secrets no more, my old friend. The world wants to see these treasures."

"Sergy, you are a dreamer like my brother. I cannot understand how you made such a fine scientist when all you do is dream. Do you not think if such treasures existed men would have found them by now? My friend, the Hindu Kush is a vast garden of ice and to search the mountains one by one would take a man the whole of ten lifetimes."

I pictured Baba smiling and pointing up at the giant map of the world on the wall. Two circles of the earth, gold and ivory, tall as a man and as wide as the banquet table where guests sipped smuggled whisky and vodka and gnashed their teeth against roasted legs of lamb.

She listened from the top of the stairs with her head resting against the wall. I smiled.

"Are you all right?" Shaima said.

I shrugged.

"Their conversation interests you?"

"Yes. It does. But you know Baba will not allow me in there, so I listen from here, as always."

I patted her soft hair as I passed and shuffled along to my room.

"Do you think Baba will send me to Moscow to study? When I am old enough?"

Her questions held me in mid-stride. I turned around to see her eyes gleam in the lamplight. "Is that what you want? What would you study?"

She leaned towards me and glanced down the stairway, as if we conspired to hatch a plot.

"Archeology. I want to do what the professor does."

She nodded, arched her brows, then tilted her head up and gave her chin a slight jerk to the right, asking me with proud eyes what I thought.

"I don't know. You know Baba better than I do. Do you think he will allow this?"

"I hope so. Will you help me?"

"What can I do?"

"You can talk to him."

I almost laughed, but the pain in my back put an end to such aspirations.

"Baba listens to no one. However, he sent me to America. Perhaps he has such a plan for you."

"I hope so."

She looked up, her eyes all aglow.

"Imagine Moscow, the city lights, the university," she said. "Yaan showed me pictures. He still comes here to teach, and he said I should go to Moscow to learn about the world.

I sensed her longing and wondered how much of it had started today, outside by the gate, when the dashing professor smiled and she trembled at my side.

I opened the door and stepped into my room. Uncle sat facing the glass doors to the garden.

"Sit down, Omar," he said.

Sighing, I trudged over, took a long shirt from my closet, and sat on my bed. Uncle looked tired and older. It shocked me for a moment until I remembered the wedding.

"I won't stay here and turn into Baba."

I spit the words out. Hearth fire crackled as Uncle stood and tossed in a fresh log. The thick black robe transferred heat to my body and I warmed. My back stung beneath Purdill's linen bandages, but more than anything, my pride called out, and for once I felt Pathan blood burning in my veins.

"You cannot fight destiny," Uncle said.

I felt the anger rising inside. "Why? I can fight it. I will fight it. A man can determine his own fate."

"Can he now?"

His tone warned of danger, and I desisted for a moment to gather the threads of my argument.

"I don't know. I think so. Why not?"

"America has given you a voice, turned a mouse into a lion. Something your Baba did not consider when he sent us there. You have forgotten that an Afghan son has no rights except for those his father gives him."

Uncle nodded, emphasizing his point.

"This is no longer that Afghanistan. I'm not just an Afghan son."

"You can change. Your father will never change."

He pushed his queen pawn forward and the game began.

Hearth fire washed the room in amber and gold. I glanced at my brother's bed and his tiny birch wood chair. An old walnut chest peeked out from beneath his bed. The piece of knotty pine he found by the river lay on a shelf above with a mob of little green army men. I thought of how time had stopped in that lonely corner of the room while my clock ticked ever faster, sweeping me back and forth, in and out of happiness and sorrow. I still lived his life in the blur of my dreams, images of waves crashing on a rocky beach and a sorrow deeper than anything I had ever known. His dark images lost me within complexities and ambiguities, and I could not think of where to search for him. I often thought if he had remained with us, he would be the one to stay with Baba, leaving me free to do as I pleased.

My thoughts disturbed me, for they proved I had become the spoiled and selfish son of a wealthy warlord, unwilling to help his own people. I suffered the guilt that comes with such betrayals, yet I knew no other choice remained for me. Contrary to my words, my life now took its own road and I walked along it helpless to change direction, and the road narrowed every day.

I pushed my queen pawn forward. I would try the Nimzo-Indian, long my favorite and one that gave Uncle difficulties. Then I set forth with the plan I had worked out in the shower.

"Uncle, I cannot marry a twelve-year-old girl."

He shot me a look, then shook his head and studied the board.

"You think you are American because you have lived in America for a few years." He chuckled and moved his king knight pawn one square, a new fianchetto he found in his chess books no doubt.

"This is how we do things here. Most do not live to reach forty. We marry young, have children, and then we die. This is our life."

I adjusted my Nimzo opening while the plan solidified in the back of my mind.

"But that is no longer true. Look at Baba, he is well past forty."

He spirited his bishop over to the fourth rank, a favorite tactic of his and one that gave me problems until a year ago. Like a fool, I determined to chase his rogue bishop, to trap and to take it, giving up a two pawns in the bargain.

"Your father is blessed by magics you do not have the benefit of."

"Magics? What magics?"

I had heard about these magics and I had tried to pry, but to no avail. Magic infiltrated every aspect of life in our mountains where villagers remarked on an ominous cloud, red moon or lingering shadow as portents of poor fortune. Gypsies, *Koochies*, sang songs of magic and even the elders shook their gray heads, stroked their white beards, and carried tiny parcels, *taweez*, wrapped tight in cloth, words from the Koran, as guardian against the evil eye. I often saw old women read Koran aloud and blow the words over their grandchildren, bless the water and parcel it out to their families. These things formed the essence of life in our world.

"I won't marry her."

He chuckled. "Then what will you do? The wedding is in three days. Hassan arrives with his daughter tomorrow."

The middle game turned into a positional duel, knights deployed to crucial squares and rooks dancing and dodging in the back ranks. The fire cast long shadows across the black and white squares, omens of days to come.

"Uncle, every summer I travel from a modern world to this ancient one. I move from an enlightened age to the Iron Age, from civilization to barbarism and constant war. I travel through time. Back and forth... and... I cannot find myself in all this motion. I am not even sure who I am anymore."

Uncle sighed and ran a hand over his thick hair and down the side of his cropped beard. He looked tired in the firelight, as if age had caught him and I thought of Baba, and how the years had not yet drawn a single line on his face.

"Not only this, but there is Jennifer, and..." I stammered, not knowing if I should reveal that Jennifer and I expected a baby in seven months. I chose not to divulge this, not knowing exactly why.

"How can I betray Jennifer for this child? What can I say to her? And he wants me to stay here forever and never return to my studies," I shook my head.

"I cannot do these things. I do not want to be a warlord, grow opium, and butcher my enemies. This cannot be my future. Help me, Uncle. What should I do?"

Uncle set one rook behind another, preparing for a spearing attack into the heart of my position. Next he planned Alekhine's Gun with his queen while his knights stood poised to sacrifice their lives for king and country.

"Omar, there will always be another woman. This Jennifer you think you love, she is American. They come and go like the wind that blows through our valley today and through Hassan's valley tomorrow. I have seen such women and understand the bewitching power they can wield over a man. You must be strong. Do not think at twenty, you have met the love of your life. It never happens that way in America."

I prepared as staunch a defense as I could muster against his attack, lining my own rooks and pulling my queen back to strengthen my weakened king.

"Why have you never married?"

I thought to distract him, take his mind off the board just long enough to delay the inevitable.

He laughed.

"No. Marriage is not for me. I've got my hands full just taking care of you."

He began the attack, my attempted distraction, a failed tactic. Baba would have sent men to scurry him like a rabbit into a trap. I possessed no such finesse and saw the end approaching.

"My place is at your side. My destiny runs with yours. They say our fates are on our foreheads, written in God's hand. No matter how far you run, you cannot run away from your fate." He paused and moved his queen closer to my king.

"But I will go where you go, for it is my duty to your mother."

Duty again. In this world, duty and the iron fist of a vengeful God ruled all aspects of life. However, I did not see God's hand in this world. I only saw a deceiver and I wished for something better, something more. I knew Baba did not believe, and I agreed with him. Uncle always carried prayer beads and a hundred times a day mumbled a prayer beneath his breath, touched his ears, and held his cupped hands out to the sky, begging forgiveness for his sins. I often caught him on his prayer rug and I waited until once finished, he washed his face with his hands and folded his beads and placed them in a pocket. Only then might I speak for interruption of prayer amounted to a sin for which the punishment would hurt him far more than I.

"Well then, we must leave this place. We must leave before the wedding and if you are staying with me, then you must leave," I said.

The final declaration, my last defense, and he sacrificed a pawn, a knight, then another knight and my king cringed in his corner with Alekhine's Gun lined up to blast through my bedraggled defenders. Tonight Uncle played much like Baba. I remembered swallowing dirt and squinting at the sun through clouds of dust. I realized that like an angry child, I wanted to hurt Baba because he wished to take my freedom and lock me down beneath duty and tradition.

Why give me a taste of the world if he only meant to snatch it away at the sweetest moment? Silently, I cried out against my fate and determined to free myself from this torment while my King wailed in the corner, howling out for help. I had little aid to give.

"Hassan will not take the insult to his daughter lightly," Uncle said.

"I will leave tonight when everyone sleeps. Perhaps you can distract the guard just long enough?"

Uncle shook his head. "Your father will count this as a betrayal. Tonight you stay. Tomorrow the guard will leave and I will go to Zebak and prepare a jeep. Tomorrow night while your father sleeps, you take old Jaheel and ride him out through the canyon. I will wait for you in Zebak."

"Old Jaheel? Isn't he too old?"

Uncle laughed and leaned forward.

"He is still faster than his son. No need to worry."

I nodded. It sounded like a good plan. Hopefully.

"You know Hassan may take revenge for this by raiding across the border. They may kill our people in vengeance," Uncle said.

"What will happen to Jennifer if I never go back to Virginia. No. I cannot stay here. I am sure no one will die because of this. He will probably welcome my escape so she can marry a Tajik prince once she reaches an appropriate age," I said.

Like an idiot, I believed my own words.

"His daughter will become a woman and marry a man more suited to this world. I am not that man."

My temples throbbed and I thought of the time left between now and tomorrow night and how long it might take to ride into Dushanbe and the plane ride back to Virginia and my Jennifer and then to place my hand on her filling belly where my child slept oblivious to its father's dilemma. Then a shadow passed over my heart and like my ancestors, I worried about grim omens, superstitious fear ingrained in my very soul.

"I believe the end is near. In three moves you will have lost your Queen, and with her, the game," Uncle said.

I reached down and laid my king on his side.

♦ ♦ ♦

25

A Secret Overheard

Shaima hesitated at the door. Baba's voice thundered through the halls. She leaned back near the door to his room and gripped the rough granite wall with trembling hands. Uncle's voice cracked and groaned as if in pain. Another voice murmured, low and cool. She peeked through the crack in between the iron hinges. Baba faced Uncle while the assassin stood in the middle as a barrier between the brothers. Purdill and Yaan stood in the corner.

"You did not send an army to search for Sikandur," said Uncle.

"I sent you."

"How many years will you search for this one, this American son?" said Uncle. "You don't even know his name."

"We must find him. I must have all my sons back."

Uncle stood still as a statue. His face flushed with emotion, he spat on the stone floor.

"She is American. You know you will never find her unless she wants you to," said Uncle.

"She was angry then. By now she has forgiven me."

"People do not forgive. They talk about it, but they never truly forgive. And what woman could ever forgive you for what you did?"

Baba glared at Uncle. Then his gaze drifted down to his left hand that held a scrap of paper shining with a dull brilliance in the sunlight filling the long windows. She maneuvered to get a better look. A small photograph with worn edges shook in fluttered in Baba's trembling hand.

"Excellency," said the assassin. "We have already searched and found nothing. I can send more men, but-".

"Then send more men. Omar is useless as a fighter. Find the family I stayed with as a student. Ask her family where she is. I have a right to see my son, even if he is half American."

The assassin nodded but remained standing between the two brothers.

A son in America. How? She needed to see that photograph. She wanted to know everything about this boy.

"Come, my friends. The gypsies have brought fresh horses. They wait in the courtyard," said the assassin. He took each brother by an arm and headed towards the balcony. Baba stumbled a bit, then slowly placed the photo on the chess table and let the assassin pull him outside into the brilliance of the day. Uncle followed and they stood looking down into the courtyard while the assassin pointed and murmured and nodded.

She cracked open the door and slipped through. Rushing forward on tiptoes, she snatched up the old photo and then slid underneath Baba's bed. She heard steps and moved further back into the darkness. The door opened and someone entered. She recognized Purdill's leather sandals and baggy black pants. She peeked out as he walked past the bed carrying a tray of rattling cups and a steaming teapot. They would drink tea and look over the new ponies, and Baba might even smile. She moved to the edge of her hiding place and studied the photo.

Faded colors, a blonde girl holding a baby with a shock of almost white hair, and most fantastic of all, a very young Baba, clean-shaven and smiling, stood there with an arm around the girl. She had a lean classical face, and eyes of striking blue. In the background lay a wide sand beach and colorful umbrellas and women strolling in swimsuits that left arms and legs uncovered, pale and dangling in the sunlight. She stared at this tiny piece of another world as distant from her as the moon, and as unreachable.

She tried to think of a story that went with the picture but could think of nothing other than Baba looked so young and thrilled. Then silent tears came and did not stop. She wanted to know more, so she slipped out from under the bed and hid in his half-open closet among coats and cloaks imbued with the scent and feel of him. Leathers hard and soft, a sturdy rough-hewn belt with two holsters. Pearl-handled revolvers sitting on a shelf behind her, glinting in a thin shaft of light. A rocket launcher sat on the table where he tinkered, and the smell of gun oil clung to the wintry wind that blustered though half-open windows. She waited there, surrounded by all things Baba, his scent, his touch, his very essence, this closet where she had spent so much of her childhood, exploring, hiding, or just sitting and falling asleep with her face against his overcoat.

Purdill left and the assassin retired to his alcove off the balcony where he sat and sharpened knives. Now, only the brothers remained inside the room. They played chess and argued and so she listened once again, hoping for more news of the beautiful girl and the child with the shock of snow-white hair. Back and forth, they discussed Gods, mountains and magic, things she did not understand, some of it in a language she could not decipher. Then they argued again.

"If your God exists, then he plays a cruel game with us all," said Baba.

"You will call down his wrath with such talk," said Uncle.

"Wrath? What more can he do? He murdered our parents by the hand of a Tajik. He took Elizabeth and the boy from me in the blink of an eye. Sikandur is dead. Arya lies entombed in the mountain. Omar is a weakling. I have nothing left to lose but a daughter. If he thirsts for her blood too, then let him take it and mine in the same day."

"You blaspheme brother. You have always let anger rule your heart."

Elizabeth... the girl in the picture, but the boy, could he be a true son? An eldest son destined to inherit everything. She understood why Baba wanted to find him now.

"You have no anger. You are milk and yogurt. Like your nephew. You are two of a kind. A matched pair."

"You have not seen my anger."

"No. You are bereft of anger. You were born from mother's left leg, I from her right, the leg that kicks. I cry out for vengeance for what they have done to my country. You meekly ask for patience. What will patience bring us but more misery and death?"

She held her breath and leaned forward, dislodging his black coat. Before it hit anything, she caught it, wiped away her tears, and hung it back against the wall.

"In this land where all believe, how can you lead so many while you do not believe? Where will you end up, brother? What will you do when you face God and he asks why you did not love your son? This does not surprise me, brother. Your heart has no room for a son, so how can there be room for God? What will you do when presented with proof of your errors?" Uncle said.

Baba replied as he usually did when pushed beyond his tolerance by slamming a fist against the chess table, scattering pieces across the floor.

"You condemn, but you do not look at the darkness that consumes the world. Imperialism, colonialism, democratism, communism, extremism. Why should my people suffer any of these masters? I want them free from any yoke around their necks. Soon we will plunge into a last war without salvation. From this end of all things, our people will emerge into a new world. Until that time, I will rage against fate or God or whatever name you give your weakness."

"Ali, one day your anger will drive you to murder an innocent and in this crime you will find your own end. In this crime against God, you will see the horror of your own life. And even you cannot face that."

So it went back and forth. They discussed history, men, and nations. They argued about the old king, and his conniving cousin, and the events of that fateful day the Russii invaded like a swarm of gray ants across the Amu River.

She trembled in passion of their voices, two brothers so different, like night and day. Her fate lay in Baba's hands, the same hands that condemned her mother, and so she knew she must escape the grim fortress before she too fell beneath the cold arms of hatred.

◆ ◆ ◆

26

Flight

I aimed Jaheel towards the moon hanging just above the canyon rim. Bullets ripped the air, cracked against cliffs and scattered rock shards in our path. I veered the stallion to one side of the gorge, hoping to give them a hard target. Shouts echoed down. A bullet sliced through my sheepskin coat and tore away a piece of my arm. I shouted a pained curse and urged the old stallion to greater speed.

The guards did not recognize me for I had slipped the sash of my turban over the lower half of my face and rode away thinking no other horse could catch Jaheel and I would be safe even if the guards woke from their opium dreams. However, with Russii inside our walls, the grumbling guards had not slept and a bullet is faster than any horse.

Leaning into Jaheel's mane, I slashed left to ride beneath the inky shadows of jutting rock formations. Greeted by a fresh barrage of gunfire, I saw any chance of escape fading. To make matters worse, I kept thinking if I escaped, Baba would surely send the assassin to hunt us on the other side of the world. I imagined him finding me and Jennifer, slashing our throats, returning with our heads in a sack to Baba who would nod and ride away into a copper sky.

The Nuristani, a pale killer who rarely spoke a word, sat in the darkened corner of the alcove until Baba nodded. Then he vanished and another warlord, rival, or bandit died. His body dangled over the Nuristani's saddle while his head rested in a bloodstained sack brought back to verify that he had completed his task. The Nuristani lurked in the shadowed edges of my life, waiting, smiling, and smoking a brown pipe. Even the servants fled his presence when he wandered the hallways, gliding over the ground, barely disturbing the air.

A cold weight fell to the bottom of my belly, gnawing at me like a hungry worm.

"A Pathan will wait a thousand years for his revenge..."

Baba's words echoed in with the thunder of stallion hoofs and the wind rushing past my ears. I twisted in the saddle to glance back at the neck of the canyon. A moonlit dust cloud above the cliffs revealed pursuers. Shouts and curses filtered through the rush of wind and shattering rock.

"Stop you fools. Stop the artillery. You will kill the horse."

The horse. For Afghans, it is always about the horse. The tank blasted again. The left side of the canyon collapsed and I veered right, hugging the wall. A chasm loomed ahead, and the stallion leaped up and over the torn earth. As we soared over the abyss, I imagined my death and what an inglorious one it would be.

They would name me the cowardly son of his Excellency Khan Ali Khan, the Bear, killed running from his wedding. Tajiks, Hazarras and Uzbeks laughing for a thousand years. Songs sung and stories told near campfires by weathered faces unable to imagine the dishonor of violating their father's wishes.

We landed on solid ground with a jolt that drew a lightning bolt of pain from my torn arm. I glanced at the rip in my coat, stained black with moonlit blood and droplets flying backwards through the pale night.

The trail ahead curved like a black and white snake in the moonlight. As we entered the area where the gorge twisted back upon itself and through sheer cliffs, the bullets stopped flying. We hurtled past shadows. Wind blurred my vision. I clung to Jaheel's neck and our spirits fused as they did those many years ago when I rode him secretly through the night, practicing to make Baba proud. His hoofs pounded, his speed multiplied, and the sounds of pursuit faded like a spent thunderstorm. My eyes closed. I held tight to the reins to keep myself from falling. Bleeding, vision dimming, I felt myself slipping away. My arm burned. I undid my belt and tightened it above the wound. I leaned down into Jaheel's mane and rested my cheek against his powerful muscles. Within minutes, my head cleared and my eyes focused once again.

Granite cliffs, a small stream, I looked as if seeing for the first time. I sat up in the saddle and glanced behind us. Nothing there, not even dust rising over the canyon. I took a deep breath and felt the cold air in my lungs and my head cleared. Then I turned forward and faced a giant of a man standing on the distant rim of the canyon, just below the moon.

I felt the bullet before I heard the crack of the gun. It smashed into the upper left side of my chest, nearly ripping me from the saddle. I shouted his name and the stallion burst ahead in a surge of power. My chest felt wet beneath my shirt and I glanced down inside my coat to see a widening blackness.

I heard Baba's voice in my head, "Tactics bachaim."

"Yes Baba."

His voice haunted me as I fled.

I felt my anger rising and determined that Baba would have to make his choice now. Kill me or let me go, for I would never stay by force. Jennifer's face flashed before my eyes and I whispered an unbeliever's prayer, begging for one more chance to see her in our cabin by the green banks of the Potomac. I imagined her swimming in the moonlight, calling for me. However, having given up belief in God long ago, I sensed the futility of my begging.

Standing next to Baba, the assassin's blonde hair gleamed white beneath the moon. A puff of smoke from the gun revealed a bullet coming. I ducked into Jaheel's thick neck and slipped to the side of the saddle, my face buried in his silver mane. The bullet cut the air an inch from my head. I peeked over Jaheel's neck to see Baba's black silhouette chiseled from a glittering field of stars and charcoal sky. He reached out and snatched the Nuristani's gun.

He wants the thrill of the kill for himself.

I drew closer, soon to pass directly beneath them. How had he known? Betrayal? No. Baba needed no help in such matters. He somehow knew everything I had done and perhaps everything I would ever do. Fathers come imbued with such insights. I waited for the bullet. I raised my face and rode within range of his voice. He raised the gun and aimed. I saw moonlight flicker in his eyes and I knew I would die. A calm resignation took hold of me and I nodded. However, instead of felling me with his bullet, he flung the gun into the canyon and shook a massive fist at me.

"Run, boy. Run back to your woman. Run coward. But never come back. Do you hear me, boy? Never come back."

I looked up to see his face gripped in shadow. Then a tiny sparkle, a gleam, or perhaps the reflection of a star fell on his face, but I could not be sure. A tear? I shook my head and laughed. Ridiculous. Absurd. The Bear never shed a tear and never would. A man cannot wring water from a rock.

♦ ♦ ♦

27

A Secret Shared

I have no one else. You are now my only heir. What you see here you must never reveal. Do you understand?"

"Yes, Baba," she said.

They rode through a narrow gorge, sheer walls on each side and a jagged blue sliver of sky high above. The horse had its own mind and paid no attention to her coaxing. He stepped lightly over the snow and enjoyed bucking every few paces, gentle teasing hops. The old woman soothsayer said spirits possessed the black, but Shaima thought Arad merely preferred to carry her brother's weight and did not understand. She rubbed his neck. He shook his mane and snorted, settling after a brisk morning of sidestepping fun.

This world seemed sharper in her vision, perhaps because she now rode deep inside its heart instead of observing it from windows. Here, the ice clung to rocks in clear sheaths. She saw every crystal, billions upon billions of blue, white gems glittering.

"What is this place we're going to Baba?"

Jaheel snorted and shook his head. They rode in silence while she wondered if he heard. Just when she thought to ask again, he spoke.

"She will teach you the way she taught your Uncle and I and all those who came before."

"Yes Baba jan."

"Your grandfather and his father and all our fathers rode this path. Their footsteps frozen in the glacier remind us of our duty, our eternal calling."

The secret, he told her, remained hidden inside the mountain for thousands of years. The secret she must protect. Baba had so many secrets. She considered asking him about the woman and the boy in the picture, but this filled her with dread and she would not violate the respect that she felt for him and the love that kept her from causing him discomfort. This prevented words from forming and her voice from rising from the small of her throat. So she rode Arad, followed her father's broad back, and she marveled at the purity of the world around her.

◆ ◆ ◆

28

On September 11, 2001, terror slammed into New York City and Americans reacted. Friendliness left American faces, replaced with a level of anger that changed everything. On October 7, 2001 United States bombed Afghanistan. On November 9, the battle for Mazar-i-Sharif began. US bombers carpet-bombed Talib forces. On November 13, the capital city Kabul fell to Northern Alliance and US forces. Hatred consumed everyone and everything in its path.

♦ ♦ ♦

29

Rescued by the Russii

S and nigger."
"Hit him again, A-Rab bastard."
"Kill him."
"And bury him between the goalposts."
"Like Jimmy Hoffa."
"Yeah."
"We told you to go home A-Rab."
"Yeah, you brown piece of shit."

They have him pinned against a chain-link fence surrounding the University football field. Nicks in the chain cut into his face as two of the young men hold him by his shoulders and head. A third and fourth take turns punching and kicking.

Now common on this college campus, these beatings are what dark and dusky students watch for and avoid. For this, they often walk together, worried eyes darting in every direction, checking shadows, gripping backpacks like life jackets, especially the foreign girls. Several raped and beaten, the culprits never caught.

Armon Badil walks alone, daring them to come, for though they cut and bruise him, they cannot hurt him. He has seen much worse.

The devils merely fortify his hatred and affirm the teachings of Mahlim, the whip of Allah.

He reads in the student paper half-hearted condemnations of violence and surprising arguments in favor, and it occurs to him that these future doctors, lawyers and politicians will rule the world. Mahlim's words mix with the drone of angry voices, the whip slices through the air and the cold smell of blood and steel invades his nostrils.

"It is a world filled with hate, war and death. And they revel in it. War means money, jets, tanks, helicopters. Oil and blood run across the land. The poor die in the streets. The rich laugh and drive their BMWs to the beach. This is the new world order. This is America."

It is all just as Mahlim said it would be.

His face presses against the wire. Lights of the Dean's tower flicker behind the tall glass windows of Freedom Library in the distance. Through the haze, he catches sight of a tall man with cropped blonde hair running up the hill from the gymnasium.

"Hey, you. Stop that."

He shouts his English with an accent, familiar but from another time, another place. The boys let go and he hears them scramble down the hillside towards the dormitories. He spins and grabs one by the wrist who had not resisted the impulse to smash a last fist into Armon's kidney.

Long blonde hair half covers vacant blue eyes that sit over a razor thin nose that Armon crushes with one blow, dropping the ruffian to his knees. A knee to the face lays him out flat. He hears the big man's heavy steps just as he drops an elbow to the boy's stomach. The boy exhales hard, a wide-eyed, breathless look on his sparrow face.

"Hello Professor," Armon says.

"You know me?"

"Professor Sergy Volkov, Moscow University, lecturing on the history of Asian antiquities with particular emphasis on the search for Alexander's tomb. I am auditing your class."

"You must sit in the back."

"I enjoyed your slides and the Hindu Kush film."

ANTHONY STONE

"I took those before the war, when there was still the blush of innocence on Afghanistan."

"Innocence," Armon who was once Snow Boy says, "Nobody knows what that means anymore."

"You look familiar to me. Very much like someone I met long ago."

"I remember you as well. We had you in a cage near our village. Helena and her father and I. You taught me about journaling."

"I know. I wondered if you would remember me," the professor said. "It is good that we remember each other. It is a good beginning."

They stand together, looking down at the gasping boy. Armon glances towards the walkways and parking lot in the distance. The snow-covered football field and hillside stand empty now. Seconds ago, this same air sizzled with hatred.

"What should we do with this one?" the professor says.

"They wanted to bury me beneath the goalposts, like Jimmy Hoffa."

"Is that so?"

The boy's frosted breath slows while his nose bleeds into the snow, bright red spreading on white.

"I have a van, let's get him to it," the professor says.

They pick the boy up and half carry half drag him down to a dark brown van. The professor opens the sliding door. Armon shoves the boy inside, then follows and pushes the boy into a backseat. The professor closes the door, walks around to the driver's door and gets in. The engine cranks a bit and then rumbles. He pulls the van away from the gymnasium and down a road that runs around the campus and past the dorms where Friday night parties illuminate three story fraternity houses and students stumble back and forth across the street. Hard rock music twists through a silver mist that hugs the ground, and the smell of beer grows strong as they pass each crowded doorway. A thick layer of snow covers everything, hedges, rooftops, parked cars.

"Well then, Snow Boy. Well met, again."

"My name is Armon."

"They called you Snow Boy in the camp. What happened? You changed your name? How did you come to America?"

The professor drives through the University town and onto the highway, heading west.

"I arrived in America as a prisoner of a holy man. I've seen his face in the news."

The professor casts a glance in the rear-view mirror and their eyes lock for two seconds. The Russian's eyes sparkle, blue and steady.

"Prisoner of a holy man. Now that is something you do not hear every day," Volkov says. "How did this happen?"

Taking a deep breath, Armon describes the man Farook El Bahar. The man they called "*Mahlim*".

"There is a bounty on that man's head. That is probably why he abandoned you and ran," Sergy said.

Armon slams the boy's head against the window with his forearm.

"There should be a bounty on people like this. People who hate the wrong people. Why don't you hate the Saudi's? No tongue in that racist mouth of yours. The Saudis bombed your towers, not Afghans. Go find some Saudis to play with next time."

Armon releases the boy's neck. The boy shivers and looks down. He picks at blood drying on his shirt. The Russian looks into the back seat. Armon glares at him.

"It is you Russians who invaded our land. You killed many with your bombs."

"Not my bombs. I left the army and joined the University. I never killed a single Afghan."

"Are you certain of that?"

The professor does not answer. Armon stifles the urge to kill the Russian. A big man, strong around the shoulders. He calculates the weight difference between them.

"The war is over for us. We have more dangerous enemies to fight." The professor nods at the boy.

"He is just a boy," Armon says. He rubs the half-moon scars along his forearms, itchy, burning scars that hurt all day, every day. Tires rumble over a frozen road and windshield wipers slide snowflakes back and forth.

"Are you cold?" says the professor.

"No," Armon responds.

"I talked about this when we were together at the camp where you put me in a cage," the professor says.

"I did not put you in the cage."

"No, I suppose not. Anyway, as I told you in the camp, your people could be descendants of the Greeks who came with Alexander," the professor says. "The Nuristani are Greek descendants as are other northern tribes. You are likely from the northeast, perhaps from Badakhshan."

Snow falls harder. Crystallized pine trees enclose a frozen stream that curls between rolling white hillsides.

"I wouldn't know." He picks at the half moon scars on his forearm.

"Have you seen any mines? Great gaping holes in the mountain from where men bring rocks," the Russian asks.

A vision burns in Armon's memory. Fires on the south side of the mountain. Away from the wind, the northern side sits in darkness. Blue rocks packed on donkeys that trudge and stumble over mountain trails. Armed men watch everything, eyes dark with kohl, beards white with fine sand. Gunfire and mortars explode in the distance. Men fall. Rocks shatter and crumble. More guns burst fire across the mountainside. Men shout and women scream. Donkeys pack the rocks across the mountain and he huddles with her between three tall boulders, waiting. Helena with the green eyes. So long ago.

"It is a small village. There are some caves, but no mines."

The Russian rolls down the window an inch, letting in cold air and swirling flakes. White fields streak past. The boy stares out, his profile dark against the snowfields.

"There are many legends. Some claim Alexander's tomb is somewhere in those mountains."

"Yes, you mentioned a few times in your lectures. You have an obsession."

The professor frowns.

"Can you find your village again, if you and I should go back one day?"

"Can you take me back?"

The professor turns his head and gives Armon a measuring look from head to toe. The van swerves to the right. The professor turns around and straightens the van back down the center of the icy road.

"You look like a man without a passport. I can fix that. Can you find your village and your teacher, this Mahlim? You know the Americans have placed a very large bounty on that man."

Mahlim, the whip of Allah. The thought of seeing the fat man sends his mind reeling for a moment, but he calms by thinking of the ocean and the cave. Ship lights on the horizon.

"Not sure what a bounty is." Armon says.

"They pay a price to whoever can bring him to justice or kill him."

Armon thinks about killing Mahlim. Can he do such a thing?

"Your village? Can you find it again? It has to be in Badakhshan."

"I don't know. I was very young."

The professor suddenly releases a torrent of words, energetic, persuasive. He has a mission to find Alexander's tomb and he wants Armon to help, but Armon is in his own thoughts. Helena's face haunts him every night.

The highway runs through the snowbound forest, a wet black ribbon leading straight into a thick fog rolling in from the sea. The snow and fog mix and form a crystalline soup, and the professor slows the van.

"I can help you. Together we can find this Mahlim and your village. You can see the girl again. I will pay you very well."

"Why do you need me? You can go yourself."

"There are a thousand such villages in those mountains. A man could spend a lifetime looking for the right one, the one where your holy man might hide today."

Armon rips a scar open. The old wound bleeds. He rubs the blood into his palm and squeezes his hands together.

"Where are we taking him?"

The professor rolls up the window and stops the rush of frosted air and a flurry of flakes.

"Next month I return to Moscow. It will take a year, maybe two to get the financing for a new expedition, but once I do, then you and I will find your holy man, bring him to the Americans, and collect the 10-million-dollar reward. We will also look for the lost tomb of Alexander, one of the greatest mysteries of all time."

The professor nods, smiles, and glances into the rear-view mirror.

"What do you think of this plan?"

"Where are we going?" Armon says.

"Not far."

Armon leans back and watches the boy flip his blonde hair back to reveal narrow spaced eyes, blood caked on his mouth and chin. He tilts his head up and he glares, unafraid, defiant.

An hour later, they stand on the edge of a cliff overlooking the ocean. Armon knows this place. Just a few hundred feet from here sits the cave where he read about the Civil War and John Brown. He looks over at the Russian, imagining him in a turban with a yellow beard. A memory flickers, revealing nothing, but he senses it there, teasing him. He does not reach for the memory. If he does, it will vanish. Instead, he waits and hopes that one day the memory will grow careless and he will catch it, tear it open, and find names for all the faces and places that haunt his days and wake him during the nights. And he will speak those names and he will know the faces and he will understand where he belongs. Certainly not here. Everywhere he sees hate. Americans are too angry and do not seem to like each other. He knows he is different. He does not belong here.

Who am I really? Does anyone know?

The professor will help him. Perhaps, in their searching, they will both find what has eluded them for so long. Perhaps in their search... and the thoughts run fast through his mind, his heart racing alongside.

"Why are we here?" the boy says.

He shivers. Now he looks strangely thin, his pinched face trembles. Jagged teeth clatter.

The professor reaches out and takes the boy by the neck, pulls him close and smiles.

"I hope you have a mother and father. It would be a shame if nobody missed you."

With that, he pitches the boy over the edge of the cliff. His screams fade into the crash of waves far below. "I never liked Americans," Volkov says.

"He was just a boy."

"Not a boy. A man who would have killed you without thinking. I have seen too many like him. Now he knows what it feels like."

Has the professor tested him with this action? It does not matter. Life happens. Control does not exist. Free choice is an illusion. Your destiny is already waiting.

They stand a few feet apart, looking down. Armon feels nothing for the boy. He remembers twisted and broken bodies of women and children stacked and burning, the smell of sweet poison in the air, a metallic salt taste in his mouth and the girl crying, holding him close. Moonlight shines on dead faces. Unseeing eyes reflect the stars.

◆ ◆ ◆

30

West Meeting East

Did I mention the American? Ah yes, and his story starts here. Perhaps he is real, perhaps not, but in this place where East meets West, where all roads cross and cross again, why not an American? It is the summer of 2002 in a mountain village near the Wakhan corridor.

Smoke curled from a bullet-riddled corpse. The acid stench of burning flesh hung in the gloom between crumbling mud huts. Blood gathered in a dark pool. A girl wept next to a scorched body. Her fingers wrapped around a charred hand. She touched the blackened face, held the charred hand to her cheek and sobbed.

"Mac, pick that little woman up and get her over here."

"But Colonel-."

"Come on Mac, hurry."

"Damn it, Colonel." He shifted his rifle to his shoulder and took her arm. She flinched and pulled away. He caught her wrist in a tight grip. Screaming, she slapped and scratched his arm. He stood her up and wrapped his arms around her. Her small buttocks pressed against his groin and he felt guilt, as good Catholics must, burn the tips of his ears.

"God's hand reaching down," Father Dodd used to say.

"You feel that boy? You feel that in your ears? That is God's hand reaching down and teaching you."

Reggie's voice intruded on Mac's rush of shame.

"God dammit Mac, get that little bitch over here right now."

"Yes, sir."

The doorway to the mud hovel hung open and hardly contained Colonel Reggie Gregory's heavy shoulders. Reggie's eyes swept her slim body. The girl cried out and turned, threw herself against Mac. Firm breasts pressed into his belly and again his ears burned. He picked her up and carried her.

"Sergeant Black. Keep those Ghans in line. Stand that towel head up. Get him on his feet."

"Yes, sir."

"Are you just going to stare at them, Errol? Ask them about the lapis mines," the Colonel said.

"Yes, sir," said Sergeant Black.

Mac handed the girl to Reggie, who shoved her to the back of the hut where a hole in the ceiling cast a bleak circle of light on a dirt floor. Clay pots lay strewn across the floor and in one corner, a prayer rug hung from a wall riddled with M-50 holes.

"Stay here Mac and watch those hills. More Taliban out there than scorpions," Reggie said.

The old wood door slammed shut in Mac's face.

Father Dodd's eyes flashed lightning and the wrath of God. Hands bled, angels shined beneath muted sunlight and stained glass. Father Dodd lurked, hovering, frowning. Hushed voices murmured while invisible ones sobbed within the shadows. Shoes clapped against wood floors. Ruler slapped against bleeding palms. Holding in tears, he sat with his hands facing the high-arched ceiling. Mother's hands gripped his shoulders from behind, Father Dodd in front with the hard ruler, gray eyes gleaming in the dim light of God's house.

Mac fought a tremor in his stomach and blinked against the solitary ray of sunlight that streaked through the ceiling of smoke above the village. Removing sunglasses from his pocket, he counted several ways to block out Black's shrill voice. None appeared viable now.

"Dirty Af-a-Ghan bastard. Where are the mines? Lapis, yeah, lapis. Do not shake your head, boy. You *will* tell me. I will shoot your woman."

A pistol cracked. A Ghan fell. It continued. They would not talk or they did not know. In between gunshots came sounds of scuttling feet. Reggie's voice, a hot knife cutting gashes into his memory to bleed, forever.

"Come here, girl. Heck, you are almost a woman. Stop running. I won't hurt you."

Mac cringed.

Help me, Father Dodd.

But why should he care? Any of those ragged Ghans might be a Talib, Al Qaeda, or even Russian. They deserved whatever they got. After September 11th, who cared? Bitterness filled Mac's mouth. Flesh burned, smoke billowed, and Black fired into the line of Ghans standing with their hands stretched high over their heads.

"Lapis mine!" the sergeant screamed.

Heavy smoke twisted around a naked patch of sky. Below this spot of blue, a skinny little beagle with wet eyes stared while a motley crew of chickens squawked and skittered about the prisoner's legs. The bleating of sheep floated down from the hillsides.

Mac heard chopper blades and looked up. Through shifting clouds of black smoke, a gunship formed a solid shadow against the sky.

"Colonel. Chopper incoming." Mac said.

"What?"

Mac repeated his alert louder. The door opened and Reggie stepped out of the darkness.

"Look there," Mac said.

"Relax, Mac. It's probably just headed back to Kunar," Black said.

Black stood over six, perhaps seven bodies. Nobody counted

bodies anymore. Nobody wanted to know about dead Ghans. The line of living Ghans wavered, their baggy clothes whipping in a wind that swept away the smoke and left the village visible from high above.

"Yeah well, Kunar is south dumbass. That chopper came out of the west," Mac said. He caught Black's grimace and flashed back a middle finger.

"That's a Blackhawk. None of those in Kunar. That Hawk came from Bagram." Reggie said.

The Blackhawk hovered for a moment and then floated down, landing in a nearby field. Six men in fatigues spilled out and ran towards the village. Four carried M16s. Of the remaining two, one stood head and shoulders taller than the other. This man wore a pakool peasant's hat over a square rock of a face. A thick black beard hung to his chest. The man held Mac's eye until the flash of hardware on the smaller man attracted his attention.

Mac snapped a salute and stiffened. "General Martinez."

"What in the name of holy shit is going on here, Sergeant? What the hell are you jackasses doing and why the hell are all these people lined up?"

The pug-nosed General stomped over to Black and looked down at the dead bodies lying at his feet. He snatched Black's gun out of his hands and threw it away.

"What in the holy name of Cracker Jack? Reggie? What are all these people doing with bullets in their brains?"

The giant moved too fast for a big man. In a blink, his hands fastened around Reggie's neck. Martinez shouted and tried to pry away the man's thick fingers. Mac stood at attention but turned his head just enough to observe the giant shaking Reggie in the air while Martinez clung to the big man's arm and screamed.

"You again," said the big Afghan. "I'll kill you this time, Gregor."

"Commander Ali, get your hands of the Colonel. I will deal with these men. I promise you they will not go unpunished."

However, the big Ghan did not release Reggie, not until Martinez pulled his pistol out and cocked it just under the giant's ear. Then the big Ghan tossed Reggie against the mud wall and stood over him shaking, veins bulging in his bulwark of a forehead.

"What have you done?" the big Ghan said.

Reggie laughed. "Well, well. It is Ali Khan, Khan of Khans. You are one big ugly Ghan."

Reggie stood up and dusted himself off. Then he gave the Ghan a look Mac had seen before, back in Alabama. The tree. The rope. The man swinging.

Mac shook his head. Reggie kept his distance from the Ghan,

"One day, we will meet again. And you will not have this wetback to save you," Reggie said.

"I look forward to it, Gregor."

The Ghan ran his forearm over his face, clearing the dripping sweat. Then he shook his head and walked towards the mud hovel where the girl peeked from the edge of a dark doorway, her eyes red, her dirt covered face stained with tear tracks.

"Place the Colonel and his men under arrest," said Martinez.

The four Marines relieved them of weapons. Reggie rubbed his neck and glared at Martinez.

"Got something else to say, Colonel?" said Martinez. "I'm dying to get to base and add to the list already forming in my wetback mind."

Reggie smiled and prattled out well-rehearsed lines. Village full of Taliban. Training grounds for Al Qaeda. Interrogating the people for information regarding the whereabouts of the terrorist Farook El Bahar.

Martinez's face trembled, razor thin mustache quivering. Reggie stopped talking and smirked, assuming a look of defiance and arrogance, reminding Mac of the time Father Dodd caught them in the rectory smoking cigarettes.

"Colonel, I relieve you of your command. Get in that chopper and I mean right now. You too," Martinez nodded at Mac and Black. He shook his finger at Reggie.

"You dumb son of a bitch. Your ass will fry for this you low life Alabama redneck."

The big Ghan stood in the shadows and watched Reggie scramble into the Blackhawk. His dark face twisted in a scowl and his deep-set eyes flashed pure hate. That kind of man would not rest until he saw them dead. Mac knew men like that. He sat next to one on the chopper. He looked over at Reggie who wore a crooked grin, and Mac knew it had all just begun.

♦ ♦ ♦

31

Shaima's Future

Looking down from her mother's window, she watched Baba ride in through the outer gates followed by a two long rows of horse mounted Mujahideen. In the distance, ragged infantrymen turned towards gray barracks that stood like worn out matchboxes leaning against the mountainside. Several old jeeps crept along at the rear. Baba's army grew smaller every month, deaths and defections to Talib taking a toll.

Her gaze drifted over the field and the stained post where her mother died and her own future loomed down in the dirt and scrub grass. Sharia, the strictest interpretation of the Koran, now prevailed in most provinces and women bore the harsh brunt of its dictates. Unless she escaped this mountaintop, she too might end up tied to that post or another much like it.

In the distance, fading afternoon light dropped mountain shadows on farmers bent to the last harvest of the year. They cut and scraped the poppy buds, collecting the last of the thick brown opiate before the chilly night descended. Beyond the brittle poppy fields, in the elbow of sheer rock in between soaring mountains sat a dust-covered conglomeration of tents, shacks and mud brick homes where children chased each other from alley to alley while mothers baked bread, hung laundry, or swept dust into small tornadoes. Next to the village, a glacial falls filled the stream that flowed in a dark ribbon through the fields and meadows just now filling with tired horses freed from their saddles. A cool wind brushed her face and she felt the frost coming that would turn this old world once again to quicksilver.

Everyone left. Omar and Uncle together in America. Only she, a few servants, and the ghosts of her ancestors remained inside these old walls. Outside the walls, a dozen soldiers walked the ramparts while a hundred more camped around the fort. Night fires burned. Rough voices crashed into each other. The soldiers kept the plateau safe and the Talib out of Baba's stronghold. She turned away from the window and lay on her bed, starring at the wood ceiling.

She often slept during the day. The nights she devoted to gazing at stars through narrow windows high in one of the two rear towers, which stood two levels higher than the front battlements and Baba's long balcony.

She waited until he dismounted in the courtyard and the men led his horse to the stables. Then she turned and hurried from the room. Shuffling down long hallways and two flights of circular stairs, she prayed the battle had gone well enough that he would smile. She knocked on his door. No response. She turned the rough iron handle and pushed the heavy door open just enough to slide in.

"Salam Baba."

He hunkered in his armchair, gazing at his chessboard. She hurried over and kneeled beside him, taking his hand and kissing the rough backside. He reached out and lightly touched her hair for a few seconds before lifting her face to his. Tired lines on his face spread and curled with a forced smile. His eyes still held a faint spark of life. The years had consumed his fire.

"How long are you staying this time, Baba?" she said.

He smiled and nodded, though his eyes remained vacant. Her mother had had the same habit. She would stare at Shaima unaware, lost in worlds of her own creation. She sat at her mother's knees while Fatima told stories of Mazar and her father and mother and sisters, all the time shedding tears. A mother's tears break a daughter's heart, and a broken heart has a very long memory. Those memories pushed her plan forward.

She stood and felt his eyes follow her to the opposing armchair where she sat and moved a pawn forward. She knew he wanted to play. It took his mind from bothersome thoughts and freed him from the ghosts that followed him. How many good men had he lost? How many mothers would he have to tell? She felt these things with a daughter's natural intuition.

He sat back for a time. She kept her head down, respecting him and fearing his instant turns of temper. She could not meet his eyes for long. She had watched him strangle a man into unconsciousness for such impudence. Such straight in the eye looks smacked of arrogance and disrespect, and he was not a man to abide such things. She glanced up every so often and fiddled with the folds of her black cloak. A scent permeated the air, the scent of Baba, a heavy scent that came from sleeping in tents and riding his warhorse and the blood of vanquished enemies. Pale yellow dust encrusted his beard, lips, and eyelids. His turban, once a brilliant blue, now turned a dark green, soaked in sweat and dirt.

"You have been a dutiful daughter. Perhaps it is time you took a husband."

She tried to sit still and keep her eyes on the black and white marbled squares, but all at once, she sat up straight and shot a glance at his square face. She looked down quickly. She knew his mood now, and she measured her next words with care.

"I don't want to marry. I want to study archeology. I want to go to Moscow."

He let out a long breath and slumped in his seat and somehow he appeared smaller, shorter as if her words had chopped a piece of him away and now he teetered like a great tree about to fall from the axe of a relentless woodsman.

◆ ◆ ◆

32

Shaima in Moscow

Ice crystals hung from rooftops and the crenellated edges of minarets. A stiff wind sent snowflakes spinning. The snow. The Russii with their great long coats and bombastic fur hats. The thick-walled architecture of Moscow buildings, thick as the fortress walls and impenetrable as Baba's stubbornness.

She thought of Baba fighting the war for thirty years, alone and so far away. If only she could pry him from his war to see this city, so magnificent that it wrenched tears from a place deep inside her. If only she could bring him to these brilliant lights, she might soften his brutal will, unfreeze his heart and breathe life back into him. Still, the brilliance of Moscow included a certain austerity, a sense of immense size and power. From this city came the invasion of her country.

She shuddered. Fresh snowfall crunched softly beneath her leather boots she purchased yesterday from a heavily bundled man along the Moskva riverbank. He laughed, his pink face crinkled and his frosted beard glittered like Christmas tinsel on trees. She had never seen Christmas decorations. She had smiled and remembered thinking, "I'm smiling. How strange."

The massive principal building of Moscow University inspired awe. White marble and pale red trim combined to issue a sense of impenetrable formality. The central tower stretched high into the dark belly of a giant storm cloud. Flurries thickened as quiet students plowed past her and into the mouth of the white building that swallowed them like Ahab's whale swallowed sailors.

She hugged her book bag, tucked her chin and thought about the past week she spent walking over all forty-nine bridges of the Moskva and visiting Saint Basil's Cathedral. The sheer bulk of the redbrick Kremlin stunned her, as did the Triumphal Arch on Kutuzov Avenue and the Cathedral of Christ the Savior. Both she visited at night, so the gleaming floodlit walls stood out against the stars and night sky. The scene stole her breath away. She had never imagined such grandeur, and she cried while her elderly aunt held her hand and took her on a sleigh ride through Filevsky Park. Trees wrapped in snow and ice. Silence but for the jingling of bells and soft swish of a sleigh passing over snow. All the while, her thoughts kept running back to the image of a dashing Professor, his eyes reflecting the sun, his hand stretched out to her that day beside the fortress.

Today, her first class would be with him. She worried he would not remember, but when he lifted his head and took her registration paper, he froze for two seconds until that smile burst across his long face. His blue eyes sparkled. She trembled, hands shaking as she pulled a notebook from her backpack.

"Hello. How are you?" He looked down at her papers, "Shaima. How is your father?"

She smiled, and it began like that. She felt his eyes follow her to the seat he pointed out, and when she sat and looked up, he smiled again. She knew her face gave it all away, but she did not care. Everything would be all right now. They began with small talk about family. She told him about her mother. He frowned, his eyes filled with emotion, and she stirred within.

A month passed and they moved to working together on his research. He said she could give him insights of great value and he kept asking about mines, caves, and he had an especially keen interest in Alexander's tomb. She knew what he wanted and she could give it to him, for she had the secret Baba gave her, a secret so wondrous that to reveal it would mean betrayal and dishonor and death. No, it would be all right. A Professor, a man of intellect and culture would never desecrate or destroy. She assured herself of this more and more each day and yet, a part of her flashed a warning.

One night in his office, he reached for her and she stiffened. He ran two fingers along the line of her cheekbone down to her chin. His thumb brushed against her lips. She calmed and leaned against him for support, warmth, and so much more.

She had dared to dream and those dreams brought her to this place and she looked up into his eyes. Sparkling blue, deep, and wide, an ocean where she floated lost and breathless. Then she remembered herself and where she came from and a large part of her rebelled at his advance, that intrusion upon her Afghan honor, and for many days she stayed away from the University, hiding in her aunt's home. She grew thin and sickened. Her aunt called doctors and they placed a tube in her arm and against her will, she gained back her strength.

She had wanted to die. She could not reconcile her desire for him with her culture and morality. Her actions amounted to the greatest of sins, and the punishment for those sins reminded her of that day long ago when she watched from the window while her mother succumbed to her father's justice. Still, her desire for the professor grew and she could not control it as it consumed her mind and body. She felt on fire though she had not yet gone to Hell.

He stood outside her window for weeks. Her aunt refused to allow him in. The phone rang and rang, and then her male cousins came and ran him off. He came back, but they beat him and sent him away. It went on like this and she struggled for months.

Unable to resist, she went back. She wanted the degree and the freedom it meant for her. She thirsted for the knowledge, and even more for the sounds of the city, and most of all she missed the bustling students and their laughter in the cafeteria where their voices danced on her ears like sounds from heaven. She worked hard to achieve this small sliver of freedom. She would not give it back.

In the full measure of her life, she realized the only thing that mattered to her, the only thing that would ever matter. He stood in front of the class, eyes searching and worried. Then one stormy night he approached her once again and this time, unable to fight any further, she succumbed. He touched her, she touched him, and it went like that. This feeling, she hoped, would never end.

◆ ◆ ◆

33

Rites of a Secret Society

She stood naked but for the mask, a black fluttery veil that covered her eyes. Pale, long-limbed, a reddish fall of Lady Godiva hair, lips painted a feverish, glittering pink. She swayed to the tangled music of the masquerade ball.

"Now that's a woman," said Louis XVI.

Mac murmured agreement while pushing the fake feather of his own privateer's hat to one side. His costume fit poorly, and he shifted his shoulders to keep the ruffled white shirt from falling. A tag in the collar scratched his neck and the black gloves caused his hands to sweat even more than the woman who stood surrounded by Zeus, Poseidon and a gaggle of Don Juan De Marcos. She towered over them all, the centerpiece of the ball.

Above the pale Godiva, a massive crystal chandelier trembled from crushing sound waves emanating from a band of Musketeers playing just behind Mac, on the balcony that overlooked a maze of high hedged and cobbled walkways where naked bodies intertwined and undulated beneath the moonlight.

"This is one insane party," Mac said.

"She is incredible, Mac," said Louis XVI.

Mac turned and stared at Reggie dressed in powder and white wig. He had avoided looking for most of the night. The brummagem costume and the fan in hand and glittering globs of rouge in Reggie's cheeks formed a truly horrifying picture.

Mac turned to the woman who arched her perfect back and beckoned her man to dance. Truly, thought Mac, women held the power of God in their bodies. He tore his eyes from her to the glittering decorations and portraits of famous Brotherhood leaders hanging on the walls.

At one end of the large ballroom, an enormous portrait of Albert Pike looked down at the revelers, his gaze fierce and determined. In one hand, he held an open book, and in the other rested a quill. Mac and Reggie had argued over whether the book in his hand could be his famous, *"Morals and Dogma of the Ancient and Accepted Scottish Rite of Freemasonry,"* which each had read and that still sparked arguments between them.

At the other end of the hall, woven into a massive white tapestry, hung the blood-red cross of the Templars. All around them, gold and silver memorabilia encased in glass depicted the history of the Brotherhood, from birth to the present day. In each corner of the room stood shining suits of armor adorned with the red cross on the left shoulder and across the chest, pennants attached to pikes, and great gleaming broadswords, one enclosed in glass, reputedly the sword of Hugues de Payens, first grandmaster of the Templars.

Moses walked in. White hair and beard aflame with glittering streaks of red and purple and gold, eyes wide and pale blue, staff in hand and long white robes. Behind him, six men dragged in a ram made of gold leaves. And Moses led them like that time long ago, his great staff pounding the floor, drawing all attention. The men wheeled the golden calf to near the center of the room.

After a few moments, Moses walked over and stood next to Reggie. Reggie stood shorter than Mac, and Moses stood taller than both.

"We have reached an accommodation," said Moses.

"I understand," said Reggie.

"You will have no prison time. The incident washed. The higher ups are distracted now by the war in Iraq. There will be a department for you to head. You will have Mac, Black, and Harris as your team. You'll do exactly as you're told."

Mac turned and thought of Father Dodd. He thought he could hear the choir singing from so long ago. Christmas nights walking the old neighborhood. Colored lights, eggnog, presents. He thought of his mother, long passed. Angels beat frosted wings against Mac's ears.

♦ ♦ ♦

- Part IV -
The Conflict

34

Armon Badil, Once Named Snow Boy

Five more years pass in our story. Some things stay the same and some things change. Over the years, my connection to my twin grew stronger and thus I knew he lived and suffered, but I had only his dreams to show me the way and that way loomed dark and full of portent.

A rocket explodes against gray cliffs. Rock shards rain down and a giant cloud of dust swallows everything. Women scream and reach for children. Chopper blades churn the air into a spinning vortex of leaves and dirt. The girl huddles over, protecting him with her body, the scent of her sweet in his nostrils. The gunship drifts closer. Their clothes whip and snap in the whirlwind. She snatches his hand and pulls him to his feet. They merge into the wave of villagers moving up the mountainside. He clutches her arm. She leads him across the rocks, past twisted walnut trees and up the bank of a slender stream. Behind them, guns roar and bullets pound into the swarming mass of humanity. A woman limping next to him bursts into a cloud of red mist and a boy cries out. Clear water turns to rust and he sees an arm floating, then a foot, an empty boot. She pulls him up the hillside. He falls to his knees and the girl lands beside him. He turns.

Shadows move in her green eyes, whirling blades and black cannons spitting fire. Smoke and devastation everywhere. She pushes him towards thin arms stretching from the darkness. He holds tight to her hand, and for an instant he thinks they will make it. Then her hand rips away. He turns. She falls and bullets tear a line of death towards her. He runs out screaming, reaching for her.

Darkness pulls him down. Screams fade and the clatter of helicopter blades dissolves into new rhythms. He rises through this fog of dreams into a dark room, a spinning ceiling fan and hot thick air. Her heartbeat flutters against his back. Sweat trickles, her breasts swell and wane as her breath cools the back of his neck. He drifts in the lilac scent of her.

She turns away, leaving his scars exposed. Opening his eyes a crack, he watches her reflection in the dresser mirror. Lightning flashes a pale glow through the open window above the bed. Her alabaster skin glistens beneath tiny pearls of perspiration. She bends and slides a short black skirt up and over her small tight buttocks. A pink tank top leaves her bejeweled belly button exposed. She fastens the black choker around her neck and runs narrow fingers through her waterfall of blonde hair. A hot draft pushes through the tattered screen to lick the scars on his back but he remains still, enchanted by her slow delicate movements.

She reaches over to the nightstand. He squints, feigning sleep. She picks up his wallet... rifles through... takes the bills... folds the wallet and places it back, just so.

She turns and gives him an icy look, aloof, untouchable. Stuffing his money into her purse, she gives him a final glance and moves towards the door. He rolls and lunges. Grabbing her arm, he spins her around and pushes her up against the wall. Dangling against the pale blue paint, she flails, kicks, and scratches his wrists, fighting to pry his fingers from her arms.

"Thief," Armon says.

She scowls and breaks away from him. He reaches for her, but she is fast and gets out the door before he can stop her. Her shoes clatter down the stone steps and Armon looks out the window to see her running down the street with his money.

He walks into the bathroom and stares at the dry bowl of a rusted sink. A cracked mirror reflects his face twice. He grimaces at the double image. He has not shaved and looks rough around the edges.

Thunder rolls over the city and rattles the window frame. In the withering humidity, walls sweat and paint peels. The room smells rotted. He breaks his gaze from the mirror when a sudden burst of hard rain pounds a drum beat on the old wall mounted air conditioner.

He tries the shower, the water trickles, sputters and then blasts. He gets in and turns the knob to the coldest cold. He unwraps the tiny soap and lathers up, rinses off, gets out dripping, pushes back his long hair and runs a hand over the stubble on his face. He thinks about growing a beard like John Brown and the image of a man that haunts him during sleep. A tall man with a John Brown beard. He remembers the dream and it puzzles him.

A gray stone castle nestles between snow-capped mountains. In the valley below, purple and white blossoms shiver beneath a liquid sun. Women and men bend and straighten, moving through the field. A white stallion prances in a sparkling stream. A woman with dark blonde hair stands at a tall narrow window, her back turned towards him. She sings and bends over flowers, but she never turns around. He hears voices, trickling laughter... water falling... a cool mist on his face.

Where is this place? I know this place, I cannot remember...

The storm rages and the rain thickens, splashing through the screen, off the windowsill and down on the bed. Cool rain splashes on his back. Thunder rumbles. He gets up and is about to close the window when he sees a lightning bolt slam into a transformer on a telephone pole. Sparks fly. Streetlights flash and neon signs flicker. Below the open window, passing prostitutes squawk and cackle.

The loud clang of a garbage can and feline yowls draw his full attention. He flattens his body against the wall. Fat raindrops bash into the screen and splatter on the sill where decaying flies sit in a graveyard of wet dust. Outside, a black SUV sits beneath a burned-out streetlight. A tiny glow in the front window reveals at least one watcher. A cat saunters down the road.

He kneels by the side of the bed and reaches underneath to pull out a black briefcase. Dialing a combination into the latches, he cracks opens the top revealing gray-green cubes surrounding several fusing devices. He brushes his hands across the cubes, picks up a small one and closes the case. In his right hand, he kneads the material into a small button. Reaching down, he retrieves his jeans and slips them on. He pulls a black t-shirt on over his head, grabs his leather jacket from the stained armchair. Gathering his two small bags, he opens the door. He closes the door and slips out into the hallway.

◆ ◆ ◆

35

Mac the Dreamer

She crawls across dead bodies, curved blade gripped sideways between her white teeth. Blood smears the length of her body and long black hair frames her young face. Behind her, the village burns and the Colonel stands in the flames, grinning. Mac tries to stand, but his body refuses. Nausea churns his stomach. He tries to crawl away, but an unseen force holds him in an unbreakable grip. Her dark eyes flash pure hate and he knows with sickening certainty that she will kill him, gut him, and eat him. She reaches for his foot. His scream echoes between gray mountains.

"Mac, wake up."

"No."

"Come on Mac, you're snoring."

"I don't snore."

"You sure as hell do snore. Wake up."

Voices cracked through radio static. Harris breathing, prostitutes laughing, footsteps on wet concrete. His eyelids opened to a collage of streetlights, hotel signs, and rain on the windshield, all melding into a brilliant multicolored waterfall. He wiped sweat from his brow and remnants of sleep from the corners of his eyes. A cat skittered across the Ford's hood, screeching, claws sliding like chalk on a blackboard. Mac let slip a few curses.

"Why the hell did you wake me up? All you do is stare at the prostitutes. You don't need me for that."

"That bastard's window is wide open up there," Harris said.

"AC probably broken, typical for these old hotels."

"Yea. Typical," said Harris.

Harris slipped something into his wallet.

"What's that?" Mac said.

Harris placed the wallet in his jacket pocket and stared out the half-open window. Mac lit a cigarette.

"Picture mom gave me."

"Yea? Of what?"

"My father."

"The one you've never seen?"

"Yea Mac. The one I've never seen."

The edge in his partner's voice held Mac back from the obvious. He coughed a couple times, inhaled, and blew out the cigarette smoke.

"How's your mom doing?" he said.

"She's dying. How do you think she's doing?"

"That... I'm sorry."

"Yea," Harris said. "She never mentioned him all these years, then yesterday she gave me the picture. Ten minutes later, she fell into a coma."

"Damn," Mac said. "I... uh."

"Yea, I know."

Mac slapped cigarette ashes from his pants and concentrated on sights and sounds to stop thinking and feeling and remembering. Rain hammered the Ford. Neon shimmered against the wet road. Water rushed and gurgled into gutters, surging towards the river.

The shrill laugh of a woman cut through the storm. Silent screams, dark dreams. Darkest flashed the memories.

A voice cracked out of the black speaker on the dashboard.

"Mac, Harris, you there? What the hell are you two doing?"

"Colonel never sleeps," Mac said.

"Yea," said Harris.

Mac reached for the radio.

"We're watching the guy. He is upstairs with a hooker. Has not moved in hours."

"Make sure you don't lose him."

"Don't worry, Reggie," Mac said.

Mac looked up through the windshield to the second floor. The radio crackled and spit again.

"Look Mac, you and Harris get up there and use the snooper... I want confirmation that he is still in there. If Farook contacts his son, I want to know."

"We're heading up." Mac slipped the radio into his pocket. "Hey, you know where the snooper is?"

"It's right behind your seat," said Harris.

"Yea. I knew that." Mac reached around and grabbed a small metal case. Opening it, he checked the gun shaped device topped with a small video screen, closed the case and shoved it under his raincoat. "Ok, let's go."

They splashed through puddles, crossed the street and huddled beneath the hotel's sagging awning. A torrent of rainwater fell over the sagging front edge of the canvas awning and a homeless man scurried from the shadowed corner of the vestibule, a tattered windbreaker over his head, his eyes wild and fearful.

"Niagara Falls," said Mac. He watched the man limp away and duck into a doorway.

"Yea," said Harris.

Hotel windows stained by cigarette smoke, dark red armchairs, a television lounge, a stained carpet. One clerk at the desk, baldhead perched on a palm, thick eyelids drooping.

Harris opened the heavy glass door and walked through. Mac followed. The startled clerk swiped at spittle dangling from the side of his mouth. Mac waved his badge, put a finger to his lips and pointed up the stairs. The clerk nodded. A narrow-carpeted stairway, oxidized brass railings, steps creaking. A single archaic brass wall lamp waited at the top. Mac sent the fiber optic camera under a gap between the bottom edge of a door and the frayed carpet. He extended the cable until he saw that the entire room.

"I don't see him in there," Mac said. He glanced at Harris who stood next to him, gun in hand, back pressed against the wall. Harris leaned forward and looked at the screen.

"Great. Chief will not be happy."

"Right, well, let's get in."

Harris kicked open the door. Mac slid into the room and pressed his back against the wall while Harris moved towards the bed.

An explosion rocked the hotel, shattering glass and knocking the ancient air conditioner out of the wall. The force sent Mac reeling back. He over-compensated, pitched forward and fell against the window screen. From there he saw the top of the Ford lift, fly over the street and land in the window of a liquor store.

Down the street, a pawnshop imploded. Alarms clanged. Neon signs melted, a telephone pole fell. A man with half a turban dangling from his head stumbled out a doorway, tripped over parts of the SUV and fell into the street holding his bleeding face with one hand and something that glinted gold with the other. Sirens shrieked in the distance.

Time slowed and Mac's memories flashed visions of burning shacks and the awful, unforgettable stench of charred flesh.

A gas tank exploded, spreading fire to cars parked along the street. Another gas tank went up in flames and fire fell with rain, bathing Mac in honey-colored heat. His ears rang and pressurized. He felt lightheaded, as if floating far above it all. The cigarette fell from the corner of his mouth. Then, from the depths of his memories, he heard sergeant Black's gunshots and felt the heat of that day from long ago.

There, a movement in the flame's blue edges, a burst of heat, and ash falling. She crawled towards him, knife gripped sideways between her teeth, blood running down her arms.

◆ ◆ ◆

36

Chaos in Georgetown

Windshield wipers slap and squeak in rhythm to the low rumble of the engine. Lights flash in the rearview mirror, fire and police responding. He sinks the gas pedal too hard and the black Corvette fishtails towards M Street and the next target. He mouths the words to an old Woodstock song playing on the radio. Richie Havens voice is like his own.

"Sometimes I feel like a motherless child. Sometimes... I fee... eel... like a motherrrrlesss child."

The streetlight turns red and he taps the brake. Alone at the intersection, he turns the radio down. Heavy raindrops and windshield wipers drown the DJ's voice. A slight movement on the right draws his attention. Outside a narrow doorway with a faded black and white Café sign, a man stands alone holding an unopened umbrella in one hand and a mug in the other. He wears a uniform of dusted gray or faded blue with a circle on one sleeve.

Lightning flashes on the man's dark face. The corners of his thin-lipped mouth droop and curve down and the skin beneath his eyes sag. Deep vertical lines on his face give him a fierce and ancient look as he glares into the rain. His shoulders sag and he leans crookedly to one side. The eyes draw the greatest attention, angry or haunted by some terrible pain, or perhaps the ghost of someone loved and lost.

The stoplight turns green and he pulls out slow, watching for flashing lights. The terrible pain in the side of his head has returned and he blinks now, trying to focus on the nightclub and restaurant signs along M street. The target sits somewhere in this street with small neon lights and clouded windows.

A girl, an umbrella, her arm in a man's arm. He wears London Fog and a bow tie. She wears a clear raincoat over a tight skirt and naked navel. They enter a doorway.

Armon Badil slides the Corvette into a spot beneath a dimmed streetlight, a few dozen yards from a little French cafe with an undecipherable sign painted in light pastels. Warm light streams through the windows onto the sidewalk. A chalkboard sits on an easel and potted plants wilt in the humid air beneath a pale green awning. He peeks through the window into soft lighting, folded blue napkins atop linen-covered tables, men and women sitting and laughing. The restaurant Sergy has selected caters to the very rich.

No dark corners, dark faces, or dark hair inside. Perhaps they prefer another of the many restaurants along the street, or they cannot afford the twenty-dollar baguettes and cream cheese, the ten-dollar mocha latte or the 18% gratuity added to every bill, according to the menu sitting in a wood and glass case beside the door.

He checks his jacket pocket for money and counts it facing the wall. She had more than she tried to steal. Typical. People always wanting more even when they have it all. Washington, a city where poverty stalks the streets while affluence hides behind marble, steel and tinted glass.

He pulls open the door. A bell tinkles. He takes a seat near the wall at a table for two. Heads turn. Two girls at the next table give him cold Nordic stares. Their suited consorts swing pale eyes up and down his jeans and leather jacket. They lean towards each other and whisper, the girls giggle. The men nod and grimace.

He waits for ten minutes. The waitress passes him four times serving bow-tied men and long-legged women who look like Paris or Britney, wrapped in tight minis and button-down shirts that come to just above their glittering navels. Another ten minutes pass. A menu lands on his table, slapped down by a waitress whose red lipstick spreads too far past the outline of her lips. He picks up the red leather booklet and flips pages. Done, he closes the menu and places it near the edge of the table. Another ten minutes, making it nearly half an hour before she shows up to take his order. Her face flushes a tortured red as she swishes up the aisle towards him, her chin down and her eyes measuring him, his faded jeans, his jacket, the black t-shirt. Then she rests blue eyes on his chin, not his eyes, and she sighs before asking, "So, what do you want?"

The lipstick moves like a crooked line of smeared blood on her face, and a straw-colored ponytail hangs out the back of her pastel blue hat. Her face droops, protesting the pounds of makeup hiding her age, which he guesses to be closer to forty than thirty.

"Coffee, please. Regular, nothing exotic." His lack of accent appears to take her by surprise. One of her bleached eyebrows wiggles like a worm. Her eyelids flutter and her blue glare softens. She leans down on the far corner of the table with her left hand and curls the order book behind her back with her right.

"Why sure hun. I am sorry for your wait. It's been a hard night, very busy."

She sounds like West Virginia, like Harper's Ferry. The river town he visited on his way here. He saw the tiny armory where John Brown died. He walked across the trestle bridge, climbed up the cliff and watched the people run while fire engines wailed and smoke curled high into the sky.

"No problem, I'm not in a big hurry."

She smells like sweat and bacon. He leans back and holds his breath while ordering an omelet. Coffee arrives in the hands of a new girl wearing a sparkling gloss of pink lipstick.

From the other side of the room, a brunette waitress with butterfly earrings and cat's eye glasses glances at him. Her hot pink lipstick grooves to the beat of a chewing gum smile. He nods. She blushes. From other tables, frigid eyes sweep up and down his peasant clothes. He does not belong and they want him to know. They want him to stay in his "station in life" so they may feel superior. These pasty-faced fools who never had a hard day in their pampered lives. He wants to kill them all.

He pulls a paperback Nietzsche from the pocket of his jacket and reads that God is dead. Thus spoke Zarathustra.

A plain omelet shows up in the hands of his new waitress, whose dimples grow deeper by the second. He likes dimples on a girl. They exude a sense of unending bliss and bring back margarita memories. Dunes and seagulls, bungalows and boardwalks, sunbaked sand burning the bottoms of his feet. He wants to take dimples, make certain she gets out before it happens.

He rubs the stubble on his face and picks at the omelet. She bounces over to him full of energy, asks if he needs anything. Her smile flashes, disarming, genuine. He makes small talk and learns she gets off work in half an hour. Men at nearby tables frown at a man chatting with the hired help. Girls flash bitter looks his way and stare at the waitress as if she just walked out of a trailer park.

"I have to meet a friend soon, but it's dark and wet out there. Can I help you to your car?"

She hesitates for a few seconds. He waits and she nods, chewing her lip.

"I'm parked nearby," she whispers.

Her voice reminds him of Helena, the girl with the green eyes, young and full of energy. He gets up and walks to the back of the restaurant. Faces turn and watch him enter a narrow hallway leading to a tiny bathroom the size of a broom closet. He takes the explosive pack out, fastens it to the rear underside of the sink and sets the timer for two hours. He turns to exit the closet but hesitates, thinking about the timer.

Setting the timer to the hour Sergy instructed might kill the girl. Even the other waitresses did not deserve to die. The customers. Well, they only do what someone taught them to do. He has heard of this thing called peer pressure. He thinks it must be everywhere in America.

Truly, Sergy hates these people, but it is one thing to kill a man face to face. Another to murder women this way, without honor. Even Mahlim would not approve. If Sergy complains it will be too bad. He can kill the Professor. Take his new passport and go back alone. He splashes cold water on his face and walks out.

Back at the table, he waits until she appears. Faded blue jeans hug slim hips. A raincoat over her shoulders and an umbrella fighting with her purse. He walks dimples to her car. She parked her Volkswagen behind the restaurant in the alley. The alley is dark. Stained brick buildings menacing on either side. A ragged figure hobbles down to a dumpster and lifts the top. A smaller figure follows, holding a third shadow, a female, by the hand.

He turns back to the girl. Hot concrete steams beneath cool rain. Beneath her umbrella, they huddle for a moment. He asks her to go to the beach with him. She laughs and flashes a smile that lights the darkness. Then she drives away. Three shadows dissolve into the rain. A child, a man and a woman.

He pulls the Corvette away from the curb and cuts through water puddles on M Street. The rumbling exhaust drowns out the never-ending storm.

♦ ♦ ♦

37

The Hotel

Chief's here," Harris said.

"About time he showed up," said Mac.

The night clerk limped back and forth, wringing his hands until a paramedic took him by the elbow and sat him down. Smoke drifted in the shattered windows and hugged the ceiling, spreading and billowing like a thundercloud.

Mac walked outside to meet Reggie. Two giant lights swept back and forth across walls and rendered the street in near daylight. A helicopter floodlight lit nearby buildings and streets. Emergency vehicles flashed red, white and blue across the bewildered faces of a mob that surged against yellow police tape and shiny wet lines of the riot squad. The press arrived and aimed cameras at medics working on a blood-soaked man lying on the ground.

"Chief, Hey there, Chief Gregory."

Lights flashed, cameras whirred. Reggie pulled his trench coat tighter and straightened the gray Fedora on his head. Mac blinked and saw Reggie through a time tunnel, standing in a crumbling doorway as the village burned around him.

The mob pushed and shouted. Sirens wailed. A man with a bullhorn demanded attention. All this pandemonium amplified between buildings into a cacophony of pure sound. Everything moved in a wave of brilliant colors splashing on a concrete coastline. Rain dropped trails of silver from the sky, a thousand giant threads spinning down.

The action slowed. His heartbeat pounded against his temple. Voices combined into a roar. Lightning flashed, thunder hammered and stunned the crowd silent for just a few seconds. Then, once again, they surged against the yellow tape and voices rose in one raging bellow of anger. Officers pushed back and bedlam ensued at the edges of the mob. Batons cracked down and the mob flinched and pulled back, all except the frenzied press.

"Chief, over here. Channel 4 News. Chief. Is this related to the armory bombing in Harper's Ferry?"

Reggie moved towards the cameras and held up his hands, nodding and penitent like a politician. A sudden frightening certainty tingled in Mac's brain. Reggie at the podium and ten thousand delegates screaming. Mac threw his cigarette into the gutter where a river of rainwater carried it down into the sewer system.

Reggie drew a paper from his pocket and held a hand up to the cameras.

"I'll give you what we know. Suspect still at large. A man sent by the Afghan warlord, Khan Ali Khan. We do not have a photo of this man, but reliable sources have informed me that the General is retaliating for what he calls 'the illegal occupation of Afghanistan'. The Pentagon has knowledge of the situation. Ask them what solution they are working on. I cannot stop Ali Khan. I retired from military life. Now the Army has to stop him."

Waving his hands, Reggie dismissed the barrage of questions and headed over to Mac.

"Room 310 Chief. Third floor," said Mac. Harris in tow, Mac pointed Reggie upstairs and down a dim hallway lit by emergency lights. He opened the door, the men stepped inside, and Mac shut the door. He listened for footsteps in the hallway. After a moment, Mac turned and faced Reggie.

"Well?" Reggie said.

Mac pulled the threadbare drapes open, allowing roving floodlights to flicker beams in and out of the room. Reggie stood there in his dark trench coat, his profile cutting sharp against the lights.

"He got by us and blew up the Ford while we had the snooper under the door," Mac said.

Reggie paced back and forth in front of the cracked window.

"Not really that big a deal. One more thing we can slap on that bastard Ali. Soon the Generals will have no choice but to go after him. Even his own people have to be on his ass by now."

Mac nodded. "There's a lot of damage out there. The guy on the street will probably die. Eventually, one of those reporters will start asking the right questions." Mac paused.

Reggie turned and stared out the window.

"Colonel."

"You worry too much, you always have. The Brotherhood planned this down to the smallest detail. Soon the Russian will go back into Badakhshan. He will get us Farook and we will get the reward. Ali Khan will be too busy fighting his enemies to stop us."

"Americans are dying."

Gregory paced, took off the Fedora and played with the brim like Bogey in the *Maltese Falcon.*

"Look Mac. Ali must go. With him there, we cannot get in to find Farook. The Pashtun warlords will not give us the Arab. We must take him. With news of these bombs spreading worldwide, Farook will surely recognize an opportunity to reclaim his son, and that will be his last mistake."

"The hell with Ali." said Mac. "You are really after the lapis. Are you not?"

Reggie smiled.

"I am not giving up the lapis. Poor Mac. Do you ever stop to think who really runs the world?"

Reggie shook his head.

"You and I don't matter. We are just pawns. These people are powerful. They controlled the world for the last thousand years. You and I will not stop them."

Reggie stopped pacing. Smoke circled the room. Lights glimmered on the long cracks in the window.

"How's your mother, Harris boy?" Reggie asked.

Harris looked up. "Doc said any day now."

Reggie nodded and shuffled his feet, scraping the old carpet, colorless and absent in the black and white moment.

"Look Mac, you think you going to get rich working this job? You think you are going to make enough money to retire? Not in this America, not with the Hindus and Jews taking all the good jobs, making all the money, shoving real Americans back into the trailer parks and homeless shelters. Ya Mac, trailer parks where all old soldiers like you and me end up, or else like those wandering homeless veterans on the street you see babbling to themselves, drooling, drinking from a dirty brown bag. You want to end up like that? I do not. One job ain't enough in America anymore. If you do not have something on the side, you end up homeless and ain't nobody going to give a shit Mac. Nobody. Everybody is out to get their own. Nobody cares how many enemies of America we had to kill, how many times we got shot. If we don't catch this bastard Farook and get that ten-million-dollar reward, we will end up in some trailer park like old man Guthrie and John Jacobs and all the rest of them that sit around down by the Dairy Queen all day summer long, soaking up the air-conditioning cause they ain't got none in their trailer. Not me boy, not Reggie Gregory. I'm getting mine."

Reggie kicked at the carpet, his shadow dancing against the wall like a wraith.

Mac nodded and knew.

"All right. The next target is in Georgetown. You guys get down there and get me the gist of it. I have a report to phone in. Remember, we cannot get close to this guy. I don't want him getting caught doing something stupid." Reggie paused. "A lot of money and planning went into this project. Don't screw it up."

Floodlights swept into the room for an instant. Their eyes met.

"Poor Mac." Reggie shook his head. "Look. They kept us out of prison, and this is the price we pay. Everybody pays Mac."

Reggie walked out. Mac opened the window and pulled the screen out, tossed it into a dark corner of the room. He leaned out into the rain and let it smash against his face. Voices broke into his torment.

"Fucking raghead. Got what he deserved. Probably set the bomb."

"Shut up, asshole. That is Mr. Jeffrey. He owns that liquor store. He's as white as you or me."

A moment of calm descended as two ambulances drove away. Then the first man spoke again.

"Kill them raghead bastards, every one of them."

"Who are you calling a raghead?" said another man.

Voices intensified into shouts. A fight broke out. Police rushed to the area and the mob pushed forward.

Sirens wailed. Mac drove down M Street in a cruiser commandeered from a uniform cop. Harris stared out the passenger window. Buildings loomed dark and deserted in a gray and black landscape. In the distance, clouds burned reddish brown against the horizon. Mac's brain fired away. Too many cups of coffee, too many ghosts, too much history.

"The Brotherhood," said Mac.

"What?" said Harris.

"Nothing. Just, well, just what do you know about the Brotherhood?"

"I know a lot. I read Albert Pike's book. He claimed Lucifer to be the God of Light and Adonay the God of Darkness. He claimed the Christian God to be an imposter and evil. Lots of blood oaths, Masons, Illuminati, secret societies."

"Jesus Christ," said Mac.

"Yea. Jesus Christ too."

"You don't believe that crap do you Harris?"

"I don't believe in anything."

"Yea. Me neither."

The police radio crackled, static mixed with voices. Flashing red, white and blue lights caught the homeless scurrying from one sheltered spot to another. Faces twisted in wet fear. Adults and children lost in a strange and incomprehensible world. Terrified, they huddled in dark corners. A man stumbled down the sidewalk, his long hair stuck to his narrow head, white beard dripping a waterfall. Older memories played a movie in Mac's brain.

Frosty nights and dodging bombs amid shelled out buildings while snow fell and painted Kabul streets in white. Dead bodies piled everywhere, half-naked ghosts dashing from one pile of rubble to another, looking for shelter, a scrap of food. Kabul city leveled to a ghostly ruin enveloped in fog. He and his squad crouched in the shadows, watching Afghans butcher each other. Women and children lay in the streets, their decaying skin like pale wet blossoms dotting the ruins. A sky scorched with tracer fire, gunships and screaming jets. Did he dream it or it happened? He could no longer tell the difference.

Now the war arrived on his doorstep, and he scowled at the cost of Reggie's revenge. Americans killing Americans. Like a hammer against his head. What could he do? Who could fight the Brotherhood? Nobody. They had grown too strong, controlling everything from the price of oil to who got medicine and who did not. These people decided who lived and who died. Everything turned upside down. Nothing made sense anymore.

Memories of that night played on Mac's closed eyelids like an old flickering black and white movie.

Mac shook himself from his recollections and barely avoided slamming into cars parked all along M Street. He rolled the window all the way down and took a deep breath of humid D.C. air. He coughed and turned the air conditioner up.

"Are there any umbrellas in this cruiser?" said Mac.

Harris looked around, tossing a glance into the back seat.

"No umbrellas. Probably in the trunk."

Mac pulled the cruiser over behind a crowd that thrust themselves against a line of riot police. He and Harris exited the cruiser and pushed their way through. Buildings on the south side of M Street burned. Electrical signs sparked and shattered. Firefighters scrambled over scattered debris, broken windows and cars knocked on their sides. The blast had leveled the block, leaving the charred remains of ruined brick and iron rods poking at the sky. Emergency vehicles parked at odd unmatched angles all around the street as teams of paramedics rushed in and out of buildings. A paramedic had found a man, a woman, and a child crushed under piles of concrete and brick. A curtain of firefighters in yellow raincoats gathered around the dead.

"It's a homeless family," said a fireman.

"Terrible," said another.

The sky burned and ash fell between the raindrops. Firefighters struggled, adding more hoses to their onslaught. Sirens, radios, bullhorns blaring in the street. Mac pushed wet hair back from his forehead and looked around for an awning to stand beneath. Behind them, police held the line against the angry crowd. The press corps struggled to get through, screaming at everyone.

Morrison, the explosives expert, walked over as Harris crossed the street and disappeared inside a smoldering building.

"Plastic explosive, Lieutenant," Morrison said. He held out debris that looked like a French delicacy.

"You can tell that from this tiny piece of-"

"Yep. C-4. He doesn't care if we know how, he just wants to blow shit up."

"Where would he get this?" He had to ask the right questions. It had to look good. Mac wiped the rain off his face but more just fell with the ash, Morrison's yellow raincoat turned gray. Lightning flashed, striking somewhere close. The crowd roared and pushed forward. Soon the FBI and ATF would arrive if they had not already. Mac looked around for their dark lettered jackets. He did not want to share information. He just wanted to go home.

"Well, they still use this all over the world. He almost destroyed the entire block with this stuff. The originating blast blew one restaurant and two stores nearby. The rest of this mess is all from the fallout."

Morrison scratched his ear while rolling the charred material around in his palm with his thumb.

"Any casualties?"

"Not one. Everything in this block had shut down just an hour ago."

"Why blow it up at all? This does not seem like terrorism," Mac said.

"I don't know, maybe he's just some nutcase who lost his mind. Why would he blow up an empty restaurant? Don't terrorists usually go after people? Transportation, subways, buses, military installations or government buildings. And why this time of night? Nobody around this late. Makes little sense," he said.

"We got lucky this time," Mac said.

Morrison nodded.

"Yes. Lucky."

Harris came lumbering out of the used record store across the street. His height dwarfed Morrison and everybody else.

"Anything?" Mac asked.

"Nah, nothing. Nobody saw anything. The owner was doing inventory and then, boom, yelling, screaming and burning. Nobody saw a thing."

"Nobody ever sees. It's a blind world."

The black limousine pulled up and Reggie got out. The press swarmed around him. He nodded at Mac and then turned to face the cameras.

◆ ◆ ◆

38

Bad Dreams, Good Life

Rain fell in pearlescent strings, reflecting the flash and flicker of lightning. Thunder grumbled and pine boughs creaked. She tugged on my hand, guiding me through the woods towards our cabin that sat in a clearing of trimmed grass. I heard the Potomac surge on the far side of the cabin and imagined it rushing like the blue green Amu where Baba dropped the bodies of gray and red soldiers.

"Let them float home," Baba said.

"Allez, allez!"

The men shouted to each other, tossing bodies from saddle to saddle.

"Oiy!"

They tossed the bodies in, one by one or piece by piece, and the mass of gray floated and bobbed in the blue-white rage of water.

"Omar."

Her voice filtered through from far away, over the gorge and from some distant high valley...

"Wake up."

She turned. I caught her in my arms and our lips met, driving all thought from my mind. The soft edge of her tongue, the pale outline of her lips and the perfect sweep of her eyebrows gave me an appreciation of the artistic hand that drew her so enchantingly. A fat cool raindrop fell inside the collar of my raincoat and down my back. I came up for air and she smiled, turned and splashed towards the door. I followed. She giggled. I caught her at the door where she fumbled in her purse for keys. I reached around and hugged her to me. My hand slipped inside her jacket and found the beat of her heart. She leaned back and turned her face to mine.

The door opened and we fell on the blue and red rug Uncle brought from Ankara for her birthday. She giggled, lying on her back, blonde curls splayed around her head. Lightning flashed, casting the garish shadow of a pine down on us. Bad omen, I thought and kicked the door closed.

"Bedroom," she said.

Uncle was mistaken. She did not pass like the wind into another valley. I picked her up and carried her up the stairs. We worked up a sweat and then she slept through the storm while I watched treetops sway and lightning flash through the skylights. I fell asleep as morning lightened. Then I dreamed.

A whip cut across my back. Pain in the side of my head. A white mountain and a cave, the ocean surged below. I looked down at my feet dangling in the air. A wet mist sprinkled over my face. Blood everywhere and Baba stood in the middle of a red river, his eyebrows knitted in that familiar way. He reached out, touched my face, and called me by my brother's name. And the drummer played again, that slow sad march. Still, I could not find him, even in my dreams.

Her finger traced the edges of my mouth.

"Having fun?" I said.

She pouted. Her lips took the shape of tulips, the ones she grew behind the cabin in the flowerbed where we planted a blue spruce the day we knew she carried our baby.

"You whimper in your sleep."

"What? I do not whimper. Girl's whimper. Not men, and never an Afghan man."

"Yes, you do. You whimper in the mornings. You dream and you whimper. What did you dream about?"

She had this way of insisting and I could not dissuade her from it.

"I don't whimper. Perhaps you dreamed I whimpered."

That argument sounded good to me, but she ignored it.

"So what were you dreaming hunny?"

"You know, I don't remember."

"Your brother again."

"I don't whimper."

"Yes, you do." She smiled and leaned over, kissed me and ran her fingers through my hair. "Maybe we should cut all this long hair off your head, like your father did."

"I don't think so."

"You don't think so?" And the tickling commenced. I learned to go easy, tickling her gently, so she turned a very pale shade of lavender, like the soft sheen of her darkening eyelids when we made love. Pulling away laughing, she picked up the remote and I lunged. As we fought for control, the television came on. I heard my father's name and I looked over at a stocky man in a Fedora standing by a burning building.

♦ ♦ ♦

39

The Big Picture

A dim hallway led to a library that served as Reggie's office. Wide bay windows looked out over a large portico supported by polished marble columns. White trimmed French doors lead to a bubbling hot tub. Two walls filled with books while a third boasted a bar, flat panel television screen and an expensive stereo. His desk sat in front of the windows, facing into the room.

"You remember Sergy Volkov from Afghanistan?" said Reggie.

"Big guy, KGB double agent."

"And for many years now, Professor of anthropology and archeology at Moscow University," Reggie said.

"A great cover," Mac said. He found an ashtray and killed the cigarette. Reggie lit up a Cuban and rolled it around in his fingers.

"He worked for our side in Afghanistan. He's the only one could get close to Ali Khan after, well you know." Reggie spit Ali's name out with a piece of cigar. His face crinkled.

"Yea, I know," Mac said.

"Anyway, Now Ali don't allow anybody into his mountains. He tossed everybody out since the Lion's murder. He made deals with the Tajiks and the Russians who protect his northern borders. From the south, only one pass leads in and no army has ever crossed over that, not since Alexander the Great. Now look at this."

Reggie picked up the remote control and the television flickered to life. Three turbaned men sat inside a dimly lit room. On one side sat piles of blue stones, and on the other, a scale and a bearded Caucasian man who smiled and nodded.

"Five million dollars' worth of lapis sitting right there. Big blue gorgeous rocks. The same lapis decorates the mask of King Tut, from the same mines. We must find the mine those rocks came from," Reggie said.

"Oh sweet Jesus, not the mine again. You heard Sergy. The mines failed. Only junk lapis comes out now."

"Does that look like junk lapis to you? Anyway, we're going for more than just lapis."

"Colonel, assuming you got inside Badakhshan, you wouldn't last two days in there. Ali Khan will find you. Then he will skin you and feed you to his dogs. That is a very angry man. Especially at you."

Reggie chuckled and took a drag of his cigar. The windows cast his face in total shadow but for the mad sparkle in each eye. Reggie's eyes took Mac back to Alabama, Cicely, and Father Dodd. Blood on the grass and Cicely tied like a hog, and Reggie sat there, drenched in red. Blue eyes sparkling insanity. Memories turned to nightmares and now they played during his waking hours. Torment and terror, weapons of an angry God.

"Help me, Father Dodd. Where are you when I need you?"

Reggie took a long drag on his cigar, coughed and continued.

"We have General Ali's daughter, or rather Sergy has her. She will lead us to the burial crypt of Alexander the Great."

Mac laughed. "Alexander the Great? You are going to find his crypt? Are you crazy?"

"No Mac. I am serious. I will make you rich."

"Reggie, people searched for his crypt for centuries. Nobody has ever found it. You think you're going to find what the world has been looking for since his death?"

A puff of smoke vanished in the blades of the ceiling fan. Chopping, hacking blades like the Blackhawk landing in the field and Mac pictured the giant lumbering towards them, stone quarry face, eyes like green fires.

Reggie grunted and chuckled.

"You know what Ali will do if he finds your Russian with his daughter?"

"Ali will be busy saving his own ass. Why do you think we are doing all this?"

Mac shook his head and stared at trees bending beneath the storm. The sky remained hidden for weeks. Hurricanes wandered north, one after another, and Mac dreamed more than ever during these violent nights.

"Ok, the crypt of Alexander. And?"

"And the Brotherhood wants his sword and shield and they want something else."

"What else?"

"DNA."

Thunder shook the French windows. A branch scuttled across the patio.

"DNA. And what will they do with Alexander's DNA?"

"Think genetic engineering. Imagine what they could do with the genes of the greatest general the world has ever known."

"You're kidding me."

"It's not as crazy as it sounds. His body is there. She has seen it."

"Who has seen it?"

"Sergy's woman. Ali's daughter."

Mac rubbed his eyes and then his temples.

"They want his DNA. What will they do? Make another Alexander?"

Suddenly, it made freakish sense. So much sense that it set Mac's brain reeling back to Albert Pike's book.

Jacobins wanted their own Anti-Christ raised from the dead. A clone of Alexander trained and coddled and in 40 years, President. A man like that might conquer the entire world and place it in Brotherhood hands.

"They already have Hitler's, Churchill's and John F's and a dozen others. They want Alexander's and our job is to get it." Reggie stopped for two puffs. Mac lit up another cigarette and shook his head. "They are giving us five million up front."

"Five million dollars?"

"No, five million donuts. Don't be a dumbass."

Mac sat in the chair facing Reggie's desk.

"How do we know the girl has the location?"

"Sergy guarantees it, and the Brotherhood will take the risk for Alexander's DNA. So, we are his back up. He takes his expedition in first. We go in a few days later in case Ali finds out and follows his daughter and Sergy. This ensures we have Ali between us in case he gets... frisky."

Reggie trimmed his cigar, rubbing the red tip in the square ashtray.

"Now this is the history that Sergy gave us. After his death, Alexander's funeral procession left Babylon and headed into the desert. Along the way, they got lost, never arriving at their destination, which was the Oasis of Siwa and the temple of the Egyptian god Ammon. For thousands of years archeologist have searched and theorized. Some say the procession vanished in the desert sands perhaps raided by devotees, fanatics who stole Alexander's body and took it all the way back to Persia and his wife Rokhshana. Some even say the sarcophagus arrived in Siwa, but they buried a fake sarcophagus and hid the real Alexander. A few think the earthquake that sank Egyptian temples into the Mediterranean buried Alexander's sarcophagus."

Mac's head felt like a cold bucket of ice and Reggie's voice, a pick stabbing.

"This is where the girl comes in. She claims Alexander's sarcophagus rests inside a mountain some distance from her home. Sergy will find this mountain."

Reggie's voice slowed at the end, dying to a whisper as he rummaged in his desk, pulled a map out and spread it open.

"Look here." He stuck a pencil in the corner of Badakhshan and drew a line to the Wakhan Corridor, a thin strip of land pointing like a crooked finger at China through the Himalayas.

"There, somewhere in that mass of white is her mountain. Her people have kept this secret for many years. We will bring it to the world. Do not let your guilt eat you. We're doing a good thing, boy."

"Terrific. Let me get this straight. This girl, who is General Ali's daughter, claims to know where they have Alexander. You believe her and you plan on following her and Sergy into Afghanistan?"

"Not me. You, Black and Harris. If something goes wrong, you and Black know the lay of the land."

The Hindu Kush ran into the Himalayas just above Pakistan. The same area of Badakhshan where they left behind a burned landscape, pillars of smoke and a girl with blood in her eyes. His hand trembled as he lifted the cigarette.

"So, when do we leave?"

♦ ♦ ♦

40

A Truth Overheard

Night retreats and daybreak brings a morning mist that drenches everything in a layer of earthy perspiration. Coming over a hill, the road divides. The western fork turns to muddy gravel and narrows to half the normal width. The other, paved and shiny, leads north. He checks a small hand-drawn map and then turns down the muddy road. Heavy leafed oaks and dark wet pines turn the winding way into an emerald tunnel. Midmorning light flickers, muted by the canopy. He leaves the headlights on. A hard curve. He fishtails out and speeds up to keep the tires from sinking. Pebbles ping and rattle against the underside of the car.

Two hours pass.

The tin mailbox sits half-hidden and leaning forward behind hanging branches. A faded Confederate flag painted on the side. A thick tangle of brush encloses the narrow driveway. The dim passage holds him captive for a half-mile or more and then releases him to a dilapidated two-story farmhouse with a wraparound deck that squats in some ten acres of drowned wheat grass. Beyond the house, spread in a semi-circle, several faded red barns hunker, roofs sagging beneath their own weight. The side of the farmhouse faces him and two darkened windows riddled with spider vein cracks stare down from the second floor. Below this, a weather-streaked gray door sits between the porch and the awning while at the very top of the crumbling monolith, old shingles cling to the roof, grimly determined not to fall. He parks the car next to a black Escalade and checks the house for signs of life.

The dark reflective windows bring a chilled memory of the house where Mahlim ripped and slashed raw horrors into his soul. The scars on his back hurt and the pain in his head returns. He lights a cigarette. Hands shake just enough to make things difficult. Echoes of a man chanting, a whip cracking in cold air, the rotting stench of death. He rests his head against the steering wheel, the cool leather sensation pleasing enough to push the voices from his mind.

The rain slackens, and he gets out of the car. Sounds drift from inside the house. Metal slides against metal. Voices and laughter. Floorboards near the door creak. The farmhouse door opens and a man stomps out.

Professor Sergy Volkov has gained weight in the shoulders and chest, a little around the waist, adaptations to an active man's late forties catching up to him. A wide grin breaks over Sergy's face.

"Armon. Welcome to Maryland my friend."

"Professor Sergy Volkov, Moscow University, archeology, anthropology, and a few other less cerebral activities," Armon says.

They shake hands, hug awkwardly, and break apart.

"Well, I never liked Americans," Sergy says.

"And you are Russian."

"Only half. I'm half Afghan."

"You? How could you be?"

"My father was a Pathan, like you, from the mountains. Came to Moscow and met my mother, and... here I am." Sergy laughs and slaps Armon on the back. "So we have more in common than you thought."

"I don't know what I am."

"Oh, you are Pathan. I am certain of this. I knew it the first time I saw you. Your height, your eyes. You are a warrior Pathan from the mountains."

"Perhaps we are cousins then," Armon says.

Sergy laughs. He worries about Sergy's ability to laugh easily at anything and everything. Though he has searched for the place inside himself from where laughter might come from, he has found only a vast darkness from where nothing but a burning rage exists.

"Lots of action in D.C. last night," Sergy says.

"I had visitors. I think they were CIA."

"Not CIA. They are comrades sent to monitor us. The men paying for all this, we will just say they are unusual."

"They should be more careful."

"Yes, they should."

They stand in on the porch, Armon smoking and Sergy leaning on a thick post.

"Do you like the car?" Sergy asks.

Armon nods.

"The second target burned down late. No casualties," Sergy says.

"My mistake."

"I don't like mistakes."

"Or Americans."

Sergy laughs. The front door creaks. A small woman of startling beauty steps out onto the porch. Straight coppery hair hangs to her shoulders. Cleopatra bangs on her forehead fall above unusually large eyes unadorned with makeup. She drops a gun that clatters on the wood porch.

"I hope you did not load that gun, *lastochka*. Dropping loaded guns isn't such a good idea," Sergy says.

Sergy bends and picks up the dropped pistol, a nine-millimeter Berretta. Armon watches the girl, something about her rings in his head.

"The man you are staring at is Armon. The friend from Oregon I told you about."

She bites her petulant lower lip, a rare pink color almost bronze but not quite. Her eyes sweep up and down his length, then narrow and glint in the gray light of the storm.

"What are you doing here, Omar?" she says.

"Omar?" Sergy says. "Your brother?"

The look on her face is fear mixed with cunning or something... predatory. Her presence is hawk like. Her hands small. Fingernails painted blood red. She moves sideways and slips halfway behind Sergy. At the edge of his vision, Sergy smiles, like a cat toying with a mouse. Armon notes all the signs of a plot. A fresh new torture designed to shake him. They will regret this game, but he will play to see where the game leads because he has not seen Sergy in three years. He receives instructions and carries them out. Now he wonders if he is the target and the girl is to take his place.

"Meet Shaima, daughter of Ali Khan and our guide to the lapis mines."

"Shaima," Armon says. "A beautiful name."

She appears electrocuted.

"Sergy, this man is not who you think he is," she says.

No one moves. Armon fingers the switchblade in his back pocket. He wonders just how fast Sergy is and calculates in his mind the two-and-a-half steps, slashing Sergy's neck. A spin and the girl lying beneath him, her neck in his hands. Then he stops and blinks.

"Omar?" Armon says.

"Omar. Come on. Quit pretending," Shaima says.

"Why did you call me Omar?"

The name touches something buried deep inside. She stares at him. He looks at Sergy. She toys with a diamond necklace, red fingernails, diamonds, pale skin. Her light scent of jasmine and honeysuckle. More than anything, it is the eyes that scare him. Something about the eyes.

"Sergy, why did you bring my brother here?" Her voice cracks, a soft lavender whisper in the darkening day. Rain picks up the pace, pounds his face and beats a loud metallic barrage on the cars.

"Brother?" says Armon.

She tugs on Sergy's arm. They move back a step. Panic has invaded her face and her hands tremble. Lightning cracks the sky and their faces turn ghostly. Almost invisible. Black and white. Shadows and light.

Visions flash. A bloody whip in thick hands. Shimmer in a black sky, a jet, a gunship, a spoon descending. It all starts with the woman. Something about her makes him nervous and angry and... he pulls the knife handle closer in his pocket.

"I'm not going back, Omar. I'm not going back to die beneath the same stones you killed my mother with."

Sergy coughs and appears to choke.

"Stoned. What stoned? No. I am not this Omar. I don't know you."

"This is Armon Badil from Oregon. He is not your brother."

"Armon Badil," she says. She squints and frowns. "No, no. He cannot be. This is my brother Omar. He's lying to you, Sergy."

Armon shifts his weight.

"Lying to me? Have you lost your mind, woman? I have known this man for years. He is a good friend. He took my classes at the University. He has done work for me. I bought him that car."

Sergy shakes his head and pushes the door open and pulls the girl inside. Armon releases the knife, pulls his hand from his pocket and follows. He crosses the threshold and steps into a different world. Rich wood floors, modern kitchen on the left, and a hallway that leads to a living room torn from the pages of a magazine. Complete with designer couches, a bar, and a plasma television tuned silently to E channel.

"Shaima, upstairs. We need to talk. Armon, make yourself at home. I will have the men bring food and coffee. Got a feeling we will need it."

"Where did you find this girl, Sergy? She's cute but daft."

Sergy laughs.

The headache pounds while a vision buried in the dark well of his past fights for attention. Then, in a split second, it comes closer and with it comes the pain. This girl's face, familiar and yet different, angry, wide-eyed, shouting at him, and the pain in the side of his head stabbing like a sharp knife. Something about that face haunts him. The frustration sets his teeth against each other as sweat bursts over his back. He feels dizzy and weak. He picks at the half-moon scars on his arm.

Sergy and the girl walk up the stairs at the far end of the room. They murmur to each other, the girl adamant, forceful. Sergy nods and smiles. They pass to the second floor. Their footsteps recede down the hallway. Armon walks to the foot of the stairway and listens. At first, he hears only murmuring until the words take shape, coalesce, and settle on his ears.

"Sikandur." she says. "He must be Sikandur. But how?" She laughs.

Sergy closes their bedroom door, but Armon can still hear them.

"My God, he is Omar's twin brother, Sikandur. He must be. The face is the same, though I have not seen Omar in years. We only talk on the phone now."

"You saw him two years ago, when you visited America without me," Sergy says.

"Yes, for my Uncle's birthday. Sergy, this man looks exactly like Omar. Exactly."

Armon takes out the switchblade and opens it, runs it over the half-moon scars on his arm. The woman's words rip fresh wounds into his soul, and wounds should bleed.

"Twin brother? It's not possible," Sergy says. "Your brother Omar who lives in that cabin by the Potomac in Virginia? The one I saw covered in dirt that day we met?"

"Yes. He must be. Don't you see? Omar's twin brother Sikandur disappeared one night in a snowstorm at a very young age, six, maybe five. A year before I was born."

"Yes... perhaps... No, it cannot be," Sergy says.

She approaches through shifting shadows until the fire lights her enormous black eyes. Horse eyes, he thinks. Dark hair whips around her head. She looks different, darker hair, larger, angrier eyes. Eyes without pupils, massive black marbles set inside giant white orbs. She comes closer and lifts the log over her head. He blinks. The world goes dark.

"They always suspected my mother of murdering him, but she didn't, because he's here, downstairs, in this house."

"Where do you think he was? Why didn't my father find him and bring him back? He did not even search. He was too busy fighting his war."

Shock steals his breath and spins his brain. His eyes sting and his ears ring. Unbearable heat, and yet he sits and listens. He cuts into his damaged arm, tearing a scar open.

"Allah is my God and Mohammad is his prophet."

Blood drips on the stairway. He whispers and rocks.

"Allah is my God and Mohammad is his prophet."

The words give the only comfort he has ever known. The words repeated in the special rhythm that he could not help but learn from the constant drone of the man in the video. Hour after hour, day after day, the words became part of him, part of his soul, and they comfort him, but only a bit. He cuts another scar open and then runs the blade across his palm and curls fingers over it. He pulls the blade out. Blood comes with it. His body shakes against the wall.

"Why didn't your father look for him? What happened?"

Father? What father? I know nothing about fathers.

Her voice interrupts his thoughts.

"What happened? I do not know. Maybe they did not want to find him. Maybe they gave him away. Maybe they sold him. People do that in my country. We should call Omar. He lives nearby, well, three hours away, in McLean Virginia. He could come and take care of Sikandar."

"We don't have time for that. We need to get to the airfield and I'm not bringing Omar into this. He is not like us. He will go to the authorities."

"Well, we have to do something. He's my brother after all."

Brother. Her words burn him. His hands shake, then his arms. The shaking increases, crazy violent shaking, his arms and legs convulse and he chokes. The world turns black and gray. He slides down the three steps and lies on the ground, jerking for a moment until he can reach the knife. He struggles to stand up, take a step up the stairs, kill her, kill Sergy. Watch their blood flow and wash away his pain. Every time he steps forward, the stairs move away. He blinks and stands there, shaking. Images flash like a lightning storm. Mahlim. Kumar. Pain. Only pain.

He retches on the steps. Choking, spitting, gulping for air, his mind searches wildly for a way to shut out the images in his brain. He runs out, slams the car door and drives. His hands shake against the steering wheel, sending the car sliding through the mud. One thing can help him now. Action will drive the pain away. Constant movement will push down the rising demons. He pounds the accelerator to the floorboard, opens the window and welcomes the rain and wind on his face.

He drives for a long time before something clicks in his mind. A terrible plan rises like a black beast from a deep well of blood. From the depths of his torment, his mind wraps around the one thought, the one concept that may lead to his own salvation. Only one thing will drive away this pain. Vengeance.

He will find this brother. He will kill this brother and rid himself of the pain and the memories. He will bury the twin deep in the ground and in this, he will bury himself and he will be someone else then, without Mahlim's hands reaching for him, without Kumar's hot breath on his back. Yes, he will become the twin.

The cracked mirror, two faces, lightning flashing behind him, casting shadows and light against the strange vision. Something dark passes over his heart. He blinks away raindrops and slams the accelerator down.

◆ ◆ ◆

41

A Twin's Life

I ran. The bear gave chase. Pushing past thick branches, stumbling around tree trunks, splashing over streams, through this misty world, unfamiliar yet familiar, and the bear grunted its panting breath on my heels, at my ear, in my very soul. I passed my mother standing in the tall window of a stone tower, her hands pressed together and her hair blowing in the wind. Jaheel ran beside me, his hoofs pounding a forgotten beat into the wet ground. Then I fell. Down I spun through the air, and the bear fell with me, swinging its great black paws, its square face familiar and yet unfamiliar. I kept dreaming the dream, and I kept waking only after knowing my death.

A clamoring attack on the front door froze my hand around a coffee cup. Jenny smeared orange marmalade on the tip of her nose and a small piece of toast hung from the edge of her mouth. The battering repeated and she dropped the toast.

Years ago, I told her about the assassin and she knew my fear that one day, in a rage of accumulated fury, Baba would send the stalking Nuristani to take, under the Pathan code of honor, his due measure of revenge. I often imagined opening the door and his curved blade sweeping across my neck and then staring out through the worn threads of a bloodstained bag in which he would carry my head back to Baba. I blinked and took a breath. Jenny cocked her head and raised her eyebrows. We stared at each other, wondering if he stood out there, his knife in one hand, his bag in the other.

"Well?" she said.

I smiled and winked. More banging on the door and I heard laughter outside, little girl ripples of joy.

"Melissa", I said. Smiling in that way she does that drives me crazy, Jenny took another bite of toast.

I pointed at her nose and said, "You have orange smegma on your nose."

Orange marmalade really, but I refused to say marmalade because the word bothered me. I hopped off the bar stool and headed for the front door.

She ran into the kitchen hollering and spraying mud over the carpet, the kitchen floor and my robe. Right behind her stomped Julie Jingles, whose real last name was Jameson, but Melissa called her Jingles and they loved each other terribly as 10-year-olds will do. They shouted about going to the mall and arcade and the rest I could not follow, nor did I try for such is not the duty of the father, but the mother, whose permission comes first before approaching the father who then meekly chauffeurs the girls from mall to mall. This took some getting used to coming from another world. One might say the opposite world where women hide beneath burqas and tremble in the sanctuary of windowless rooms while men roam the bazaar, Kalashnikovs dangling in the sunlight.

"Hi Roger. Thanks for bringing her home," I said.

"No problem. Julie loves having her over. Matter of fact, it's impossible to separate them."

Roger Jameson stomped outside the door in his London Fog and flashed a smile through his trimmed blond beard and mustache. He looked too much like the assassin, and I sometimes wondered if the killer had not somehow taken Roger's place and stared back at me from behind blue eyes.

Standing in the doorway, I felt a chill in the July heat and glanced at the woods in front of the house where a dark shape slipped behind a trunk of a pine. I dismissed it as deer roving through the forest as they did every morning when they gathered in the backyard and watched us watch them through the glass wall of our dining room.

"No hunny, no mall, no more adventure today. Tomorrow you go to camp with Julie and you're getting a bath and packing a bag tonight."

Melissa turned to pouting, and her little face tore at my heart, but a father must show strength in such situations.

"Daddy?" she said.

I shook my head. "Mom's the boss."

"Mommy's not the boss."

"She is in our house," Roger said.

We stuck up for each other like that. Roger and Emily, well adjusted, well to do, well bred. Everything seemed so perfect, so... well, American. Still, I could not help but feel as if I looked in from the outside of a glass ball.

Truly, I found I slipped in and out of a world that only half accepted me. Who knew what Roger and Emily said about the Afghan next door while they drove to the mall? Had they watched CNN today and heard the news? Did dark thoughts lurk beneath Roger's smile? Had they already reported to Homeland Security that they lived next door to an Afghan?

Therefore, I suffered this sense of vibrating, oscillating, shifting between two worlds, and I could not tear myself from one nor did I fit in the other. When I walked with my Uncle, I felt my Afghan blood flowing thick in my veins. We spoke Farsi, we laughed at Afghan jokes, and we shut America out and gazed on their skyscrapers, highways, and perfectly trimmed parks. A fairyland, it did not really exist for us for we had shifted back to primary existences of living in a land of white scorpions crawling through windows without glass. Mud and straw adobe huts, winding trails of smoke rising from clay ovens, fields of white and purple poppies.

All this and more walked with us when we wandered together in America. My sense of not belonging surrounded me, and I could not run from it. When they prattled on CNN about Islamic extremist, terrorists, evildoers and the axis of evil, we looked to each other and a thousand words crossed between us, unspoken. They had canned us, labeled us, and shipped us to the land of woebegone. A political shanghaiing as effective as placing millions of innocents behind barbed wire and marching them into ovens. Now I could not look at an American face without wondering about the mistrust and outright hatred that lurked behind their eyes. I shook myself from these thoughts and returned to watching Melissa smile and bounce on the kitchen floor.

My daughter came into the world in a hospital in Virginia, much to my great relief, and they would not call her Afghan or Arab or even foreign. Her blonde curls and pale skin fit in and thus she would live without the curse of sharp-edged insults, stares and murmuring whispers I strived to ignore. I felt even more sensitive and worse than before, in the beginning, when it surprised me.

A frown, a tight edge of the knife response from an angry American, and I would sit and ponder. A flood of emotions drove me, a red and wilting shame, a simmering anger, and a fire burned inside and I hated, and this more than anything, made me think this place would not hold me for all my years.

Julie Jingles and Roger left. Melissa and Jenny chatted at the kitchen table. I went up to the loft, tuned into CNN, and watched Georgetown burn.

"Ali Khan, warlord and opium king. American occupation". The words faded in and out of my reeling mind. Words spoken by the short, eagle faced man, a Chief of something. I picked up my cell phone and called my uncle.

"Come to the embassy," he said.

ANTHONY STONE

I looked at Jenny but wanting to protect her and keep her from a combusting world, I told her I had to go to the studio, to develop a roll or two and build the set for next week's shoot. I lied to her for the first time in our lives. I fretted about that while driving into D.C. to see my uncle, and once again, I oscillated between worlds.

♦ ♦ ♦

182

42

Missing

Where did he go?"

"How should I know?" said Sergy. "I think he believed you about being your brother. He is probably wandering around in shock."

"What are you going to do?" she said.

He picked up the heavy phone, an encrypted line, and pounded a number into the face.

"Colonel, we have a problem."

She listened from the bed, staring out the tinted window at treetops bending to the force of the wind. Rain hammered a beat on the old roof and thunder sent a tremble through the floor.

"He has vanished, we don't know where," said Sergy, "and there's something else. He could be the Shaima's long-lost brother, a son of Ali Khan."

She heard the shout from the phone.

"I don't know how the hell... she says it's him, I don't know, could be I guess."

She took a sip of water, pulled the blanket over herself and curled up. Sergy hung up and walked back over to the bed. He stood there for a moment, staring down at her.

"Are you sure it's him?"

She looked into his blue eyes and smiled.

♦ ♦ ♦

43

'A Lost Feeling in the Heart'

He watches from the edge of the forest. In the clearing before him, a log cabin nestles within a fog. The Potomac rushes past in a hurry to empty into the Chesapeake. Two white BMWs sit in the long driveway.

A thunderclap directly overhead pounds waves of pain through his head. An aura scars his vision, a shimmering polygon. They said migraines, but he knows better. The old pain never left him. He could not recall the source of the long scar above his ear. Not until yesterday. Now the woman haunts him from a world he cannot yet find. An old fortress, mountains, and ever-falling snow.

The cabin door swings open. A man steps outside. Long wavy black hair, same eyes, same face. A woman steps into warm light. Golden curls, petite, like Sister Mary, that pale skin, that same slight lavender tint. She glows in the doorway. The door closes. The twin, his wife, and everything so perfect. Laughter from the cabin reaches his ears. His anger surges almost to that point...where only pain relieves the pressure. His teeth grind. Twins. Could he really be a twin? What made his life charmed and Armon's a living hell? His life.

Should have been mine.

He leans against the tree and looks up into the wet boughs. Fat raindrops cool his hot skin. He looks back at the cabin. Sudden confusion grips him.

Why am I here, what am I doing? He pulls the switchblade, flicks it open and drags it across his forearm. Congealed blood breaks and flows over the cuts.

The door opens. The twin kisses the woman, hugs the little girl. He gets in the BMW and drives away. The door closes.

A few minutes later Armon steps out from the cover of the forest. He walks in a dream, wrapped in his anger and thirst for revenge, wielding them against the memory of Mahlim's whip. Voices in his head, whispers, shouts, screams. The ozone of fresh rain sparkles and tickles his nose.

His hands shake for a moment, then settle as he breathes in the wind and rain. He knocks. The door opens and the woman stares at him, at his clothes, his face.

"Hey. You must be, but you can't be," she says. "Come inside out of the rain."

He steps in and shuts the door behind him.

"Can't be who?"

"Sikandar? Is that you?" she says.,

"No. It is not."

He advances on her and she moves back and takes the little girl's hand.

"Who are you," the little girl says. "You look a lot like my daddy."

"I noticed that too," he says. "I'm going to find out."

"Wait. What are you doing? Who are you then?"

"My name is Armon. Don't you know me?"

"Yes. You must be his brother. His twin brother."

"I am not anyone's brother. You are coming with me."

"What? Where?"

"To Sergy. He will know what to do. Yes. Sergy will know."

He grabs her by the arms and pushes her down on the couch.

"Sit there. Hold the little girl. I'll be back."

"But wait. I don't understand. Who is Sergy?"

He moves away and looks around. A pinewood sofa sits between two recliners, several remote controls spread across the redwood coffee table, and a plasma television hangs on a bare cabin wall. Vaulted ceilings release a murky glow through inset skylights. He heads up the stairs and into the bedroom. A large bedroom decorated in the color of a fair cloud, sheer curtains on a windowed alcove that looks strangely familiar. In fact, the entire house is familiar, as if he had lived here in some other life or dreamed it many times.

A noise interrupts his tour. He looks over the loft banister just as the woman gets to her feet. He heads down the staircase. He rounds the corner to find her behind the kitchen counter with a gun pointed at his face.

"I'm not going anywhere. Now you need to just calm down. I am going to call Omar. Come here, Melissa."

The girl runs and hugs her mother's waist. The woman pulls out a cell phone with one hand while holding the gun in the other. He waits for the moment her eyes move, then he strikes her hard in the face. She sprawls across the kitchen table and falls to the ground on the other side. The gun clatters across the kitchen and vanishes down some stairs.

His stomach twists with the pain of striking a woman, but without enough time to think of a plan, he picks the woman up and sits her on the couch. Strangely, he finds a thin rope in the first place he looks. Minutes later, he pulls the car out of the long tree-lined driveway and heads back towards Sergy's compound.

She wakes up coughing, spitting, and struggling against the ropes. With a raspy cracking voice, she groans.

"Melissa?" she says.

"Mommy?" The girl is in the rear compartment of the Corvette, her hands tied together.

"What are you doing? I told you I can call your brother."

He does not answer. She shifts around. Her hands tied. She's looking for something, feeling around the seat.

"Where's my gun."

"No guns. You will be fine. Sergy will know what to do. I promise."

"Who is Sergy?" she says again. "What do you mean?"

She fights the bonds harder now, but the more she moves the more the ropes tighten. Ultimately, she settles back, breathing hard. The windshield wipers swing back and forth, beating back the relentless rain. He turns the radio off, one less distraction.

"Are you Sikandur?" She whispers this like a secret they share, her voice shaking.

"You must be Sikandur. There's no other explanation."

He turns and stares at her.

"Are you Omar's brother?" Her breath still runs fast and ragged. "Why are you doing this?"

He spits out the open window and drives.

"Is he soft? Do you like soft?" He pauses, then turns to her and says, "I am not soft."

She shifts around until she can see her daughter lying in the cubbyhole behind the front seats.

"Oh, my God. What did you do to my daughter? Why? We did nothing to you."

He ignores her.

"Where are we going? Why are you doing this to us? We are family. I can help you. I can tell Omar. He will be so happy to see you."

He looks at her. "Happy?"

"Yes, happy. Why not? You are his brother."

"You think to save yourself with lies, but it will do you no good. Now be silent and let me drive."

"Where are you taking us? Please, may I see if she is all right?"

He glances over his shoulder at the girl.

"She is fine."

"What will you do with us?"

"Sergy will know what to do with you."

"Who is Sergy? You don't understand. Omar has nightmares. He thinks it was his fault they took instead you of him."

He turns and glares at her.

"Yes, it was his fault. You will pay for that. You, your daughter and then him. Sergy will help me."

"Why don't you listen to me?" She grunts and grits her teeth.

He pulls the car over, gets out and paces in the rain.

"What are you going to do? No... no... please."

He makes a gag from a strip of cloth and ties around the little girl's mouth. She is so scared she does not move. Large blue eyes stare at him mercilessly.

"Stop! Untie me you, idiot!"

He muffles the woman's scream with a small gag.

"All right now. Be silent. We have a long drive until we get to Sergy. He will know what to do. I cannot decide."

Several hours later, he parks next to Sergy's Escalade. Darkened windows glare like eyes from above the front porch. He scowls back. The door opens and Sergy steps out with a cigarette in hand. The copper haired girl clings to him. She grins until she spots the woman in the front seat, then her face pales and her long, elegant eyebrows pinch in the middle of her forehead.

"Oh my god. Look at that," Cleopatra says.

"What is this Armon? Who is in the car?" Sergy says.

The plan did not include explaining it to Sergy. He coughs and watches the diminutive Cleopatra, her dark pupils firing off a storm of old memories. He feels weightless, transported back to a dark room. Large black pupils surrounded by white emerge from the shadows. His head aches so badly he shuts his eyes. Still, he feels weightless, as if he existed only as a shadow.

"I don't know."

"You don't know?" Sergy approaches the car and looks inside.

"Who are they, Armon?" Sergy's voice moves into an unfamiliar pitch, high, tense, and edgy. He glances at Sergy and then at the woman in the car. The pain in Armon's head increases and he rubs his temples with both hands.

"They are my brother's wife and daughter." Cleopatra's low voice sinks into the humid air. She glares at Armon. Sergy blinks. He shakes his head and tosses his cigarette into the mud.

"I don't know what to say. What are you going to do with them? They are witnesses. They have seen our faces. This is a disaster."

Sergy paces in front of the car. Cleopatra's voice rises.

"Why bring them here?"

"Shaima!" Jennifer yells. "Get me out of here. Get these ropes off of us."

Shaima runs to the car and opens the door. She kneels in front of Jennifer and begins untying the ropes.

"Come on. Get out of there so we can get Melissa," Shaima says. She pulls Jennifer out by the hands.

Sergy picks up the rope and takes Jennifer's arms to tie them behind her back.

"Wait. Why are you tying me?"

"Stay here until we are out of the country. Clearly, this was not in our plans."

"Shaima?" Jennifer says. Melissa climbs out of the car and runs to her mother, grabbing her leg and shifting herself behind for safety.

"Are they going to kill us, Mommy?"

"No!" Shaima says. She kneels in front of Melissa. "You just have to stay here for a few hours. Then you can go back home."

"Stay here?" The woman named Jennifer looks around. "But where? Is it safe in that house?"

"It's perfectly safe. Don't worry. I have a room just for you," Shaima says.

"Well, then." Sergy runs fingers through his short hair, squeezing rainwater back and off his head.

"Take them inside. They are yours to deal with."

He walks over and claps a hand on Armon's shoulder. Armon stiffens but does not resist.

Sergy leans down and whispers to Armon.

"My friend you must fix this. They have seen your face and they are Americans. If they live to tell that you are alive, the CIA will chase you all the way back to Afghanistan. Do you understand?"

"Yes." Armon rubs his face and takes a deep breath. "I understand."

He really does not understand. Sergy wants him to kill the woman and child? Armon did not plan for this. A sinking feeling in his stomach grips him.

"Ok. The plan stands. Tomorrow you do the third target. I have your documents. Catch a plane at a private airport in West Virginia for a flight to Cuba. From there you fly to Dushanbe and make your way into Afghanistan. You will have plenty of money and be on your own. I know you prefer that. You can meet us near Zebak. We will find Alexander's crypt. I have maps for you. You find this Farook. We report his location to the American base and get our reward. All right?"

"You get me there. I will find him."

"Good. Then after we go inside, you move them upstairs. Then get yourself a shower and shave. Make sure you take care of them before you leave. You can leave the bodies in the bunkers under the barn. Nobody will find them there."

Sergy takes the Cleopatra by the hand and pulls her towards the house. She slaps him. He laughs and picks her up, carries her inside. The floorboards of the old porch groan beneath Sergy's weight.

Armon orders the woman and child into the house.

"Come. Your room is upstairs."

When they get upstairs, they walk down the hall. Armon pushes the door open. Small, with one window over the bed, it is a child's room with colorful décor, yellow window frame, blue bed railings, and a red footboard, naked white walls. He ties Jennifer to the bedpost and Melissa to a child's purple rocking chair. Tears stain her face.

She reminds him of a girl... a girl with green eyes. He turns to the woman. She glares at him. She glances at her daughter and back at him and fear pales her face.

"What will you do with us?"

"Do not fear. I do not want to hurt you. I... I want you to talk to me... like you talk to... him. I want you to-" He shakes his head, "tell me about him."

She looks like Sister Mary. Sister Mary arose from the dead at last.

Red and yellow petals melt beneath the sun. Sister Mary cries. Her black robes flutter in a soft wind. She crosses herself, whispers, reads from the tiny book, and crosses herself again. Naked wisps of blonde hair tremble from the edge of her cowl.

"He is your brother," she says. "He searched for you. He still searches in his dreams."

Armon shakes his head.

"Nobody came for me. I still cannot remember what happened. They just left me out there."

Outside the window over the bed, rain slants down at a sharp angle, casting distant woods in a gray haze. Armon sees a man with a rifle wander past the old barn, stare into the forest, light a cigarette and shift the rifle from one shoulder to the other. The man wears military slickers, camouflaged dark green and tan. Sergy's man.

She lunges for her daughter. The rope stops her. She falls back on the bed. She mumbles and her eyes fill with tears. The daughter slides down a bit in the rocking chair. The mother whimpers.

Sister Mary's frost blue eyes stare into heaven. Whispering, her lips weave spells as she sways in the wind. Her power wanes. Night comes and Kumar turns into a demon. Spoon flashes in the moonlight.

"Where are we?" She says. She twists around to look out the window behind her.

"Omar thought about you every day," she pauses. "What will you do with us?"

She has magic. He can sense her power. The power of beauty rivals the finality of death. Forces come together and clash. He feels that tightness in his stomach again... *what is it?* He stares at his hands.

"He searched for you for months, for years. He will be so happy to see you. You can stop his nightmares. If only you knew. If you only knew your brother, you would love him as I do."

He feels her power spreading, bearing down on him. She looks like an angel but spins a web of deceit. The room has already taken on her aura, radiating with the pale colors of her skin and hair, the suffused glow combining with the wet, clean smell of her. These are manifestations of her power, her magic.

"Searched for me? You are lying."

He feels something, doubt, hope, or just complete exhaustion that will not let him reach out to stop her magic from flowing into the room. It puzzles him. Her magic is powerful. He tries to ignore it. He thinks to strangle her now before she works any further spells, but his feet will not move. She has frozen him, charmed him, and he is powerless against her. Then she speaks and her voice burns.

"Now you know my name is Jennifer. My daughter who is also *your niece* is sitting there in that chair. Her name is Melissa. She is your family. Will you murder your own family?"

Sister Mary stands in the moonlight, head high and proud. Pale skin, willow thin body. Her hands reach out and she calls his name, Snow Boy. Snow Boy. I will save you. Come with me Snow Boy.

"Well? What are you going to do?" she repeats.

He stares out the window. Another man joins the first. They light cigarettes and puff smoke into the rain from beneath camouflaged baseball caps. The edge of the forest blurs in the distance, dark and wet.

"If he is my brother, where has he been? I will tell you. Here, living comfortably with you and her. Nobody looked for me. He lied to you."

Rubbing his temples, he coughs and continues to mutter while staring out the window. He is afraid of the woman. Her magic.

"Perhaps I did something terrible for them to sell me to the tall man. No doubt he would have fed me to his tiger had I not escaped. You say I had a family, but I ended up with nothing. No. They sold me to the tall man. I know it. I feel it in my bones."

"They didn't sell you to anybody. Someone kidnapped you. Omar and your uncle searched together for years. They just could not find you."

Teeth grinding, he looks away long enough to break her spell.

"You are a powerful witch. Your words are like honey, but I know the truth. They never wanted me."

This infuriates him.

"They never wanted me." He punches a hole in the wall next to the window. Her voice fades.

He takes a deep breath, walks down the hallway into the bathroom and splashes water on his face. Two faces stare back from the mirror, his own, and just behind this, the shadow that has lurked there since he can remember. He slams his fist into the mirror, then again, until the mirror cracks.

"They did not want me. Why?" He mutters.

A long fracture divides the mirror. A sharp pain in his head drives him down to his knees, and he grips the sink to stop from sprawling on the floor. He reaches for the water, the sound of it to drive the pain away, but no, it increases the pain to a blinding white lightning bolt. Struggling to his feet, he slams a fist into the mirror, shattering it again. Then he leaves the bathroom and enters the bedroom again, approaching her carefully to protect against her magic.

"Why him? Why did they keep him and send me away?"

"Send you away? No. They did not send you away. Your stepmother had someone kidnap you so she could eventually have her own son inherit father's lands. Then she poisoned your mother."

"My mother is dead?"

Jennifer nodded and touched his arm. He pulled away. The lady in the tower window. That must be his mother.

"But a father? I have a father?"

A heavy, hot drop of water falls to his lip. Salt water. Tears? Not remembering ever shedding a tear before, he considers it miraculous. However, this state of elevated wonder last only a single moment. Time stops, suspended for a strange emotional freefall as he hurtles through a dark abyss. Then, the feeling evaporates, the darkness vanishes and the floor rushes up to meet him as he leans forward and heaves.

Family. What does it mean?

Heaving several times more, he gathers himself up and stumbles back into the bathroom. He locks the door.

Think of something else. Anything else. Shower.

Armon takes a long, deep breath. His hand trembles reaching for the water faucet. He finds a dainty little soap dispenser, flowers and butterflies on the side, and frowns. Rubbing hard, he washes away the seen and the unseen as water massages his shoulders. Then on his face, like the rain outside, yet fiercer, angrier, and he welcomes the pounding on his skin.

He slides to the remaining long shard of mirror and stares at himself for some time before he remembers the razor and the shaving cream and the task. Filthy, ragged three-day beard disgusts him, though in the past he has gone for weeks without shaving. He shaves quickly, frantically, cutting himself several times. Rinsing the remnants of the lather off, he looks at the face that left the cabin earlier, the face of his twin.

A good healthy face, not the face of a killer. Next to him, on the other side of a crack, stands the killer, unchanged and smiling.

You can never run from me, you can never leave me behind.

He turns away from both reflections, wipes the steam off the window with his towel, and looks out at old barns sitting in wet yellow grass. He puts on fresh clothes. Opening the door, he sees the copper haired vixen.

"Hello Sikandur," she says.

She has a strange smile on her face, teasing, taunting, or perhaps her face just is this way, like those haughty English actresses with their immaculate lips.

"My name is Armon Badil."

She laughs, bends over and giggles. He almost smiles, another new thing for him, and he glances in the mirror to see what it looks like. She straightens to face him again.

"Do you know what Armon Badil means?"

"It is my name."

"No, it is not a name. It means *regret* or *anguish* or maybe like this... how you say in English: *a lost feeling in the heart*. That is what Armon

Badil means. There is no such name in our language. It is merely a phrase. Your name is Sikandur. If you want to call yourself Armon Badil then go ahead, but our brother and our father will call you Sikandur... when you meet them," she pauses, studying his face.

"Yes, I am your half-sister. We had different mothers."

She slides past him, takes his hand, pulls him into the bathroom, and shuts the door. He notices she likes to get her way. He lets her for the moment, still shocked that she declared herself his sister.

"Your mother is a cruel woman."

"Our father murdered my mother." She spits these words out like a child that tasted something horrid and wants no more.

"She was your father's second wife. She looked like me, but much darker hair."

His head hurts. The side where she hit him. He remembers those eyes appearing from within the shadows. Rushing at him. Arm lifted. Something gripped in a claw like hand. The pain.

"Your mother hurt me." He rubbed the side of his head. "Here. I cannot remember anything before... the giant cats in the cave."

"Cats?"

She appears softer, gentler than the witch. The eyes are the same. And her magic, strong, bends men to her will. She is a great witch. He must be wary of this one. Her magic is vibrant, effusive, not slow and delicate like the woman in the room. Yet both possess a similar strength, an overpowering push towards domination.

"Why would your father kill your mother?"

"Because my mother killed your mother." Now she looks angry and small and even ashamed.

"It seems we come from a family of murderers," he said.

A light passes behind the curtain of his simmering rage.

"We come from a violent world. Now, what are you going to do with Jennifer and Melissa?"

"What do you think I should do with them?"

"You cannot kill them. I know Sergy wants you to, but they are your family. You cannot kill Omar's wife and daughter. Omar is a good man. His wife and daughter are innocent. You must find a way."

She turns, stares out the window and wrings her hands. He watches her carefully, wary of her tricks. There is a color that radiates around her, a hungry firestorm of red.

"You must get them out. I have a plan. Later today Sergy and I leave for the airstrip. You must get them out before we leave or he will kill them. Sergy is a dangerous man, but you know that don't you?"

"How will I do this thing?"

"I don't know, but you must. It is not Omar's fault. It is my mother's fault. I heard the stories, but I did not believe them. Everyone thought you died. You cannot blame Omar. Blame father, a cold, angry man. You know nothing, and I do not have the time to tell you all of it. You will understand it all later. You must believe me. Now you must save them. Go now. Find a way."

She pushes him out of the bathroom and closes the door behind him.

"Armon, come downstairs when you can. I want to show you the bunkers and give you your papers," Sergy shouts.

Armon shouts back down the stairs.

"Be there in one minute."

He goes back down the hallway, into the child's bedroom and shuts the door. Taking no time to think, he takes two steps and he reaches for her neck. She screams. His hands close on her pale skin. He tightens his grip. She struggles, fingernails digging into his arm, legs kicking against the rope. White light invades the room from the window. Everything glows with her magic. She grunts. He looks away from her face, lifting his view to the distant gray forest. He thinks about the cool wet of the trees and he squeezes. Rain slams down hard against the window. Floorboards creak behind him but he, caught in the rough grip of a runaway madness, ignores the noise. He hears a shriek, fast steps, and then something smashes into his head. He slides down, fading in and out of consciousness. In the wash of light and shadow, he hears voices, rapid and breathless, drifting in the passion of driving rain.

"Go, get out the window and run."

"But Melissa."

"She's not hurt. She's still asleep. Get Omar... no police. We leave in an hour."

"But he will kill her."

"Nobody will hurt her. I promise. Run, Jennifer."

"Run where?"

"Through the woods. To town, call Omar. In an hour we will leave."

Armon Badil sinks into a dark place.

"Oh, Snow Boy. My silly Snow Boy. There is but one God. Don't talk about Jesus here, it's dangerous."

Suddenly, he sees Helena, the girl with the green eyes. Then everything fades away and darkness descends.

He wakes. Cleopatra holds a gun to his face.

"Listen carefully Armon or whatever the hell you want to call yourself. Sergy is waiting in the bunkers with your passport and money. Go there. Do not come back here. If I see you again in this house, I'll kill you."

Her face pulses with pure hate, like her mother those many years ago.

◆ ◆ ◆

44

Omar Jaheeli

On the television, former Marine Colonel Reginald Gregory claimed Baba sent a man to bomb Harper's Ferry, and a restaurant in Georgetown. I thought of the Nuristani. He never used bombs. His family died beneath bombs, crumbling mountains and bleeding earth. He killed with his hands and the knife he sharpened in the alcove, day after day, the grindstone and the knife scraping against each other. He used his sweat from his arms to wet the blade as he pulled it down the stone. Then, with a gnarled thumb, he tested the blade. A blood drop hit the stone table he set his knives upon and there he sat, that smile lighting up his sharp features.

On nights plagued with heavy winds, I heard the faraway echo of his blade sliding across the stone in a steady rhythm that sent me back to those cold mountains, the Buzkashi field and the Russii lined up against the tank. Baba standing with his Nuristani on the rim of the canyon, shaking his fist beneath a fat moon.

My cell phone rang.

"Omar Jaheeli," I said.

"Omar. Oh my God. Omar."

She cried. I heard voices and somebody else took the phone.

"Is this Jenny's husband?" a woman asked.

I stood up. "Yes, what's wrong?"

"Come and I mean now," she said.

"Who are you?" I turned to Uncle, who stood up and somehow knew. The voice in the phone echoed in the large room that served as Uncle's office.

"Omar, they have Melissa. She said no police or Sergy will kill her." Jennifer's voice from the background sounded small and tired and-.

"What? Where are you and Melissa?"

I kept her on the phone, got the address and felt sicker by the minute. Then she told me about Sikandur. I could not think what she meant. Uncle asked, I told him, and his face paled and his hands shook as he took his phone and issued instructions. Within minutes, I heard feet pounding and men shouting. In the hallway, men ran and we fell in with them, ten men, then twenty and more, all in step, a wave of black shirts heading in the same direction.

◆ ◆ ◆

45

A Promise

You will not hurt her Sergy."

She held the Beretta up and took his gun, a Walther PPK from the nightstand.

"*Lastochka*, my love-."

"I mean it, Sergy."

"Princess, I wouldn't hurt her. You don't have to hold a gun on me."

She studied the way his eyes crinkled on the edges. She wanted to believe.

"I heard you, Sergy. You said to kill them. I won't allow it."

If she shot him, that ended everything. If she did not, he might kill Melissa.

The corner of his mouth twitched. Then he smiled again.

"Lastochka. You know I never hurt a woman or a child."

She tried to hold the guns steady by placing them against each other and holding them with both hands.

"You promise me Sergy."

"I promise lastochka."

His face beamed clean and angelic, unlike Afghan men who

frightened her with their violent raging tempers, wild beards and fanaticism. She wanted to trust Sergy. She had to. All her plans depended on him.

"Lastochka, I gave your brother all his papers, and his money. He left for the hotel so tonight he can take the last target. Come now. You know you can trust me."

He stepped towards her. She moved back and held the gun higher.

"Your plan fails without me Sergy, you know that. If you hurt her, it's all over."

"Did I have her mother followed when she escaped? No. She cannot hurt me. I'm not coming back, but they saw yours."

"I don't care. I'm not coming back here, anyway." She sighed and lowered the gun. Sergy stood there for a few seconds, then walked over and hugged her.

"You're such an Afghan."

"Yes, I am. A Pathan and don't you forget that."

She pulled away and laid the guns on the bed. The phone rang. Sergy went to answer.

"Ya. Ok Jeffrey. Ya. Ok we are leaving. Tell the men to get going. Yes, all of them except you and your group. Ya. I need you to bring soup and a sandwich for... Shaima's niece. Ya."

Sergy turned towards her. She sat on the edge of the bed, pulling on her boots.

"Ya do that. You know. I'll see you over the satellite on the laptop from the other side."

He hung up and she sensed him watching her.

"We have to leave. My man outside your embassy said your people are heading this way with an army."

"Good."

"Too bad we don't have time for a little you know."

"Sergy, you're so bad."

"Ya. Ya. I am bad." He laughed.

She thought he loved her, but who could trust a Russian. She remembered Baba's words, "Tactics. You must have a plan. One day, you will need this skill".

They left the room and headed for the car. She listened at Melissa's door. She heard crying and soft mumbling. She gave Sergy her blackest look. He ducked his head and went down the stairs. She followed.

♦ ♦ ♦

46

The Plan to Save Melissa

I turned the car into a graveled driveway next to the mailbox that read, "Daniels" stenciled above the address. Oak trees lined the road until I reached a clearing, a white fence, and a blue Dodge truck. A garage on my left housed a brown Hummer. The picket fence surrounded a ranch house constructed from stone and brick with three chimneys.

I got out of the car just in time to catch Jenny in my arms. She trembled and sobbed. Wet hair hung all around her face, and her skin had turned the color of snow. I held Jenny close, touched her face and wiped away her tears. A man ran out of the house followed by a woman, both in clear raincoats and carrying extras.

"Hi, I'm Bob, my wife Belinda. Bell for short. Raincoats, put them on, keep you dry."

"I'm Omar. Thank you."

I could not express what it meant for him to save my Jenny.

"Come inside, we can call the police and figure this all out. I know your wife said no cops, but I really think we need some help," Bob said.

The rain thickened and thunder rolled over our heads.

"No police. Kidnappers will kill her and we do not have time. We must find my daughter now. She must be near if Jenny ran all the way here. Do you have any ideas?"

"There are only two farms close to us here. The rest is forest. Jennifer came from the east. There is an old farmhouse about three miles from here. Old man Jacobi owned that farm, but he died about ten years ago. Since then I have not seen too many people there, except this one black truck that I figured belonged to a real estate agent."

"Yes, a big black SUV," Jenny said. "There's one in front of the farmhouse."

"Then that's Jacobi's place. I can take you there."

"You don't have to take us, Bob. Just tell me how to get there."

"Let me get my gun and I'll be right back. You have a weapon, Omar? Hang on. I'll get you a pistol." Bob spit a stream of tobacco on the ground and smiled.

"Country boy and Marine, my Bob will help you," Belinda said.

I failed to smile, my mind entangled around old fears and my heart assailed with new ones.

Assassin in the alcove, blade on the whetstone, stroke, stroke, wet the stone, stroke, stroke, and time melted away.

My daughter in a farmhouse with killers. Now I expected to find the assassin waiting at the farmhouse, hovering over Melissa with his bloodstained bag. I left behind that world of violence, and yet I had not escaped. I thought about fear and how life held little else but the constant threat of death, even here, even for my poor girls.

"Come on baby, get in the car. Lead me to the farm."

I tried to get her around to the passenger door, but she had no strength in her legs and sagged against me. I picked her up in my arms. Then I saw the bruises around her neck. I choked back my rage and held her against my chest.

"Who did this to your neck? What happened? How did you end up here? I left you at home."

"Your brother happened. We can talk about it later. We need to find Melissa."

"My brother? No. It simply cannot be. You must be mistaken. How would he get here?"

My questions flustered Jenny so I took a deep breath and kissed her forehead.

"I will fix this. I will get Melissa back," I said.

"Wait, we'll take the Hummer. Much better in this weather than your BMW," Belinda said.

I looked around at muddy fields and nodded my agreement. She ran for the Hummer. Bob splashed his way back towards us with a pistol and rifle. We piled into the big Hummer and Belinda refused to stay behind or even to leave the driver's seat. I thought it best not to argue. We did not have far to go. Within minutes, Belinda pulled to the side of the road a hundred feet past a driveway and an old tin mailbox.

"Old Jacobi's farmhouse is back there, down the driveway, but I think we shouldn't just walk right up. Hoofing it through the woods might be best," Bob said.

"Thanks, Bob. I will find it. Can you keep Jenny here with you or take her back to your farmhouse?"

"Forget it. I'm coming with," Jenny said.

"You can't, you're too weak," I said.

"I'm coming to get my daughter and that's final."

I looked at Bob for help.

"Me too," Bob said. "I'm coming. Don't worry. I'll keep you safe."

I could not think straight and Bob sent my equilibrium further askew, but the cell phone ringing in my pocket erased these issues. I told Uncle we had found the farm and he replied that with the GPS sensor in my pocket, he would track me. He told me to hold on, to wait, but I said no. Ten minutes later, Jenny, Bob and I stood in the trees at the edge of a rain flattened yellow field. I still had Uncle on the phone and described to him the five old barns and the farmhouse in the center. He told me not to move, he would be there. I argued.

"A guy with a gun is coming our way," Bob said.

We ducked down, I pulled Jenny close behind me, her breath hot on my neck. We moved behind tree trunks. I found a group of ferns with a canopy of leaves that served as an umbrella. I pulled Jenny down beneath this and covered her with my body. She trembled and I felt her hot tears on my hand. I stroked her wet hair and told my Uncle to hurry.

♦ ♦ ♦

47

Omar

The gunman stood at the edge of the field, his eyes sweeping the forest. Had I Bob's gun I might have shot him and ran for the farmhouse, but they would hear the shot and kill her, I reasoned, long before my feet touched the front porch.

The man reached down and pulled a stake from the mud, wiped it off and jammed it back in. He kneeled and turned it, so that a small black spot on the stalk faced the edging of the forest. Finished, he ambled off to our right, walking the tree line, throwing regular glances into the brush and the trees. I stood up and walked to the stake. It looked like some sort of transmitter.

"Look, a man with a tray heading towards the farmhouse," Bob said.

He slipped the pistol in my open hand and I looked down and remembered Baba and the Russii lined up against the tank and blood flowing around my feet as Baba shot and felled them all while I retched. Now I needed him here. He would know what to do.

"Tactics," he said. However, no tactics would save Melissa. No approaching enemy column, no Russii, no tanks, and he never taught me how to save a life, only how to take them.

"Uncle, a man just entered the farmhouse," I said.

His voice buzzed in my ear and kept me from running out into the field. The gunman still lurked by the barns, walking around one and then another. Every so often his eyes turned to the farmhouse and I remained that ten-year-old coward, frozen in place.

"Can you hit that man?" I said.

"I can," Bob said.

"If I run out there, can you make sure he doesn't get me before I get to the farmhouse?"

"Don't even think about it. We do not know how many other gunmen are out there, or what kind of technology they have in that field. Take it from a Marine, this looks like a serious operation. They don't have sensors and assault rifles for a group of cultists," Bob said.

"Let's move closer, along the trees," I said.

We slid along, crawling through undergrowth and mud, making our way close enough to look across the field into the second-floor window. Peering through slashing rain, I saw Melissa sitting by the window and looking down, her little yellow curls disheveled and her face pale. Jenny whimpered behind me and Bob cursed.

"Look," he said.

A man loomed over her. He wore thick glasses, his red hair a mop on his oddly shaped head. He reached for her and she turned and screamed. I dropped the pistol and ran for the house. I heard Bob cursing, Jennifer shouting, a shot, a bullet tore past my ear, then a shot from behind and then... nothing. I ran.

◆ ◆ ◆

48

Tactics

From the window, Melissa's eyes met mine and she cried out. I reached my hand towards her as I ran, but sensed movement on the edge of my vision. Then I fell. Down I went, into a trench or a hole or something deep, wet, and sloppy. My feet hit ground and drove my knees into my face. I rolled and shouted, holding my ankles and falling to my side. The trench collapsed.

I had fallen into a long deep gouge in the red earth some ten feet deep. It ran from the far end all the way to the tree line. Looking down the trench through the thickening rain, I saw a massive black beast splashing in my direction. My eyes could not focus and water rose quickly to my knees and higher. I looked up and saw muddy red walls leading to gray clouds and nothing else.

Lightning flashed on the beast, illuminating the monster in shocking white. Drool hung from his open mouth, his black eyes gleamed, and he came fast. Whispering Jenny's name, I braced myself for impact. I knew, all these years, that eventually I would meet this bear in my waking life and that he and I would fight and only one of us would live.

Just then I heard my daughter scream from somewhere above and gave me a surge of energy. I felt around in the mud for a weapon, a rock or sharp stick, anything to use against this nemesis of my dreams. Fate written on my forehead? This would my fate? Frantic, I tried to jump for the lip of the trench. What the hell is a trench doing here, anyway?

The bear's jaws gaped at me as he let his rage loose. I knew then I had no escape. I stood and waited.

A gunshot cracked through the downpour. For a split second, the bear hesitated before crashing against the trench wall, knocking chunks of mud down and breaking away a gap for more water to crash down. I looked up, Bob stood at the edge of the trench, his rifle smoking in the storm, and standing next to him, Jenny, in her hand the pistol which she lifted, aimed and fired. I shouted for her to run, get out of the field, but she kept shooting and missing, and the bear kept coming.

Bob dropped to a knee and fired again, hitting the bear. It slammed into the wall and stumbled. Shaking its head from side to side, it rose and splashed forward. Again, I heard Bob's rifle crack and the bear fell about ten feet away. There it stayed, staring at me with dark raging eyes so familiar that a shock tingled through me from head to foot. The black mane on its head jutted straight up in the air and the squared muscular face, so much like another face I knew. We watched each other for a time, both of us panting in syncopation. A strange rhythm of rage, brutality and fear, and then he died.

I heard another shot and looked up. Jennifer vanished from my view and Bob stared at the spot nearby to where she had stood. He looked at me, his face a white mask in the downpour. Then he vanished too, and I lay there alone with the bear.

I struggled up to my feet and jumped, but could not reach the edge of the trench. I called out her name, but no answer. Uncle appeared on the other side of the trench, looking down at me, then to where Jenny had stood and then back at me. I felt a sudden rush of cold. A feeling of dread and impending doom. A dark, heavy thing took hold of me and shook me. I thought of a vengeful celestial being that resembled those old wise Greeks with their long gray beards and white robes. They laughed and drank wine and wrote on concepts that meant nothing, ideas that had no value to me until this moment, when all ideas connected and all lives became one life and all questions became one question.

"Where's Jenny?" I said. They pulled me out. I heard guns and saw Uncle's men fighting gray-clad men near the barns. I remembered a chess table and two kings, a lonely pawn. Russii lined up against a broken tank, blood on the snow and the river raging, bodies floating belly up. Violence would not let me go. Destiny written on my forehead, he said, and I denied it all. Like a fool.

Men entered the farmhouse, I heard a shout, crashing, and banging, but I did not hear my daughter. I turned around to find Jenny and a man brought a plank of wood for a bridge across the trench. She lay in the grass, Bob on his knees beside her, his face down. I kneeled on the other side of her and watched a faint wisp of smoke rise from the hole in her pale and perfect forehead. It felt like a dream.

"Wake up!" I shook her and looked again. "Wake up."

She did not. I slumped on the ground next to Jenny, holding her hand and shaking my head. I remember talking to her, but I don't remember what I said. I closed her eyes with my hand.

Men came with a stretcher and a blanket and took her body. I did not ask. The earth kept sliding away beneath my feet and I could see in my mind's eye, Baba and the Russii lined up beside the tank, my hand shaking and blood everywhere. Had I shot the Russian, would I have lived to see my Jenny like this? I kept asking this question and cursing my cowardice.

"Melissa," Uncle said.

I got up and followed him into the house, Bob sloshing along in our wake.

◆ ◆ ◆

49

In the Farmhouse

Four Afghans descended the stairs, pale faces above long black raincoats. Between them, the red-headed man stumbled along, thick glasses askew on his crimson face. They pushed him down the stairs. Tumbling, rolling, he ended up by a couch. A frail man, thin face pocked with tiny volcanoes of red and purple, he scrambled on the ground for his glasses. A man kicked him in the ribs, dropping him flat.

"Melissa?" I said.

In my vision, Jenny lay in wet grass, her eyes open, smoke and a thin line of blood oozing from her forehead. Flashes of my stepmother tied to a post, her sallow face melting in red snow. My sins, or my father's, caught me, and caught my Jenny.

Then I faded into a shadow world where nothing lives but pain, sorrow, and endless seconds of regret, ticking one after another, squeezing my chest and eyes and brain, sucking the air from my lungs and burning me, burning me alive. My consciousness came loose from the anchors that held it together and I struggled to think, concentrate, and find my daughter.

I tried to get through the men but they held me back, so many of them, gliding and mixing and moving, a wall of dark wraiths. The wraiths parted and Uncle walked through and up the stairs. Then the black wall closed again and I remained, bending and groping for a way until Bob took my arm and stood me straight.

A minute later, a small man descended the stairs. He rubbed an eye and shook his head and looked at me. The black wall parted. He walked past, took an umbrella, opened the door and left. Then Uncle came down and in his arms, Melissa. Her head lolled too far back for my liking. I rammed myself against the wall of black, and they caught me and handed me slowly forward until I stood with Uncle, looking down on my angel. Her eyes closed, her breath stopped, her curly blonde hair hanging to my waist.

Try as I might, I could not touch her.

♦ ♦ ♦

50

Back at the Embassy

W e found DVDs in the bunkers beneath the barns. You'll want to see this," Uncle said.

He slipped a silver disk into his laptop. I stumbled around the wide desk. French windows open at my back. Thunder rumbled and rain crashed. They said a hurricane approached, but I knew God fumed over a burning city.

Uncle's laptop came to life playing a grainy video. A big man got into a black SUV followed by a girl whose back looked uniquely familiar. When she turned and opened the car door, I saw her face.

"Your sister and Sergy Volkov, a friend of your Baba from Moscow," Uncle said. "This explains why we have not heard from her in several months. Now watch this."

He slipped another disk in place of the first. A man stepped out of the house. At first, I thought I watched myself as the man got in a sports car and flung a backpack down on the passenger seat. Confused for a few seconds, I thought back to something I had forgotten, something important.

"Your brother is alive." Uncle's voice shook.

Thunder roared. I felt a sudden rush of blood to my head. I squinted against the brilliance of the brass light fixtures in Uncle's ballroom sized embassy office.

"Sikandur," I said. "How can it be?"

I felt the words slip from my mouth and I wondered who spoke them, for I could not believe the capacity for speech remained in this, my hollow self. I suspected the man in the video to be a fake, a doppelganger, a trick, perhaps a mask.

Still, I knew he lived, for I still dreamed his life and on those nights, I would wake and wonder in the darkness. His life confused me. I could not understand the strange colors swirling around stranger images, blood and screams, fire and destruction.

"It is him," said Uncle. "Don't you think so?"

I had no reasonable answer.

"But how?" I said.

"Yes, how, and why, and where, and so much more. Look what else we found."

He pulled a map out of Central Asia, tagged with blue and red dots all along my father's lands and the mountains of the Hindu Kush. I saw marks and names and in the borders, tiny notations which I could not read. They had used a code to keep some secret.

"What does it all mean?" I said. "And why would they need my family for this? Ransom?"

"Let's go see what it all means," Uncle said.

We shuffled around a corner and down a hallway, part of the Embassy I had never visited. Enfield rifles, aged tapestries and jeweled scimitars hung inside glass cases along the walls, but these only grazed the periphery of my vision while I suffered doubt, regret, and sorrow.

I felt as if someone had peeled the skin from my body. Everywhere I looked her face floated in front of me and if I looked away, then Melissa lay in Uncle's arms and called to me, "Hold me daddy". What could I have done differently to avert this fate? What could I have done to save them?

"Your fate is written. It cannot be changed."

Uncle's words from that night kept echoing in my mind. My destiny, sealed and inescapable, kept creeping back, seizing control of my life no matter how I struggled to free myself from it.

An old elevator sucked us down, then jammed us to a stop. The door opened to gray concrete walls and another hallway, long, dark, and winding downwards. We passed a half-open door from which a shaft of light fell onto the floor and opposite wall. As we passed, I looked in, but the brightness of the light blinded me. When one door faded behind us, we walked in darkness, then another door appeared, lighting a slender piece of the hall and then past that, more darkness and then light again.

I wiped a wet mess from my eyes as we descended deeper into the tunnel. From below, a man screamed and mumbled and it sounded like prayers, fast, breathless chatter, then another louder scream that pushed stale air towards me like a barrier of raw terror. We kept walking, our shoes clacking against the cement floor.

"Help me, God," he said.

I shuddered but stayed beside my Uncle whose leaning, limping form seemed to grow and straighten as we approached the next door. A polygon of white light from the room fell upon the gray hall where a fat black cockroach fought to climb up and out of this dark hole.

The room had gray cinderblock walls, three metal folding chairs, and a black and red Bokhara rug on the ground, a steaming samovar set with china cups on a red tablecloth, a seated man holding a cup of tea in his right hand and passing beads through his left. He had a beard speckled with gray and tanned flaps of bagging skin hung below his eyes as if he stood in the Afghan sun for a hundred years and then in a wink of an eye appeared here in this naked room, with his samovar, his cup and the old, burnished pistol laying on his lap.

A scream from the next room, a bone cracked, something fell on a wet floor, and my mind pictured a desperate scenario.

"Salaam Vizier sayeb," he said.

He stood and bowed, placed his teacup and gun on the table and bent to kiss Uncle's hand. Uncle withdrew his hand, placed it on the man's shoulder and straightened him up. Another man walked out from the doorway of the next room. Short, slightly rotund, a red fez and dangling tassel on his head, a thick blonde beard and sparkling blue eyes. An older squatter version of the Nuristani bowed and approached my Uncle who leaned down, hugged and slapped hands against each other's backs.

"Omar,, meet Yousef Marhoob, formerly of the Turkish Army, now working for us."

Yousef Marhoob bowed and I bowed. We shook hands like civilized men, and then he ushered us into the next room.

Never had I imagined such a sight as this.

A metal plate lay across the concrete floor and on this plate, spreading pools of blood and two metal straight-backed chairs and on the chairs, two men sat naked, both unconscious or perhaps dead.

We walked around the far desk and took our seats against the wall. Then I turned around to face the horror of it all. Uncomfortable with such sights, my eyes, full of their natural inclinations, took to avoidance by wandering over blood splattered concrete walls. However, like a perverse magnet, the carnage pulled my eyes back to where two armed Pathans stood at attention behind the occupied chairs.

I looked to the nearby desk upon which lay several metal instruments. Jagged, ripping, tearing, curving blades and things with blood, meat and small chunks of bone stuck to them. I felt the room spinning and my mind fastened to my family, waiting for me on the other side of death.

"This one here, you know, of course," Uncle said.

His voice brought me back and saved me from certain humiliation. I looked at my Uncle and followed his line of sight to the red-headed man from the farmhouse.

He sat with his head lying back on his shoulder. Eyes glazed and mouth twisted in a final despairing scream. His arms hung down and at the end, the stumps of his fingers, and on the metal plate, lying in that thick crimson pool, small fat sausages.

A raw, bitter thing choked my throat and burned my eyes.

"This one here, they found outside the embassy, in a surveillance van."

This man still lived, if one wished to call it that. They had chopped off the tip of his nose and ears, cut open his chest, and peeled away strips of skin.

"We watch them, they watch us, only God sees everything," Yousef Marhoob said.

He possessed a child's voice and he spoke with hushed reverence. He held his hands together, cupped and raised them to the ceiling like the old man in our courtyard so many years ago. He whispered a prayer, blew it into his hands, and then washed his hands over his face. After completing his small prayer, Yousef took a thin blade and cut into the man's chest with great concentration, which resembled gentleness and care, but the man screamed anyway.

We sat there for some time. I squirmed in my seat, fighting waves of nausea and dizziness, while Uncle sat straight as a board, folded one leg over another and watched. The man cried out, begged, swore and at his very last and final point, he laughed the laugh that comes from madness and terror and the very last inch of life. When at last he died, I took a breath, realizing that for many moments, I had neglected this and shared in his life, in his last heartbeats. I had witnessed nothing so terrifying.

They say God tests man and requires him to suffer like Lott and Abraham and many others, but I say that is crazy. Why should we suffer? To prove our worth to enter heaven. If so, I did not want to go. Why should I want to sit in heaven with a God as cruel as this? I heard God laughing and it sounded strangely like the drummer absent from these many years. He played with my life like Baba played chess, delighting in my every tribulation. I vowed once again to turn my back on the cruel jester.

We sat there for some time while Yousef sat behind his desk and scratched a pen to paper. I did not move, my thoughts growing into the bars of my prison. Uncle sat still as a rock while in the heavy wet air the scratch of his pen sounded like a knife tearing into my soul.

The two dead men sat there, eyes glazed like sheep sacrificed in the old way, with a village elder praying, a woman washing the blood away, but no one prayed here, and the blood slowly fermented to a stench. I imagined that hell smelled much like this.

Thinking of what lurked beneath the earth a sudden panic gripped me. A worry that even in death, I would never see my family again, for if hell existed surely a burning pit waited for those such as me. Cowards who said and did nothing as men died at the hands of other men.

"What information have you gleaned for us, Yousef?" Uncle said.

Silence shattered like glass and I stared at blood on the walls, trying to recall something lost in the mists of my past, something important that now fought to escape.

"I have prepared a report and will send it to your office, Excellency."

"You have no further need of us here, I take it?"

"No Excellency. I shall inform you by phone if something else comes to my attention, but you will find my report complete. I will leave nothing undiscovered."

After the traditional lengthy session of handshakes and cheek kissing and thanks, tea offered and humbly declined, we left, my Uncle and I, and it once again resembled a dream, all of it, the entire day. As I floated back up the long hallway, I grew hopeful in some giddy walking on air way that I would wake, all this would vanish, my Jenny would smile and laugh, and in the next room our Melissa slept, her blonde hair spread against her pillow like summer's wheat grass.

However, I did not wake from the dream. We sat again in Uncle's office, he behind his desk with the map and thick sheath of papers and I in front of the desk staring at the painting of Band-i-Amir, a lake sitting like a blue mirror in a green canyon some distance from Kabul. Though I stared, I saw almost nothing, my vision unfocused, my thoughts a jumble of unknowns. I felt myself shaking, my atoms moving fast like Greek philosopher postulated long ago when he claimed free will to be an illusion. And I heard him laughing in his garden.

Why do all paintings of God look like old Greeks?

I had lost my mind. I tried to reason with myself, to settle and calm and calculate everything, find out where I had made my mistake, like a mathematician. Where had this life led me? My choices made freely or not, determined everything and now my girls lay dead. If I had stayed ten years ago and married Hassan's young daughter, Jenny would be alive and Melissa too, for I would not have returned to them and this would not have happened.

If that bullet had found its mark that night as I escaped on Jaheel, or had Baba shot that gun instead of tossing it in the canyon or had a hundred thousand other winds blown across different skies. Or maybe not. Maybe it would all still happen, unchangeable, the pattern uninterruptible, like a book written, a classical play performed through the ages of man. And nothing I did might ever change it.

They say time happens all at once, like the crash of water against a rock, all in one instant, past, present and future. But the gods? They just laugh at us. Puny humans cheating time.

"We are flying to Tashkent and from there, we will find Volkov and rescue your sister and I hope, your brother," Uncle said. "We can use these maps to follow them."

I heard him like a distant cannon or thunder rolling over a hillside, and though I heard, comprehension somehow escaped me, for a minute, then two and three, and then I felt his words as they unbundled themselves and settled into a form that I understood.

"I'm not going anywhere," I said. "I will bury my family. Why would I go? She is no prisoner. She went with him willingly. Who are we to rescue?"

Uncle flipped a page and kept reading, as if he had not heard my voice at all.

"We don't have time right now to bury them. Your sister has betrayed us. They are going, according to this report, to take what has been our family's duty to protect for hundreds of years. There is mention of your brother and an Arab, Farook El Bahar, and some sort of connection. We must find Sikandur before they kill him."

Too many words, jumbled together and falling apart. They meant nothing to me. I could only think of Jenny and Melissa.

Protect what for hundreds of years? Must be the land. Sikandur, or the strange look-alike who took my girls. What did I care if they killed him? Still, I wanted something, craved something, but what? I tried to separate all the emotions but failed. I felt the exhaustion in my very bones.

"I'm not going. I don't care about any of it."

"They may have forced Shaima to do this against her will. She might be a prisoner in this man's hands. You will do nothing to help?"

"What good can I do? Everything I do or touch turns out like this, a horrible mistake. You are better off without me."

I heard him turn in his seat. I looked up into his eyes. Green blazing fires. His face turned red and his massive shoulders came forward as he leaned towards me.

"You feel sorry for yourself. I understand. But I am telling you to get over it. The time for weakness is past. You have hidden in America all these years and I have asked nothing of you. I have always stood next to you in everything."

He stood up and looked out the windows behind his desk for a moment.

"This must be a dream." I said.

He turned around and glared.

"I will give you some time." He sat back down. "But do not test me, Omar. I have little patience now. They are my family too, and I intend to get them back. Events are in motion now and you will have to face them like a man or you will choose another way and that way will not include me in your life."

In his eyes, I saw no pity, only disgust.

"You would abandon me now? Now when I have lost everything? Now when I need you more than ever before?"

He picked up the report and read for a few seconds before replying.

"I have never pushed you. I kept hoping and waiting, but you never hardened the way I thought you would. Your father was right. You are soft. This will either kill you or strengthen you. Decide. But know this. I buried your grandmother after a Tajik mullah, a Jihadist fanatic murdered her before my eyes. As you can see, now your father will not allow mullahs into the valleys."

He paused and took a deep breath.

"Your father, tough as he is, could not face seeing the brutality of this mullah's twisted beliefs released against our parents. He turned and ran. I buried our father after the same mullah beheaded him. I was nine years old. Your father was twelve. You are thirty years old now and still you act a *child*.

You think you have suffered? You do not know suffering. You have lived here in this soft country while your father and your people fought for their lives and their land, and I stayed with you and share this guilt. However, that time has passed and a new time has come for us both. I go back to rebuild our homeland and defend our people and to find your sister and brother."

He paused here and averted his eyes from my face, and then he whispered his next words as if speaking to himself.

"You have nothing left here. And I am tired of coddling you as if you were still a boy."

"I just lost my family."

Stunned by his words, I rose from my seat, lost in a world I no longer understood, my head spinning with recent revelations. A mullah murdered my grandparents. I did not understand, and yet I did, for Baba always had that look, that haunted, ripped apart visage that I always sensed as his inherent nobility, his sacrifice, and I had not comforted him.

I had not given him joy. I felt the weight of my sins crushing me now, and I had nowhere to run.

"I lost my family at nine years old. My entire family except for your father. I went into the river to find my father's head so we would not bury him without it. Your Baba could not do this, and to this day, he has not forgiven himself. Anger and guilt consume him every day of his life.

Yes, you lost your family. They were my family too. Do you see me fainting like a woman? I am Pathan and I want my revenge! I want to see them pay with their lives. What do you want?"

Why did I not feel it too? I felt nothing as I looked inside, just a black thing choking me, squeezing my neck in a tightening fist. And then it happened. It all turned into something else.

Slow and silent, it crept up on me, pushing out from the inside. I began to loathe. At first, I loathed life and everything associated with life, and then the loathing crystallized and formed an image in my mind, an image of myself cowering behind a rock with my hands across my eyes. I tried to shout but as I opened my mouth, the loathing tightened and robbed me of my voice and all that squeezed out from my lips sounded like a whisper, a ragged denial of a futile life lived only for its own pleasure.

Then, while trying to breathe against the building pressure in my chest, I began a slow battle to crawl out of my skin. Years ago, Baba turned away from me. Now I wished he had shot me the night I rode Jaheel to freedom. I knew my weakness killed my family, and suddenly I could not stand still.

I stood up and paced across the wide room, pushed away the desks, pounded my fists against the walls and ripped down paintings of dark-eyed men in karakul hats, lines of medals on their chests, generals and kings and men who lived their lives with honor, men whom I hated and yet revered. I groaned and fell to the ground, got up and shook my fists in the air like Baba that night, standing on the rim of his canyon, silhouetted against a crisp round moon.

◆ ◆ ◆

51

Armon

He places several charges in the corners of the flat rooftop and straps wrapped explosive bundles to pipes and duct covers. He ties larger charges to long wires, which he lowers into three chimneys.

Lightning scorches jagged white lines against black clouds, illuminating the rooftop. During each lighting blast, he hides behind a wall or behind a humming air conditioning unit. His nerves are calm while doing this work. Destruction requires concentration, awareness.

The twin, the farmhouse, Sergy, and the girl fade into the deeper parts of memory. He hears whispering, like the wind blowing across the mouth of a cave or the soft voices of dead villagers, friends speaking to him, assuring him of the righteousness of his acts.

He sets the primary charge and the timer, slips it down a tube and then into the chimney. Job finished, he runs and leaps from rooftop to rooftop. Finding a metal ladder, he lowers himself to the fire escape and drops to the pavement in a dark alley. He runs into the cover of warm steam clouds rising from grates in the ground. For just a moment, he allows himself to wonder about the twin and his family.

Do they still live or did Sergy kill them? The woman, Cleopatra, she might have something to say about all that. He rubs the persistent knot on the side of his head and frowns.

♦ ♦ ♦

52

Explosions

Here we go. Philly cheese steak on a rainy night. Here, I got you one," Reggie said.

Mac unwrapped the sandwich and set it atop the dash. Rain fell in sheets over the windshield, turning the night into a smeared and runny Van Gogh.

"Maybe we should start it up and turn on the air, get the wipers running so we can see the damn target. Which one is it?" Mac said.

"Hell no, you crazy?"

"Well, I can't see much. How will we know if anybody's watching?" Mac said.

"Who will be interested in us?"

"Well then crack the back windows to get some of this steam off at least."

"You were always a complainer, even back on Front Street."

Reggie turned the key and lowered the back windows, letting in air and calming Mac's claustrophobia.

"You know Colonel, we should stop hurting our people. All this destruction is getting out of control. Somebody is liable to get killed."

"Don't worry, boy. This is the Tajik embassy, nothing but rag heads and sand niggers. Soon as Hassan, the Ambassador's father, learns his son is dead because of Ali Khan, he'll go storming over the border to kill him. These bastards love their sons and their vendettas, and they love to kill each other. It is all they have to fight their boredom. Dumbasses. You'd think after five thousand years they'd get a clue."

Mac took a bite of his sandwich. Reggie slurped, sucked, and chewed, wet, loud, lips smacking.

"Remember boy, you ain't no cop at this scene. And you do not know me. You stand back, out of sight, and let me do all the talking."

"Yea, I don't know you."

The sandwich tasted good. A noise startled him. He looked to his right. A homeless woman with a plastic bag for a hat pushed a shopping cart through the rain. She looked old, pale skin sagging from the sides of her face. She stopped, turned her head and stared directly at him. Mac stared back. Their eyes locked. She smiled, two teeth shining in a scarlet mouth. She held a plastic-wrapped sandwich in one hand, half-eaten, and this she held out to him, offering. He looked away.

When he looked back, she had walked away and vanished in the rain. Homeless came out at night in the capital. Nobody wanted to help them. Nobody wanted to admit the greatest nation in the world had millions of homeless, and no Americans seemed to care about them. He shook his head.

He knew she would die out here one winter night, in the snow and cold and freezing wind. Some cop would find her beneath the awning of a bus stop, her mouth wide-open, eyes staring at nothing. Who would go to her funeral? Who would care? He felt a sudden panic, as if the earth had opened and he had fallen into this bottomless pit of regret that tortured and terrified and consumed all things within its emptiness.

Rain slanted through the back window and splashed the backside of his head. He looked straight into silver edged water cascading down the front windshield. A BMW parked in front, across the street, two limos and a Mercedes. Five, six, seven, more limos pulled into a long-curved driveway, a party at one of the embassy's that lined Massachusetts Avenue.

The sandwich lost its taste.

A limo door opened and five young women got out. Long legs and dark umbrellas. Four uniformed men ran out to usher them into a marbled doorway.

"Look at that," said Reggie.

"Yea."

"I want one for tonight."

"Goddamn it, Reggie. We will get caught."

"No, we won't. Did we ever get caught in Alabama? Stop worrying. We got caught one stinking time by that bastard Ali and you are going all soft on me. You were not like this before that. Get your head on straight, boy."

Reggie reached over and slapped Mac on the back. "You will be so rich you won't have time to piss. So take it easy and let me handle it."

"What if just one body floats up in this goddamn rain? Will not matter how much money we have then. I should never have helped you. Electric chair. That's where we're going."

Reggie stared at him, thick gray eyebrows arched, eyes gleaming.

"You're a damn pussy. You did not kill anyone. If anybody gets the chair, it is me. Stop your damn whining." Reggie pulled out a cigar and lighter.

"If you weren't my very own flesh and blood, boy, I don't know what I'd do with you. Your poor mother. If she knew you'd grow up to be such a wimp... she'd have strangled you in your crib."

A moment passed before Mac chuckled, soft at first, like a man choking on something bitter. Reggie joined in. He lit and twirled the cigar. The laughter grew, infectious. They laughed aloud, rolling, thigh slapping, bone fracturing guffaws. The car shook from side to side and rain pounded a marching band beat on the roof.

A rapid succession of explosions shook the ground and the car bounced, the back window shattered. Gold flames lit the cascading water on the windshield, bathing them in a molten flow of yellows and reds.

Reggie rolled his window down. The embassy broke apart in pieces. Flying chunks of debris crushed cars on both sides of the street. Fires erupted in the adjacent buildings, but they appeared mere matchsticks to the inferno raging in what remained of the Tajik embassy.

The structure kept perhaps one fourth of itself. Columns of brick and stone and steel girders and iron bars stuck up in dark crooked angles against the flames. A woman ran out and screamed. Her clothes burned away, one arm hung at an unnatural angle.

A pale gray nebula formed between the fire and the clouds above. Night turned into day. Sirens wailed. Men appeared from the shadows and the dark edges of the ruined street. One took hold of the screaming woman. She swooned in his arms.

A thousand things happened in the square of Reggie's open window and Mac saw them all, every flicker of every flame, every shouting man and falling burning shard of concrete, wood and steel, melting glass and bodies in the street, black burning husks that once laughed and cried. They never knew. Never saw it coming for them. The hungry fire.

♦ ♦ ♦

- Part V -
The Trek

53

Tashkent, Tajikistan

O pening the hotel room door, I found them with faces pressed together, bodies bathed in the halo of the rising sun. All around them floated a thousand specks of dust. A cosmos within a cosmos within a cosmos, and so on.

I cleared my throat. They jumped apart and she stumbled on black high heels. He wiped a quick hand across his mouth.

"Well," Uncle said. "You came in quietly."

"Sorry," I said.

A fresh morning breeze pushed the sheer curtains aside. I shielded my eyes against the light in time to catch her blush and smile. Her slender form, willowy and delicate, angelic face, hair falling in flaxen curtains reminding me too much and too soon and tears filled my eyes. I choked them down and swallowed the hard lump in my throat.

"My nephew Omar."

He looked at her, then me, then back to her. I had never seen him nervous before, or in the arms of a woman.

"Meet Natasha Cherpinski, an old friend and representative of the travel ministry, and our passport for the journey."

Uncle had friends in every town. His heart shined outward, towards people, and they gravitated to him. In contrast, I possessed a dreary heart. One that stood apart from others. Sometimes I felt as if I did not belong in the story of his life and like a ghost, I hid in the edges, the corners and the dark places.

She circled the long sofa and flashed a dazzling smile with a hint of pink lip-gloss. She extended her hand palm down in the style of those old grand dames, and I felt compelled to bend and reach for her hand to plant a kiss in the air just above her skin.

"Pleased to meet you, Mr. Jaheeli," she said.

"Call me Omar."

"I am sorry to hear of your loss," she said.

"Thank you."

I had the Tashkent newspaper under my arm and when she moved to the love seat, I sat on the opposite sofa, pulled the paper out and flipped it open. She made me uneasy, uncomfortable, too much like Jenny, and I could not look directly at her.

"Jaheeli. What kind of name is that? I have never heard it before," she said.

"We stole the name from his father's horse," Uncle said.

"From a horse? Well, I never heard of that before."

I asked her last name. I know Uncle mentioned it, but I could not recall.

"Cherpinski," Uncle said.

"Well, you don't have to say it like that," she said.

"Just kidding," Uncle said.

I went back to my newspaper, holding it up in front of my face. Cyrillic type mystified and so I looked at the pictures of round-faced men sitting at a table discussing something. Tajiks, who hate us and we learn to hate, their close-together eyes and wizened skin and I felt guilty and ashamed so I opened to a new page and gazed at modern buildings of glass and steel set behind old green Russian statues in a tree-lined park. Old Tashkent and new Tashkent mixed and blurred in my eyes. I closed the paper for a moment and rested. When I opened my eyes, I found her staring at me.

She curled her long legs up under herself on the loveseat. Pale Russii eyes peered from beneath long Sophia Loren eyelashes. Uncle sat down next to me with a glass and I smelled the whisky on him. I flicked open the paper. I knew some Afghans drank the vodkas, as did Baba, and now for the first time I saw Uncle drinking the amber liquid that smelled of overripe decadence. I found myself unable to wrap my mind around this thought, and even less able to comprehend the woman sitting across from us. Uncle pulled his prayer beads and passed them through thumb and forefinger.

"Natasha will be a great help to us. She can explain," said Uncle.

I flashed him a look.

"What?" he said.

"Nothing," I said.

"I know that look. What is on your mind?"

Silence dominated for a moment. Only the wind rustling curtains made any sound. Then a man selling milk on the main street sang out his familiar rhythmic chant I had heard so many times before. His voice drifted in with the rising sun. She broke the mood with a sigh, her legs unfolding, rubbing against the fabric of her chair.

"Well... um... thank you Mukhtar."

She purred excellent English wrapped in a Russian accent.

"I am pleased to be of help in this terrible situation. I have prepared everything. More jeeps arrive in the morning along with permits, passes and all other documentation we will need for travel. One issue poses our largest threat. We cannot inform the military or the police because your enemy, Hassan Khan is an important member of the new ministry. He controls all the southern borders with Afghanistan, and that presents us with difficulties. You know about the assassination of his son at the Tajikistan embassy?"

I shook my head.

"Well, they have attributed the bombing of the embassy in Washington D.C. to Sardar Ali Khan. Your father."

She nodded that way people trained to sell things nod. I covered my eyes from the risen sun now flashing directly through the window. Uncle took a long sip of his whisky and coughed.

"Double agent Sergy Volkov has already crossed into Hassan's lands, and so we must travel covertly as mountain climbers and photographers. I have arranged such permits. In addition, your jeeps will have cold weather gear and climbing equipment since we will probably catch Volkov in the high altitudes past the Amu Darya. I have weapons hidden in your jeeps, all courtesy of your friends at the Russian embassy."

"Very good," Uncle said.

I wondered how many friends he had at the Russian embassy. Once our enemy, then our ally, and now our good friends. Russii played a strong game of politics. She snuggled her shoulders up as they do in those old movies like "The Thin Man".

I caught the motion from the edge of my vision. I wondered how many of her cousins Baba killed during the war. If she held any animosity towards Pathans, she hid it well.

"How did you two meet?" I said.

Her head turned quick, feline and smooth. Her neck, chalk white, the hint of blue vessels just beneath the surface. The neckline of her buttoned blouse revealed nothing, stiff sleeves and collar, almost a man's shirt.

"University. He came to study. We met in the snow beneath the stars, New Year Eve I think."

"You never told me, Uncle."

"You were... and I was... very young."

My mind drifted in the warm Tashkent morning and I thought about home, Baba, and the canyon where I should have died from the bullet still wedged an inch from my heart. If I listened hard, I heard them crying and if I closed my eyes, I heard them scream. I had not slept more than an hour at a time for three days, lying on cool sheets, staring at stucco ceilings, waiting for the darkness to consume my heart.

◆ ◆ ◆

54

Euro Snow Dogs

She dozed through the night, half awake, sensing disorder in the world so close to Baba's lands. During hot days of driving into the mountains south of Dushanbe, she felt a presence and she recalled her mother's warnings of deadly mystics, dangerous men, and dark nights on the mountain.

She lit the kerosene lantern, shivered, and watched Sergy sleep. Thoughts ran wild in her head and she fretted over this, but most of all she fretted about her own unalterable destiny that Baba so often pointed out. Fated to marry a ferocious Talib whose ideas included the burqa, and domination. No, not her. She decided years ago.

She meant to change her fate and that of her family. She meant to get them out of these mountains and most of all she meant to release Baba from his duty and free him from his cold fortress so he might live once again. She even dreamed of one day reuniting him with the woman in the picture and the baby boy with the shock of pure white hair. Family reunited, a dream she had once as she felt her mother whisper one snowy night.

"Be free my daughter. Run, run for your life."

SECRET OF THE HINDU KUSH

The certainty that her family would come for her gave her hope and dread, joy and sadness, anticipation and anxiety and she shivered beneath that pale blue moon, half expecting old magics to awaken and take her to a long-ago time full of monsters, magicians and madmen running all around.

A shout outside the tent, a man ran by breathing heavy. Metal slid and clicked against metal as men pushed magazines into guns. Sergy stirred in his sleep, mumbled and turned over. She shook him, slapped his face, still he did not respond. A gunshot, then the rapid fire of an automatic pistol and Sergy jumped to his feet, snatched up his pistol and ran out of the tent. The camp exploded in confusion, men running, shouting, and Sergy giving orders.

She pulled on the sweatshirt that Sergy had specially made for everyone. It featured "Euro Snow Dogs" stenciled above a cliff where a man dangled like a spider. She picked the color, pale blue like the sky... and a piece of ribbon her mother gave her years ago. She pulled on her cold weather pants and a dark green parka, picked up Sergy's parka and left the tent.

Men scrambled. A shot flashed in the darkness at the edge of the forest, light beams swung in every direction and in the middle of the mayhem, Sergy stood listening to the merchant Abdul, who sold them ten jeeps in Tashkent. She walked over. The merchant spoke in rapid little bursts of Russian.

"Your man is gone. The Italian taken from my tent as I slept and the guard, he is missing."

The little merchant coughed and stuttered, shivering in the chilly night, soaked in something dark and thick.

"And blood, so much blood."

She jerked and took a fast breath.

"Blood? Nobody said anything about blood." She turned towards Sergy and eyed him suspiciously.

"What's going on? Is everyone alright?" Shaima said.

Abdul the merchant shook his head.

"This is terrible. I am afraid. Maybe we turn back?" Abdul said.

"Show me," said Sergy.

They walked to a tent set at the edge of camp in the gravel base of a snowbound peak. Cold air dampened their footsteps and the only natural sounds came from a stream set back in the trees to their east. A tremor moved the ground. Shaima slipped. Sergy caught her.

"Earthquakes here all the time, nothing to worry about," he said.

She gave him a look. "I know."

"Yes, you do, Princess," he said.

"Stop calling me that."

"No. Not going to stop." Sergy gave her a kiss on her cold cheek.

Men muttered behind her. Something about bad luck, women and demons.

"Did you see it?" said one.

"No," said another.

"What are you shooting at?"

"I don't know."

"What happened?"

"Nobody knows."

"Bad luck."

"Misfortune."

"Evil on this mountain."

"Did you see it?"

"I saw nothing."

"Yes, bad luck."

"I need coffee."

"Best thing for you."

"Who is missing?"

"Grimaldi and Bola."

There came a live silence for the next few moments. The wind whispered through the forest and set the leaves to singing and she felt the magic awakening. Earth and air spirits rising to flaunt the night. Voices drifted on the wind, and moon shadows shifted beneath spruce and pine groves growing along the riverbank. They found Abdul the merchant's tent ripped open from the rear, shreds of wet green canvas hanging like bloodstained teeth. She gasped. Sergy told her to go back to the tent.

"You're not in charge of me," she said.

"Oh God," he said.

"Russians have a God?"

"I am only half Russian."

"So you believe with half your soul?"

He shook his head and issued orders.

"Set up a perimeter. I want every foot covered from the stream all the way around. Luwenthal, get over here and track this. Whoever took Grimaldi and Bola, I want to know everything."

Men scattered. She stood next to Sergy, looking up into his face, waiting.

"I know Professor. I know who took your men," Abdul said.

Abdul's turban tilted on his head and his bushy hair stuck out on one side. He licked his lips and reached a trembling hand towards Sergy's arm while peering into the trees around the camp as if he expected a monster to charge out and drag him away.

"Who?"

"Not a who. Something else. Professor, something high above us. Perhaps... a demon."

He nodded and shook visibly.

Sergy moved closer to the poor man and placed a hand on his shoulder. Abdul continued his halting, out of breath Russian.

"I know him. He killed my family with an avalanche. He destroyed my village in one night. When I come back from Dushanbe, I find them buried under a mountain of rock."

"Abdul, who are you talking about. Calm down and tell me."

"Professor, I am telling you. They say he is half man, half god, he cannot die. He takes shape of leopard or wolf or hawk, and if you go to hunt him, you will not come back. People fear him from here to the Himalayas. They say he is born from a race of giants, the son of a God chained to a mountain long ago."

"Prometheus is a myth, Abdul. There is no such person or god or even half-god," Sergei said.

The merchant shook his head and waved a hand back and forth.

"You must not go further, Professor."

She knew this legend. Her mother spoke of mystics, who transformed into birds and flew from mountain to mountain. Half-breed sons of Prometheus whom Zeus chained to a mountaintop while he sent Pandora to plague men and bring evil to the world. Prometheus lay with human women and gave life to the *Dau*, giants destined to wander the glaciers for all eternity, cursed by men and Gods.

Old legends never die, they just move over for new ones, but in this ancient world, new legends do not exist and so the old ways remain fastened to the very root of every man, woman and child. She knew. She felt the root inside, pulling her closer every second. The intense magic of her land so real, so vibrant, and so utterly dangerous.

"That is all remarkably interesting, Abdul, but first we must find the men. We cannot just leave them bleeding on this mountain."

"But Professor, they are dead already. Please, you must not leave camp. Much danger out there."

Sweat beaded on the merchant's face.

"Sergy, I have the trail." Luwenthal stood some distance up the mountainside, pointing at a snow-covered peak jutting into the moonlit sky.

"Up there, it leads straight up this mountain. We do not need ropes, but we had better hurry. There's a lot of blood up there."

Sergy picked eight men and told them to get their gear.

"I'm going too Sergy," Shaima said.

"Oh, no. You are not going up there. It is dangerous."

"No, Sergy. You are not leaving me down here. I'm coming with you."

He mumbled a few words and rolled his eyes.

"Get your pack and your pistol. Stay with me, right behind me, understand?"

She nodded. Moonlight turned rounded boulders into giant pearls. All around her mountains soared, snow caps shimmering. Years ago, Baba told her that only the old Gods walked among these peaks, home of the noble bird Simorgh who with a human head and claws of a lion could carry away animals as large as an elephant. She recalled Baba's stories of the giant bird that saved Prince Zal.

Abandoned on a mountaintop by his father King Saam when Zal came forth from his mother's womb an albino. Simorgh raised the young albino prince as her own, and when the prince grew to adulthood, she gave him three green feathers with which to summon her.

Zal rejoined the world of men and married Rudaba, who later nearly died in childbirth. Zal used a green feather to summon Simorgh, who taught Zal how to save his wife and child with caesarean section. Rudaba then gave birth to the great Persian warrior hero, Rostum.

"You should wash that blood off your boots and get your gear," Sergy said.

"I can take her to the stream. She can wash up there," Abdul said.

Shaima shivered in the cool air and headed for the stream.

Abdul kept up a steady rambling dialogue while he followed. Sitting on a boulder near an eddy, she washed the blood from her boots.

"Ugh. Gross. So much blood," she said. "Nobody said anything about blood."

Abdul stammered warnings. He claimed to see the shadow of an eagle flying against the moon and his incessant voice cut through memories of her mother whispering in the hallways, running her hands over walls or sitting by the window, and telling her stories of the *Siddhi* and his mischief.

The Siddhi, the wild man some called *Malang* and others called *Sufi* and still others named him *Jinn*. She never met him, but the stories of his cannibalism and magic terrified her. Those stories kept her awake long after she went to bed. Some nights she hugged her pillows, listened to the wind shake her window, and watched strange shadows melt together and split apart. Pushing the memories from her mind, she slipped into her boots and snatched up her rucksack.

Luwenthal led. Sergy climbed next. She followed. Light and nimble, she maneuvered around boulders and over rocks. In these mountains, her ancestors developed into small boned, quick stepping climbers. She possessed the genetics for this. In Moscow, she studied the anthropology of her people and, with Sergy's help, obtained her doctorate. This trip would ensure her position as a professor able to teach in any university and guarantee her freedom forever.

"Hold on Princess. It's going to get rough in a bit," Sergy said.

She held on to his rucksack strap and let him pull her, saving her strength.

"Look up there," Luwenthal said. He pointed at the snow-covered crags.

"What is it?" Sergy said.

"Well, it looks like a cave. There, that shadow up there on the mountain."

"Looks like a shadow to me."

"Yes, but what could cast such a shadow up there?"

"I see your point."

"One more thing."

"What?"

"Whatever took the men picked them up here and carried them the rest of the way. Look, smeared blood along these boulders. This is not at ground level. It is not even a level where a man might carry something."

"Carried them? What could pick up two men and carry them?"

"Look," Luwenthal said. He pointed his lantern at scratches and smears on the rocks.

"And there is a big track right here under the blood."

They leaned in and flashlights lit up the blood-filled track. Nearly a half a foot across and over a foot long, the track shimmered black and reflected the moon.

"Not a wolf or a leopard. Maybe a bear?" Sergy said.

"There are bears in these mountains," she said. "People mistake them for Yeti all the time."

"A few," Sergy said. "They've been hunted, and bears drag, they don't carry."

"Then what else could it be?" she said.

Quiet settled again over the mountain, silence sulking beneath the sound of footsteps. Her ears tuned in to her own breathing. Wind gusted for a moment and then vanished. Sergy stopped. She bumped into him, stopped and looked back down the mountain.

The camp sat lonely in the gorge. A line of men, breaths chugging like tiny smokestacks, curled below. A white fog hovered and swirled over the river. A shifting silver ribbon between pale tree trunks where shadows moved, and childhood monsters waited.

Luwenthal appeared next to her, materializing like magic from the shadowed side of a moonlit boulder.

"It could be brigands or cannibals maybe," Luwenthal said.

"Shut up. Get going, Luw," Sergy said.

"Cannibals?" she said.

"No cannibals, Princess, he's just being funny."

"Better not be cannibals," she said.

"Probably cannibals," Luw said.

"Shut it, Luw," Sergy said.

"I can wait for you here," Shaima said.

"Oh, no you don't. You wanted to come. Now get up here in front of me," Sergy said.

"He said there are cannibals."

"There are no cannibals," Sergy said. "Do you think I'd let a cannibal eat you? Just like that?"

She looked up at him.

"You better not let any cannibal eat me," she said. She walked in front of Sergy with Luw walked ahead.

After what seemed like hours, they reached the cave. Its mouth dripped long, smooth icicles, giant teeth shining in the moonlight.

"No tracks going in," Luwenthal said.

"How can that be? They have to be somewhere up here, right?" Sergy said.

"Yes. Look, smeared blood against this wall."

"But no tracks?"

"Don't ask me." Luwenthal shrugged. "You want to go in there?"

"Ya. They make me mad. I am going in to find my men. Everybody stays behind me. You keep your eyes on Shaima."

"I'll be right next to her," Luwenthal said.

"Everyone have headlamps?" Sergy waved his headlamp in the air, signaling the men to get them on. He switched his headlamp on and then showed her how to fit one to her head and turn it on.

"Ok, I got it." She pushed his hand away, annoyed at her own deficiency.

The cave widened. They huddled in the cold dark. Light beams flashed off granite walls. Searching the cave, they found a tunnel between two rocks. She followed Sergy into the narrow passage and down a tight path through sharp-edged rocks. He stopped and she ran up against him. He turned and squeezed her hand for a second, his beam blinding her. She pushed his head forward.

Water dripped in the distance, echoing the slow, deliberate passage of time. Her ears alternated attention from one sound to another like a butterfly unable to choose a flower.

In one area, they had to squeeze between two huge rocks. Sergy's parka zipper dragged across one surface. She could hear everything so clear.

From there the passage opened wide enough for them to walk in pairs. The ceiling receded in the darkness. She cast her light up into rock outcroppings and ledges high above where drawings of muted, ancient faces stared down. Sergy stopped and remarked if he only thought to bring a rope and a camera. Like a child, he wanted to investigate every new thing while she ached to get back to camp. The tunnel made her nervous and she held his hand tight, pulling him to a stop every few steps. A faint breeze carried a horrid smell past her nose. She gagged and they stopped for her to recover.

"That smell. What is that?" she said.

She saw Sergy's head turn towards Luwenthal, but neither said a word. Behind her, feet shuffled against rock and sand. The men mumbled words she could not hear, but their angry tone she understood. They walked for a good hour or more before he stopped and held a hand up, pointing to his ears. She listened to a faint crunching and a soft melodic chanting. Sergy signaled for quiet with a small flashlight illuminating a hand to his mouth. He switched the flashlight off and peeked around the edge of the passage. A faint light glowed in the distance. Sergy signaled headlamps off. She reached up and doused hers.

He leaned down and whispered in her ear. "Stay here, Princess. I must see what is up ahead. I will be right there. You can see me from here."

She squeezed his hand and held on tight, shaking her head, no, no, no.

He took Luwenthal's arm and put her hand on it. "Stay here with her. Send the men ahead with me. Don't leave her under any conditions."

Luwenthal placed a hand on hers.

"Don't worry," he said. "He'll be right back. Nothing can hurt him. Look at him. What could be big enough to dent that man?"

Sergy led his men into the darkness. The men moved in silhouette against the backdrop of diffused light. He signaled for them to file past and move forward. His inkblot shape beckoned with a hand and she moved up to the edge of the tunnel.

She saw a cavern, cold and vast. A hole in one side allowed moonlight to stream down to the cavern floor. In the center of this light stood what she could never dream. She nearly screamed, but Sergy's hand found her mouth and clamped down. She squirmed in his powerful hands, trying to tear her eyes away, but failing. She stared, mesmerized by the horror of it all.

Dismembered limbs hung in the mouths of white leopards. Scattered meat and bones lay in pools of blood and the moonlight gave it a pale fuzzy coating, like old movies run on a patchwork screen. Standing tall in the middle of the mayhem, the shimmering outline of a hulking giant stooped and raised a... man's arm to his mouth.

Her breath caught and she swallowed a hard lump of scream in her throat.

She clutched Sergy, pulling him down to whisper in his ears, "We must run. Run. It is the Dau".

Sergy held a finger to her lips, moved across and to her right. She studied the thing, a legend come to life. As the pounding in her chest calmed, she realized the immensity of the... beastman. The importance of such a discovery. If she could capture or kill it, bring it back, her name would live forever in the world of archeology. She could write a book, two books, and a movie. This must be the creature mistaken for Yeti all over the Hindu Kush and Himalayas.

Excitement took hold like a windstorm and sucked the air from her lungs. She calmed herself and made mental notes of its dimensions and movement so she might draw it later.

It stood in the half-light and she could not determine its height though it stood much taller than an average man. A prominent forehead loomed over deep eyes, flat nose and thick jaw line. From there, a muscled neck led to wide shoulders. Long muscular arms flexed while the torso sat atop a pair of thick legs. Its dark bluish body gleamed and glistened in the light, wet and gothic, like a gargoyle or... She remembered. A winged beast painted on the side of an ancient monastery she observed years ago when traveling the high mountains with Baba.

Suddenly the giant moved out of the moonlight. His movement appeared unreal, dream-like. She gripped Sergy's arm and pulled him down.

"Wait. What will you do?" she said.

"I will kill them all. That big thing dies first," Sergy said. "Get back, Princess."

She moved back and bumped into Luwenthal. She cringed and leaned out to watch Sergy and his men. Moonlight and shadows played tricks on her eyes. What beast can chant and hum melodic music? Yes, it must be a hominid. Her interest peaked. She wondered if killing it...

Sergy moved away and she jumped when he let loose with a barrage of gunfire. In less than a blink of an eye, the giant vanished into the darkness. Sergy roared and guns spit into the dark cavern, and the noise grew into a long blast of thunder that forced her hands up and over her ears.

Leopards dashed across the circle of moonlight to die, cut to shreds. A frenzy of white fur and shattered bone and black blood splattered everywhere. Within seconds, the cats lay strewn about the cavern. Gunfire slowed and then ceased. Silence and smoke spread throughout the cave. She stood, unsure and dizzy, so she groped for the wall to steady herself.

Then, from the high reaches of the cave, a scream broke. A piercing long shriek and when this stopped, boulders fell and shook the ground. Rocks rained down from all sides. Sergy signaled a retreat. He took her by the arm and pulled her back down the tunnel.

"Avalanche," he said.

They stumbled and lurched along, banging against rocks and bumping into each other. She looked up and saw him sweating and his eyes wild, and she felt the raw energy flowing through him. Once outside, he picked her up and carried her down the mountain. She wrapped her arms around his thick neck and leaned into him, thinking of her mother and the thing in the cave and her strange melancholy brother.

"He is following us," shouted Abdul the merchant. His hands waved in the air, stirring the fog that climbed the mountain, hiding rocks and ground. They slowed and felt with hands and feet the way down the mountain.

"Hurry!" shouted Abdul. "Come on. It is catching up!"

♦ ♦ ♦

55

Uncle's Story by the Campfire

We drove past Dushanbe among a throng of pedestrians, bicyclers, yaks, donkey carts and dilapidated automobiles. Grey clad soldiers patrolled the streets in groups of two or three, Kalashnikovs dangling, cigarettes stuck in the edges of weather-beaten faces. Eyelids crinkled against the sun's fire. They watched every lorry, truck and person. They stopped and questioned the rough or ragged and lingered longer with men wearing black, the color of extremists driven north by Americans and Afghan militias.

The official government emblems on three of our seven jeeps worked with grand effect on the guards. They waved us through checkpoints without so much as two glances. Uncle drove and Natasha sat up front while Aziz sat next to me in the back. I called Aziz my brother, though we had no relation by blood, but his father fought with mine and died in Dora beneath the grinding track of a tank while holding a bomb to his chest.

Aziz often said, "My father died shaheed. What better end to a warrior's life?"

Uncle adopted Aziz in a manner of speaking. Since the day of his father's death they became like uncle and nephew and Aziz would visit our cabin, laugh with my wife and play with my daughter and now we stood together, wondering about tomorrow.

"We will drive into the night. We are likely two days behind and need to make up time. They will slow once they arrive at high altitude and we can catch them," Uncle said.

He drove up and over the Fann Mountains and headed for the Pamirs that loomed high, rugged, and snowcapped. From province to province, the guards waved us through. Smiling, bowing and stumbling over themselves to glimpse Natasha. Our jeeps bounced and lurched along the narrow and pot holed M41 highway, which snaked through the mountains, unpaved in places. We passed through a semi tropical valley that held a mud bricked town, Kofarnigon, "where Kafirs do not go" and Uncle joked with Natasha who slapped his shoulder and then leaned over and laid her face there, like a lover. I gazed out the window, nervous to meet Uncle's eyes in the rearview. Aziz chuckled and then caught himself. Natasha slipped her arm through Uncle's.

We stopped to buy pistachios and almonds at a line of shacks along the highway. Children swarmed Natasha, so we gave them money to buy things and while they ran in different directions to retrieve the items, we loaded the jeeps and drove away or else these smiling, hospitable folk would have waylaid us for days with food and song.

We kept on through sheer fall-away cliffs on one side, towering mountains on the other. Sometimes our narrow ribbon of road ran muddy from melting glaciers and snow. We got out and pushed jeeps from deep muck until we discovered a towrope in one, and then we made use of this to pull out our stranded comrades.

With ten jeeps and four to a jeep, we had forty in our group counting a cook and his assistant. If nothing else, we ate well each evening and then slept. At night I dreamed my brother's nightmares. Shadowy images of his life. A dark-eyed monster and strange four-legged beasts. His dreams mixed with my own terrors and the faces of my dead family. Some nights I fought tears so that Uncle might sleep undisturbed.

Uncle drove for hours until crumbling precipices hiding in the dark night forced us to halt. We drove off the highway and followed the stream that curved behind a hillside and opened into a small glade surrounded by conifers and mountain poplars. Thick grasses along the stream provided a fair campsite, so we pitched our tents and lit fires.

The night air cooled quickly. Soon we huddled in blankets around a central blaze. The cook prepared kabobs and bread. We passed steaming teacups round in a circle. I gazed up into the white peaks, a sky full of stars and a near full moon, and I wondered where under this same sky my sister and brother slept.

A thousand thoughts ran across my mind, leaving tracks and furrows. I saw Jenny and Melissa walking in a moonlit desert. I heard the wind rustling through the willow trees in Baba's courtyard. I pulled the blanket tighter around my shoulders and sipped my tea.

"Tell us a story, Mukhtar," Natasha said.

I found refuge from my thoughts by concentrating on two beetles discussing a crumb of bread between my feet.

"A story... hmmm... what kind of story?" Uncle said.

"Tell us the story of the giant and village girl, the one you told me in Moscow."

The campfire lit Uncle's face a reddish-gold and the muscles of his jaw quivered as he bit into a hard piece of *rhot*, something like dried cornbread we brought from a merchant sitting cross-legged in his wooden stall beside the road outside Dushanbe.

"Well then, this story comes from my great-great grandmother, who should know the truth of it, for she lived in the village where it happened, or perhaps her mother did, so long ago, who remembers these things."

The red beetle crawled on top of the black and tried to smother it, pushing its face into the sand.

Warmed by the fire, I heard Baba's voice in a faraway roll of thunder and I looked to the gap between two mountain peaks where lightning slashed from dark clouds. I sensed him waiting there, standing on his balcony, the assassin at his side, both knowing that I approached soon to violate his last command to stay away, forever away. Yes, I deserved it all, for I had abandoned my people and my land and now I suffered, as I should for those few years of pleasure I had stolen from my father.

I returned to the battle at my feet.

"There was and was not," all our legends and stories started with these words, "many thousands of years ago, when our ancestors from the north first settled into these mountains. Here they came upon an ancient race of giants who, as the legend says, descended from the old Gods and their unsanctified unions with mortal women."

The delicate lines of Jenny's face interrupted the tiny battle at my feet, and her fingertips touched me in the passing breeze. Creation, a misery, a farce, and I watched two beetles brawling for a scrap of bread. What mattered? Nothing. My girls lay beneath rich Virginia soil.

Uncle continued his story.

"One of these giants, a cave dweller, grew restless living alone. His ancient race teetered on the brink of extinction, and he could not find a mate. He took notice of a new race settling along the rivers and streams far below. One dark night lit only by a sliver of moon, he descended to a village to learn more about these new beings. Hiding at the edge of a forest, he observed a young girl. Slender hipped, with an enchanting face. The poor giant fell in love, so he waited and when she came to wash by the riverside, he stole her away and took her back to his cave."

Now the warring beetles lay on their backs, feet kicking in the air while a line of black ants formed. These newcomers cut the bread into grain-sized bits and carried them away. One ant, larger than the rest, stood guard and when one beetle had nearly tipped itself over, the ant pushed it back and I heard laughter, tiny chuckles, but someone fed the fire and crackling sparks drowned all sound but Uncle's voice.

"The next morning her father raised the alarm. They gathered the men and marched up the mountain in search of the girl. They found scraps of her torn gown and tracks that frightened some with their great size and many turned back claiming the Gods had taken her and they dare not interfere. Her father went on with a handful of young men and found the giant. The battle raged for many months, through the winter and spring. They hurled spears and arrows and dodged enormous boulders tossed like pebbles until they slew the giant and cut his head from his body. From the severed neck, his spirit rose into the air and screamed that they had killed the son of a God and his Father would give him the power to live forever and torment the race of men until time itself stood still. And they say his spirit wanders these hills today and in the dead of night steals children, the old and the very weak, thus fulfilling its promise. So my dear Natasha, never turn the tent lamp off at night, for if the giant comes he will surely steal you away."

Natasha laughed and pulled her seat closer to Uncle.

"I have heard such a story," one soldier said.

"So have I. My father says it is true," another said.

"He is a cannibal."

"They call him Dau."

"I have met him," said one. "He is a man like you or me, but he is also a giant."

"I met a giant once, a *Malang*. Wild hair and eyes, murmuring his songs and beating his drum, he cut men down as they ran from the guns of Russii and then he slew the Russii, killing an entire brigade in one dark night."

"Aye, I have often heard of that night."

"I was there," said a man, "and I alone escaped the mountain by falling from a cliff into the great Amu."

No one argued that, and silence took hold of us all.

The beetles righted themselves and crawled about, looking for the bread but finding only dirt, they whipped their antennae around and kicked with their tiny legs. The ants laughed from afar and the beetles, in a frustrated rage, fought again, scrambling in the dirt for territory and defiance.

Later, standing at the edge of the stream, Uncle and I listened to the passion of falling water and observed a pale mist rising, swelling and twisting around trees and over rocks.

"You can find peace in the words of God. Any God will do, they all say the same thing," said Uncle.

I thought of the many questions I did not ask that day on the ramparts when Baba warned me about the power and seduction of prayer.

"I wonder if God had wanted such devotion, such unquestioning compliance and most of all, such knee bending, totalitarian worship. Why not make us ants whose entire purpose is one purpose and who devote their entire existence to the nest, the queen and the propagation of their species. Or why not keep us as spirits in an incorporeal world without light and without love so we might never know passion and pleasure, temptation and hate? Why create this blue sphere of mountains, oceans and plains and make us all different colors and distinct races so we could not help but wage war and destroy all the goodness in the world? Do we speak of a benevolent God or an evil jester?" I said.

"Through the ages men have asked these questions however God's intent is as incomprehensible to us as we are to the ant. Our duty is not to question but to accept and have faith."

"Has anyone ever proved the existence of any God? You give rationalizations that defy logic and mathematics and science. Such thoughts only appeal to weak and frightened men, those who look at the sky and imagine someone looking back. You have nothing to offer in recompense for the multitudes that have died for your God but a word. Faith," I said.

"It is all I have."

"Men who believed strongly in their Gods have committed the greatest crimes in history," I said. "Baba is right. Religion is just something that seduces people in believing they should murder others who believe in a different God. You are all just blind men dancing in a field of dead poppies."

He said nothing more.

The mist spread, billowing, reaching up and over us, warm, wet, and shining in the moonlight. I felt a comfort for a moment, but only for a moment, and I knew the things I should know and the rest remained just heartache without salvation or peace.

I knew it would always be this way for me for my questions would go unanswered and yet I somehow reasoned that another world must exist and I believed in this illusive world just as Uncle believed in his God. And in my belief, I found a peace and I looked forward to that day I would meet my girls again in that world of mystery and once again feel their smiles warm my soul.

"No sounds of animals or birds," Uncle said.

I said nothing, for from beneath the moonlit blue and silver stream, I sensed Baba's dark eyes watching. Baba and his unfathomable face revealed nothing.

◆ ◆ ◆

56

Close to Her Father's Lands

The yellow-brown town of Eshkashem sat in a valley between gray mountains. The collection of mud brick and adobe structures shimmered in the high-altitude heat while the blue and white Amu Darya River rumbled along on their left. Sergy parked the jeep on the edge of town, near the river but a respectful distance from the bridge leading back into Tajikistan. Voices filtered through the swirling dust, and children from the outskirts of town gathered and waved. Two old men and their stick-laden donkeys scurried out of the dust cloud kicked up by jeeps full of Sergy's men pulling up against the hillside.

"I told you don't stop here, Sergy," she said. "It's too close to my father's lands."

"Look Princess, stay in the jeep if you're afraid someone will recognize you."

"Oh, sure. And this is not glass right here," she tapped on the windshield. "It is dirty, but do you think they can't see through this?"

He gave her a look, then stretched his arms over his head.

"Where the hell is that camel merchant? Wait here, Princess."

Sergy shouted out the window for Abdul, who ran over from the last jeep in line, his turban a dazzling blue in the swirl of yellow dust.

To her right, fields of poppy shivered against the wind and a thin line of villagers moved like colorful sails through the sea of purple and white blooms. To her left, Sergy's enormous head and shoulders blocked her view.

"You have a huge head," she said. "I can't see anything out your window."

He flashed her a look.

"What?"

She pointed at his head.

"Your head. It is too big. It's blocking my view."

Sergy laughed.

"Ugh. Forget it," she said.

She went back to worrying about someone seeing her. All along the drive, she had felt eyes watching her. Perhaps the elusive cave giant or someone else, following, waiting. Sergy refused to take her back up the mountain and refused to look for the strange humanoid creature. He said he would bring her back for her proof as he chiseled his dead men's names into a massive white rock, a gravestone of sorts. He said some words beside the rock and Luwenthal lit a fire. Then they drank the vodka, smashed their glasses, got in the jeeps and left.

She shivered. She recalled the apparition she saw while watching stars flicker from her stepmother's window where the scents of lavender and jasmine drifted in the cool night air. That night she looked down into the garden and beheld the glowing outline of a thin woman with her mother's face looking up at her, mouth twisted in a scream. She listened to the wail of the ghost and learned what freedom meant. Her mother spoke. The wind whispered through open windows and clear water slipped from pool to pool in the garden. She remembered the everlasting minutes of that night and the tiny luminous angels that flew up the walls into her window to dance about her ears, singing like bells chiming far away.

"Xanadu, take me to Xanadu."

For years, she wondered about Xanadu until she learned from the tutors Baba employed for her education that Xanadu lay in China, in the old kingdom of Kublai Khan, sometimes called Shangri-La, and sometimes, the Forgotten City. This mystical place held some unknown charm or wonder for her mother; she remembered listening through the locked door to her mother's calloused feet scuffling and sliding along the stone floors. Once again, she heard a long-forgotten scream drifting in the Eshkashem air.

"Shaima, oh my daughter, what will become of you? Escape these evil Pathans or you too will end like this."

She looked around but saw only spinning eddies of yellow dust and men moving through like shadows, indistinct faces without substance. She looked back up into the mountains, expecting a cloud of dust and the thunder of horses pounding down towards her, Baba in the front astride Jaheel, his whip gripped in his teeth and his beard frothing with anger. If he caught her, she knew he would tie her to the same wooden post as her mother and...

She sighed and took a sip of bottled water.

The camel merchant stood listening to Sergy for several moments, then took a jeep and made for the street leading to the bazaar and flies by the millions laying eggs in slaughtered meat hanging in butchers' stalls.

"You told him not to buy the meat Sergy?"

"Yes, I told him."

"Good. We can purchase sheep from farmers along the way."

Rusted hulks of tanks and trucks littered the riverbank where children pretended to shoot each other and fall to the ground. She watched and smiled despite a heavy sense of dread. Then, in one second of flashing light, the smile died on her face.

Kalashnikovs on their backs, turbaned men advanced on horseback, six in front, and she could not tell how many rode behind. Jeep doors opened and slammed shut. Sergy's men gathered behind him and she trembled even though the heat at 9,000 feet broke a sweat across her brow.

Sergy leaned into the open window, "Are these your father's men?"

"Probably. These people tend the poppies. Farmers and their families, some government people in the town, and the militia. Everyone is loyal to him. Listen, Sergy, you mustn't kill anybody." She squinted into the morning sun to get a better look at the bandoliered men.

"Of course not. What do you take me for?"

She recognized the leader, Zia Pasha riding up front, dressed nicely for a militiaman, a forest green cloak with gold threads looping in a flowered Tajik design. His white turban wrapped above his tanned face where tight spaced eyes marked him as Tajik. Still, he worked for poppy money and this outweighed ethnicity in these valleys. Money bought loyalty, and Baba bought much. She ducked down behind the gunmetal gray dash, leaving just her eyes above to watch while she listened through the open window.

"Mondah nabashi," Zia Pasha said. He stopped his horse and patted the neck, settling the black pony while his men lined their steeds to either side of him. She whispered the correct response to Sergy through the window.

"Zindah bahshi," Sergy said.

"Hello, you speak Angleezi?" Zia said.

"Yes. How can we help you?"

"Where are you going, big Angleezi?"

"Nowshak Mountain. We come from Germany and France and England to climb the great mountain."

"Oh yes, Nowshak enormous. Yes."

Zia fingered his narrow beard as if he wished to pull it out further than where it hung just low enough to cover the hair on his chest peeking through the top of a brown shirt.

"Why do you have so many guns?" Zia said.

"Protection, my friend. We heard about the kidnappings in Uzbekistan, you know, the four climbers, and now others, so we brought men and guns for protection. You know, one must be careful." Sergy nodded and smiled.

Sergy's men spread in a wide arc to the other side of the road, securing positions from which each man had a clear shot at the band of riders. Her breath quickened and steamed up the windshield. She ducked lower and shifted her attention back to Zia Pasha.

"Do you have permits for those guns?"

"Yes, we do. Are you the local commander? I can show you if you wish."

"We are farmers, Angleezi. We protect our crop from strangers and warlords from the north."

She watched a hundred or more flies, tiny specks against the blue sky, circling and diving at the men and horses. A smell reminiscent of her father's stables blew in the window, horse dung and filth, and she held her breath until the breeze passed across the Amu rushing along behind her. Zia suddenly pushed himself up in his saddle and peered through the windshield, straight into her eyes. She pretended to fumble for something beneath the dash and came up with a cigarette and a lighter. She puffed furious billowing clouds of smoke in front of her.

"Who is the girl with you? She looks very familiar."

"She is our guide and knows this area. She also knows Sardar Ali Khan. Do you know Sardar Ali?"

A wave of laughter broke through the horsemen, soft rolling chuckles, deep in the chests of bearded men. Their horses edged forward, tails swishing away the flies. So hot.

"Everybody knows Sardar Ali. We are his men. We farm his lands."

Zia swung a hand around himself.

"All this, between the three mountain ranges, this valley and the next two are all Sardar's."

Zia swung his Kalashnikov back and over his shoulder, hanging it by the strap thus showing peaceful intent. The never still ponies dipped heads, stomped feet and swished tails.

"Yes, I too have met the Bear. I fought with him against the Talibs," said Sergy.

This appeared to impress the horsemen. They muttered and nodded to each other.

"Then you must come to my home, you and all your men, and the woman. We will roast young lamb for you. Come, what do you say Angleezi?"

"*Tashakur*, thank you very much. We can stop on our way back, but we need to move along now and get to the mountain. It is late in the climbing season and the weather changes quickly. We have only two weeks of climbing weather left."

Zia Pasha leaned forward, stared into the jeep, squinted his eyes, and smiled.

"Well then you must stop on your way back. You must stop and eat and tell us stories of your adventure."

Sergy nodded. "I would welcome the chance to visit a new friend in my favorite land."

"Then we see you in few weeks Angleezi."

Zia Pasha turned his horse slowly, and in unison the other men turned their mounts and followed. In the distance, a dust cloud hovered behind Abdul's jeep. Shaima threw the cigarette out the window. Zia turned around again and waved.

"Just ask for Zia Pasha, someone will direct you to my home."

Sergy waved back and nodded. The horsemen followed Zia, slow and steady, hoofs clopping in the sand and gravel. Zia summoned a rider to his side and leaned over to speak to the man. The man glanced back, and Zia grabbed his cloak in a fist and pulled him forward. A minute of chatter and the man rode off at a gallop, dust flying from his pony's hoofs. Her heart thrust up against her throat.

"Sergy, get in. Hurry. Zia has sent a rider to my father. He knows."

"What? Are you sure?" Sergy signaled with a hand winding over his head for his men to get in their jeeps.

"I think so. Zia has been to the fortress many times. He may be simply curious, or he may have recognized me or..."

She took a sip of bottled water and played with her hands, clicked one pink polished nail against another, then she twisted the deep blue lapis ring from her mother's jewelry box around her finger.

"Stupid. I told you do not stop here. You never listen. The rider will reach my father tonight. He will most certainly follow us."

"Well, hmmm. No worry. They will look for us on Nowshak and we will be much further inside the Wakhan Corridor. They can't find us, can they, where we will go?"

She trembled and looked up at clouds gathering at the jagged tips of black mountains.

♦ ♦ ♦

57

What Does an Elephant Know of Salt

Stepping from my tent into a bright morning filled with the comforting fragrance of fresh coffee, I heard Aziz crooning an old song that reminded me of my mother's hair reflecting the sun while she tended her window flower box and sang a song of heroes and giants and winter storms. I never learned those songs. Things happen. Life takes a man and burns him and then, as Baba once said, he is never quite a man again.

Aziz stopped his song and shouted for a man to fetch water from the stream. I bent and picked up some dirt, light brown and sparkling with flecks of granite and mineral. Genghis, Marco, and Timor all walked here so many years ago. Perhaps this same handful of dirt lay beneath their camps. It had an ancient feel to it, unlike the fresh black soil in Virginia, so new, as if God just bought it at the home improvement store and laid it down next to the dark waters of the Potomac.

A breeze stirred in the leaves of white birch trees spread along the stream. For a moment, I lost myself in memories of our cabin in the forest. Melissa laughing and jumping on our bed in the mornings. Jenny smiling so bright even on rainy days I felt her shine brighter than any sun.

"Come Omar, have some tea. What are you doing, holding dirt in your hand? Put that down and come here. There is cream and sugar for you westerners who cannot live without such extravagances. Here is honey. You should try the honey and tea, do not reach for the coffee, for only the tea will fasten your root to this land again. You'll feel this earth reach up and grasp you and pull you back to her bosom and speak to you in a voice you only heard as a boy."

"You are a poet, Aziz," I said.

"Yes, he has always had that talent. But his singing could wake a dead man from his eternal slumber."

Uncle emerged laughing, dressed like Crocodile Dundee with a vest like Baba's, black leather and gold stitched pockets.

"Yes, well, my father had a saying, what does an elephant know about salt,"

Aziz said. "Come, my overlarge Uncle. Come and have some tea."

Aziz handed a steaming cup to Uncle, who ran his hand over his forehead and pushed strands of silver hair back from his face.

"I think nephew, stick to your cooking, for your singing has chased away the birds and the worms have dug deeper into the ground. What do you say, Omar, how is his singing? Did you not rise from your bed this morning thinking that world had ended?"

"Do not listen to the big ox. You keep on singing every morning."

Natasha gave Uncle the chastising eye, emerging from her tent with her hair tied tight behind her head. "And you are just jealous because you cannot sing. I would love some tea Aziz please."

The crack of a rifle shot echoed between the hillsides a full second before the bullet smashed into the rocks at my feet. I stood there stunned until Uncle tossed me by the collar down the embankment of the stream. We scrambled for safety among the rocks and boulders while the camp roiled beneath a crescendo of gunfire. Bullets danced across the ground kicking boots, cups and plates up in the air. A propane tank exploded and flames shot into the sky. A yell from above, a whoop and holler, and another cascade of gunfire ricocheted across the rocks, pinning us to our hiding spot. I glanced at Natasha who cringed behind us, trembling.

"Do not move." The voice came from the hill. "Nobody move or we shoot. Men are coming to relieve you of your jewels and money."

"Stay down. Let me handle this," Uncle said. "Aziz sneak down in the river and get around them, perhaps we can flank them. Take my pistol." He handed over his gun and Aziz crawled down between boulders and slipped into the water.

"Hassan's men?" I said.

"Who knows? I should have posted guards." Uncle shook his head and let a few curses slip.

"Perhaps the IMU."

"IMU?" I said.

"An Islamic extremist group with links to Talibs. They have been impotent in the last ten years since the Tajik government routed them. Now they wander in small groups, robbing and kidnapping tourists."

"Bad luck," I said.

"Then again, they could be Hassan's men. Won't they just love finding the two of us here?" said Uncle.

"Yes, thrilled. Can we reach our guns?"

"Do not provoke them. Wait for Aziz to begin something if he can."

The gunfire ceased and I heard a man's boots crunching against gravel. Peeking up over my rock, I spotted a large rotund fellow carrying a Kalashnikov and wearing a faded brown turban.

"You may rise and come out from behind your rocks. If you turn around, you will see men across the river with guns aimed at you."

Uncle signaled for Natasha to hide between two large boulders, and then he and I stood together and strode into the camp. Brigands dressed in a haphazard collection of dirt-encrusted grays and browns descended from the hillside, rounded up our soldiers, and pushed them into a line.

Memories flashed of a tank and men lined up. The hair on my neck and along my arms tingled. I tasted a familiar bitterness in my mouth. The large fellow smiled, gun dangling in one hand, weathered skin dotted with bleached pink patches on his face and neck. A thick black mustache bristled above ingrained dirt and stubble. Not extremists, for they would have long beards. Shaving brought dire consequences for fundamentalists. I glanced around. Some had beards, and some did not in this mixed group of ragged men.

"You have cigarettes?"

Uncle shook his head. "I do not smoke."

"Good and bad. I do not smoke, but Abdullah smokes. It will disappoint him."

The man had one tooth in his mouth and he flashed this like a badge at us, nodding up and down as if he entertained thoughts of eating us without delay and merely wondered how many pounds of meat hung on our bones. I felt my Uncle tensing and hoped he had no ideas of jumping this man and taking his gun. The man must have felt it too, for he lifted the barrel and pointed the Kalashnikov at Uncle's belly. I heard hoofs clopping and from the bend of the mountain stepped a black stallion carrying a tall man, thick in the chest and shoulders, wearing a long black cloak and a turban above hawkish eyes and a hooked nose. He stopped his stallion behind the one-toothed man and gave us the same look as his friend. Sweat dripped down my back, my throat tightened.

"They have no cigarettes, Abdullah."

"Get the woman. She hides in the rocks by the stream." Abdullah said.

One tooth shuffled off to the stream and pulled Natasha from her hiding place. She yanked her arm out of his grasp, strode with her head high to a spot next to my Uncle, and took his arm.

"Your woman?" Abdullah said.

"Yes. Mine," Uncle said.

Abdullah looked her up and down and turned the stallion just a nudge and I caught sight of amber prayer beads in his right hand, near his saddle, while he held the Kalashnikov in his left.

"There is no law in these hills but mine. Do not rely on my generosity for your lives. Give me everything and you may go, otherwise, I will kill them first."

He nodded towards our men who stood emptying their pockets and removing watches and rings from their arms and fingers. "I will also take your woman since you are incapable of protecting her."

"What do you want with her? She is Russii, your wives will object," Uncle said.

It just then came to me that Abdullah spoke Farsi in our own dialect and therefore must have come from our own northern provinces.

"Don't worry. I will keep her for a few days, then I will send her back to Dushanbe or perhaps I will kill her. You are correct. My wives would object."

"I will give you everything you want but leave us our jeeps and the woman. We just want to get through the pass to Badakhshan. I am sure you know the place as you are Afghan like us," Uncle said.

"Like you? No, not like you. You are rich and stupid. Westernized Afghans, soft and fat. You will not survive here without your jeeps, your kerosene stoves, and your clean clothes. I will let you go, because I can see that you were once a soldier and years ago, I knew a man like you. But do not think you can follow us."

He spat a black wad of tobacco on the ground at Uncle's feet. "Your jeeps cannot climb mountains and your feet have grown delicate, like a woman's."

"You may not take her," Uncle said. He moved in front of Natasha.

"Is that so?" Abdul nodded to one tooth who swung the Kalashnikov fast, and like Baba's hands in the days of my youth, I only saw a blur and Uncle fell to the ground, a bleeding gash along the side of his head.

"You are no Afghan." I shouted. "You have no honor."

Dropping to a knee next to my Uncle, I felt for a pulse while Natasha kneeled and held a hand over the wound in his head. She cried and touched his cheek and mumbled something that I could not hear because of the roar in my ears and the visions of blood and snow dancing in my eyes.

"Silence dog. You have no right to say anything to me. You soft pampered thing. You are not even a man. Did you fight the Russii? I think not. Go home, coward. I can smell your fear even from this distance."

He turned his stallion round in circles and showered me with curses and fury, but all this had no effect on me, though perhaps it should have and there lay my shame, but I had no concern for anything other than the pulse still beating in Uncle's neck. I heard a gunshot and one of our men fell, the rest cursed and shouted their anger. The light brown dirt I had held in my hands now ran red but I did not care so much about that as I did my Uncle whose eyes rolled back into his head while I tore my sleeve and held it against his wound.

And so the brigand's voice trailed off into the distance and I barely noticed when they dragged Natasha away and then left, kicking up dust that swirled and settled on us while I held his head and shouted for help.

◆ ◆ ◆

58

Armon Travels Alone

He runs the palm of his hand back and forth against the edge of a sharp rock, cutting, slicing and with this action feels his own substance and assures himself that he is not just the shadow or reflection of the man kneeling in the dirt across the stream.

Blood drips and dries beneath the sun. He glances down, then turns back to where his twin shouts and cradles a man's head on his lap. Men run over and one dips a bucket into the stream just a few feet away, but Armon's camouflage gear blends in perfectly against the gray and brown hillside. He stretches his legs out and shifts his backside for comfort and waits to see what the twin will do. So far, he has shown only weakness, indecisiveness and empathy. These are the traits of a common man.

Armon Badil wants to see the other side, the side like his own so he can study it and in observing this dark aspect from an exterior vantage point perhaps, he can remember and find the source of them both. However, he has little time.

Sergy travels a day, perhaps two ahead, but Sergy has burdened himself with many men and a woman. Though Sergy has jeeps, he cannot travel at night. He will not know the calm of riding beneath the moon and stars. Nor can he take the high trails and travel the straight line.

The brigands leave the twin on his knees. They retreat quickly up the mountainside and vanish over the crest. He turns and walks an opposite trail that leads up and over the southern ridges. His horse stands down river, hidden in a cluster of alpine trees, face bent to sparse grasses, nibbling. He mounts and glances once back down the river where the twin mourns, then he rides south towards the mountains of his youth. He feels their call and the cool wind on his face and from somewhere past the great river Amu Darya he hears a soft voice calling.

59

A Soldier's Honor

Help me remove this cloth from my head and let me stand."
"You should rest a moment, Uncle. The bleeding has
stopped, but you look a little pale," I said.

He trembled a bit and reached up for the towel.

"It is not good for the men to see me on the ground. Get me up."

He stood there contemplating the camp. Men wandered, necks bent
with respect, picking up pieces of this and that and sifting through boots
kicked into piles, the best taken by the brigands. So we had men without
boots but for Afghans that is not unusual and they made the best of it
without complaint. They would buy new boots along the way.

Several men had wrapped in linen and buried our felled brother,
Jamal, who had an Afghan father and French mother. They lived in Paris
and I knew them well. They attended my wedding and Jamal's mother
gave Jenny lapis earrings and a gold bracelet. Jamal and I attended
Georgetown together and we laughed together, went to movies, and
had many dinners at our home. He helped me cut trees along the forest
edge and together we chopped them into firewood. Because of his
French goatee, we called him "Musketeer" and he loved those old
movies full of swashbucklers and damsels in distress.

Yet who could know that for all these years his destiny waited in this place for him to come and find it. A bullet just for him and his life ended in the space between one second and the next. I wondered what I might say to his parents. How might I justify taking him back into danger and when his mother's eyes looked up at me, what answer would I have then?

I kicked some dirt and tasted a sour coating on my tongue.

Our weapons remained hidden in the jeeps, which Abdullah's men did not find, or if they had, they did not steal for reasons that escaped my understanding. Uncle called it a matter of soldier's honor and left it there for me to mull over.

"What are you staring at boy?"

"Nothing." I looked away and kicked a pebble into the stream.

"I suppose you thought a knock on the head would do your old Uncle in?"

"No such thing entered my mind." I lied.

"Has Aziz returned?"

"No, Uncle."

"Then he will follow Abdullah and mark a trail for us. Get the men and the guns. We leave immediately."

I gathered the men and distributed two dozen Kalashnikovs and four banana clips per man. We followed Uncle up into the mountainside, some with shoes and some without. Each wielded a grim set to his jaw and often cursed the brigand and they named him Abdullah, the bird nose.

We had a long walk and the sun beat down on our heads. The men preferred, like me, the light skullcap which sat like a fuzzy cup on the head and let the cool mountain air-dry the sweat beaded on our brows.

We left seven men with the jeeps. The rest of us climbed and walked across the ridges and over the hills and up into the snowline where solitary conifers bent by wind and storm leaned south like old men beaten down by life.

The sun plunged behind the mountains and the air chilled. Blue night wrapped us in a frosted cloak. We followed scratches in the rocks left by Aziz, which Uncle pointed out and smiled like a father proud of his son's first steps.

Our men climbed and scrambled across the mountains as if born for it. I recalled the long rides with Baba and his troops, leather saddles creaking, wind snatching up sand and dashing it across our faces.

None spoke. Expressions remained grim, memories of a fallen comrade and prayers whispered by his grave.

Deep in the night, we crested a high ridge and stood in the snow. Some distance below, the oil lamps and torches of Abdullah's camp glowed while armed men stood along narrow paths and goats and chickens sauntered about, sleepwalking. Old-fashioned animal skin yurts and huts made of straw and mud sat near a stream and a pasture where horses shook their manes, snorted, and fed on long grasses.

"Guards on the hillsides, Commander." Aziz appeared from a group of rocks just behind us and gave Uncle a report, pointing out which bluffs held sentries. They whispered together for a moment, and then Uncle motioned for me to join them.

"What would you do?" Uncle said.

I suddenly wondered if Abdullah knew we would come for him. Had he planned it all along, his own death and that of his people? If so, what dark hand squeezed his heart?

A soldier's honor, Uncle said. What honor might we find in this? However, my Kalashnikov no longer hurt my shoulder, so the years had some effect. Then a lightheadedness came over me and I found the words spilling out from a dark well of turmoil inside. Like a stranger eavesdropping, I listened to myself talking in a hollow voice.

"Where are they holding Natasha?"

"There, in the large tent by the pasture, this side of the village," Aziz said.

"Then I would send men to a spot near that tent so when the shooting starts they might free and protect her. And I would send men to the far end of the ravine to push them towards us, and thus we can squeeze them from front and rear."

Baba's voice, soft thunder in the distance and my thoughts flew past these mountains to a faraway fortress where I knew he sat next to a fire and a chess table, alone.

"Tactics my son. It is all about tactics," he would say.

All those years and his constant efforts changed me after all. I recognized the change and I welcomed this evolution and held on to it, hugging it tight, for this alone might define me now that my girls lay buried in Virginia soil. I felt the tear fall hot against my cheek. I ignored it.

Aziz left with half the men and we spread out and descended from rock to rock, silent shadows in the moonlight. I looked to the right at the silhouette of a man who lifted a rifle to his face, rubbed the barrel against his beard and flashed me a grin and a nod. On my left, Uncle stood with Kalashnikov gripped to his chest, eyes burning bright in the moonlight.

I never shot a man, but no doubts crossed my mind and this disturbed me. I could only think my Jenny and Melissa's deaths had obliterated all sense of caution or self-preservation, or perhaps I longed for my end. And so I took up my Kalashnikov, aimed it at a man standing at the edge of the village, and waited.

◆ ◆ ◆

60

On the Glacier

She timed her motion to his breathing. Swing one arm. Stab a pole in the ice, step and slide, breathe and repeat. This rhythm pulled her forward over the glacier while a counter beat of apprehension grew inside.

Sergy stayed close on her heels, sometimes pulling even with her and flashing a smile. His cheeks blazing pink in the altitude. He often turned and shouted to keep the yaks moving or he made a joke to Luwenthal that threw her rhythm off and she had to stop and gaze at the cobaltite sky and the miles of perfect snow.

The glacier stretched like a field of white linen surrounded by a towering curtain of ice that sat just below white peaks, jagged, jutting and magnificent. She stuck a pole in the ice and surveyed the blue green apron of cliffs that ran around the entire glacier, encircling it like the walls of an ice rink.

"There." She pointed at the western ice face. "We make camp there. We find the entrance tomorrow when the sun comes up and travels directly above the big mountain to the west. A shadow on the mountainside will mark our entrance."

Sergy nodded and moved ahead. She pulled her pole out of the ice and followed in his tracks. She floundered, concentration scattering. He cast an enormous shadow and it grew long and ominous. Last time she came here, she followed a strikingly similar shadow. Baba led, she followed on Arad, and now every rock and ice flow reminded her and left her no peace of mind. The guilt of her actions almost too much to bear.

They set up camp along the ice wall. Sergy instructed Luwenthal to contact camp one, ten men they had left behind 2000 feet below to watch for Baba or any others that might approach. Sergy unpacked several battery packs, which he claimed would last for two weeks. They also packed small generators and these sprang to life, rumbling and sputtering. The sound reminded her of the thing in the cave and the thunderous gunfire that still reverberated in her head. She worried about the mountain and the secrets within. What terrible things might happen. Then she realized with sudden shocking clarity that none of them might leave this place alive.

♦ ♦ ♦

61

Captives

Wrecked tanks rested along the riverbank. Fat barrels pointed at the town where a crumpled old man shook a tambourine. A rag-clothed boy drummed on a tin can and a small monkey leaped and spun in the air. A one-legged man juggled pomegranates and a man with muddy eyes shouted out his inventory of walnuts and pistachios and hot kabobs served on a stick and wrapped in flat bread.

Children puttered about Mac and tugged on his clothes while their parents stood back and watched with wary eyes. The very next minute, shutters slammed on merchant stalls, burqa clad women shooed their children behind pale blue doors, and grizzled old men shuffled into narrow side alleys. Sergeant Black cursed and Mac turned to see why.

Dust settled, flies buzzed all around, and Mac reached for his belt where an empty holster greeted his fingers. From both ends of the alley, Kalashnikov toting men in baggy traditional garb and black turbans approached them. One man stepped forward and put his gun up, resting it on his shoulder.

"Bismillah Rahman, eh Rahim. Allah is most merciful," he said. "Good day, gentlemen. We prayed for your return. Allah rewards the devoted."

He spoke flawless English and a smile flickered across his face. Laughter rippled through the ranks of his men. Guns pointed with aggressive intent.

"You have mistaken us for someone else," said Mac.

"No, I don't think so," said the man. "Hassan Khan has requested the honor of your presence and as you can see, replying in the negative is not an option."

Mac agreed about the options when he realized Black and Harris had also hidden their guns in the jeep. Left without viable alternatives, Mac followed the turbaned men towards the river. They put Mac, Harris, and Black on mules, the reins controlled by their captors. The men rode fine horses, surrounded the captives and crossed a cracked concrete bridge back into Tajikistan past unconcerned border guards. They continued for three hours in a southerly direction. Turning east, they rode for another two hours.

The sun showed no mercy, its heat slamming down directly on their bare heads. The skin on the inside of Mac's legs burned, his lips cracked, and a raging thirst plagued him. Their captors refused them water. They rode until they reached fields of thick wild grass surrounded by steep hillsides, and beyond this sat a village nestled against soaring gray cliffs. At least two dozen yurts reflected sunlight from animal-hide roofs. Between the yurts, children laughed and scampered away from a shouting woman while an old man hobbled along with a bundle of sticks tied to his back. Younger men leaned against fences, smoking and chatting while a thin man sat in the shade of a twisted tree. A small prayer rug beneath his feet and beads in his hand. Goats, chickens, and sheep wandered through the village and the smallest children played with these, pushing and prodding them along with sticks.

Pulling them from the mules, their captors shoved them through the village towards a huddle of large yurts sitting next to a stream. Across the water, a hazy meadow languished like a vision of lost

Eden, diffused rays of sunlight filtering through birch trees and warming a multitude of yellow and orange highland flowers where flocks of butterflies beat pale wings against a honeysuckle breeze. Next to this perfect meadow, a slender thread of water fell from high cliffs to a clear pool where large fish swam in place as if unwilling to move forward or back, content with their little piece of paradise.

They led Mac and his friends to the last yurt. Two armed men stood outside the small door and two others circled the perimeter and more sat and chatted on dark red carpets at the riverbank. Their captors gathered while the speaker went inside. He came out and nodded.

A foot against his back sent Mac sprawling into the yurt. He heard his two partners fall next to him. Their captors pulled him to his knees and faced him towards a wooden platform where a tiny man sat on an elegant carpet festooned with thick velvet shams and pillows. He stroked a long white beard with one small hand while in the other he passed brown beads on a string. His lips moved in silent prayers, which he finished and then blew over himself as if blowing dust off his embroidered cloak.

Two enormous men stood on either side of him, baggy pants and thin vests over hairless, sweating chests. Mongols, thought Mac, as he ogled the long-curved swords hanging at their sides. The sight of this wizened Aladdin and his storybook guards almost seemed absurd. Mac stifled a chuckle, barely. The situation sobered when one man smashed something against Mac's head, knocking him to the dirt.

Unknown minutes passed before he recovered and struggled to his knees. He glanced around. Rugs and tapestries hung from wooden wall beams, a shining samovar, a long rifle he recognized as a British Enfield, notorious in the 19th century for decimating invaders. Two girls bustled in and out dressed in *hijab*, all but their eyes covered, carrying teacups and trays of white sugared almond candy. An old hound stared at them from the little man's feet, flies buzzing all around them both.

The past three thousand years had not touched these people. Only the gun divided them from their bow-wielding ancient ancestors.

"The mighty Hassan Khan, the Sultan of the south and descendent of Darius the Great and Xerxes the Mighty."

The announcement came from the English speaker who stood on Mac's left. Mac nodded. Next to him, Harris squatted on his knees, his face impassive as a brick. Black kneeled on the right out of Mac's vision, but he could hear the small man shuffling and grunting on his skinny knees.

"CIA?" Hassan said. He fingered the beads and did not look square into his prisoner's eyes, rather, he kept a dialogue with his beads, counting, massaging and chanting some solitary phrase, interrupting himself only to utter, in contemptible fashion, a few words.

"Police, your highness," Mac said.

"I think CIA," Hassan said.

"No, sir. Not CIA. Task Force on Terrorism," said Mac.

Hassan whispered his prayer, passed his beads, and stared at Mac. He stopped and blew again over himself, sliding a hand down his white beard, smoothing it against his chest.

"We have information that a group of heavily armed men passed through my land. Are these your men?"

"No... Your highness."

The beads continued to move through his fingers and his thin lips whispered loud enough for Mac to hear him repeat the same phrase endlessly. Some sort of religious chant, no different from Father Dodd's sermons, really. Or perhaps more like the choir. Yes. No. Mac shook his head, still foggy and not thinking straight.

He stopped the movement of beads and looked up at Harris, boring holes with blue eyes behind gold-rimmed glasses. A strange juxtaposition in this, a world lost in time. Mac considered the irony but dismissed it as simplistic and futile. One could not measure time with human senses and human logic. Time happened, all at once, like a rush of the wind, each atom perhaps the life of a single man or a single planet and then, to repeat itself all over again, the cycle of life and death, endless and eternal. Mac's forehead blistered. Sweat stung his eyes.

"You, the big one. You look familiar. Do I know you?"

Harris shook his head. "My first time out of America."

"Will be your last, CIA man."

The beads moved again, and he whispered his prayer and Mac felt himself hypnotized by it all, heat broiling inside the yurt, sweat falling from his brow down over nose and cheeks. Then he heard chains jangling and something heavy dragging through dirt. A big man dragged an old English town stockade into the yurt and set it down in front of Hassan. Rusted chains hung on thick wooden beams ingrained with dried blood.

"Take the small one," Hassan said.

The two big guards snatched Sergeant Black up and shoved his head into a hole, shutting the top beam down and trapping him. They stuck his hands through two more holes and clasped them with iron bracelets. His legs they left to dangle in the dirt. Black looked desperate, like when Father Dodd caught him taking from the collection tray instead of depositing. He licked his lips and twisted his neck to get a look at Mac. Mac nodded.

What would he tell Constance if he made it back without her brother? Constance with her long white legs and pouty lips. Hell, he probably would not make it back either. Somebody else would have to tell Constance. His tongue swelled and his heated brain skittered from one thought to another, nonsensical absurdities, irrelevant details lost and floating in a dark void.

"I am aware of my son's assassination. He died beneath the rubble of our Embassy as the result of a plot by CIA and Afghan militia. Perhaps you are not happy with Iraq and Afghanistan, you wish to conquer Tajikistan as well? You call us terrorist and yet you invade our countries, kill our men and women, murder our children, lay waste to our land and steal our resources. How would you feel if a foreign army invaded America? I tell you now. Your demon armies will never set foot in my country. Do you hear me, CIA? Do not expect any mercy from me. You are the real terrorists of the world, you Americans."

One big turbaned fellow took hold of Black's right hand. Hassan passed his beads one by one, whispered and nodded to the big man. Fingers snapped like kindling in a silence disturbed only by Hassan's whispers and Black's grunts. The hand lasted perhaps thirty seconds, five fingers, six seconds each, Mac calculated and then thought of Constance and running naked with her in the moonlight and Father Dodd, now white haired as Hassan, and just as devout. He remembered the slap of the ruler against his palms and the twinkle in Father Dodd's eyes while Mac bled.

Black did not break, at least not right away. It took his other hand and those five fingers snapping in the dead air, and only then did he blubber and mumble what he knew about Sergy, the girl, and the mountain.

The prayer beads stopped at the mention of the mountain, and when Black mentioned a treasure, Hassan's eyes widened and Mac noticed how fiercely those dark orbs glittered. Hassan nodded to the big man. Big man pulled a pistol from his belt and walked behind Black. One shot in the leg, the next in the buttocks, and the third shot in the back, and Black breathed out and then hung motionless. A blow to Mac's head turned it all to darkness.

♦ ♦ ♦

62

Rescuing Natasha

They died, bodies twisting in a storm of bullets that struck from every direction. Our men had toted the 50mm across the mountains, and now it tore holes through tents and mud walls.

Within seconds, the village vanished beneath a cloud of gun smoke and I saw nothing. I heard only a few lingering screams that sounded strangely like the bleating of sheep. An image formed my mind. Jenny with a smoking hole in her forehead, and I turned my gun towards the sky, held the trigger down, and emptied it into the pale blue of a new morning. Uncle shouted and the gunfire died slowly, like fireworks petering out during New Year celebration at Baba's fortress.

I do not know if any of my bullets had hit, but I thought probably some had, and this had no effect on me. Instead, I pushed my thoughts towards long buried desires. How proud Baba would be on this morning and then I knew he would not because the smoke cloud lifted and I saw women and children and goats, sheep and even chickens sprawled and silent in the dirt.

Revenge for Jamal, I thought, but that helped little.

We found nothing alive. Abdullah had met his end at the hands of the men sent to save Natasha. They now stood guard outside and nodded to me as we entered to find her with a blanket wrapped around her body. She saw Uncle and fairly leaped into his arms.

"It's about time," Natasha said. "I knew you would come."

I turned for modesty's sake and heard her voice muffled against his chest. He spoke Russian to her, and she murmured, and I heard them kiss, so I walked out and looked up into the eastern mountains and watched the sky turn nine shades of sapphire and the sun peek out. The air warmed and the stench of death arose. Our men walked like shadows floating through a morning mist. I suddenly heard Baba's voice as if he stood next to me in this smoldering village of death.

"Do you see God down there, my son?"

I remembered the suffering of my people. Their blood and screams and the children wandering aimlessly in the swirling dust, looking for a father or mother that could no longer hold them in both arms and wipe away their tears. I remembered and I bent over with the pain of it, as if a hand reached inside me and squeezed. I felt the guilt of all my sins in that one solitary moment.

◆ ◆ ◆

- Part VI -
The Mountain

63

Shaima's Doubts

I have to do this. Right?" She shivered. "I'm not a bad person. I want to be free. Baba will understand. Right? I must escape these mountains. There is nothing but a hard life to look forward to in Afghanistan."

She had not meant to say it aloud, much less raise her voice. She glanced at Sergy.

"Of course you must, Princess. If you do not, your father will marry you to a stranger. You would not do well in that situation. Sometimes we have to fight to change our destiny."

"Shut up, Sergy." She turned around and slapped him in the chest.

He smiled, always a gentleman and yet so violent. She had to be careful with him and his men. She would limit the number of men she would take inside, hoping the oracle would listen to reason. Nothing could go wrong. Especially if her father found out. She had to get in and out fast. Sergy would get his photos and proof, and then they would head back down the mountain. She bit her lip and sniffled.

It seemed so simple and clear back in Moscow. Love's delirium took her to heights from where she wished for things that today's cold reality told her could never happen. She knew this now, but she kept leading them to a place from which they would likely never leave.

She led them through a thin chasm, barely wide enough for a man. Sheer walls of snow and black rocks soared high over their heads. Another breath caught in her chest, tightening. She coughed. Somewhere she read coughing helped release tension, so she coughed a few more times. The tension remained.

Two hours later, they arrived at the blue tunnel. Like a glass vase on its side, the ice walls formed a tube structure wide enough for two men to enter side by side. She led them in and smiled at the exclamations of wonder from Sergy and the men.

"Did your people make this bridge? Amazing," Sergy said.

"Silly. This has been here for billions of years. Only God could make this."

Sergy stopped and took a sample of the ice, placing it in a small thermos and handing this to one of his men to store in a pack. Outside the glass walls, columns of rock stretched in haphazard directions. Jagged ice formations and pale crystals poked up from below, and long icicles hung all around them. Massive knife blades of black stone thrust skywards. A chasm yawned beneath them, wide, sheer walled, and deep. The ice tunnel provided the only means to cross over this deep gash in the earth.

"The crevasse beneath us is bottomless." She repeated Baba's speech from ten years ago, so many of his words coming back on this ever more familiar mountain. "It stretches, they say, to the other side of the world."

"Amazing," Sergy said. He asked a man for the camcorder, but within minutes the mechanisms froze and Sergy cursed and fumed about Russian craftsmanship. They walked gingerly through the tunnel for standing on glass over a sheer drop can twist one's nerves and she barely kept her smile hidden when she noticed Sergy reaching out to the wall every few steps as if to catch himself from falling.

They left the ice tunnel and she walked out to the edge of the mountain. The sun had just crested the eastern summits and now its brilliance cast long jagged shadows westward across the glacier.

"We have to keep moving higher. Stay to the left, follow me."

She led them through a slim crack in a wall of white ice that opened to a massive crevasse surrounded by sheer cliffs with a sliver of blue sky above. The wind picked up and whistled through the gap. She heard a voice, stopped and looked around, but saw nothing.

Then the mountain shook, tumbling boulders and snow down into the crevasse. They scrambled from side to side, dodging pieces of ice and rock. They lost a man to a long sliver that fell like a needle, stabbing him through the collar, chest and belly and then into the ground. He stood with his mouth open as if to speak and then slid slowly down the needle to his knees and died in a widen-ing pool of blood. They could not break or dislodge the long ice shaft from the ground, so they had to leave him there, on his knees.

Sergy crumpled his knit hat in hands, wringing it like a sponge. She looked away from the horrible sight and gazed up into the high reaches of the gorge. At the top of its sheer walls, wisps of snow danced against a deep blue sky, reminding her of tiny angel wings shimmering up the length of her tower on a starlit night. The wail of the wind through the gorge took her back through time, and she once again heard the cold air moan as it rushed through the hallways of a distant fortress.

Memories of a blood-stained wooden post in a dusty field danced in her mind's eye for a moment. A sweat broke across her forehead and bridge of her nose. Then she saw something. A shadow moving fast along the top edge of the crevasse. She stumbled forward, realizing that with every step she advanced closer to her own death. What did it matter where she died, here or tied to a stake or at the edge of a heavy curved blade in the hands of a man with a thick black beard and wild eyes? A lifetime prison beneath the burqa or death at the hands of an extremist frothing at the mouth with the desire to kill and die. Only these alternatives waited for her without Sergy. The closer she got to the entrance, the tighter this dread gripped her.

"What's wrong, Princess?"

"Nothing."

She led them around a sharp corner of blue ice and Sergy let out a yell. He rushed over to a granite lion the height of three men. Carved from one massive block of black granite, encased within a thick sheathing of ice, the great lion posed as if ready to pounce.

"Look at this. The perfection of this smooth, curved surface. This entire lion cut from a single rock and then polished to this... and the eyes. Are those sapphires or diamonds? Look at the size of those jewels. It is impossible. Nothing like this exists anywhere in the world."

Sergy darted around and under the lion, touching carefully, as if at any second this treasure might crumble and vanish in a cloud of dust. He shouted for a still camera and snapped pictures while she stood and watched. She had to smile despite the cold, the dread, and the voices in her head.

"Come on, Sergy. There's a lot more to see."

He followed, subdued, looking around like a child in wonderland. She hoped he would stay like that inside the mountain. The trail twisted back and forth, always climbing higher up the mountain. She rubbed her gloves over her exposed skin and breathed into her cupped hands. They kept on until a gap in the rocks. Sunlight streamed in and warmed the air. She shook her rucksack off and leaned against a boulder for shelter from the wind.

"We can rest here."

"Only for a few minutes." Sergy said.

"You're eager to die," she said.

He glanced at her. He looked puzzled, as if she had joked with him all this time. She took her thermos from the rucksack and poured coffee into the top.

"How much further?" Sergy said.

"Not far. Look up there."

She pointed to a spot high on the east face, just past a wisp of a cloud. He nodded and sat next to her. They shared the cup, passing it back and forth in unspoken rhythm.

The men gathered and set their rucksacks down. Some took out oxygen tanks and took their measure, passing the tank to the next man. Others ate energy bars and some chewed tobacco and spit angry dark stains on her pristine ice. Strange, she had not thought of it as her ice until this moment, but now she did, and the stains angered her. Her face burned in the cold air.

She gripped the coffee cup tighter and stared hard at the men, but they ignored her. She imagined the stains coming to life, a raven, a bear, a great black cat, and she shivered. Sergy put an arm around her shoulders and she nestled against his body and tried not to cry.

◆ ◆ ◆

64

Into the Mountain

L eave your guns here." She pointed to a group of rocks near the
entrance. "No weapons allowed inside the mountain."

"No weapons?" Sergy said.

"It would take years to find your way through the labyrinth. You'd
die of thirst or hunger long before that."

He approached her. His blue eyes locked on her face. He liked to
do that and get up close and make her lean back. She pushed him
away.

"You've only been here once," he said.

"I got us this far. I won't go further with weapons."

He flipped the headlamp on, set the little automatic and his
Walther PPK on the ice, and took a few steps into the cave. A minute
later, he emerged.

"Do as she said. Put your weapons in a bag behind the rocks there.
We keep our picks, hammers, rations and everything else. I will mark
our trail as we move through."

She shrugged and kneeled, retrieved her headlamp and strapped it on over her woolen cap. Heaving the rucksack across her shoulders, she walked into the cave. One man said something. She did not hear the words, but the cackle of laughter progressed down the passage. She stopped and turned around.

"No talking. No reason to let them know we are here. Not unless you all want to die today instead of tomorrow," she said.

"Wait. Look at this," Sergy said. He had his face pressed to the rock wall where his lamp illuminated faded pictograms of dwarf-sized men yielding spears and bows against giants.

"Here, drawings of giants remarkably similar to the humanoid in the cave. I have never seen cave drawings like this before. This shows a great deal more skill than it should, considering the chronology of human evolution in this area."

"They are the stonecutters, the original peoples, the small ones. They fought a long war against the giants. They won with my people's help. Stories say they pushed the giants east, into the Himalayas. I always thought of them as just a myth, but... I do not know anymore. That thing in the cave that took your man might be one of their descendants."

"Your stonecutters could be a lost tribe of Neanderthal lineage. Look at the prominent brow ridge and the large wide nose. Give me the camera," Sergy said.

A man handed him a Nikon. He snapped photo after photo in rapid fire.

"There are giants in the Bible, a tribe of Canaanites, east of Jordan. Some cave drawings depict them, but none so clearly as these. Also, a tribe of Kushites, south of Palestine near Hebron. David slew one named Goliath."

Sergy mumbled more to himself than anyone else. The excited ramblings of an archeologist with a new treasure.

"Are you ready to go on?"

She knew the diagrams. Baba had told her all about the stonecutters. Soon Sergy would learn what he needed to know. And then what? What did he expect her to do? Could she do what she had intended? Her doubts multiplied as they stood in the dark with headlamp beams crisscrossing over the black granite and ice.

"I suppose I can take a tracing later. It's not like these will go anywhere."

"Yes, you can come back later and get tracings or whatever you need. If we live that long."

Using markings left by ancient masons, she found her way through dozens of false passages and dead ends. Descending at a near 25-degree angle past many small tunnels and caverns, she kept to one recognizable passage lined with luminescent sparkles of a remarkable green mineral that had Sergy baffled. He ran his thick hands over it, picked at it with his icebreaker, took samples while making excited faces.

"Look here, Princess. Just look at what may be an entirely new species of bioluminescent algae. Maybe they can call it 'Volkov's night algae'. Yes?"

She sighed and nodded. She experienced the algae blooms on her trip with Baba.

Ugh. Baba.

The thought of her father made her stomach churn with anxiety. Did that rider go to him and if so, when would he arrive?

Water trickled into rivulets. The walls turned wet and the floor more slippery as they descended. A man fell and muttered. She had to stop several times to signal for silence. When they reached a wide cavern with a dark pool of water in the middle, she stopped, unleashed her rucksack and sat it on a rock.

"Keep your voices down. Come here, Sergy." She pulled him over to sit down next to her.

"You must tell your men to walk silently from now on. There are guards and other... things down here."

She looked up into his square face, her lamp flashing in his eyes.

"If I told you before you'd want to bring weapons, so I couldn't tell you."

"That's great. Will they attack us?"

She stared at the dark water, still and mirror-black, thin traces of green phosphorescence along the edges. Memories flashed of her father wielding a great scimitar over the bare heads of prisoners and his men lined up with guns, waiting for his word. His secrets, his world, all this belonged to him. These thoughts cooled her blood and sent shivers up her back.

"They will kill us all. How do you think this place has remained a secret for thousands of years?"

He directed the men to remove their metal crampons. She got up and led them down the passage. The temperature warmed as they descended. She took off the heavy parka and stuffed it in the rucksack, leaving her sweater and cap on. They came to a place that smelled of death, a wide circular cavern with a churning vapor cloud billowing from the ground.

"Stay along the edges. Do not go near the cloud. There's a big hole there."

The cloud covered more than half the cavern so she could see nothing on the other side, but she knew the passage she needed.

"From here we can go to the city or the crypt."

"The crypt. I can get the proof I need and we will get out of here. After that you can talk to your oracle and get permission to enter the city."

"She will never give you permission. Not unless you promise not to leave the city. No one may enter and then leave, not unless..."

"Unless what?"

"Not unless you are a member of an old family such as," she paused for a moment and turned around to face him in the dark, "such as my family. You would have to marry me and even then, your men could never leave. Only you and I, and that is not a guarantee. You would have to earn the trust of the people."

She pivoted away from him. She did not want to see his reaction. Nor did she have time. A low deep growl and a flash of white swept past her and then the whispers from every direction that she heard more with her mind than with her ears. She reached back for his hand and ran, pulling him along.

"Invaders." Voices echoed the words down the passageways. She feared they would not get the chance to speak to the oracle.

"Run!" she said.

He did. Behind them, the growls grew to roars. A man screamed. Sergy stopped and turned. She pulled his hand, but he would not move. Then she saw them.

Long, lean cats ripped into the men, knocking them down like bowling pins. The cats should have been on the other side of the mountain during the day. They never wandered free this way.

"I'll marry you," he said.

"Too late. Run!"

She led. He followed. They slipped and stumbled down the wet passage. Screams and rapid footsteps came from behind, but she dared not turn to see how many men survived the attack. The whispers faded, but the growls did not. She hoped defenders had not yet blocked the way forward.

"Hurry, we can hide in the crypt."

The passage dipped at a steep angle and she grasped at jutting rocks for support as she ran. Then she gave up and just let herself slide, pushing with hands and feet, tumbling and rolling until she burst into the cavern and there, stretched across the cave, a stone wall and in that wall sat the huge wooden doors that led to the crypt.

She heard Sergy behind her, cursing and grunting in the dark. She heard no one else. She stole a glance and here he came, tumbling into her, alone. No cats. Silence in the passage, only the trickle of water and the crackling of torches burning high along the walls.

Sergy picked her up in one arm and ran down to the cavern floor. He made for the doors, opened them and slipped inside. A roar from outside and a weight thrust against the door. They stood there breathing hard.

"Why didn't you tell me?" The words blew out on the edge of his ragged breath as he leaned against the doors, holding them closed with his bulk.

"We need those weapons. We can't fight these animals with our bare hands."

"I tried to tell you, but…"

"But what? You said nothing about tigers or panthers or whatever those things are." He pushed against the door. The cat roared outside.

"My men, my poor men. They had families. What do you want me to tell their wives and children?"

"I'm sorry, Sergy. I hoped they would let us pass. I did not think they would attack us with me in the party. At least not without warning us first."

"What now? We can't get out this way."

She slid down against the door. "I don't know."

"I have to get something to brace this door." He looked around. She sensed him tensing, and then his breath stopped.

◆ ◆ ◆

65

Magic Words

In the cavern men lay strewn about, dark lumps in the darker underworld. Iron and smoke particles drift in an angry cloud, unable to escape. Tight, claustrophobic, yet strangely comforting. He unfolds from his vantage point and sneaks down the rocks.

The cats dash away in pursuit of Sergy and Shaima. Three powerful leopards, thick-furred and fast. They do not stop to taste their kills.

Squatting, he feels for a pulse. Nothing. He moves to the next man. No need to feel. The torn throat and glassy eyes say enough. He sees the cat just one instant before it sees him. They eye each other. Cat jaws drip dark blood. A memory flashes of a tall man chanting.

Magic words.

The cat leaps, but Armon's blade is fast and his strength is uncommon.

Magic words.

He matches the cat's speed with his own and twists, slashes twice, and stabs deep. The leopard jaws snap shut on empty air.

He takes the smallish leopard by the neck and slams it against the wall, pinning it with an arm under the chin. Claws rip at him, tearing the temperature resistant carbon fiber down to the armored vest. He stabs deep, eviscerating the beast, releasing the innards to fall on the ground. The cat paws the air once, twice, opens its mouth, but no sound comes out. It pants a few quick breaths and then the light in its eyes flickers and dies. He releases and the cat slides to the ground.

Sergy's men litter the ground. A cat growls further ahead. He slaps the knife against the rock wall. The leopard charges from around the bend and leaps. He crouches low and slices up with a long blade that works like a short sword. Entrails spill out and the cat tumbles down on its side, eyes wide, panting. He moves on.

He checks himself for damage. Not a scratch.

Magic words.

Long tapered stalactite columns drip water. Breathtaking curtains of limestone give the cavern the appearance of a cathedral. A rough-hewn stone wall stands at one end of the cavern, and within the wall sit two immense arched doors. He takes the goggles off and slips them into the backpack.

A snow-white leopard larger than any of the others paces in front of the doors. Armon backs into the passage, scrapes his knife along the rocks, and waits. The cat runs past him and stops. He strikes, leaping on its back and slashing twice across the neck and then stabbing it just behind the front legs, up and in and twisting the blade, ripping through muscles. The leopard collapses, still as the rocks.

Armon has never felt more alive.

♦ ♦ ♦

66

Only the Oracle May Enter

W hat is it Americans say? Oh my God," Sergy said. "It is simply, a wonder. Magnificent."

Parallel lapis columns at least thirty feet tall led in rows down a long, wide hallway. Gold and emerald engraved marble floors lay between the columns, while a huge engraving of a leopard done in silver and emerald hung on the wall, torch light playing on its velveteen skin. At the far end of the long room, perhaps fifty yards from where they leaned against the doors, between two huge lapis columns sat a massive green sarcophagus, Egyptian in design, inlaid with rubies, lapis and emerald.

"Alexander," Sergy whispered.

"His son brought him from Egypt. The Oracle said it took thirty years to find his body and thirty more to bring back."

"His son? His son died very young," said Sergy.

"Not that son. The huntress Nimah bore him twins, a boy and a girl. The descendants of Alexander and Nimah also bear twins with uncommon regularity. You may learn the history if we live long enough."

"I love history," he said. "I could study history for the rest of my life and be happy." Sergy slid to the ground and sat next to her. The cats no longer scratched and growled.

"I don't hear them out there," she said.

"At least for right now."

They faced each other in the soft glow of gas lanterns set along both walls.

"Shall we go have a look at the crypt?" Sergy said.

"Not unless you want to die. You will get no closer than this. The room is a trap. The floor falls into a chasm and you have no rope. Only the Oracle may go there. A door in the back leads to her private rooms."

"What? Why bring us here? Why didn't you tell me?"

"You wanted to *see* the crypt. Take pictures. You have the camera in your pack. I did not bring you here to desecrate or to steal. You wanted this so terribly much, so here we are. Your proof must be pictures."

He sat there for a time before speaking.

"Eight men dead for nothing but pictures. It cannot end this way."

He listened with his ear to the door. Apparently satisfied, he turned back and stared straight ahead for a long minute. Then she felt his hand on hers and she rested her face on his shoulder.

He looked in the pack. "No camera."

"I will talk to her. We can still get your proof if she will allow it. I'll talk to her for you, Sergy." She reached up and touched a hand to his cheek. He kissed it.

"I need to see Alexander's remains. I need a sample for carbon dating and testing."

"I'll get you one, but not now. We must get out of here. Then, I think I must come back alone. Perhaps I can get a sample in a day or two while you wait outside. You can't come to the city or they will kill you."

"Even if I marry you?"

"Well, maybe if."

He chuckled and put an arm around her shoulders.

"How are we to get out of here?"

"I don't hear the leopards," she said.

He stood up and pressed his head against the door. "Stand back."

She moved behind him. He cracked the door open and looked out.

"They're gone. I don't know where but let's get out of here."

She took his hand and they ran.

♦ ♦ ♦

67

Armon Observes

D on't stop," she says.

They run hand in hand until they stumble over the dead leopard. They give each other a look.

"What happened here?" says Sergy.

"I don't know. Maybe one of your men killed the cat."

She shrugs, takes his hand and scampers up the passage.

Armon follows, blending into the darkness. His thick neoprene soles ensure quiet passage through the mountain. They panic, slipping and sliding, the girl leading. They run for long minutes that feel like hours.

Sergy looks for marks he chiseled in the wall on the way down. He appears unable to recognize his own marks, but the girl seems to know the way. When they reach the cave entrance, they stand with hands on knees, bent over and panting. He senses something following. Hiding behind a black boulder, Armon observes unseen.

Sergy picks up a pistol and then turns back to the cave.

"I think someone is following us," Sergy says. He checks the gun and crouches in the cave entrance, a gleam in his eyes. Shaima pulls on Sergy's arm.

"Come on, Sergy. We must go. You're not safe here."

Sergy peers into the cave for a moment, his eyes moving from side to side. Then he relaxes a bit but does not move away.

"Yes. I must contact the Colonel and camp one. We need those men."

She looks shocked, her face twists in obvious pain, but she does not relinquish her grip on his arm.

"Come Sergy. You cannot shoot anybody here. You promised."

Sergy nods and runs his fingers through her hair, pulls her in and kisses her on the mouth.

The day has passed and moonlight turns everything a pale and lonesome blue. They put their parkas on and stand there just a moment, hand in hand.

Armon thinks they look... majestic.

They go back towards the camp far below. A brisk wind picks up. Armon waits for the thing behind him to reveal itself. Nothing comes, but he hears feet shuffling, whispers, and then silence. Then two women dressed in brown leathers with bows in hand emerge from the darkness. Framed in the shadow of the far passage. Small in stature with elegant pale features, they bend their hooded heads together and whisper in perfect Dari.

"I tell you it was her."

"No, it couldn't be. Her father would be with her."

"I know it was her. We must tell the oracle. Perhaps she is a prisoner."

They vanish back into the tunnel. He has no time for them now. He leaves the cave, climbs and follows Sergy from the heights of the glacial plateau.

They arrive back in the camp late that night and the men greet Sergy with shouts until they hear news of their fallen comrades. After the men listen to Sergy, the circle of darkly bundled individuals breaks apart and they trickle like lost creatures back to their warm caves and out of the cold bitter wind that has risen in just those few moments. Silence pervades the camp, and only Sergy's voice drifts as he talks on the satellite phone.

Armon finds a spot above Sergy's camp. In between some ice-encrusted rocks, just a few yards from a small cave where he stashed his pack and horse. A trail from the other side of the cave winds down and through a ravine back towards a narrow gorge leading to this place.

He wraps a thick sleeping bag around himself and settles in, watching strings of light in Sergy's camp glitter and tremble in the wind. Just before he falls asleep, he catches movement on the far side of the glacier. Small dark shadows shift against the glacier wall. He gets up to investigate.

He climbs back to the edge of the ice curtain and begins the long circuitous route around the plateau. The ethereal landscape glows silver and blue beneath stars and moon as he thinks about how close he must be to the orphanage and perhaps the cave of the tall man with the magic words. The proximity of his past raises a sudden gut twisting apprehension.

However, this night holds something more, something dark and malevolent. He hears it all around him, whispering and laughing, beckoning him towards sharp edges and long ice flows that appear as waterfalls frozen in time. Their otherworldly beauty a wondrous attraction to a swift and certain death. Now the wind blusters with fantastic force, as if to knock him loose from the high rocks and send him tumbling.

He pulls his crampons off, stashes them inside his small rucksack and drinks some water. He unwraps a protein bar and eats slowly, all the while turning and searching the shadows for whatever hides there, watching him.

After another hour of travel along the ice, he arrives at a point above and to the right of the shadows he spotted from Sergy's camp. The sound of footsteps, crampons crunching and whispers. The wind drowns the sounds for a moment. He moves for a better vantage point.

Down below, men in black and white camouflaged parkas make their way through a slender gorge to a large stand of tall alpine trees somewhere just beyond the glacier. He can see the very tops of the trees and this draws him forward, climbing, sliding along the ice flows until a stunning vision opens up, shimmering in the moonlight.

The valley hides in a deep depression surrounded by icy peaks. Throughout this pristine forest, steam rises over the trees and dissipates into the air, most likely from vast underground hot springs that give both water and warmth to this strange place. A steaming river runs through the center of the valley and in the distance, deer wander and mountain sheep, and giant goats called Markhor sleep standing in high crags, and he shakes his head and looks again, hardly believing. The vision remains.

Amazingly, in this high mountain range only footstep from the Himalayas sits this small, perfect valley. Only these few men seem to know of it, and now they camp, setting their tents against the tree line and gathering firewood. One man stands out against the rest, tall and wide shouldered. His face hides within the parka hood, but his eyes glitter in the reflection of ice and moonlight. He gives orders, stands to one side and stomps like a bull while another man whispers in his ear. A thick beard hangs out of his parka hood. Reminiscent of a picture in a book Armon read inside a cave on the other side of the world.

A tingle raises the hairs along his neck. He crawls along the rocks, moving closer to the big man, close enough to hear the two men's conversation.

"No, tell the men not to kill her. She has betrayed us, but only I can decide her fate," says the big man.

"Allah be praised that she lives," said the smaller man.

"You don't understand. She betrayed us for this Russii."

"Shall I prepare the men to attack tonight?"

"Not in the dark. We will attack as the sun rises behind us, blinding them. They have twice as many men. I will not waste mine. Make certain the men do not shoot her. Also, make certain they know that not one of these invaders may leave here alive. No prisoners."

"Yes, excellency."

"Thank Zia Pasha for me as well when you see him. Without his keen eyes, we would not know of this."

"I will see to it, Excellency."

The tingle spreads along Armon's neck to his arms as he listens to the big man's voice. That voice bothers with a familiarity that pulls on something deep inside, as if the man's voice comes from his own stomach. Then he spots something in the tree line, a fog bank perhaps, or a low-flying cloud. The big man spots the movement as well and points.

"Purdill, look over there," said the big man.

"What is it, Excellency?"

It flickers and shimmers in the trees, sliding across the ground. The thing stops between two trees and hangs there, small and thin, almost like a flower blooming in the dark night or a piece of steam broken away from the hot gasses rising from the canyon floor.

"A ghost," says a voice below him.

Then a long cry breaks through the quiet night and the men stop, stand up and glance around. One man falls to his knees and prays. The other men, some twenty in number, all stand and stare at the apparition.

Then it glides closer, and a voice in the wind whispers a name. Then, incredibly, he hears a giggle, like a young girl and a whisper, soft and seductive. The wind dies. Treetops straighten. Pine needles quiet. The strange mist coalesces into a shape. He stares, unbelieving, at the form and face of the dark-haired witch from his dreams, the one Sergy's girl claimed as her mother.

She stands with her pale face bloodied and bruised. Her clothes in tatters. The big man lets out a long, loud breath and drops in the snow to his knees. The shorter man scrambles to pick him back up, but the big man refuses to move.

She laughs wildly for ten fast heartbeats, the sound like the rush of thawed spring waters. Then she vanishes behind a tree trunk and slips back into the forest, darting in and out of silver moonbeams, moving further from the snowline and deeper beneath the dark canopy of tall alpine trees. She disappears, but her laughter rings through the forest and he feels the heavy shadow of evil pressing against this remote paradise.

♦ ♦ ♦

68

The Drummer Returns

After we crossed the blue waters of the great Amu, I heard the drum beating once again. I had forgotten the drummer in America, just as I had forgotten so many things.

We passed many villages along the way, and in one I asked about the drummer. They laughed and walked away. An old Jewish woman in a village of Hebrews brought me a poultice wrapped in a scarf of many colors and told me to rub the material on my temples at night, and I would not hear the drummer. I smiled and nodded. What else can one do when confronted by an old woman and her kindness?

Other villages claimed they knew the drummer and that he passed through only a day or two ahead of us, and they told stories about him. I grew excited. They said he lived nearby, the son of an even greater drummer who lived high in the mountains.

This father had tossed the son down the mountain as a child. No one knew why. Some speculated that a soothsayer told the old man that the son would play a greater song than his father. This made the father jealous, and so, before the son grew to his full potential, the father threw him down from the mountain into the deepest of pits and buried him alive.

"Did not the father hear his son screaming in agony beneath the dirt? I asked.

"He heard, we heard, nobody wanted to listen," an old woman said. "Now let me continue."

She gave me a stern look and a wag of her finger. I smiled.

"As I was saying, when the father thought the son dead, the boy escaped and slaughtered a goat, from its skin, he fashioned himself two small drums, and these he played as a child wandering from village to village, earning himself a piece of bread, a bowl of yogurt. Never having much, he thanked God for what they gave him and blessed each house, and each of those houses saw good fortune.

I asked if the drummer was still a young child and they said oh yes, he is still young, like you. They said that he fell in with a band of gypsies and they wilted under his spell, following him from place to place. They danced while he played, and their dance lasted the whole of the night and into the next day.

I asked what the drummer looked like and they could not tell me. One said he was tall and another said short. One said fat and another said thin. One said he had no hair and another said he had long pale hair and even another said that a flock of birds nested in his hair and when he played, they flew all around and sang their own sad song.

Several nights we drove deep into the darkness and I heard him. He played nearby, perhaps around the very next bend in the narrow road, or up above us on the sheer cliffs, or below in the deep valleys where lights of villages dotted the night. I asked Uncle if he heard the drummer and he smiled but said nothing. I grew angry and anxious and urged my Uncle to drive faster. Aziz gave me tea from his thermos, but this did nothing to calm me. I wanted, no I needed to catch the murderers of my family. Looking over at Uncle's face, his stone visage looked the way I felt.

Frustration became our constant companion as we drove past a dozen tiny hamlets and towns. Every once in a while, I heard a voice, or thought I did, only to realize that it was the wind slamming through the gorge or the tires bouncing along the rugged road. We passed people of many religions, Buddhists, Moslems, Christians,

Hindus, and a dozen others, all living close to each other and yet all living in peace.

This confused me more than anything, for I had grown accustomed to the rantings of fervent men with strong bonds to their separate Gods. Men who fought over words in a book or the sand in each other's deserts. Then I realized these people only cared about surviving the next day, gathering the next harvest, milking the next goat and feeding the next child. They had no time to waste on war. And as I looked into their smiling faces, I saw a river of clear water full of life still flowing in the hearts of these good people.

♦ ♦ ♦

69

Mac and Harris

Hassan raised a hand in greeting to a man who sat next to a campfire just inside the mouth of a cave. Darkness fought with firelight. A woman in a pale blue burqa hustled around the bend of a leaning boulder. Feet shuffled, guns rattled, horses whinnied, and the seated man stood with prayer beads in hand.

"*Salaam alakum*, my brother. I have brought you two American CIA in the name of Allah, the most high," Hassan said.

Snow mantled mountains loomed all around, stretching towards the night sky. A cold wind cut through the gorge. A thousand feet below, glittering in the light of a nearly full moon, a pearlescent river rushed through jagged black rocks. To get here, Hassan dragged them for days through frozen passes and narrow canyons and secret trails known only to these weather-beaten men.

Farook El Bahar moved out of the cave into the moonlight. Two men followed a step behind.

"Mondah nabashi Hassan Khan." Farook El Bahar smiled through the long gray wisps of an unkempt beard. The years of fugitive living had shriveled his once thick frame and his neck stretched forward like a vulture's.

Hassan's bodyguards tossed Mac and Harris down on the dirt near the cave entrance. Men appeared from the shadows with guns pointed and pushed Mac against a rock. Mac understood a bit of Arabic, so he watched and listened, waiting for a mistake that might lead to freedom. A man poked him in the ribs with a gun barrel and laughed. Others joined him in this delight. They spoke of a fire and a long stick through his bowels, and Mac felt dizzy. He looked up, took a few deep breaths and listened to Hassan discuss Ali Khan and the mountain and the two of them laughed. Dark turbans pressed together. The scent of roasting meat drifted by on a breeze, and Mac realized he had not eaten in so long that his stomach had shriveled and stopped hurting. Harris lay in the dirt, his face to the rocks, silent.

"Harris. You alive?"

"Yeah."

"What are you doing? Sit up."

"I have to tell you something, Mac."

"What's that?"

"My mother died last week."

The big man leaned back into a boulder and closed his eyes. Mac found his own eyes closing. He fought to stay awake but sleep took him and once again he saw her standing in the fire with that knife in her teeth. She smiled and drew close, her long black hair a silk curtain surrounding high cheekbones, slender small nose, and lips pale as poppy flowers.

Mac wanted to run, but he could not tear his eyes from her full breasts, narrow hips, and tan skin glistening with blood. And so he released himself to her. She smiled and ran the knife blade across her stomach, wiping away the blood and leaving a dark trail on her skin.

He woke to the thunder of hoofs and a man running past him dangling a Kalashnikov. Voices drifted. Hassan laughing, Farook giving orders. Men crowded around and yanked him to his feet. Two more pulled Harris up off the ground and tied a rope around both their waists. They tied one end to a horse and a man jumped in the saddle and led them away. Mac twisted around to get a look behind him. A gray line of horses and men curved around the bend and beyond the cave. Hassan and Farook rode in the middle, chatting and pointing towards the east where the moon hovered.

They walked for two days and on the second morning, the sun turned blue moonlight to a deep purple morning haze. The trail led up into a gorge, sheer ice cliffs on both sides and a serrated strand of sky above.

Mac shivered, teeth chattering. He pulled his down jacket tight against a blustering wind. The cold air gnawed at his face, cutting and burrowing deep into his body. A roaring in his ears kept him from falling asleep on his feet. He stumbled along, cracking the ice beneath, the sound like guns firing. The ice stopped cracking, the gunfire kept on and he shook his head, thinking himself caught in some delirium. He leaned against Harris for a moment and they stood there, listening.

"Guns," Harris said.

A man poked Mac in his back and pushed him forward.

"Move CIA," a voice said, "move or die here."

Sounds of gunfire drew closer the higher they climbed. The line of men and horses stopped. Hassan and Farook rode up from the rear and stopped within listening distance. Men and horses bunched up just behind the two leaders.

"Look, they fight each other, not knowing their true enemy is behind them," Hassan said.

"Blessed is Allah in his wisdom," Farook said.

Mac shuffled up next to Harris and leaned out past a finger of rock and ice. The glacier spread in a wide circle. Men along the distant west ice wall fired automatic weapons against men huddled in the rocks far to the east. All along the edges of the glacier, men lay sprawled, black lumps marring the dazzling surface.

"What say you, Hassan, old friend? Are you prepared for battle?" Farook said.

Hassan chuckled. "Look at the Americans. They are always interested in war."

The Arab looked down. A man kicked Mac from behind. Harris turned and glared. Hassan chuckled and picked slivers of ice from his long beard.

Farook withdrew a small Koran from within his long black coat. He kissed and passed it over his black turban three times, then held it out to Hassan, who repeated this action. Then he held the book out and each man dismounted, walked up and kissed the book, passed beneath it, turned and kissed it again, passed again and then one more time. During this process, Farook slipped beads through his hand, mumbled prayers, and blew enchantments on each man as he passed. Gunfire rattled from the glacier, sometimes fast and fierce, sometimes sporadic and hesitant. The battle appeared stalemated.

It took the better part of an hour for all the men to receive the blessing and separate into their respective forces. Now the sun flashed from nearly straight above and the wind died. The sky turned into a blazing dark blue umbrella. Guns reflected sun, boots crushed ice, men moved onto the glacier. Three ruffians pushed Mac and Harris behind the Arab. Farook led the way into the sun. His men streamed along the glacier's edge. Within minutes, they began firing rounds into the western camp.

♦ ♦ ♦

70

A Leader Falls

The noon sun blazes overhead. Armon hunkers down between ice-covered boulders and watches a familiar man approach on horseback, white teeth flashing inside a gray beard. Gunmen stream past the horseman and attack the rest of Sergy's forces that hide in cracks and crevices along the ice curtain. The horseman rides dressed in all black and sitting on a black horse. Mahlim lives, but he looks wraithlike, his face sallow, eyes gleaming deep inside his skull.

He reaches for his rucksack and extracts the pistol and silencer. Mahlim stops and looks around. The horse steps gingerly over the ice. Two men in front test the ice, picking the path for Mahlim.

The battle stands in his favor, and Mahlim looks almost bored and disappointed by it all. Three men around him shout across the ice to their fellows who have the Professor and the girl surrounded. Armon descends from rock to rock, drawing closer to the man who changed his life.

Now he stands twenty feet away and calls out. "Mahlim sahib."

Farook-whom the faithful call Mahlim, twists in the saddle. His eyes widen when he sees the gun trained in his direction. He raises the Kalashnikov, but far too late. The bullet strikes in his forehead just below the black turban and Mahlim topples. Two men rush forward, Kalashnikovs pressed against their shoulders. A third man kneels over Farook's body. Armon slips behind a tall boulder, drops, spins to the other side and fells all three men with three silent shots.

Others do not notice. The silencer worked. He will need more of them. They wear out so quickly.

Mahlim's forces have rushed ahead to cheer and shake their Kalashnikovs in the air over a small collection of prisoners while many dead lay strewn all across the glacier. They still have not noticed their leader has fallen. Armon turns and climbs back to his observation point.

♦ ♦ ♦

71

Shaima and Baba

If my hands were free, I might kill you now.

"Like you did my mother. Yes, I know."

"She murdered your stepmother. She deserved her fate."

"I don't plan on dying like her, in your hands or the hands of any man you choose as my husband."

"Yes. So then what will happen? You choose your own fate, but still it is not you doing the choosing. Fate, working through you, guides the path of your life. It is the same for all of us."

"Did she tell you that? Has she ever been mistaken?"

"The Oracle?" Baba said.

Shaima nodded. "I mean she can't be right all the time, can she?"

Her father shook his head and sighed. He stared a long time at a spot on the glacier before speaking again.

"How could you do this? How could you bring them here?"

She did not answer. Hassan's men stood all around. She peeked to her right. Sergy sat against the blue ice wall with two Americans and a few wounded men guarded by a contingent of Kalashnikov toting militia. She glanced at Baba's face. He kept it down, hidden in shadows, steam raising a fog around his bare head.

She looked away, unable to overcome that inherent genetic code preventing direct eye contact with an elder. Respect, such an overwhelming aspect of Afghan life that some sank beneath it and floundered. She preferred Moscow, where she moved freely, held her head up, and Sergy gave her life a purpose beyond suffering and dying young. Here, she trembled like a slave brought before her master for punishment, and this infuriated her.

She took a breath of cold air, slow inhale and quiet exhale. She felt like a thief stealing his air. Glancing up, she saw her father's temples bulge, teeth grind, shoulders working to loosen his bonds. If he got loose... her neck muscles twitched in anticipation. She turned her head, getting another look around.

The camp smoldered in ruins. Ashes and embers marked where Sergy's men had slept. Some tents remained standing, the small generators still purred, and Hassan stood by the red glow of a heater, surrounded by men staring at the body of a man spread on the ground. Hours went by. The sun crossed the sky and sank behind the western peaks. Dark came quickly on the glacier. Many prisoners fell asleep. Bodies and blood darkened acres of once unblemished, blue ice.

The mountain cried in the rising wind and she recalled a certain night, standing at a window, her mother's spirit in the garden and angels climbing the tower to whisper in her ear.

Lanterns remained lit as they dug fire pits and the men searched for timber. Horses formed a line to a distant gorge and back, carrying wood across their saddles. A man tended the wounded with a halogen lamp that cast a brilliant white glare onto the ice cliff. The man stood and fired a pistol, and another man jerked on the ground and then lay still.

The American soldiers slid and shuffled towards each other, the smaller one with eyes wide but not with fear so much as madness. The big one strangely familiar, his eyes blazing beneath a square forehead, the jaw jutting and his white hair sticking straight up like a brush.

She looked back at Baba. His profile cut shadow from light like a razor and she felt him holding it all inside. He swayed back and forth and shook his head like a man praying. She turned her face down and whispered to him.

"Please, let it be a swift death from your own hand. Don't let them stone me."

♦ ♦ ♦

72

Armon and the Leopard

The thing leaps from boulder to boulder, its silhouette shimmering against the light blue glacier. A hundred feet below, dead men pose. Flaccid bodies scattered over rocks and ice. Camp lanterns shine in fuzzy circles, holding the darkness at bay. The battle long over, most sleep while two guards stand next to heaters that radiate red.

It moves again, a tall amorphous collection of energy bending over dead bodies. It straightens and forms a clear adumbration against the rocks. Muscular and yet nimble, its thick chest tapers to sinewy legs. The thing looks human and animal, both and neither. The head, a grotesque thing, sits on wide strapping shoulders. All of it, from head to foot, appears almost insubstantial, like a dream or a gothic nightmare.

Again, it bends over the dead. Suddenly, it leaps away at impossible speed, over boulders and up the mountainside, a body dangling from its powerful hands. It tosses the frosted dead man over a shoulder and runs higher, slipping past him and into the darkness above. Then it fades away and but for its lingering luminous shadow, almost disappears.

He fumbles in his pack and pulls out the night goggles. Darkness gives way to a suffused green glow and he sees the thing, a monster or a man, standing tall and regal. Promethean, it possesses a hideous beauty. The edges of it glow incandescent in the moonlight. A spirit, a phantasm, a thing intangible. The beast stops and turns its mighty head and shoulders side to side and a cord strikes, a memory reaches Armon from somewhere and tugs.

Nightmares echo. White faces. Fetid breath chanting and the icy blades of a bitter wind. Something crawls on the edge of his consciousness as the beast-man moves in and out of focus, dragging death high up the mountain. Armon follows. He climbs and scrambles until he too is on the backside of the jagged peak, but the thing has vanished into the heights. He takes the goggles off and scans the mountainside.

In the night sky millions of diamonds sparkle and glitter. He climbs. Beneath a crag and next to a sheer drop, a large black hole gapes in the mountain's face. Long white icicles hang from the upper edge like sharpened teeth.

Memories shift, ghosts rising from a ripe darkness.

He stops just below the cave and huddles in the middle of three ice-covered rocks. Whirling crystals dance across the ice. The hands of God play with creation while his eye, the swollen moon, laughs as if saying:

"You there, puny human hanging on the edge of the world. Look at me, your creator, and weep."

However, he has turned from God. Anger does that to a man and fury does more. He creeps to one side of the cave. Sneaking a peak around the cave's edge, he spots a narrow passage slicing between two massive slabs of rock. He enters. The crack widens to a path that looks chiseled, carved from stone. In some places, great crystals of rock jut upwards, polished smooth as monuments. On these, an ancient people have carved etchings of men with spears and at the very top, a faded outline of the beast-man wearing a helmet from which two great horns protrude. A man dangles from its mouth and other men bow or lay on the ground with open eyes, as if dead and waiting for some purpose unfathomable.

He creeps past this and down the passage. The walls loom higher, icicles drip, tears of the mountain. Twisting around and down, he follows the single hole until it flares and widens to a small cavern. He stops at the sheer corner of rock that leads into the cavern and listens. Ripping and tearing sounds echo in the frigid air. Then a chanting, or a soft lullaby, melodic and repetitive drifts through the darkness. Far away, water trickles and a low moan leaks out from some unknown place. He peeks around the edge.

Wind gusts across his face. Moonlight streams through a gap from above. This diffused light illuminates a single white leopard of enormous size. Muscles ripple beneath its quicksilver coat. Massive jaws stretch and slam down on dead limbs, ripping meat from bone. The beast-man has vanished.

His eyes search the dark corners of the cave, focusing on shapes and shadows, a field of luminescent green and white crystals clumped and stabbing into the air. He hears chanting from above, but in the darkness, he cannot determine its exact origin.

The leopard lifts its face and blinks baleful eyes in his direction.

Armon Badil retreats around the corner and slams his back into the wall. The bitter cold of the rock penetrates through his torn outers. He has repaired most of the rips during the night, still the cold slices through and he shakes, his mind slows and he closes his eyes for just a moment.

"You returned. I knew you would."

The voice, deep and resonant, sends a bolt of lightning up his spine. He cranes his neck around the corner. The leopard has vanished. He turns and searches the deep shadows for any movement.

"Who are you?"

"You know who I am."

A sliver of light on his right side draws his attention. He spins and crouches, preparing for the attack. None comes. He turns to the shaft of moonlight, a slight comfort in the darkness. Then he sees it towering over him, eyes like amber fires.

A face covered in a layer of ice crystals reveals human lips and nose and wild hair matted to an oversized head. The smile flashes razor-like teeth and images explode in Armon's mind, teeth ripping him apart, tearing out his throat, chewing on his limbs while he screams into the cold night. The flashing images force him to instant action.

He does what he knows. He slams into the giant, knocking him back against a wall where he hammers a fist into the blue face. The giant laughs and pushes him down on the rocks. Armon rolls and yanks the giant's legs out from under him. The giant falls hard, his head slamming into the ground. He kicks and escapes from Armon's grasp.

"Fool. What are you doing?"

The giant attacks, leaping in, slamming Armon into the wall. They bounce off and roll. The ground gives way. They plunge through a dark void, arms and legs entangled. They tumble, bounce off ledges, and burst through tangles of vines. They come to a stop. Night vision goggles knocked from his head spin off into the darkness. Walls glow with a pale green phosphorescence in which he can see the brute rising from the ground. He leaps on the broad back, gets an arm around the thick neck and squeezes. The giant stumbles and slips, and then they fall once again.

Armon Badil loses his grip and they part, each grasping for the other. A dense cloud accompanied by a fetid stench swallows them, growing thicker as they fall. Then the cloud vanishes, a mystery, but the stench remains and the seconds drag like hours. They fall, bounce, and knock into each other. The air turns warm and humid. Thick vines dangle like crooked ropes along the glowing walls. Armon grabs hold of one and though he cannot stop his fall, he slows his descent by dragging his feet along the wet rocks. The vines end and they fall through a wide space, spinning in the air.

He hits water with a force that knocks the air from his lungs.

♦ ♦ ♦

73

Another Secret Revealed

Hassan laughed as Sergy backpedaled from Baba's kicks. They had bound both men's hands in front of them so they could slap and strike. An activity that Baba pursued with his entire heart but Sergy dodged and ducked his way behind a pillar of stone and ice that bore a strange resemblance to a woman, robed and hooded.

Tired, Baba came back and sat next to Purdill who had established his position as her protector, keeping all others from sitting nearby. Sergy squatted near the pillar and flashed a smile. His spirit seemed undaunted by their predicament, and she took some heart from this. Still, Baba fumed, and Purdill had to keep an arm on him just to stop him from getting up and kicking Sergy again.

To the east, the early morning sky lightened into ultraviolet and cobalt and the wind blustered across the glacier, lifting and spinning ice crystal into pellucid whirlwinds and gyrating tornadoes that resembled spirits trapped and unable to find the road to their promised heaven.

Baba growled and stirred. She scooted closer to Purdill. Wounded men sat along the ice wall with their backs bent against the wind. On the other side of a small circle heater, two Americans sat alone, the small one moaning in his sleep, the larger one staring at Baba with a strange look in his eyes.

Hassan had erected cloth and steel wind barriers around Natasha's blue tent, which he now claimed as his own. His men gathered round him, laughing and slapping one another on the back. A small man carried a tray full of steaming cups from person to person, distributing what smelled like green tea. How her parched throat ached for just a drop. She shifted out of the wind, keeping Purdill between her and the cold gusts.

A guard walked by the group. His Kalashnikov pointed first at Baba and then at each of them in succession as he passed. He stopped by the Americans and kicked the small one in the boot. The big one snarled and at that moment, she felt a shock, electric and deep.

She studied his face, the angry expression so familiar. Two more guards came over from further down the line of prisoners and they laughed and taunted the big American. He ignored them, his eyes drifting back to Baba and then to her. He smiled.

His tormentors appeared bored and wandered off muttering. The American again fixed his gaze on Baba and she saw something in that face she knew and yet could not understand. The big American crawled over to Baba. His hands tied behind his back, he fumbled for a minute, then rolled over and dropped a wallet on the ice.

"Open it."

Baba reached for the wallet and flipped it open.

"A photo... in there." The man nodded, his eyes locked on Baba's face.

Baba picked through the contents. The photo fell on the ice and though yellowed and stained, she recognized it immediately. That mournful smile, long hair swept aside by the breeze, seagulls floating, waves crashing, and the boy in her arms, the shock of white hair.

"Hello, Father. Hello from the CIA. We knew we would catch you sooner or later. I was recruited and trained just for this day. By the way, Mother died recently in case you even care."

♦ ♦ ♦

74

Mystical and Magical

He plummets into the liquid depths of a black womb. Eardrums bursting, he sinks and water fills the back of his throat. A long dark shadow brushes past his legs. Sharp teeth close around his ankle and pull. He kicks the attacker away and flails in a panic. He spots a shimmer of light and makes for it. Suddenly, something snatches him by the back of his vest and pulls him up and out of the water.

The momentum of his exit sends him flying to land on a large flat rock. He lies there, coughing and gathering shocked senses. He kicks in reflex to the memory of sharp teeth on him. He lays there trembling for a moment, then rolls to his back. A vaulting ceiling of rock extends like a starless sky, peaking somewhere behind high mists. He lifts on an elbow to look around. Dim green phosphorescence lacing the walls casts a bizarre, otherworldly light in the cavern.

The giant sits at the edge of the rocks, his back turned, his great ugly head swinging from side to side. He turns, and the corners of his mouth curl in what Armon can only imagine as a sneer. Past him lies black water.

A vast lake, the far side hidden by a phosphorescent fog that curls and shifts along the surface. In what appears to be the center of the lake sits an island, and from this, a massive tower of rock extends upwards, vanishing in the dark recesses above. Around this thick column of rock, green threads radiate and curl upwards like ropes, entwining, sparkling. The sight is striking, fantastic.

Around him, a beach of rock and sand and all along this, red eyes glow from cracks and crevices. He stands and reaches for his gun, but it has fallen and the holster sits empty. He draws his belt knife and looks around. Something reflects and bobs in a pool at the water's edge. He reaches for it. Night vision goggles. His luck holds even in this unearthly bowel. He dons the goggles.

Lizards stare with shining eyes, some larger than Komodo dragons, others small as his foot. He hears them swishing their tales and slithering about. He calculates their prey to be each other or fish foolish enough to get close to the shoreline. He recalls the teeth around his ankle and he shudders.

He remembers his enemy and he spins around ready to defend, but the creature sits at the side of the lake, washing itself and staring up into the heights of the cavern. A shriek breaks the silence, a piercing angry wail from somewhere high above. The giant stands. Another scream and then chittering, like leaves rustling in a fast wind.

Winged beasts plummet and skim the lake surface. Then they hover for a few seconds, staring at Armon and the giant. They fly like bats, perhaps a species undiscovered and undisturbed for thousands of years. They soar and dive, chatter and shriek. All their terrible voices combine to form a symphony of raw noise.

"My magic protected you well," says the giant.

Memories flash, the cave, the tall man praying, and the white leopard.

"That was you." He states it rather than asks, unaccustomed to asking for anything. He refuses to start now, with this... thing.

"But you are not a man."

The giant chortles.

"Son, there are descendants of gods and demi-gods in the Himalayas. There are mysteries you never imagined. I am a man, but I am also much more as you can see."

"Those giant cats in that cave. They almost ate me."

"No. The white tiger protected you. It would never harm you."

Armon shook his head.

"Why do you fight me then."

"You attacked me, remember?"

Armon nods.

"I thought you could be a Yeti or Yeren."

"Many have made that mistake. This form keeps them away from our sacred places where we go to find mates and live."

"This is unbelievable."

"And now I will take you home where your ancestors will greet you and explain a great many things"

"Home?"

"That is why you came back."

They walk together along the edge of the lake while lizards scatter and slither out of sight only to close ranks behind them and make dark sounds, tongues slipping in and out of scaly mouths, rough skins rubbing on rocks. Dangerous horrifying noises, the scampering of a thousand feet at once and Armon turns this way and that, wiping condensation from his goggle lenses, always on guard for the attack. The giant makes a low sound in his throat. Maybe laughter.

After a long walk, they enter the strange fog and hear voices in the distance. People laugh and chatter and suddenly the fog gives way to a white sand beach intermingled with tiny sparkles of green phosphorescent mineral. All along the beach, men and boys prepare to launch small skiffs laden with fishing nets. Out in the water several boats already manned by two-man crews toss their nets and drag them up full of pale-skinned fish with wide flat bodies and small faces. The nets also hold squirming eels that spark tiny lightning bolts and these form a dazzling sight as they come up from the dark water.

Some fishermen are missing an arm or a leg, hobbling on crutches, waving stumps, and they need to work in teams, for only together do they make one complete man. They pay no attention as Armon and the giant walk past. It seems they cannot see them or do not want to. Perhaps because of something in the giant's walk or in the way he hums a low tune as they pick up the pace and pass the fishermen.

Extending from the lake, a deep black river channels off into the distance and the giant turns this way.

"Who were those people?" says Armon.

"Did you not recognize them?"

Armon searches his memory but cannot find anything remotely familiar.

"Is this hell? Have I died?"

The giant says nothing. They walk on. Soon the sounds of working men drift back towards them. Cracking, pinging, shattering sounds float through the semidarkness and down the long river cavern. Here and there, pockets of shimmering mist still hover, ghostly emanations from the earth itself. More voices filter down, and the rush and flutter of wings sweep past and up into the heights. Echoes of men singing and working grow louder as they round each bend.

"These are your people. They come here as war refugees, most without an arm, leg, or perhaps more. But here, they are equal and here they stay, helping each other, living together in peace."

"My people? I have no people," Armon says.

"You have more than you know," says the giant.

They come to a widening in the channel and on their left, fields of pale grass sway in a stale underground breeze. Dark shapes bend and straighten in the grass and as Armon draws closer, he sees they are women, young and old, carrying reed baskets, which they fill with the slender shoots of pale grass.

Rock shattering sounds come from all around them. Armon spots a shadow and as they walk, he recognizes these shadows as small tunnels from where voices and cracking sounds drift down to the river. Picks, shovels, and many mining tools lay near the mouths of these small tunnels, and from one emerges a small man covered in a fine yellow dust. He too does not appear to notice them as they pass.

"How far do these caves extend?" says Armon.

"Imagine," says the giant. "It is a mystery. We sent many but few have ever returned from the Far Away."

The green phosphorescence laces rocks and water, lighting their way in that spectral manner.

"It was here men battled the great serpent," said the giant.

"What?"

"The monster from the very center of the world. She rose from the deepest chamber when she heard the ancient ones carving the city from the softer rocks of the mountain's core. My ancestors fought her in this place. In those days humanity still nursed from the breast of the world."

"You have lost your mind." Armon shook his head. "No such things as monsters."

The giant grunted and stepped over a boulder. Armon walked around the boulder and hurried to catch up as the giant spoke again.

"The serpent has the face of a woman and two curled horns that play seductive music, and no matter how many mortal men come to slay her, she charms them like a man charms a snake."

"So they sent you."

"We came because it was our task, set before us by our forefathers, to protect the ancient ones. We fought her, but she escaped into the world and since then, the world has never known peace. Now, men are born to war and will die in war, thus their beginning and end tie them like a knot that not even Alexander can break."

"What are you then?"

He seems more a man than anything else. He walks soft for such size but still he walks and only men do this, or ancient things that wander the high cold realms where men dare not set foot. For hundreds of years, thousands even, these stories and legends have frightened and terrorized the simple farmers and herders of these high valleys. Cannibals and magic, giants and monsters. Unknown species discovered every day by scientists and surely, he must be one.

"I am Abraham. I was Captain of the Royal Guard in Kabul. I saw the revolution coming, I saw the generals defecting. I warned the King. I called for your father to come and help. Only he could have stopped the revolution. He ignored my plea. They imprisoned the Royal Guard. Our families killed. I lost two sons and a wife. The Russii came and I escaped from prison."

They walked on in the dark, the man knowing the way and Armon following.

"With nothing left to live for, I traveled to the east. I wished to learn from the masters how to cross from this world to the next, how to find my sons and my beloved. They taught me many things, but not that."

Down here, I search for the legendary river that leads to the underworld. I have found many strange things, but I have not found the river. I took you because your father owed me two sons. He refused to part with you. Therefore, I had your stepmother deliver you to me. I took you in payment for my sons. And now you have returned to me. So it begins."

Armon stops walking to take in the revelation. Royal Guard. What happened to this man to turn him into this? The giant stops and turns around to face Armon.

"Come on. We have a long way to go."

So they continue, Armon's mind reeling so badly he does not even notice that he is walking again, following the... Royal Guardsman.

The river ends at a wall of sheer rock, hundreds of feet high and sparkling with long sweeping lines of green phosphorescence. It is more beautiful than any work of art Armon can imagine.

"There, beyond that doorway in the wall, you will find a passage that will lead you to the city. You will find corridors lit by torches where they study the history of this place. Stay in those corridors and you will find what you have searched for."

"You will not come?"

"I cannot. And you must not speak of me there."

"Who are you?"

"You know who I am."

With that, the giant took two steps and vanished.

◆ ◆ ◆

75

The Eldest

I searched for years," said Baba.

The American nodded but said nothing. Somehow, she knew he would be a quiet man, full of secrets and simmering rage. God made Afghan men that way and diluting that blood by half would not be enough to change anything.

"Baba, men are coming," she said.

Footsteps grew louder. Three men picked Baba up and the photo fell to the ice.

"Do not tell them who you are," he said.

"Silence Afghan pig." The short gunmen pushed him back and forth between them. He looked down and smiled. Hassan strode forward and Baba launched a thick wad of spit. It hit Hassan's beard, drenching it.

"Why are you talking to this American?" Hassan said, "I thought you hated Americans. You know he is CIA. You know we have agents everywhere now."

He did not acknowledge the spit, but his dark blue eyes flashed a madness simmering within.

"I was not talking."

"I saw you."

Hassan looked down at the boy, and then he spotted the shining piece of faded paper on the ice. He bent and picked the photo.

"What's this?"

Hassan's soldier slammed the back end of a Kalashnikov into Baba's ribs. Baba gasped and bent. Hassan laughed and then drew a deep breath, letting it out slow between clenched teeth.

"You, I recognize. We grew up together, Ali. I would know you with or without the beard." Hassan studied the photo. "A woman, an exquisite woman. I understand. You would want no one to see this picture. But the boy, the hair, the eyes, I have seen..."

She watched the little man's eyes move from the photo to the American sitting on the ice. His jaw jutted out just like his father's, the height and width the same, all of it too much to ignore.

"So, this is your bastard." Hassan said this, cold and hard like the edge of a sword. "Bring that one with his father."

Two men picked up the big American and Hassan led them towards a blue tent.

"Wait. Go get the daughter," said Hassan.

They came for her. Purdill fought to keep them away. With his hands tied behind his back, he shouldered men away from Shaima. One man slammed his rifle butt into Purdill's face, knocking him unconscious. She struggled, but she only elicited a grunt and a rough laugh as she kicked a man in the groin.

They stood side by side, placing her close to the glowing electric heaters in front of her tent and her half-brother next to her and Baba at the end. Hassan's men encircled them. Bearded men wearing thick sheepskin coats, high boots, and thick fur caps.

"What's your name?" she whispered.

"Harris."

"I'm your sister you know."

"Pleased to make your acquaintance, I'm sure."

She smiled.

Hassan seemed absorbed in the picture, his men taken with the celebration of victory. Steaming teacups passed from hand to hand.

The tiny cook distributed bread and bowls of soup with great haste and a smile. Hassan walked to her and she spit in his face. He slapped her, spinning her around and down to the ground. Harris fought to rise from his knees, shouting curses. Baba went wild. He swung his hands around and leveled two men, then ran for Hassan, but before he reached him, a man tripped him and sent him sprawling to the ground.

Hassan laughed. "They tell me you are hiding a great treasure in this mountain, Ali. I am certain you want to show your old friend, no?"

Baba spit on the ground.

"Remember, I have your son and daughter. Do not think our friendship as children will prevent me from killing them. You owe me a life for the insult to my daughter when your son ran from his marriage."

"If you want a life for that, take mine. But I warn you, if you hurt one of them Hassan, I swear I will kill you with my own hands."

Hard men gathered round her, faces leathered and tight as old goatskins. She heard them kicking and though she could not see Baba, the thudding of boots on man had become a familiar sound. A man picked her up and stood behind her. Hassan walked over and spit on her.

"Faishah, *prostitute*," he hissed.

He slapped her, knocking her down again. Men picked her up and set her on her knees in front of Hassan. A short distance away, they had Harris down on the ice, beating him with rifle butts. He bled into the ice and she could no longer see his eyes. Still, he struggled against those holding him down.

Hassan walked back into the thick circle of men around Baba.

"You will show us to the treasure, Ali. And to ensure that you know what I am capable of, I will let you choose which one of your children I will kill now."

She heard his muffled shout, the crack of a hard blow, and then silence.

"It seems you cannot speak at this moment, so I will choose for you."

Hassan walked over to her and drew his pistol. She recognized the .357 Magnum for its size and bulk, and in the little man's hand, it looked far over-matched, but he held it to her head and motioned for his men to clear a path so Baba could see. Baba lay on his side on the ground, his face a bloody pulp, his eyes swollen almost to where he could not possibly see. She smiled and tilted her head, for she understood this to be her last moment. She nodded at him and found her face wet with tears, her throat tight, breath halted. She lifted her head and glared at Hassan.

"Go ahead, Tajik animal. Kill the innocent. See what Allah rewards you with," she said.

Hassan turned and fired into Harris. The bullet shattered his skull, sending bits and pieces flying across the ice. The echo of the gunshot bounced across the glacier, dying slowly in the harsh whisper of the blustering wind. She turned her face away. Hassan grabbed her by the hair and forced her to look at her brother. His laughter, like a witch's cackle, dry and evil.

The Bear roared and roared and roared.

♦ ♦ ♦

76

The Woman with the Green Eyes

In the distance, firelight dances along the passage walls. When he rounds the next bend, he notices elaborate long stemmed oil lamps set on stone pillars interspersed along the tunnel, and it feels as if he strides down a boulevard in old Paris. Even the ground is now cobblestoned and elegant.

He walks around another bend. Stone chiseled from a solid section of rock depict an ancient people with strange tools. Lines of them work on the stone carving and cutting in unison. Among them stands a woman dressed in white, and she appears Egyptian or Greek, perhaps a rendering of a goddess, a thin gold band around her black hair. Extraordinarily large eyes and fine features. He stops and takes a long, slow breath.

Some distance ahead, a woman kneels on a rock, the reddish gold of her hair flashing in the lamplight. She holds a sheath of paper and a pencil and draws on this while studying the wall. She does not hear him or notice that he stands only a dozen or more yards away. He approaches slowly. He stumbles, shocked by her profile, the soft lines of her nose, the full lips, and the flickering light in the edges of her eyes. She sees him, stands and drops her papers, which flutter and swoop to the ground. Her green eyes lock on Armon's and he cannot tear his eyes from her face.

"You," he says. "I thought... I never... would see you again."

She smiles. "It seems Fate would not have it so."

A silence. He shuffles his feet a bit. She smiles, walks over and kisses him on both cheeks. Her hand slips in to his and she leans into him, her cheek resting on his chest.

"Your father?" Armon says.

"Dead. All dead. Gunships from the north buried my village in bullets. All the people, young and old, murdered. Only I lived."

He holds her tight. She trembles and sobs quietly.

He runs his fingers through her red hair the way he remembers she ran her fingers through his. He wipes her tears away with his hand and kisses her forehead.

"I am here now. Though I do not know where here is. What is this place?"

She looks up at him and after a moment, points to the wall.

"Look there. Read the ancient carvings and learn the history of our people."

She leads him to a section of wall where pictograms glow in the firelight. These look like the ones at the mouth of cave and there stands the giant and below him, people with spears and hammers, small chisels and strange tools. The people look smallish, squared with thick beards and protuberant noses, wide eyes.

"These small people, who are they?" he says.

"The ancient ones. They built the city and carved much of these tunnels," Helena says.

"They came in an age before humankind. For millennium they ruled this mountain range, but they live only in legends now. A disease took them all, leaving a few new humans alive, and from those few the city returned to life."

She pulls him by the hand to the next mural, a mosaic of tiles less ancient, with painted golds and blues and reds. She points to a tall man astride a red roan with ram's horns on his green helmet, his face a dusky tanned and his hair auburn.

"Then came Alexander, a king from the west," she says. "One day Nimah the huntress found him near death in a distant valley. He had lost his way and had several arrows in his body. She brought him here and nursed him back to health and they fell in love."

She pointed out each scene and now he understood the pictograms as if they spoke to him and he felt drawn into a time long forgotten and it resonated with warmth and a certain sweet longing.

"And this is Nimah," she says.

A woman with striking red hair surrounding a small and delicate face looks out, her pale blue eyes lock on his. He moves, the eyes follow, to the right or the left. The girl laughs and hugs him. They move to the next mural.

"But Alexander left and met his own destiny."

The girl points to murals depicting the history, a boy and a girl stand near a whitewashed square house, blonde hair falling to their shoulders.

"And Nimah died giving birth to twins, Alexander's son and daughter."

"Twins?" he says.

"And the son went out and searched for thirty years, found his father's body and brought it back to lie with Queen Nimah. Now they lay deep below us, together in a crypt."

He studies as they walk, history unfolding in paintings, lamplight playing on the faces. They seem almost real, alive, but he dares not reach out and touch though he feels the desperate need to do this. Instead, he holds Helena tight against his side.

"Come, I will take you home now."

They walk like before, hand in hand, only now he stands taller and she leans into him and the mountain does not roil in blood.

"My little Snow Boy."

◆ ◆ ◆

77

Mac's Prayers

A merican, here is your comrade," the man said.

They dropped Harris' headless body in front of Mac. They shouted some insults and kicked Mac in the ribs, knocking him to his side.

Memories flashed of Errol Black grinning at dead women and children. Black had an excuse of sorts. Insanity. Errol's parents spent time in sanitariums before Errol graduated from elementary school. They murdered Errol's brother, a toddler of four, by shaking him to death. So Errol came to live with Cousin Reggie, and that did not help at all. In Vietnam, war became Errol's refuge and killing his profession.

Men did these things to each other. They killed just to kill. Good and evil, not as different from each other as one might think. Is it good or evil to kill for territory, for religion, or in defense of family? Good and evil had become arbitrary and irrelevant, and nobody cared. Did this render God irrelevant as well? He wondered what old Father Dodd might say.

He listened to the wind and her sobs and he looked around, thinking she found him in his half sleep. He saw two men, smoking, silhouetted against the blue glacier, arguing back and forth, gesturing towards him and one pushed the other and the other stuck a bearded jaw out, belligerent, insistent.

Mac kept hearing the village girl scream, her voice laced into the wind in a tapestry of misery and pain. If he pulled his shoulders up to shut his ears from the wind, he still heard her cries. He shook his head, trying to dislodge her from his mind, but the fever that burned inside had weakened him. He could hardly fight now and realized with a sinking certainty that she would come for him soon. His face burned against the ice, lying on his side, staring at Harris' body. A woman wailed. Or was it the wind? Agony colored a strange shade of blue.

He pushed himself up to his knees and fell back against the rock, turning his face to the left to get a view of something, anything else. His eyes wandered to the distant depression in the eastern ridge beyond which several hundred miles away stood Everest, the king of mountains, while here, the Hindu Kush lay like a court of dukes and duchesses, kneeling in absolute reverence. Across all this, a pale moon cast its eerie light, giving frozen boulders strange shapes.

Women in white robes, a man sitting, and a giant bear with a raised paw. A series of ghostly cries ripped into him, somehow magnified by the emptiness and desolation of this place. The girl had escaped his dreams and now haunted him during his waking hours, and she would not stop. A pain in his head hammered and the heat of fever took him down. He closed his eyes and dreamed.

She crawled from the flames, knife blade gripped between her teeth. He reached out to her. She approached, eyes glittering with bad intent. Her body nearly naked, her skin on fire. How could he ask her for forgiveness? No words could do that.

"Hail Mary, full of grace, the Lord is with thee..." and he kept it going aloud, so he could hear and lose himself somewhere in the sound of it. Father Dodd appeared in the distance, ambling towards him with that familiar frown of fury. Mac kept praying.

Then, from between spinning whirlwinds of ice crystals playing on the glacier, a white stallion charged into the camp, his coat rippling liquid in the moonlight. It stopped near the blue tent, reared up and kicked a man in the face, knocking him to the ice. Rearing and kicking, the stallion knocked man after man down, and more men ran over, reaching out for the horse, but the stallion bolted through the camp, snorting and stomping and wreaking havoc. At that moment, gunfire broke out from across the glacier and the stallion ran off.

♦ ♦ ♦

78

'War Is a Seductress of Men'

We had traveled far and now stood on the brink of Uncle's plan to rescue my sister and brother from the Russian professor, Sergy Volkov. Two thousand feet below the top of the glacier, we came across the destroyed camp and ten dead Europeans. We could do nothing for them, so we continued up the glacier. Now we stood at the near summit and across the wide expanse the lights of Sergy's camp gave a carnival atmosphere to the far western ice curtain.

I suppose Uncle saw I had lifted my Kalashnikov and shot into the air at Abdullah's camp, for he had not spoken to me the entire rest of the trip. Now he relegated me to the care of the cook, thus setting me even below him, and I chaffed but said nothing. Respect for elders is the uttermost important aspect of life in this Afghan world.

So Uncle insisted I stay behind with Natasha, the cook and two men, safe in the gorge, while he, Aziz, and the rest attacked. I did not reply, too stunned, too shamed, and too weak. Baba said it all those years ago. It took stone and gristle to lead men into battle, and even Uncle did not think I had these.

I felt Natasha's eyes on me. And the men, watching the coward hide while his Uncle stood out in the hurricane. My disgust pushed me into action. I turned to the dark eyes of Uncle's men.

"You men stay here and guard Natasha. I'm going up."

"Yes, Excellency," said one. The other kept silent, but I sensed his disbelief. He must have heard the stories about the son of the Bear. The cowardly boy who would not fight, would not kill Russii.

I moved toward the glacier. The moon hung over the mountain, fat and angry like that night in the canyon when I clung to Jaheel's back. Then I rounded a great finger of ice and there he stood.

Jaheel in all his royal splendor, pranced, staring at me as if to say, "Where have you been? I have waited." And the circle closed.

All things great and small fled from my mind and I had but one purpose now, one road, one death to die and my spirit to fly to Jenny and Melissa. Rhymes kept sticking in my mind as I jumped on his bare back.

I slung the Kalashnikov to my left hand and pulled my pistol with my right. I took his reins in my teeth and aimed him at the battle. Jaheel knew the rest of the task. We had ridden too many times through black canyons, across unspoiled snowfields, and over mountain trails for him to forget me. I leaned forward and urged him on.

Uncle's men strung out along the glacier while he stood tallest in the center, Kalashnikov spitting fire, shoulders squared against the enemy, and he looked so much like Baba that day in the gorge, silhouetted against the sky and moon. Jaheel charged past him, flying over the rocks and scree, his hoofs sure and heavy, and I heard my Uncle shout but nothing could stop us now.

Jaheel tossed his head and bore down, his speed increasing, the thunder of his hoofs like... a drum beating. I saw a man and killed him, cutting him in half with the Kalashnikov. With my pistol I killed another and I felt a lust rising in me and I understood the killing fever that takes a man. I pulled the Kalashnikov close to my chest, lifted, aimed, and downed another, then another, and I screamed, the wind clawing at my eyes. And I recalled Baba's words, "War is a seductress of men," and they rang true.

I felt myself expanding in the world, taking space, conquering the ground and sky. Man after man fell to my guns and I heard a roaring in my ears like a waterfall crashing from a high mountain. I ran out of rock and ice. The cliffs loomed up and Jaheel stopped, slid and spun. He reared while I slammed another clip into the gun and leaned down. We cut across the camp again, and I shot at anything that came before me, the dead the wounded, the living, I did not care, the smoldering pleasure of it had taken me and I heard the monster inside me roaring.

◆ ◆ ◆

79

Omar Observed

A big man rode the stallion over gray rocks and blue ice and with gun barrels afire he leaned down across the horse's neck and shouted. Mac leaned back on his knees and watched Hassan's men squirm in the rage of this man's guns. He realized no other opportunity like this would present itself. He flattened to the ground and crawled towards the rocks on the left. If he could just make it, hide and wait. Dragging himself along, casting quick glances back, he saw the man jump from the stallion's back, draw a knife and plunge the blade into a man's neck.

Mac froze. The man's gaze flittered over and past him. Mac had seen that look before, and he knew the unholy death that came with men caught in the grip of that particular madness.

The man leaped on another man crawling across the ground, yanked back his head and slashed his throat, then stabbed the man overhand into his chest and ripped down with the blade, eviscerating him completely, spilling the man's guts out in the moonlight.

Mac ducked his head and crawled. He reached the rocks and tumbled down behind them. His body shaking, he peeked out. Men ran towards the crazed one, shouting. But the killer did not hear them or did not care. He walked up to man after man, kneeled, slashed, cut, and stabbed. Two men finally took him by the arm and spun him around, but he could not stop himself. He slashed at them and they backed away.

Mac experienced this before. Losing all control. Something had built up and exploded inside the man. He would be incapable of stopping himself.

A very tall man walked over and spoke to the man. This seemed to have some effect and within an unnerving number of seconds the knife dropped from the crazed man's hands and men swarmed around him, slapping him on the back and cheering. The man stood there, chest heaving, his hands and arms dripping moonlight black blood onto blue ice.

♦ ♦ ♦

80

Omar's Other Brother

I stood in a strange blind emptiness. My mind struggled to find its way back and I trembled while Jaheel nudged me repeatedly as if to say, "It's all right now. Everything is all right now."

Purdill appeared and I heard him talking to Uncle. Then my Uncle, gripped in a wild rage, slapped Purdill, knocked him to the ground, and commenced to kicking the poor man. I stood there, unbelieving.

"I told you never, ever leave his side." Uncle kept saying this and kept kicking. I had to stop him. I knew this but did nothing.

"The boy, Sardar's first son," said Purdill between Uncle's kicks.

"What?"

Uncle stopped.

"Over there. Hassan murdered him. He's taken Sardar and Shaima prisoner and is forcing Sardar Ali to take him to the treasure," said Purdill.

I heard his voice, but I did not understand.

"First son? What are you talking about, Purdill?" I said.

I looked to where Purdill pointed and saw a headless body lying there, across the camp was the head, with half the face blown away but the other half remained and, in that half, I saw my father but for fairer skin and one blue eye staring at me as if I stared from there myself. Then Uncle took me by my shoulder and propelled me towards the ice wall, all the while telling me a story I had not, could not imagine in all my dreams.

♦ ♦ ♦

81

Snow Boy Returns

The ice dome shines a pale blue, green and translucent, frozen between spindles of rock that, like spokes on a giant wheel, connect to an enormous central column. Large bats hang from the spindles, fighting for space. Red eyes gleam in an ocean of chittering madness. Several of the creatures fly slow circles around the rock column. Sweeping, arcing, diving ever closer to the ledge where Armon stands with Helena.

An impossible sight, primordial and fantastic, and yet it exists right here, dazzling and real.

Light slips through the dome. Pale turquoise beams filter down to illuminate a magnificent cavern. In the giant cup of rock below, a small city cut from stone sits like a Greek isle from the dawn of human history. Dozens of tiny lights flickering in windows and along cobbled alleys between square white houses, layered and placed atop each other, stairs leading this way and that. The entire city glitters like a jewel nestled inside a circle of white and black cliffs.

A tower sits to one side, wide and fashioned from stone with a crenellated round top. Around this tower are ramps of smooth stone held up by pillars and the ramp circles past many doors fashioned of dark wood, which swing open as dwellers wander in groups, some taking the spiraling ramp higher and some lower.

"What is that tower surrounded by the stone ramp?"

"That is the center of learning. Every citizen spends half of every year as a student and the other half as a worker. There are divisions of work, clerical, medical, defense and culinary. Some still work the mines."

He shakes his head and blinks, but it does not fade like a morning dream. He pulls her close to make certain of her, afraid that she might be a vision or ghost, but she slips an arm around his waist, and he knows.

"You live down there?" he says.

"Yes, and now you will too. In my home. If the city survives the men who come to violate and destroy."

"You mean the Professor? He does not come to destroy but to study."

"It is good that you have come now. We will need you if things go badly," she says.

"Other men took the Professor prisoner. I am uncertain what they will do."

"We will see. Come, I will show you the city."

Her skin is milk white and her lips, the purest pink. He leans down, she stands on her toes and they kiss. She tastes like soft water and strawberries, and she smells like lilacs. He lifts her up. She wraps her arms around his neck and all things fade away.

Later, as they sit on the edge of the cliff dangling their legs over the side, she points out her home and the kitchens, the grand halls and balconies built into the tower. And he laughs and laughs. She touches a hand to his cheek.

◆ ◆ ◆

82

Beasts from the Pond

Shaima hid the crumpled photograph. Later, as they stumbled down dark passages, she pressed the wet photo into Baba's hands and as she did this, she held him tight for a moment. He pulled away, slipped the photo into a pocket and turned his head away from her. A moment later, a guard slammed a gun to his ribs, bending him over and setting him to coughing. Baba spit blood that glistened dark red and sizzled on the cold stones. She wept silent tears.

Sergy hobbled along a step behind, whispering hope in her ear. She wanted to smile for him, but she could not find a ray of hope to which she might cling. She could not shake the image of Baba's eyes swollen shut. Through his knitted brows, she saw that his last remaining spark of life had vanished. He looked back at her with an emptiness so deep and vast that she feared he might provoke Hassan to murder him, if only to end the life that had so disappointed him. Too late came her desire to comfort him. The man now stood gnarled and bent. His face wizened and pale. Her heart broke to see him thus reduced.

They came to the cavern of the pool where earlier she sat with Sergy and his men. Dark waters still and silent, surrounded by sparkles of green mineral,

She thought about the dead leopards in that passage and the warriors of the guard who protected the white city. She wondered when they would attack and take her back for her inevitable punishment. She sat down next to him, held his bloodied hand in hers, and laid her head against his shoulder. He did not move for a moment. Then Baba sighed and rested his bearded cheek against her head.

"You know you will die for this," he said.

"Silence," said a man. He hit Baba and Baba laughed, a crazed, tortured laugh that slipped out like a grunt and a groan. She cried.

"Separate them. Do not let them speak," said Hassan.

A man grabbed her by the hair and pulled her up. Baba stood and knocked the man down. Another man struck and Baba fell. Sergy stood up and shouted. A man kicked him to the ground. Angry violence filled the world, sounds unheard in the mountain for countless generations.

A sudden movement beneath the surface of the pond caught her eye. Shouting, battling men stilled and quieted for a moment as the water rippled and waves lapped the rocky shoreline. A massive black shape broke the surface and next to it another and then more, swimming, entwining, and roiling in the water like a scene from darkest Hades and she fully expected to see Charon rise from the murk in his death boat.

Then a dozen or more incredibly large lizards scuttled forward. Men shouted and pushed each other towards passages that led away from the water. Pistols fired, barrels flashed, and it appeared as if a lightning storm raged inside the cavern. She choked on gun smoke as she scrambled to a ledge and watched in horror as a five-foot lizard bit into Baba's leg. He tried to kick free as two men dragged him towards the wall.

A lizard scrambled over the rocks towards her, his eyes gleaming green orbs and razor-sharp teeth. She screamed for Sergy. She turned her face from the beast's jaws and just at that moment Sergy's foot connected and knocked the leathery monster away. He stationed himself in front of her to swat and kick at lizards attacking from three directions. She heard Hassan shouting. She closed her eyes, waited for the end, imagined sharp teeth against the soft skin of her neck, crushing and tearing. She curled up and sobbed beneath Sergy's feet as he fought wave after wave of beasts, kicking them into the pond where they thrashed and fought with men, the mass of writhing, twisting darkness gleaming in the green glow of minerals and mosses all along the shoreline.

Then it stopped. The noise, the gunfire, the turmoil evaporated as suddenly as it had started. The beasts scuttled away and Sergy kneeled down next to her. Her eyes searched for Baba and found him lying face down near the water. She called out his name, but he did not respond. She screamed and a black screen filled her eyes.

She woke. Sergy held her in his hands. Two men had raised Baba from the rocks and sat him down. He stared into the air, his face the texture of pale wax. At first, she feared they had killed him, but when he took a breath, she felt a surge of intense joy.

"Get up. You will lead us to this hidden city," Hassan said.

"I will not," she said.

"Then I will shoot your father now, then I will shoot you and the Russian will lead us instead. Do not tempt me. I think that maybe my best option."

She looked into his narrowed eyes and saw madness. Hate and revulsion radiated from his face. He saw her as worthy of nothing less than death by stoning.

She stood, walked to her father and took his arm and led them from the cavern of the pool. As she looked back, a flash of movement caught her eye. On the other side of the pond, a tall man wrapped in darkness stood, beardless, long unkempt hair, wild eyes, and she felt a strange familiarity with him. Then she recalled the beast in the cave with the leopards, and she glanced around to see if anybody else saw the man. Hassan's Tajik's and Mongols stared back at her. When she looked again, the man vanished. She turned and led them into the passage that led eventually to the city. She knew this passage would take longer, and she counted on this time for Sergy to escape the ropes that bound his wrists. He nodded and understood.

They arrived at the cavern of the fog, stumbling and cursing. She leaned against a rock and caught her breath. Hassan's men poured out of the passageway and discarded their heavy rucksacks on the ground. Some bent over, breathing heavy. Others sat and wiped the sweat from their faces.

She had led them on a merry-go-round of a walk through many of the same passages twice, and they had not noticed. Just when she wondered when the city defenders might respond to all the noise, she heard the soft air-slicing whisper of an arrow. It struck Hassan's wrist, cutting through muscle and tendon and toppling the gun from his hand. The little man screamed. Two burly men surrounded him and pushed Baba against the cavern wall. Baba slid along the stones and boulders, making his way around the cavern.

Men dived for cover as arrows filled the darkness. Many died right there with half a dozen arrows protruding from their bodies while others fired their guns into the fog and shadows. Their headlamp beams jiggled and danced across the cavern, but could find no enemy. They spun around, befuddled, unable to determine where to direct their fire.

In the confusion, Baba bolted down a passage hidden around a bend in the rocks. Two of Hassan's men followed him and she found herself alone but for Sergy. An arrow slipped past her and hit Sergy in the shoulder. He fell. She had to decide now.

She chose Baba. Perhaps out of her guilt and perhaps out of love and perhaps because Sergy told her to run, run now, follow your father and get away while you can. She ran straight down the passage behind Baba. Behind her, screams, shouts, and gunfire filled the cavern of fog.

◆ ◆ ◆

83

Helena, A Warrior with Green Eyes

Old John Brown hunkers against the rocks and watches the battle unfold. His eyes glow, reflecting strands of green phosphorescence that lace each cavern wall and cast him in a demonic aura. Something about the man bothers Armon, a familiar bend to the back, the shape of his eyes, the way his brow furrows like the side of a snow-bound mountain. John Brown edges away from the invaders and vanishes down a passage. Armon turns his attention back to the battle. There will be time to catch John Brown later.

Helena kneels next to him along the edge of a churning vapor cloud that exudes a familiar fetid stench. Her bow does not rest, firing arrow after arrow into the cavern where surprised men fall and cry out. They come around the cloud, she cuts them down, but more come and soon the cavern swarms with men. A dark fog of gun smoke combines with the vapor cloud, the smell of wet sulfur and death invading his senses. Bullets spray all around the cavern as the men discharge their guns into the ethereal green darkness. Muzzle flash like lightning bolts in a thunderhead. Bullets ping and ricochet close by.

Armon pushes Helena behind an outcropping of rock and shields her with his body.

"You must retreat," he says.

"I cannot," she says.

More young women crouch up against the other side of the passage. Her friends, Dasha and Gelasia and others, clad in dark leathers and firing their bows. He knows they cannot survive against modern firepower and they will die here unless he does something.

"Listen to me, Helena. They will soon realize your location and then their guns will end this battle. Take your friends and go back to the city. I will circle around behind them, take them one by one, and only a few will live to reach the city. Go back and take positions along the city walls."

"I won't leave you here. I won't let you out of my sight again."

"Then we both die here. Your friends will die. There is no reason for any of you to die. I can kill these men. Please. You must take them back."

She looks up at him. In the dim light of the mineral, her eyes shine and tears sparkle on her cheeks.

"Don't make me go," she says.

"You must."

She shakes her head and then buries her face in his chest for just a moment before pulling back and whispering to her friends. They go, each giving him a smile and a nod. He watches them disappear into the tunnel behind him. Then he darts down another passage, already planning, already knowing the way.

John Brown must wait, for now.

◆ ◆ ◆

84

An Afghan Moon

With Purdill's help, we determined the identity of the dead American to be my brother, a secret Baba kept for many years. Purdill told me many things I did not know, among these, that Baba had searched for my half-brother and his American mother for 35 years, a lifetime for an Afghan. Now, his first-born son lay dead on Afghan ice.

I did not cry for him. I could only wonder at the fate that brought him here, to this ice bound plateau some 14,000 feet above sea level where he met the bullet that bore his name, a name unknown to me until tonight. My brother lay dead at my feet and I could feel only a sharp blade in my stomach, turning and cutting me to ribbons from within.

The moon still shined on us, fat and clear. Yes, my Afghan moon, which is far different from the moon that shines down in Virginia. The moon seems far larger here. At this altitude we are much closer to it, and yet there is something else, something ancient, primitive, and even, dare I say, divine that shines down from that craggy argentite face.

I followed Uncle into a crack in the frozen face of the mountain. Uncle counseled as he likes to do, and I listened with half an ear while the rest of me burned in the frigid night.

The oldest son of an oldest son, he gave up the safe life in America, though my Uncle could have taken his place here as Khan, but that would have burned a brand in Baba's heart and he could never accept it. Now I saw why.

This magical place, the shining ice, the rugged mountains, the secret of the green valley. Even the old yellow dirt. I felt it then. I felt the longing for this mystical ancient world in my very bones, and I wondered how I never felt it before.

"You're wrong. A father can never put aside his love for a son," Uncle said.

I cast a look his way. He stood nearby, adjusting his light, shifting the rucksack to his back. He tightened my straps, pushed, and pulled on my parka like a worried mother.

"It happens," I said.

"Not for Afghans."

"He thinks I am a coward, and he's been right all along."

"You are not a coward." Uncle smiled and turned away.

Our headlamps illuminated the passage and we descended quickly and kept to a distinctive path. Pictograms of men and strange beasts marked the stones as if telling a story and recording the momentous occasions of another time, but my mind could not comprehend it all. My thoughts filled with worry about Baba and Shaima, both prisoners of Hassan, a man who never ceased to plague Baba with his incessant raiding across the border. A man who never forgot the insult of a daughter spurned. I walked behind Uncle and Purdill. Aziz took us into the darkness.

I felt a horrifying excitement and a strange hunger for battle pulling me forward, and I realized with great trepidation that I had become a beast thirsting for the blood of my prey. We passed passage after dark passage, men strung out ahead and behind, and I remained somewhere in the middle, monitoring

Uncle's broad back while he spoke and ran his gloves along the rocks.

"He knows you needed time to find yourself. Some men need time," Uncle said.

I knew the truth.

"How did you not know about his first wife and son?" I said.

Uncle did not answer.

"Your mother came from this place."

"My mother came from a cave?"

"A tiny city in the crater of an extinct volcano. Covered by ice, unknown to the world, protected by our family for more than a hundred generations."

I thought I must be dreaming. Soon I would wake and find myself back in Virginia, and my Jenny next to me, playing a finger across my face the way she loved to do. As I touched wet stones that sparkled with a strange green mineral and breathed in the heavy dark air, she melted from my grasp. Fading like a mist fades in the wind.

Sometimes the world spins too fast and I thought to jump off for a day. To let it all shift and shudder beneath me until I found a place where my feet could land and I could stand without dizziness and nausea.

"A city inside in a mountain," I said. And a wonder so intense gripped me I felt my feet might lift from the ground and I might drift down the passage. After all, it could only be a dream.

My eyes shifted from Uncle's back to closer inspect a pictogram and then another. This caused me to falter and fall behind, but I felt an urge to look and feel the stones, listen to water trickling from frozen heights, and breathe the warming air. I unzipped my parka and let my hood fall. I stood still now and unable to move from the mouth of two passages, one on my right and one on my left. A force held me there, and my feet mired themselves in the spot. The hairs on my arms prickled and I felt a shadow pass across me, though no sun could shine through miles of solid rock. Perhaps a lost spirit or something worse.

The men walked by me, some with a hand on my back in camaraderie, other's mumbling "Excuse me, Excellency," and passing by with heads bowed almost as if praying. I found this sad and joyous at the same time. They shuffled and lurched ahead, their silhouettes swaying against the light from their headlamps and their whispers dying in the air as they rounded bend after bend.

Then, I turned my head and saw myself in the depths of a passage on my right, dressed in black, my eyes glowing in a soft green light, my hair long and wet, my face decorated with stubble.

I looked into that mirror and gripped the rocks. I took a hesitant stride forward and approached myself, only vaguely thinking of my Uncle and the men leaving me behind. This unfamiliar sight dumbfounded me. I took a step, paused, and then took another. My mirror self also appeared dazed and took a step forward, then back, and then forward again and reached out a hand as if to touch me.

I recalled the dream I had in the plane and wondered if I had died. Yet the cold heavy air and the sound of water dripping and the apparition in front of me told me no, this is real, and I reached out, our fingertips met, and a wild bolt of energy passed between us.

Then I remembered. My Jenny and Melissa, my precious daughter, died because of this me. I glared at myself.

"Why?"

He shook his head and tears fell from his eyes. I could not kill him, though I felt it my right to strangle him on the spot.

He nodded and reached out to touch my shoulder.

Falling to my knees, I wept there, and he stared at me weeping, withdrew his hand and stood tall. I saw him then. So perfect and so wild. I saw myself and I saw Baba in him. And yet, something else, something visceral and eternal.

He had the bearing of a king and the heavy muscles of a fighter, the eyes of a bird of prey and the hands of a killer. He had the energy sizzling around him like Baba, and at that moment, I realized with a shock that he should have been the one to stay and they should have kidnapped me.

He whispered in the darkness, his regrets, and a look came over him, a dark sadness, and I think he knew before I did, who and what and why.

Then I remembered him, his smile as he woke me in the mornings and pulled me from my thick quilts and took me out from under my willow tree and his laugh, the sun, the toy boats and the stream.

He vanished before my eyes, dissolving like a dream. Or did I blink and lose the image of him, a mirage, a trick of my reeling mind? I searched the air and the rocks and the dark places nearby, but he had gone without a sound and so I stood there, waiting for him, needing him to return, needing him to look into my eyes and find himself here so I might find myself in him.

My girls. Oh God, my girls.

◆ ◆ ◆

85

Awakening Memories

The giant wraps an arm around a man's neck and pulls him behind a rock. Armon slides down closer to the next man. The giant moves within the darkness, ruling the underworld, a fallen angel, a legend whispered by men gathered round ancient campfires. He watches in wonder as the former Captain of the Royal Guard kills two men in silent swiftness and then vanishes.

Armon slips the blade between the next man's ribs, cutting silently up and in, and with a hand over the man's mouth, he drags him around the corner, resting his limp body up against the rocks. He moves ahead quickly.

Another group of men comes from behind. A group in which the twin plods along like a man wilting beneath a mountain of worry. He could have killed him, but the twin looked pathetic and wondrous and... innocent.

He follows the men, sliding in and out of their wake. He slips in and takes another, depositing him down a passage. He hurries back. The Captain has disappeared. Sometimes he wonders if the giant truly exists or is merely a manifestation of some unfulfilled need, and thus the hulking man appears sometimes as a demon and other times, an angel. Still, whether real or imaginary, together they have whittled the ranks of the invaders.

Men scramble and shuffle ahead through a narrow passage, lost in the maze, frenzied with fear. The Professor led them astray, and they realize they are losing men by the minute to some unseen hand. He regrets the inescapable fact that the giant will probably kill Sergy.

Three men surround the Professor and more follow and Armon recalls the night Sergy walked up by the football field and scattered those boys and drove him to the cliff where he tossed one over the side. Screams drowned in the rhythm of crashing waves.

Now, a handful of men remain, fewer than 30 perhaps, and although he wants to save Sergy, he hears a distant voice, an echo that reverberates through miles of dark passages, perhaps the voice of Old John Brown calling him through the mountain. He decides he cannot save Sergy any more than he can save the world, and the giant has vanished. For now, Sergy is safe. He turns towards the voice and slips forward through the heavy cold air and searches through the images stored inside his memories.

In his wakening memories, John Brown stands in a snowstorm calling him by a secret name while a white stallion prances by a waterfall and a gray stone fortress hangs between heaven and earth. That frothy beard and those wild eyes pull at something buried inside, some raw and bleeding ground where he has never trodden for fear of sinking in and never rising again. He steps down the passage that leads to the man who must be his father.

A very large part of him wants to forget everything, return to the city and hold Helena to make certain she truly exists and that he has not dreamed this entire journey. Earlier, high above the city on the ledge, diffused daylight flickered over her long slender legs as he tasted her lips as her breasts trembled beneath him. She took him into her and he floated in a dream wrapped inside the scent of lilac and every tiny sparkle of her clear skin, and in that soft pale realm he found parts of himself that he had never known before, the parts he left in these mountains so many years ago. Like ghosts, they invaded his body and took up residence, giving birth to original thoughts and original feelings, and warmth that he did not remember ever knowing before.

He senses movement ahead. He quickens his pace and finds himself behind two men on John Brown's trail. They carry Kalashnikovs and pistols, and he has only the long blade sheathed at his calf. He smiles.

♦ ♦ ♦

86

Shaima's First Kill

A shadow slipped through the passage, struck down Hassan's soldiers and then vanished into the darkness, leaving behind the rapid gasps of dying men. She hugged the wall and stepped past a man lying in a puddle. Something latched on to her ankle. She looked down. The man had an iron grip. She kicked, but he pulled hard. She saw his other hand reach for the holster.

The irony of this death did not escape her. She had survived by the strength of her will for these many years to die in this dark tunnel, and once again, she heard her mother's voice calling in the distant sound of trickling water and angels singing her a welcome.

He pointed the gun at her with a shaking hand. She fell to the ground and reached for the gun with one hand while raking her fingernails across his face and eyes. His voice crackled, raspy and thick. The gun fell. Unable to find it, he reached for her with both hands, but she straddled his chest and squeezed with all her weight and power against his neck.

Still, her small size and weight could not overpower the man and she knew unless he bled to death soon, he would kill her easily. Then she heard them, the angels, singing in her ear, like bells ringing softly in the darkness. She turned her head and saw what she saw that night in the tower so many years ago.

The image of her mother floated down the passage towards her, mouth open in a scream, eyes like dark lights shining in her vaporous head. The man saw it too, and he froze. His hands fell to his sides and slapped against puddles of his own blood. She had never killed before, but she experienced a strange exhilaration as she felt the man die beneath her. His eyes rolled back into his head and after a long time, she let go of his neck. She stared at his face for a moment. A Tajik face filled with deep sun-baked furrows. The man's life had taken a toll and his journey led him here to die like this, stabbed and strangled in the belly of a mountain.

She looked back for her mother, but the apparition had vanished as fast as it appeared. The angels sang no more. The air lost its electric charge, and only she and the dead remained in this deep hole. She shrugged, got up and headed down to the crypt of the King where she knew Baba waited.

♦ ♦ ♦

87

Revenge Is the First Rule

Hanging from what appear to be stalactites, a vast number of gas lanterns splash light along the walls and smooth stone floor of the enormous cavern. A great wall seals one section of the cavern from view and within this wall two immense doors hang open just a crack. A breeze slips through this part of the mountain and he wonders where it comes from. Looking up, he sees the high ceiling extend some hundred feet or more and boasts a dozen or more dark holes that he assumes to be tunnels that reach to some outside vent or crack in the ice that covers the mountain.

Returning his attention to the glittering cavern floor, he senses Old John Brown waiting behind the doors. He has wondered since the last time he came down here, when he saved the girl and Sergy from the cat, what lay behind that wall. He steps over the body of a leopard and walks down to the open doors.

He takes a single deep breath and slips through the doorway into a long room with a dozen or more pillars running parallel along the sides, great wicker baskets sitting on benches, lamps hanging from an inlaid gold and emerald ceiling and old swords strapped to the walls. A huge tapestry depicting a white leopard shimmers in the lamplight. Liquid mercuric body of the cat trembling against the high walls.

"I thought I had rid myself and you and your foolish Uncle years ago. What trick of fate has brought you back?"

The voice, gruff and graveled, echoes in the deep chamber. Armon turns. Old John Brown, eyes burning in the lamplight, stands with a sword gripped in both hands and raised above his shoulder. The thick beard hangs to mid-chest, wet with spit and dribble and the face, a face of stone and mortar with deep cracks like dry riverbeds and thick black brows. He oozes life and vigor and yet a sense of doom surrounds him, like Old John Brown in the picture, dying and not knowing it.

Words escape him. Ideas abandon him and he struggles to find something, but he can only stare at John Brown come to life in this dark and ancient place, a billion ticks of time from Harper's Ferry.

"Why? Why have you come back, boy?" John Brown says.

"Why?" He can only repeat, stuck in shock, unable to tear his eyes away from John Brown's ferocious face. The sword hangs in the air, quivering, revealing the tremors in John Brown's hands. John Brown licks his lips and a long bead of sweat rolls over his brow and down the edge of his nose. Hysteria flashes in his John Brown eyes. Armon takes a step back.

"Do you come to beg forgiveness?"

John Brown tilts his head to one side, studying Armon. His hands tighten around the sword's hilt, twisting. The creak of old leather scratches the air.

"Forgiveness?" Armon holds his hands open, showing that he has no weapon and he needs none, for he only wishes to talk and learn of the history between them.

"No? Then where is my fool of a brother?"

John Brown chokes on a chuckle or a roar, spittle falls from his cracked lips, his eyes roll in his head and Armon thinks the man will fall or faint or perhaps die on this very spot. Armon raises a hand, palm up, and reaches out to calm or somehow comfort the man standing between the flickers of green light on one side and the deep shadows on the other. This new... Old John Brown.

"No, I don't know, I-."

"Haven't I told you a hundred times? Revenge is the first rule. A Pathan will wait a thousand years for revenge, and even then... you know the rest, you finish it," John Brown says.

"But I-."

John Brown swings the sword so very fast. A bolt of green lightning slices air, and the blade sings an ancient song of death.

◆ ◆ ◆

88

The Bear Roared

Shaima arrived in the crypt in time to hear voices from behind the massive doors. Baba's voice, high and frantic, madness laced within the words, and she hesitated for a moment before scurrying to a gathering of rocks where she hid with a view to the door, a door she dare not enter for Baba's wrath had come unleashed and she imagined her own death waiting there, as he promised.

A shout, a wild angry grunt, a whisper in the cold wet air and then came the muted sound of something hitting the ground. A few seconds passed and then Baba roared. The sound of a man suffering pure agony. She got up to run in, but her feet would not move. Breath frantic and fast, hands trembling against the rocks, she froze and listened to him roar.

He roared like the bear they named him for, and she heard him muttering and weeping, and then the door burst wide open. He emerged like a man deranged, his face and hands covered in blood and a sword, glittering green and gold, dripping wet along the blade. He crouched and peered into the dark corners of the cavern. She hid and trembled. His footsteps came closer. She held her breath. Sweat breaking along her arms, she cowered lower. His footsteps stopped just a breath away and she put a hand to her mouth to stop herself from breathing or speaking or crying.

After a long moment, a moment in which she dared not look up or around, a moment that dragged into lifetimes, his footsteps receded into the distance. She looked over the rock just in time to see his great bulk disappearing down a far passage, the green sword gripped in his massive hands, his head shaking from side to side and his mutterings, the mutterings of a man lost.

She came around the rocks, stepped quickly to the crypt door, and peered inside. The sight that greeted her she had not imagined or thought possible. The headless body of her brother lay in a heap.

A sudden cold wrapped around her. She saw a glittering essence, a ghost or spirit, a residue of life or the very soul of him approaching her, hands reaching for her. The shadow took her into the darkness and she heard angels sing the dance of water.

♦ ♦ ♦

89

Duty

My head reeled, vision darkened, and a great pain sent me to my knees. After a few seconds of deep breathing, I noticed one passage featured unique marks carved into the rocks. Chipped signs that declared a path through the mountain, and I followed these signs to a wide cavern where bodies littered the ground. Not our men, but Tajiks and Mongols lay with arrows through their necks and chests. Some groaned and others cried out, but I ignored them all, for these I knew to be Hassan's men.

I searched among them for Baba while an angry cloud churned in the center of the room. This I avoided and followed the wall, crouching and moving until from the far edges of the cloud I saw Purdill waving a hand at me. Come this way. I went. I asked Purdill if he had seen Baba, but he shook his head and kept going.

I kept looking behind, as if the apparition might appear again, my twin, my mirror image. I never thought to see him again, not in this lifetime. For this last week, I even hypothesized the man on my Uncle's laptop could not be my brother but an imposter, posing as me for some unfathomable reason.

I even ventured a thought Baba had finally sent the assassin to take his revenge, first on my wife and child, and then to torture me in this way until the end, which I felt coming like a storm on the horizon. Yet, I had no time for these thoughts as we ran and stumbled down the passage. Gunfire and shouts filtered back through the darkness. Alarmed, I pushed my way past Purdill, but he snatched me by the scruff of my rucksack and pushed me against the wall, sliding past me and running down, leaving me behind while I scrambled along to catch him. I stopped for a moment, undid my straps and dropped the rucksack to the ground. Now at a run, I followed his fast-receding footsteps into the darkness.

I burst into a stunning scene and froze. A massive cavern. A wide, towering column from where a hundred small shafts of light spilled forth from distant windows and doorways. A huge wall of stone above a channel of black water, and in front of all this, a crowd of men struggled in hand-to-hand combat.

I had no time for further gawking as a bullet flew by my head. I ducked and fired my pistol at an enemy. He fell and I saw Uncle surrounded by two men and I fired, downing one while he hit the other in the head with his rifle and split his skull. The area filled with gun smoke and bodies and I saw Purdill propped against a rock with his hand over his leg, so I kneeled by his side.

"Idiot. What possessed you?"

"Duty," he said.

Duty. Always a duty. I hated duty. I would crush duty with my bare hands if I could. I shot a man and my accumulated fury spilled forth unchecked by previous hesitations and fears. My rage knew no bounds as I shot into the crowd of men, mostly not caring if I hit friend or foe.

The fighting space tightened. I spotted Hassan and his giant of a bodyguard pinned against some rocks. His men stood all around and I emptied my pistol, drew my knife and waded into them, slashing and stabbing.

This time my mind did not flee my body. Rather, I felt a strange serenity as I slashed a throat, stabbed a chest, and yanked my blade free with a pleasing sound. I stabbed again and again, my passion mounting, that familiar wave rushing over me. Their screams, groans and curses echoed in my ears for some minutes before fading.

I could not stop. I saw a man struggling with another. I picked one and stabbed him fast in his side. He cried out and I slashed his neck twice and stabbed him again. He fell. I looked around. Only our men stood now.

Hassan groveled on his knees in front of Uncle. His huge bodyguard lay dead with the side of his head smashed open. I looked for Baba, but I did not see him. I searched the bodies. Still, I could not find him. I moved to Uncle's side and snatched his pistol from his holster. I pointed it at Hassan's head.

"Where is my father?"

"I don't know. He escaped back in the passages. Please, I am old," he said.

Without pausing for a rational thought to enter my mind, I squeezed the trigger and heard the crack of the pistol. His blood splattered over me. I turned around and all the men stood there, staring at me. Uncle stared as if he looked at a stranger.

"What have you done?" he said.

Most of Uncle's men did not move. Some backed away from my still smoking pistol. We stood there for a time, all staring at each other like strangers.

"I killed Hassan, the pig who raided us from our borders. No more will he raid."

Some men began praying fervently for salvation from god. I laughed.

Uncle kneeled beside Purdill, tending his wound. I heard a strange alarm sounding inside, but I did not think about it very much. Alarms had sounded all my life and I had listened, shivered, and hid in the rocks while other men fought and died.

Now I fought and blood rushed wild through my veins like the great Amu rushing through the mountains of my homeland. I wondered if another war would come and I would lead these men and others into battle like Baba, perhaps beside him, and together we would slash and kill like our ancestors. Like the ancestors of all men everywhere. Alarms sounded. I felt the changing inside me. I felt like a beast with many coats.

A drawbridge lowered across the black water. The gates to the city opened, spilling bright light over us. I stood ankle deep in blood pooled within a small depression and three bodies rested at my feet. Blood dripped from my hands and my elbows and I shook my shoulders and reached out to a large rock, steadying myself for a moment.

Men dealt with the wounded while I took deep breaths. I moved towards the drawbridge and saw the people for the first time, standing along the high walls, looking down at us. Most of them had gold or auburn hair, fair skin and small delicate features. I knew the history of my land and I recognized them as Nuristani or other descendants of Greeks left behind by Alexander's conquests of these mountains.

Beyond the walls, a pure white city sparkled. Cobbled alleys and a central pavilion surrounded by black water channels and these spanned by wooden bridges. While I marveled at these, a sudden commotion broke out behind me. Men cheered, guns rattled, and I turned to see what prompted this happy outburst.

A man stood in the passage's mouth. An enormous man, his beard ragged, his eyes haggard, he stared at me, his mouth moved but no voice came forth. The man looked to have lost his mind, spit and froth dripping from his lips, his clothing torn from his body, his face a mass of black and blue bruises.

I had not seen my father in many years and thus a full ten seconds passed until I recognized him there with a sword in his hand and a wild look twisting his swollen features. I had never seen so much pure emotion on his face, and I wondered where he was during all the fighting and what journey brought him to us now.

By the added light of the open gates, I could see the blood stains on the green sword, his hands and face and my mind fastened upon a warning in the moonlit gorge.

"Never come back," he shouted.

An image of a man dressed in black, his face like mine, lying somewhere out there, a victim of Baba's leering madness.

He pointed the sword at me.

"You are dead."

He spoke these words in a whisper or perhaps a groan or some other semblance of sound that I cannot describe but I heard them and though I wanted to deny it, I knew my poor brother had fallen back there behind my father whose burning eyes bored into me like green tipped spears.

"I killed you myself. Not an hour ago," he said. He waved the sword.

"With this sword. I saw your body fall and..." he looked down at the blade and lifted it to a better light. "I know... Yes I know."

"Who did you kill, brother?" Uncle said.

Father looked at him, but in his eyes, I saw no recognition. The skin on his face sagged and he looked old for the first time. Then that light or energy that always lit his face had faded and he shifted his gaze back to me, tilted his head, and shook it from side to side.

"I killed him. There, standing with the pistol in his hand. I killed my son."

"Sikandur, you killed Sikandur," Uncle said. He took a step towards father.

"You fool of a man. Give me the sword, Ali."

"Sikandur? No, it cannot be. I killed Omar the traitor, Omar the weakling."

He tensed at Uncle's approach and pointed the sword at him.

"Don't move. Do not move now, brother. You took my son from me. You are responsible for all this."

"You drove him away, brother. It was not I who dragged him around the field behind a horse."

He stared at us from a place beyond words and reason. Nothing could reach him. His face shook and fury filled his eyes for a moment and then faded and he leaned against the wall. I saw understanding creep across his face and desperate terror rise in his eyes. He did not ask where or why or when or anything else. He understood the truth of it and I saw him shrink in the light as if all his soul had fled and only a shell remained, crumbling there in front of me.

"What have I done," he said.

I watched despair take hold of him, a downward glance at the sword warned me but the instant I thought to run and take that sword away he moved so fast, faster than I had ever seen before. Uncle and I both lunged, but far too slow, far too late.

He turned the green sword, braced the pommel against a raised rock in the ground, and with the point against his own chest, he leaned forward and fell.

Men shouted and ran. Somehow, I reached him and turned him over. His green eyes opened for a moment and he said to me the words that still burn me in the darkness of every night, nights that I thought would never end.

"Bachaim, you are the light of my eyes, my one true heart. Now you must carry on. The burden is yours. The people must remain safe until the last war is over and we renew this poor earth. You must be their protector. You…"

And with that, his spirit left and his eyes closed and I caught the last glimmer of green before he shut himself away from me forever, taking all my pride with him.

♦ ♦ ♦

90

The Oracle Speaks

Yes, for a time they called it Old Alexandria, but for many millennia we knew it as the White City, or Shar Safed."

The woman they called "the Oracle" did not appear to have aged in all the years since Shaima visited the mountain with Baba. Her long hair hung dark. Pale translucent skin shined healthy, and her eyes still held that deep blue gleam that had so enchanted Shaima as a young girl.

They walked side by side through the shaft, some twenty feet wide by twenty feet high, walls painted with brightly colored frescoes of Buddha and the giant Persian bird of lore, Simorgh, and a great green bull that Shaima recognized as coming from the Indo-European period that gave birth to the Zoroastrian time. Older, far more primitive drawings and carvings decorated the lower sections of rock, and these she interpreted as left behind by the first settlers of this mountain range.

"The stonemasons of another era carved the city and this shaft and many of the passages you have seen. Much of the rock is limestone, calcium carbonate surrounded by solid granite and ice that lays thick across the mountain. The city took some twenty thousand years to carve, and our scholars have dated it to some 600,000 years old, perhaps even older."

"600,000 years? Neanderthals? Perhaps a lost tribe wandered this way from the Eurasian subcontinent," offered Shaima.

"Perhaps," the Oracle said. "It does not matter what they were, just that they existed and that they carved from this mountain a city that the old legends tell us, 'gleamed in a covering of gold. And at one time, it did. Each home, each wall and each tower has a residue of gold dust in its stone, and now, because of the vastness of time, only the stone remains. When the first stonemasons came here, ice had not yet covered the crater and thus they still received the benefit of sunlight and so the people built lush gardens and many grottos decorated with their art. Terraced waterways that ran throughout the mountain emptied somewhere beneath the great Amu. Time moved forward thousands of years and as the earth and its continents shifted. Ice encased the great mountain and thus it has remained for the last 50,000 years."

The Oracle fell silent, and only the footsteps of the procession echoed in the passage.

Baba lay in his simple wooden coffin borne on the shoulders of six men at the head of the long line of city folk while she and the oracle walked just behind Omar and Uncle. Sergy had vanished into the mountain, and patrols sent to find him returned empty-handed. He remained lost or else had escaped. She hoped he still lived.

She worried and wondered, and as they passed each branching passageway, she cast a glance into the darkness. She expected to see Sergy come running out, but as they descended, her disappointment grew and she felt the full force of an ocean of tears making that brief journey from heart to eyes. She clenched her jaws tight and dug her fingernails into her palms to stop the rush of despair.

They proceeded further into the catacombs, passing wide caverns full of gold, lapis, emeralds and rubies, all piled high in heaps, as if God himself had poured them into each room. Locks did not exist for no doors blocked the caves, no chains, no signs to beware. She found this alarming and yet strangely appropriate for this underground city.

"You do not post guards to keep this immense wealth safe?"

"Only outsiders consider this wealth. To us it is part of the city and belongs to everyone. There is no need to steal what is already yours."

"I see your point. Still, one might wonder if a greedy person would-."

"How much could one person carry from here?" The Oracle smiled. "We don't worry about such things. Those who live here know and accept the bonds the tie them to this place."

Shaima felt ashamed, as if she should have known the answers to these questions. She watched her Uncle's back as he limped down the passage. He had not spoken to her, nor had Omar except to tell her that Sikandur had perished in the crypt, beheaded by Baba.

After that, Omar had not spoken a word to anyone. She learned from Purdill about Jennifer and Melissa. He had retreated into himself, perhaps to a place where he could lose nothing more. She understood his pain and she saw it would haunt him for all his days, never giving him peace, and she knew she had caused it all.

She found forgiveness a distant thing, alien and unobtainable. Her guilt consumed her. So many dead, so much lost, all for her desire to be free. If she could curse herself, she would, but she knew that no curse of hers could be stronger than that which already haunted her.

They called it the "evil eye" and they believed, as simple people do, in all the curses and all the prayers. She had tried but could not escape that evil eye. The more she struggled, the more it closed around her and now, it would crush her. She knew this and yet she remained calm, accepting, no longer feeling a need to struggle, no longer a need to fight. She wondered if drowning felt like this. As the water entered the lungs, did one stop struggling, or did the struggle continue until the end, until that last second of life?

The passage widened and now they passed holes cut into the walls where coffins like her father's rested in the shadowed interior of each tomb. The place reminded her of a gigantic ossuary like the catacombs of Paris that housed millions of deceased. Some holes had wooden covers on which they had carved in ancient Greek, the name of the deceased. Others remained open and only the ends of the coffins held any identifying writing.

They continued deep into the catacombs where the walls stood riddled with tombs. The cavern widened to a cathedral sized room, stairways carved deep into the limestone curtain of the wall.

It appeared as a world inside a world. A majestic place that even in her imagination she could never have found. Similar though not as large as the city, the vast cavern radiated in the green light of at least one hundred lanterns hanging from a massive chandelier. Huge calcium formations hung like the pipes of a gigantic organ, and she half expected to hear Beethoven or Brahms booming out at any moment.

"You can see here why we do not allow firearms inside the mountain. Just one loud noise in this room could destroy these majestic formations. So our weapons remain the weapons of our ancestors, bows, spears, catapults along the city walls."

"Yes, I understand."

The cavern sported antechambers of smaller size and many passageways leading to unknown destinations. She could not help but wonder if Sergy had somehow found his way down to this palatial room, and so she scanned everything. The stairways, the dark alcoves and semicircular vestibules that held wicker baskets of immense size. Around the edges of the cavern stood tall towers reaching from floor to distant ceiling that at first appeared as if hewn from quartz or some other pale stone. Then she saw these stalactites growing from the ceiling down, connected to the floor, and she looked in wonder, attempting to fathom the thousands of years it took these grand formations to appear and form their twenty-foot diameters.

The procession continued across the cavern to a set of wide stone steps carved into the wall. Up these stairs they paraded, a silent gloom surrounding them all. Along the stairway, passageways opened into semi-darkness, the curved sloping halls lit by distant lamplight, flickering and shifting against stone.

She shuddered at the icy wind that blasted through one passage and unzipped her light jacket from the hot air that pushed forward from another. Along the cavern walls, various art forms recorded 600,000 years of humankind's evolution, from cave dwelling stone carvers to the great civilizations of China, India and Eurasia. She realized she might spend an entire lifetime studying these walls and still only learn a small fraction of the knowledge stored within these vast caverns.

Her eyes filled with tears. She could not help but think of Sergy. Where could he be? What could have happened?

Suddenly, she felt the need to separate herself from all sound. She needed quiet. She needed to think. She could not stand the trickle of water, the shuffling of many feet, the heavy breathing of six men who carried Baba in his coffin on their shoulders.

She broke away and ran, the sound of her own feet deafening. Cold air breezed past her face, the scent of fresh snow carried from a distant world lost in the fast blur of the past few days. She ached to see the sky, the stars, the sun and moon. The dark stone walls sent her heart racing and her thoughts to a future without Sergy, without light, with no hope of escape. She wondered what the oracle would do with her. Had they a terrible death planned? A stoning, perhaps. Oh God no, she heard herself whisper.

Then came the quiet of a dark and lonesome madness.

Taking a deep breath, she followed the passage up, calculating the angle of her ascent at perhaps 15 degrees. She realized the difficulty of ascertaining this angle with any accuracy. So she just ran, hoping to find the dark blue mountain skies by the pure grace of God.

◆ ◆ ◆

91

Baba Laid to Rest

We watched Shaima disappear down a passage. Nobody made a move to follow. What could we do? Where would she run? Back on the glacier, only death awaited. I felt suddenly tired, and my thoughts flittered back to last night's dreams.

Melissa's voice calling, Daddy, Daddy, and the darkness within which her voice echoed, complete but for a single shaft of brilliant white where two figures stood, one tall, one small, hand in hand, waiting.

"It frightened her," said the Oracle. "Let us continue with our task. Once we lay your father to rest, we will find her."

Dazed and thinking heavenly thoughts, I relented to her wisdom and my Uncle's hand on my shoulder, which directed me ever higher into this massive cathedral edged in curtains of pale calcium carbonates. Among these wall paintings and animal sculptures, I found a certain peace and contentment that I did not understand but gave into for nowhere else had these feelings come to me, nowhere that is but along the green banks of a deep river, in a cabin where two angels blessed my life with happiness.

Thus, I knew I had found my new home.

As we neared the top of the stone stairway, she pointed out the crypts of my grandfather and the many generations of our ancestors. I saw the crypt of Agha Khan, my ancestor who rode with Mahmud eh Ghazni *(Mahmud from Ghazni)* in the first millennium A.D. and many much older. Some so old that in places the stone steps had crumbled and worn flat. We approached the crypt where they would lay Baba, which I recognized by his name, Sardar Ali Khan, which they had enriched by adding his nickname, The Bear.

I waited for a ceremony or some special words spoken for this moment, but no voice broke the cool silence. Six pallbearers placed Baba inside the wall, closed the wooden door and left. City folk who had come all this way filed past us, kissed our cheeks like family and made their way back down the long stone stairway. Uncle and I stood there accompanied by the oracle who took me by the hand and showed me the next crypt in line. It bore my name and next to this, the tomb of my Uncle reminded me of losses yet to come.

"Now let us find your sister. There are dangerous tunnels in this mountain, places where our people do not go. I hope she has not found her way into such darkness," the oracle said.

We followed her back down to the passageway through which Shaima had vanished. The tunnel slanted strangely, in a way that I could not determine with any confidence whether we descended or ascended. The lanterns along the walls illuminated the way for some time until they too faded behind us.

We continued by the light of Uncle's hand lamp, a battery-operated beam that shone a brilliant white light along the walls, displaying stalactite formations above and great puddles of water at our feet. The steady drip of seeping water echoed through the passage while the smell of fresh air rushed past our faces. Sometimes as strident as a full breath of wind, other times, just a faint breeze.

"Are we close to the surface," I asked.

"Do not let it deceive you. Like other things, often it comes from long distances and small men," Uncle said.

I almost laughed.

We followed this passage while the minutes slipped away in the drip, drip, drip of water.

The hours passed and the wind faded, the air turned heavy and warm. I could only surmise that we had descended to unfathomable depths and soon would face Cerberus or some other denizen of a legendary underworld. I had pulled off my sweater and stuffed it in my half-emptied rucksack when I noticed a shadow behind us, a darkness moving within darkness. I looked again, but this time saw nothing. Yet my instincts warned that something lurked back there, following us, cloaked in silence.

Then I heard a distant scream, and the echo of that scream approached from a forgotten nightmare. Then a scuffle of feet behind me and I turned in time to see four young women dressed in dark leathers slipping past us, bows in hand, quivers of arrows at their hips. The guardians of the city, usually women because they far outnumbered males in this place for reasons I did not yet comprehend.

Uncle held me back with a hand as the diminutive warriors passed us and vanished into the curve of the passage ahead. Again, the scream echoed and I pulled away and hurried forward towards the voice I could not help but recognize.

Remembering the crows that circled on the day of her birth, I hastened to save the last of my siblings, one with hair the color of sunset, a treasure found. Uncle kept up with me, leaving the oracle somewhere behind us.

We ran forward, pulling out pistols from their holsters, prepared to battle yet another foe. I felt that passion again, this time quicker, stronger, and I suddenly realized that I had left my old self on the glacier. This new self I welcomed and yet deep inside, I feared. I feared what I might be capable of, what murders, what atrocities, what unthinking actions that would one day become apparent as grave errors with graver consequences. I no longer concerned myself with weighing and measuring alternatives. These activities occupied the mind of weak men, and I was no longer weak.

Or so I thought until I came upon a sight that sent my stomach reeling and my mind into shock.

First, the whisper of arrows marked the air and then came shouts. Exiting the passage, we came upon a large snake writhing on the ground with a man in its mouth. Three rows of shining white teeth pulled the man's torso downward into disjointed jaws. The man in the jaws turned and I saw his face.

It belonged to the man I had seen so many times back at our fortress, the man Baba called Abraham, Captain of the Royal Guard. A bigger man I had never seen and yet the huge snake had wound itself around his body, pinning his arms and slowly swallowing him while young warriors sent arrow after arrow into its black glistening hide. All around the room, bodies of countless lizards of varying size lay ripped apart, dead. The signs of battle lay strewn over every inch of the cavern, blood and guts and death decorating walls and floor.

The scream came again, this time very close, and my eyes searched for her. Uncle shone his light into the rocks, along the floor, and then the beam stopped across the writhing snake. There, half hidden by rocks and nestled against the wall lay Shaima, her legs crushed together as if combined into one, a wet slime covering her from waist down. Next to her lay Sergy, the Russian, his eyes closed, his face pale, a half dozen arrows stuck in his shoulders, legs and arms. They both bled from their wounds, their blood running together into the battle between python and man.

I rushed over to the snake and fired my pistol into its head at an angle that would not hit Abraham. Uncle joined me. Together we blasted pieces of the giant snake apart, and yet this did little to relieve poor Abraham. The snake tightened its grip and I heard the slow crushing of bones.

Arrows continued to fly, but for a monster snake of this size it would take hundreds of arrows to just slow it down. I reloaded my pistol quickly and continued my onslaught. Although I shot out its eyes and fired into what I thought must be its brain, this only caused the beast to twist and squeeze with increased fury. Uncle reloaded and fired, but the monster would not release poor Abraham whose bones appeared crushed beyond salvation. A young girl thrust a long, sharp knife into my hand and pointed.

"Cut off its head," she said.

And I did. Sawing, cutting, straining against the writhing coils of the beast that pushed me from side to side, I sliced the two sides of the head from top to bottom, behind the massive jaws until only the man inside kept the beast together. Yet, even in death, the beast continued to coil and squirm and struggle.

We had to get to Shaima, so we pushed the remains of the beast to one side and ran to her. Consciousness had left her and I saw she would never walk again, her legs smashed beyond hope. Still she lived, a pulse strong in her neck.

Uncle prayed immediately. Sergy had also survived, though I did not know for how long. The arrows had done their job, bringing down the big Russian. Yet because of his enormous size and strength, I surmised that he too might live through the ordeal. Soon more help arrived, men with stretchers who took Shaima and Sergy back to the city, and some minutes later the oracle arrived and assured us they would live.

"Our doctors are very skilled here," she said.

I believed her. I do not know why.

Poor Abraham died inside the python. As we cut him out and lifted him up, he sagged from every part of his body, his bones crushed to putty, his great heart beating no more.

He had tried to defend them and in that he had lost his own life, sacrificed for the sake of others. Once again, the heart of a true Afghan revealed itself to me and I stood ashamed for my guilt, my greed, my selfishness that drove me to America.

I felt that for these sins, I lost my family and then I understood I would live a long life so I might suffer the pain of this knowledge, and in this suffering, perhaps I would become the hand of an angry, vengeful God.

I considered this, yet my anger did not allow me to succumb and so I refused, as my father had before me, to recognize that which I struggled so hard to deny. For still I thought God must exist as a benevolent God and not a God of pain, suffering and death and this reality turned my head and my heart from any belief and so I stood and followed the devastated remains of my family back to the white city. And I knew I would never understand.

♦ ♦ ♦

92

Shaima & Sergy

You must not leave the city," the Oracle said.

Shaima glanced up at Sergy. He squeezed her shoulders, looked down and smiled.

The oracle nodded at them both. "Can you live like this? Before you answer, remember that one day you may prove yourself worthy of trust and we will have this talk once more."

Shaima smiled. She hoped the blush she felt rising in her neck and ears hid well in the lamplight.

"Yes, I can live like this," Sergy said. "There is much to study here and much to do. I could spend a lifetime here and it would still not be enough."

He looked down at Shaima huddled against his side.

"I will wed this girl, if she will take me."

She sighed, looked up and studied his face seriously, knotting her brows and pursing her lips.

"I don't know Professor. You are not of my people. What might they think?"

"But I am half Afghan."

She smiled and squeezed his hand. Sometimes a person does not really know what they want. She wanted to escape her mother's fate and accomplished that. She would never have to marry a violent man and die by religious fervor. She loved Sergy since the day she saw him outside the fortress. Perhaps she had known what she wanted all along. And yes, the hidden city must remain undiscovered, at least for now. She could live with that. What else could she do without legs?

The oracle stood and smiled. "I think you will be happy here," she said.

"The city will give you everything you need and you are free to study in the library and meet with our teachers. Perhaps one day, you will teach us." Then she turned, opened the door and left. Shaima looked up and smiled.

He stood tall, his head almost rubbing the whitewashed ceiling. The lamplight of their new home flickered in his face and his leather tunic, given to him by the city tailors, shone like armor on a knight. He walked over to her and swept her up in his arms. He carried her up the stairs and into a room, laying her down on a feather soft bed. Time stopped and she thought her heart stopped with it. Still, in the back of her mind, a plan sparkled like a piece of blue ribbon in the sunlight.

♦ ♦ ♦

93

Taj the Nuristani

Taj parked the rented Ford beneath overhanging branches of an old red leafed maple tree and walked into the Virginia woods. Pushing his hair back, he stuffed it under a black knit ski mask and pulled the mask down over his face. He put a pair of new sunglasses into his dark windbreaker side pocket.

He loved the aviator glasses. Gold rimmed, dark tinted kind American pilots wore as they buzzed over villages in their war machines. Sardar frowned on such luxuries, and though he loved his general, Taj's own vanity remained an admitted weakness.

He pushed rain-soaked branches away and studied his assignment. The white Cape Cod Colonial sat on an expanse of wet grass flattened beneath the weight of rainwater. At one end of the estate, a rounded room with sweeping windows overlooked the manicured lawn and a hot tub steamed on a patio styled in the fashion of the American White House. White portico and marbled columns. Silly Americans and their toys. Hot springs served an Afghan well enough. Ali would laugh at such luxuries.

He circled through the woods to a point hidden from observers. Last night he considered all the cameras and charted their coverage.

He knew the best path to cross undetected. He stepped out of the forest and onto the lawn, sinking in the wet grass. Sprinting to the side of the house, he left behind the slapping patter of rain on the forest canopy.

Lightning flashed and thunder banged behind heavy clouds. The dreary day depressed him, weighing on his soul. It rained in Nuristan but not like this, not unendingly, and they welcomed the rain for it fell like sweet nectar, light and full of taste. This rain smelled of death, rot, and the very essence of evil. He sensed an acute discomfort inside himself, and he attributed it to this grim weather. Still, his mother had the gift and her mother before her, and the nape of his neck tingled as it did when the enemy drew near. He nodded over his shoulder to nobody, the force of habit ingrained from many battles.

He settled to his task, mind clear and eyes sharp. He slipped a blade under a window, flicked it across the lock and lifted. The window popped open. He moved his aviator glasses from a windbreaker pocket and placed them in a safe pocket stitched into black cargo jeans. He loved cargo jeans. Yesterday he purchased ten to take back for friends.

He adjusted the ski mask and slipped through the open window. A desk and couch, a bar, books lined up on dark wood shelves. Two doors led to opposing hallways. He shut the window.

He had studied the layout of the building for two days. Ali had taught him preparation before execution. He moved down one hallway and immediately noticed something strange about the building compared to its schematic. A downstairs bedroom seemed too small, a bathroom also smaller than the diagrams showed. The kitchen, wide and with an elegant island, appeared correct, but the rest of the downstairs looked off.

Then he heard something beneath his feet. The house diagrams did not include a basement, but he heard voices, two of them, one thick and burly, a man, the other, a woman's voice. A door slammed beneath his feet. He slipped into a closet in the hallway between a bedroom and the bathroom. A light creaking sound came from inside the bathroom. He peeked from the dark closet, moving his face past the suits. A man grunted and stomped past him down the hallway towards the study. Grey hair, short and squat, a powerful man waddled along grumbling to himself. Taj recognized the Colonel. Had he worn his uniform, he would have recognized him sooner, but a man looks different in just his boxer shorts and a stained undershirt flapping against his ass.

Taj heard a desk drawer slide open, a curse and cupboards opened and slammed shut. Then a happy exclamation and here he came, back down the hallway, twirling a fat cigar between his lips and a gold lighter out in front, the flame turning the end of the cigar into a glowing cinder.

Taj slipped out and sank his blade into the Colonel's left side. He pushed up and in and felt the wall of the heart give way. He twisted and pulled the blade free and then whispered in the Colonels ear.

"Sardar Ali says goodbye."

Back at the hotel, he slept for several hours. When he woke, the muted television showed photos of the Colonel and his home and ambulance lights flashing in the background while a woman mouthed words from beneath a black umbrella. He turned the sound up.

"Chief of Metro Police, former Marine Colonel Reginald Gregory died this afternoon, a clear victim of suicide. A note left on his desk cites a lifelong battle with depression aggravated by an addiction to pain medication. Chief Gregory leaves behind no children. They will bury the former Marine tomorrow at Arlington Cemetery."

Taj laughed.

"Suicide?" He shook his head. "Americans."

◆ ◆ ◆

94

Time Spent in the White City

There remained only Natasha, Uncle, Purdill, and I. Aziz died in the mountain and we laid him to rest there with Baba and Sikandur. A month later, we left the city under the mountain and journeyed home over the glacier, down through the gorges, and back through our war-scarred land. I rode Jaheel and Uncle led the way on a great ruddy roan with long ears and a sweeping broom of a tail. I lost myself in the swishing of that tail while memories played in my mind.

I met the woman they called the Oracle, the pale thin recluse who lived in the white city and protected all the refugees from these many years of war. Uncle gave somber accounts of the Talib and American forces battling in the south and said we should plan another trip down there to bring back more injured and destitute.

I visited the crypt where they said my famous ancestor lay awaiting the fulfillment of a prophecy. His body, encased in gold and ivory, rested inside a green sarcophagus that sat upon a dais. He looked nothing like the history books or statues that the outside world had erected in his honor. Memory is a short-lived vice, after all.

I studied their art and their influential books and I met a woman with green eyes who said I resembled my brother, just not enough and perhaps too much, and she turned away and wept violent, aching tears.

I too wept for so many lost. Time would never bring me back to where I stood before. Later I learned the woman bore my brother's child and this made me happy, as it should. She came to me one day, much thinner, the agony of his loss having stolen much of the life from her, but deep inside her green eyes, a light shined, a special light I knew would lead to something good.

When I thought back to the things I had recently done, I felt my heart turning black, as black as the roan's long swishing tail.

The Oracle allowed Natasha to come with us under the protection of my Uncle. Along the road they did a great deal of handholding. I gathered some hope from this, for the time had come after all his wanderings and all his pain to settle and take a wife and have a child or an entire tribe of children. She had goodness in her. I recalled sweet goodness, and I knew he would find happiness there.

We rode through fields of poppies, white and purple. In between grew acres of multi-colored flowers, reds and blues, and then came the walnut trees, twisted trunks and bushy umbrellas full of leaves. Sunlight's slanted beams fell through this forest upon a soft ground covered in leaves and husks. We stopped and spent an evening in a meadow next to a running of small waterfalls that smelled fresh, like a world just born. This strange place with all its primordial beauty held time outside itself and I saw butterflies fluttering over tall grasses and deer wandering by as if we did not exist.

Not one of us spoke that evening. All sat by the fire and stared into the flames or up at the glittering sky. The stream dragged a blanket of mist over itself and sang us to sleep.

That night I dreamed of Jenny and Melissa and our home by the banks of a river. Green grass, thick forests, and deer watching us watch them through the kitchen window.

In the morning, we left this heaven and emerged from the forest once again into desolate mountains bereft of any apparent life.

Beneath our horse's hoofs, the ever-present white scorpion scuttled this way and that, chasing lizards back and forth across the rocks as they had for unknown eons, long before we humans set our burning feet upon this earth.

Appearing like ghosts from within the morning mist, ragged children gathered around us and called out for candy and money, and we had only a few Afghanis with us, which we gave. We passed through towns and villages and hamlets, hot springs and the gorge where the Russii tank still lay with its top crushed as if Baba's fist had smashed it in.

I looked down at bloodstained rocks and remembered that day in the falling snow, his angry face and the clatter of my Kalashnikov as it fell from my hands. The air so crisp and dry, I could almost see each molecule as sharp as each memory, and they cut me. I bled.

I found myself alive yet dead or somewhere in between, floating in a dream with nowhere to go and nobody to hold, protect, or live for. A great weight settled on my shoulders. Purdill rode beside me, his face grown dark over the last days, he looked older, his shoulders bent, and I knew that one day soon his son would ride next to me instead of him.

Then the fortress came into view. Its four towers looked old, gray, and somehow crooked. Worn down under the crushing weight of history. The yellow outer walls crumbled in places and the courtyard sat deserted. Not even the chickens scuttled about. A great sadness filled me as we entered the front hallway and I knew the stones felt the absence of him, that great bellowing voice of his, the towering height. His sheer presence brought this place to life, and without him I feared that even the ghosts of my ancestors might cease to haunt the hallways.

I stepped inside his room but found no sign of him. They had cleaned the walls and the closets, and the room had a stark nakedness about it. I wandered to his chair and the chess table and then out onto the balcony. I walked the ramparts and searched, wishing, eventually fighting tears.

In the distance, farmers walked back towards their tiny homes where children played outside. Women chased away chickens with brooms, and a red dust rose in the fading sunlight. I watched the sun melt into the mountains, then turned around and went inside.

Purdill stood in his usual place by the hearth, waiting.

♦ ♦ ♦

95

Mac at Peace

Kneeling by the fire, she turned and cast him a look over her naked shoulder. Her teeth flashed within the elegant profile of her face. Large almond-shaped eyes, a straight nose leading down to lush lips sitting above a perfectly cleft chin. She held the knife in one hand and in the other, a pear. The knife glittered and flashed in Mac's eyes. He squinted into the flames, remembering.

He walked the hills for months before finding her. They had rebuilt the village better than before, but she lived alone in the ruin of the same hovel where the Colonel took her innocence. No Afghan would have her, and she fended for herself since that day when her parents died beneath the rage of bullets.

He watched her for three days before coming down from the hills and standing beside her door with a freshly dressed out deer. He laid the deer down, stepped aside and waited. She stared at him for some time, stared and ran a finger up and down the blade, and he understood her thoughts and the glimmer of tears pooling in her eyes.

He slept outside while she slept within. He fixed her hovel, first the door, which he took off and splintered for wood. He made a new one from wood he bought in another village, for they refused to sell to him in this one. He bought glass for her window and then more wood and fashioned furniture, a bed, a stone hearth with a flume and a table and a floor to cover the dirt.

He slept outside.

He helped her in the fields until one day she brought him a cup of water. On another day, she almost smiled. He held her in his arms that night, and then another. Then, as the first wintry winds blew into the valley, they made love and she cried with her face resting on his chest. He would stay here. He would protect her until the very end.

He owed her that much and more. Over the years they grew to love each other.

◆ ◆ ◆

96

One Day Bachaim

On the fortieth night of Baba's death, a night reserved for tradition, I stood on his balcony and watched campfires burn in the courtyard and the people huddle in blankets and long coats of karakul. The September air chilled and frost settled on the fields. Next to me stood Uncle and next to him, Natasha. We too had on our karakul coats, warm and curly sheep's hair, hand embroidered, beautifully tailored work which Uncle had decided we would export and he knew a man in this city another in that town. He knew Americans who would buy the coats and sell them in America.

He wanted to burn the poppy fields and fill them instead with wheat, sheep, and cattle. I listened while the man in the moon smiled and the stars wept, their tears falling as glittering crystals of light hurtling towards us.

A long line of people carrying lamps and torches filed from the pass towards the outer gates. More visitors to honor Baba. Word spread, as it does in these mountains, and people came from all over the northeast and camped in the courtyard or the nearby fields. We welcomed them and the cooks cooked, the servers served, and we harkened to singers and poets' lamenting, each trying to outperform the other. They sang ballads and composed wondrous rhymes about the Bear, how he defeated so many and never lost a battle, and how he rode the stallion Jaheel in 21 Buzkashi, winning them all.

We ordered coats and jackets and candy from Dushanbe and a crowd gathered by the doors and Purdill stood down there, disbursing these goods among the children and the needy. I had tried to give Purdill his freedom and some land but he refused outright and tears fell down his long face and so he remained and his family came to join him in the fortress instead of living in the village. I wished to count him as my family for I had so little left and he had been there all the days and all the nights and for the first time I saw him smile and he did a little dance with his son in his arms and his wife by his side.

I could not pass a mirror without thinking of him, my brother, my twin. Therefore, I had all the mirrors taken out and given away, except one just for Natasha. We had a wedding for my Uncle, just a few of us, and now they stood next to me arm in arm and I saw him settle like sand settles into itself. She made him happy.

We kept his rule that no Mullahs come into our valley. We kept it for him and for his father. All our fathers came from a place where words did not separate men and women, and religion did not imprison them for what God would want such things.

What God would want to spoil the majesty of creation with hate and death and destruction? What God possessed such an ego he required constant prayer and devotion? Did God not have better things to do?

Baba's voice echoed in the wind, caressing our faces.

"Here, in my valley bachaim, you must make sure that men can be men and not made into a whip in the hands of any master."

So we shuffled inside and I tossed another log onto the fire and poked at it for a moment. I heard the television turn on and Natasha sigh. I turned around. She sat on the couch I had placed in front of the television. Uncle sat in his usual armchair next to the chess table, waiting. I sat down across from him. The door opened and Farid walked in carrying a steaming platter of kabobs and behind him came Nargis with a platter of rice and behind her came more food, gifts, and solemn faces. We rose to accept the gifts and kiss cheeks and shake hands.

They came in, they left and came back again with more, placing it all on the same long table by the door, Baba's table where he studied star charts, read great bound books from his library and tinkered with some contraption or other, showing me as he liked to do, the parts and the gears and the tiny springs within. I could see him even now, sitting there, his back bent over a new mechanism he had built for the farmers. His beard twitching as he bit his lower lip. He would hum, dabble, poke a tool in there and then look over at me, and say, "One day bachaim, you will bend over this table and find the little miracles that will sustain your people through the years. Come, watch and learn."

I walked to that table, pulled by some force or magic or perhaps his everlasting presence.

Then the Nuristani walked in.

I stared at him and Uncle rose to give him a kiss on either cheek. He came over to me and kneeled down, took my hand and kissed it, the way I had seen him kiss Baba's. I placed a hand on his shoulder, hugged him, and sent him to get himself some food, which he did, and then walked behind the curtain of his alcove and sat there, as he always had and always would.

Then I realized the delicate balance of life, the day-to-day, moment-to-moment patterns that repeated themselves like a clock's spinning gears and if one piece broke, it would all break and this place would vanish like a dream or a story that never really happened but should have.

I sat back down and played the game with Uncle, as we always had and always would. Better to play at war than to wage it. This chess table held all our histories, my father and his, and his before him and the rest, warrior sons of warrior fathers, they all played here, at this table and I felt them all sitting next to me, whispering in my ear.

I glanced at that picture of a young boy sitting on a bear's chest and he held my gaze and memories raced through my mind in a storm. I leaned back in the armchair that once held my brother and me and watched the dust motes play above the board again. All the old things surrounded me and I sank into them, as a man sinks into his familiar pillow.

I had struggled against my fate as Fatima had struggled against her bonds in the field below, but in the end, I too succumbed to my destiny.

I now realized that only death could free an Afghan from Afghanistan for no matter where we went, our souls fought to return and even our shadows tore away from us, running home to the rugged sky-ripping mountains that held the bones of our ancestors.

What taste was there in any life but this, what sweetness, what peace? For some, only this will do, only this can be enough. The war drove many away, but peace would bring them back, for no river flowed as beautifully as the Great Amu and no dirt held the history and magic of our dirt and no mountain soared so elegantly to scratch the very essence of the sky.

"So here we are," he said.

"Where it all began," I said.

"Where it all begins once more."

◆ ◆ ◆

Epilogue

So here you are, Mac, my friend. Your sons have grown as Afghan sons and so you all must assist my uncle's daughter as I send her to you with all my hopes that you will help her find her way for we can no longer sate her thirst for knowledge and she needs to spread her wings and fly.

I like to think he would have wanted her to be free. Uncle has passed on and his son has inherited the mantle of Khan. All the old ones who saw things no man should see and done thing that wither the soul, have left us. My heart, though broken all those years ago, broke a hundred times more as I saw my people suffer and every day I questioned and waited for answers from a silent God.

I heard my drummer through the whisper of years and never having found him, I lay down to die knowing that the wars have not ended and will never end. Evolution has deserted us. We are a dead branch on the tree of life. Beyond this, there is nothing. Like the Neanderthal, we will one day extinguish ourselves and those who come after will wonder whatever became of humanity.

I have found no answer to my singular question of Creation. If we are products of a greater being's desire to create, why then must we destroy each other in His name?

I have found no logic in our dishonor and understanding evades me, for I am but a man and have not the capacity. You and I have struggled with these questions for so many years and now as I lay upon my stone pallet and watch lanterns glitter and gleam through my window, I wonder if somewhere beyond, I will find my answers.

As death opens and life closes behind me, will I truly face the All-knowing and receive judgment for my sins or will I merely fade into an icy darkness? Will I whisper and stalk the corridors of my home like the witch or merely wander, my spirit still searching, always searching for answers that do not exist?

No one has ever come back to say what lies beyond the gates of death and so I lay here and watch stars glittering in my own little sky and still I have hope.

ACKNOWLEDGEMENTS

You would not be reading this in my book if not for the love, support, help, encouragement and tenacity of my wife, Karen. She read many, many, many iterations of this book. She helped with editing, retrieving from the cloud and printing. She recruited beta readers for me (and my deepest thanks to those special friends) and researched the ins and outs of independent publishing.

I have been working on this book for years. I'm not even sure how many at this point. I wrote most of it and then stepped away from it for a time and wrote another book (coming in a bit, completely different) and then returned to finish this story and journey. Over those years the situation in Afghanistan changed as well. I leave Omar and his descendants in a safe enclave in Afghanistan, and hope that the people of Afghanistan find the same.

My heartfelt thanks to those who read Secret of the Hindu Kush along the way and offered their thoughts.

- Anthony Stone

ABOUT THE AUTHOR

Anthony Stone lives in Baltimore with his wife and their cat. He is an Air Force veteran, a photographer and an Afghan. It may or may not be true that only death can free an Afghan from Afghanistan.

Online at www.AnthonyStone-Author.com

Printed in Great Britain
by Amazon